# THE
# Jack Creek
## HORROR

*PHIL & DARREN*

*THANK YOU FOR SUPPORTING*

*AN INDEPENDENT AUTHOR*

*ENJOY!!!*

A NOVEL BY:

## C. JOHN COOMBES

COVER DESIGN, PAGE LAYOUTS,
AND TYPESETTING BY:

# C. JOHN COOMBES

BOOK PUBLISHED BY:

## C J COOMBES STUDIO

PRINT ISBN 978-1-941623-70-1

EDITED BY:

### MARIA DENBOER

CONTRIBUTING EDITORS:

### C JOHN COOMBES
### NANCY BURKE SMITH
### MARTHA HART

First Edition

# 1

Jack McGrath felt as if he had been skewered. The pain in his neck was excruciating. Even before opening his eyes, he cursed himself for being too lazy to climb into bed. The agony showed no sign of mercy as it dropped downward to stab him between the shoulder blades and knife him in the small of his back. His ass was dead asleep and tingling. His knees were especially killing him. He parted his eyelids with care; they felt as if sand-filled and scraped.

"Ohhhhh... good mornin' world. It'd'a been easier to die," he muttered.

Jack grabbed his head with both hands and raised it carefully off his shoulder, slowly turning it until his nose pointed forward. He let out a breath as he rolled it about a stiff neck. Next, he moved to drop one of his outstretched legs off the porch banister. He knew his ears were too far gone to hear the knee creak with complaint. Sadly, he was not yet old enough to escape the pain of joints bent in reverse the whole of a night. Gritting his teeth, Jack eased the other leg off the banister in a likewise manner.

Both feet now on the floor, Jack moved to sit tall in his rocker. He teetered forward, working to straighten out his spine, carefully restacking his vertebrae until the alignment was closer to what God intended. At the same time, he worked his eyelids, scraping them up and down slowly across dry, hazel-hued irises, until parted sufficiently to take in the dim fog-laden light of dawn.

At that point, Jack was able to stare into the mists that concealed most of the swamp beyond his porch. Something inside of him felt unsettled. His mind struggled to capture the fading memory behind a sensation that hung about him like a cloak. It dissipated fast, but left behind a residue, a feeling about the swamp. Something.... Something... too obscure to put into words. Something forever lost to the dreams of night.

Grabbing the arms of his chair firmly, Jack rolled forward on the rockers, and in one fluid motion catapulted himself onto his feet. One long howl of a yawn later, he managed to steady his balance and jostle his wits. It was just a dream, he thought.

"A dream. Probably a bad one—best to forget," he spoke aloud. "What the hell is that *smell?*"

Jack tried to blow the bad air out of his head. He closed his eyes and moaned as he arched his back to tweak the morning alignment.

"Ohhhhh."

He forced a little more flexibility.

The cooling night air squeezed out its humidity through hours of rainfall that soaked everything outside and in. And yet, Jack preferred the clammy atmosphere and the occasional breezes that circulated around his rocker to the air in his bedroom, which was hardly less damp but as still as the inside of a coffin and every bit as suffocating. Again, he rubbed the back of his neck and confessed.

"Lord, there's a price to pay for sleepin' in that—"

A most peculiar sound cut Jack's complaint short. It was a gentle whooshing sound. It reminded him of a particular Fourth-of-July firework that exploded to send thousands of smaller firecrackers across the sky. A shimmering cloud, they popped in great number to make a prolonged whoosh instead of a bone-jarring bang. It was like the sound of a million bubbles rushing up through a tall glass of ice-cold soda.

Although the sound was unfamiliar, what followed was a sound that Jack recognized at once. It was the splash of fish falling back into the water. Many fish. Odd in itself, he wondered if a swarm of bugs had made the whoosh, if they had performed a suicidal dive into the water that initiated a feeding frenzy. He was heartened to hear the sound of jumping fish. The fishing had been so poor as of late, maybe there was yet hope.

As a rule, after first accepting he was yet alive to witness a new day, Jack's second morning thought was usually how bad he had to piss. This morning was no different. He turned to step away from the rocker and go inside. As his shoe came down to complete another step, it trod upon something that felt to be a stone.

8

He peered down into the shadows that concealed his feet. Had he not glanced down, he would have fallen flat on his face.

*"What the—"*

A sight slowly emerging from the murkiness jarred Jack's foggy head. It appeared to be a rotted skeleton lying spread out before him across the wooden planked porch. He leaned forward and was just able to make out an animal seemingly reduced to a stringy mess of hair, tendons, macerated muscle, stench, and all things horrible. It added up to a revolting pile of stink that rested midway along the four-stride stretch between his rocker and the back door.

Jack raised his foot and observed a faintly white stone. He then spotted another and another. They were scattered across the porch. In his seventy-seven years, Jack had seen about every eye-opener imaginable, and so at this age, he was not one to be easily frightened or put off. A mind that sought and expected rational explanations quickly subdued his initial alarm. And this explanation was easier than most.

*"Scrub*, I swear.... I'm gonna *shoot* yer ass," Jack threatened with much emphasis on the word "shoot".

Scrub was Jack's golden retriever. Scrub was not as much gold as gray, and every bit as old as he, so Jack felt little need to show compassion.

"Ugh."

Jack was more annoyed than repulsed, knowing he would be the one called to the task of dragging the carcass off the porch and tossing it into the swamp. He looked up and hollered out in a reprimanding voice.

"Scrub! ...*Scrub!*"

Jack whistled for the dog a time or two and then shook his head in exasperation. From one end to the other, he looked along the narrow strip of ground that separated porch from water. As expected, he saw neither hide nor hair of his dog. Scrub would know by the sound of his voice to keep his distance. Scrub would also continue doing what Scrub did best, nosing about, following some scent picked up in the thick morning air, and hauling that scent home.

Jack hollered into the shifting mist a final time but to no avail. The dense air muffled his call. He looked down at the disgusting mess nearly touching his feet. Even in the shadows, the carcass looked to have been decomposing in the swamp for a good month or more.

Jack was not sure what Scrub had dragged home for dinner, dessert or gift of gratitude. Scrub was good about providing, about doing his fair share. He perfected the art of bringing home deer parts, often showing up with one end of a dead deer's leg clamped within his jaws. Trouble was... he never brought home anything a sane person would touch, let alone eat.

After a good deal of growling and wrestling, Scrub would drop his catch at the bottom of the porch steps and then wag his tail proud as could be. Anything a hunter could gut, Scrub could drag home. The swamp was chock-full of animal remains that he retrieved to deposit on the narrow ribbon of sand and grass that made up the bank dividing Jack's porch and water's edge— *until today.*

"On the porch?" Jack asked aloud. "Really?"

Considering the amount of time Jack spent outside in his rocker, Scrub might as well have dragged the carcass straight into his house. The screen door was little more than an undetectable divider. It certainly was no barrier to the rancid or, more accurately, the acrid smell of the remains. A biting odor was impossible to escape within the relative confines of the covered porch.

Off in the distance, the sound of a barking dog caught Jack's attention. He straightened up and looked in the direction of the ruckus.

"Scrub! ...Scrub!" he hollered before turning his head to listen. The barking continued. "You're dreamin', Jack," he said to himself.

Jack knew that when Scrub was sniffing out a trail, there was no getting him back. He was a great companion but suffered from stubbornness, lousy manners, and a single-mindedness all his own.

10

Jack's natural ability to note the unobvious came into play. Rotted remains always possessed a smell that could turn a stomach inside out. They could draw in flies and vultures from across two rose-covered counties. He noted how the expected stench was absent, or at least heavily masked by another smell. One less repugnant, but vaguely familiar. He could not put his finger on it. It was an unpleasant odor, which forced Jack to pull a handkerchief from his back pocket and hold it up to his nose. He bent over to study the carcass. The dog must have hauled it past one of the many hidden oil or gas wells that populated the deeper unseen and impassible reaches. Anything having moved near those wells might carry a nose-pinching pong for days.

"Mercy me, Scrub…. How can this shit smell good to ya?"

The longer Jack studied the bones from behind the white cotton kerchief, the weirder things got. This was not Scrub's usual fare. It was not a deer. At first, he thought it was a fox.

"Fox."

No. That did not sit well with him. Seemed too large for a fox.

"Coyote. Gotta be a coyote. Pretty good size."

Maybe so, but still mighty large for the average coyote, he thought to himself. He wondered if this was one of those hybrid coyo-wolves. Rumors of their presence were enough to scare the crap out of everybody. They were big and aggressive. But then, why not the bad boy himself?

"A wolf?" he questioned aloud.

Jack had heard how wolves were making a comeback, hence the coyo-wolves. He remembered seeing a wolf some years back. It was watching him from a piece of high ground across the water. He had heard one or two after that, he was sure of it. However, the odds were stacked heavily against this being a wolf carcass. His desire to identify the creature gave way to another revelation, a peculiarity that equaled all else. He frowned as the words rolled slowly off his tongue.

*"What the hell…."*

As the light of day grew brighter, Jack realized that portions of exposed bone looked scrubbed clean and unusually white, as if

11

bleached. In fact, he now noticed that there appeared to be little, if any, connecting tissue between these colorless, flesh-free bones. It reminded him of bones that belonged to both roadkill and fish that littered the shallows in front of his cabin.

Jack tossed all kinds of scraps into the water as bait to attract fish. They could strip away flesh in a heartbeat, leaving nothing but bones in the bottom muck that were visible beneath the coffee-colored water when penetrated by sunlight.

Scrub was a natural-born swimmer, and all too often, he would haul Jack's roadkill back out of the shallows. Yet, hauling something this big out of shallows seemed a bit much even for him—dragging it up on the porch and all. On the other hand, as Jack thought about it, considering the size of one or two deer his dog had collected, maybe it really was not so farfetched.

Now, there was another option.

Jack gave thought to some sort of prank pulled at his expense. Yet, who the hell would take the time to do that? he wondered. It was the kind of prank one or two of his old buddies, long since buried, would have pulled off with glee. No question, rotting corpses on front porches beat burning bags of shit hands down. Trouble was, nowadays, whatever friends remained who might be remotely capable of pulling off a prank of this caliber were either stationed permanently in wheelchairs, or else hiding in hammocks with little or no gumption to stop snoring, let alone play a joke on *him*. Not to mention, most of them probably had no idea that he was even alive.

"Goddamned kids," he snickered.

That was it. Had to be kids. Jack considered his hearing. Bad enough when he was awake, non-existent when he was asleep. A couple of smart-ass kids could do just about anything if he was sawing logs in the rocker. It was certainly within the realm of possibilities.

Down through the ages, some things never changed. If the tables were turned, he would have jumped on the chance to pull off a prank of this stature. It would have made him famous. Right now, it was the only thing making sense. He looked across the banister. They were probably out there somewhere watching him and laughing their asses off. His eyes scanned the swamp. He hollered.

"Great prank! Honestly, very funny! I'll hand it to ya; ya got my ass good! Yep, you guys did good!"

In fact, Jack was sincere. A prank of this standing deserved respect. A smile crossed his face, but if there was a response to be returned from the swamp, it was nothing more than the reeds gasping for fresh air between the slow-flowing currents of mist snaking past his cabin.

At no time did Jack feel fear. He had spent all his years in the swamp. He was not one to get spooked in a place where *everything* went bump in the night. For one thing, this was bear country. The only things he felt were a fading sense of confusion, an urge to chuckle for being had, and let us not forget—a dire need to take a piss.

Add to that, a desire for coffee to sip while sorting out all that took place, the remains, how they got on the porch, when they got on the porch, why his damn dog was always running off chasing shit instead of guarding the house against pranksters, and... well... let's just say morning was off to a rollicking start.

Jack moved to step over the skeleton. His shift in position caused a flash of reflected morning light to catch his eye. He halted midway, ending up straddled over the skeleton. Squinting his eyes, he leaned over to take a closer look. He stabbed at a piece of metal below the skull with his index finger, working it out of the clutch of matted fur. He slid it into the open. It was a tag, and he did not need any more light to read the inscription.
*SCRUB*

13

## 2

Jack straightened up as if poked in the ass. His thoughts were wiped clean. If he possessed a reset button, it reset. The sight of Scrub's tag slammed him back to square one. Any urge to chuckle died before the memory of fourteen years of petting and scratching ears—all of which left Jack profoundly familiar with his dog's nameplate. He then spotted a buckle and recognized it as part of Scrub's leather collar. At any other time, he would have been crushed by the loss of his longtime four-legged friend. At any other time, he would have been moved to tears. However, emotion besieged by bewilderment overwhelmed him. He begged for a sane answer.

Jack understood he was getting on in years, but he was yet a resourceful man; he was yet intelligent. He knew when faced with something challenging, it was best to step back, relax, and look around. He let loose the initial shock.

Jack assured himself that he was no longer dreaming, and then stepped past Scrub's bones to open the screen door and enter the cabin. He walked over to the kitchen counter, rinsed out a mug from the sink, filled it with water, and took a drink. He filled it again and placed it into the microwave.

"One, two, three," he said aloud as he pushed the MINUTE button at each call.

While the microwave whirred, Jack made his way to the bathroom. He took his morning piss. He rinsed his face and hands. He stared into the mirror as his mind raced back over what he had seen and misconstrued. He was deep into speculation when summoned back by the microwave.

Jack returned to the kitchen to remove the mug of boiling water and place it on the counter. He spooned in some instant coffee and began to stir. He slipped back into his thoughts. He continued where he left off, while staring blindly at the spoon rattling around in circles.

What troubled Jack the most was not the possibility of the skeleton being Scrub, for now that appeared to be a reality, but who would commit such a cruel and heartless act. His mind raced to remember if he had wronged somebody, if he had done anything that might warrant such a revengeful deed.

The severe degradation of Scrub's body and the whiteness of the exposed bones further complicated Jack's mental scramble. How could that happen in the space of a night, seven or eight hours? It could not. Besides, he clearly remembered filling Scrub's bowl before dozing off in the rocker. Maybe somebody swiped Scrub's collar and stuck it on a carcass. Now that would have made an already award-winning prank stellar. It would if that was what happened. However, if that was not what happened, then there was not a single aspect of this mess that made sense. He was pondering the impossible.

Jack tossed the spoon into the sink and took a sip of coffee. He turned to lean back against the counter and take in the shadowy sight of what lay beyond the screen door. If this was something other than a joke....

"Hmm. What the hell could I have done to deserve this?"

What kind of person would take it out on a poor old half-lame dog? he wondered to himself.

"Nobody in their right mind."

Jack was lost for an explanation, but also nudged by thoughts that there had to be clues. He flipped on the porch light as he headed back outside. With mug in hand, he stared down at the remains for the umpteenth time. He slipped on his glasses and studied them closely. The flesh was badly deteriorated, or entirely missing, from various perfectly clean and white bones.

"Jack... only one thing dissolves a carcass that fast. Acid. That's what you're smellin', buddy. Acid."

It was utterly mystifying, incomprehensible. *Step back and look around*, he thought to himself. Therefore, leaning against the doorjamb and sipping his coffee, he began to search the porch for signs, clues, anything.

In the porch light, Jack noticed that it was rock salt scattered across the porch—not white stones. The spread was thickest

15

about his rocker and the carcass. He knew at once, from where it came. He had removed the bag of salt off a small wooden nightstand, a makeshift worktable that was perfect for tying flys and making lures. The nightstand with its single tool drawer, and its cabinet door, was tight against the porch banister. The day before, he had moved the opened bag off the nightstand and onto the banister, wedging it firmly into the right angle formed by the railing's fitment to the house.

Jack studied the spilled salt, and the bag, now draped over the nightstand, and wondered how it had fallen off its perch. Maybe the thud of its landing on the nightstand was what awoke him. His eyes followed the scattered salt crystals across the floor planks to the porch steps. His eyes descended the steps and skated across the narrow strip of land that butted up to the water.

As Jack supposed, a clue soon made itself known. With the first hints of light coming across the yard, fresh details now were apparent. The most notable one was unhidden and hard to miss. A wide random-flowing pattern similar to a track of spilled milk showed quite clearly.

Its outline was somewhat defined at the center of the steps, across the porch, and surrounding Scrub's bones. It also was visible beneath the rocking chair. The path was one of perfectly clean and pitted wood, the grain raised and pronounced. The wood looked as fresh in color as the day it was milled, the day it was nailed down decades ago. The appearance of the path was in stark contrast to the surrounding wood floor, which showed as old, dirty, and worn as the years might suggest.

Jack walked over to the rocker and leaned it back on its side. He noted the pitting that covered the rockers. All that he saw appeared attacked by some sort of very corrosive liquid. Was it possible someone poured acid all over Scrub? It was ridiculous to think Scrub would just lie there while that happened. He would have been howling and carrying on like a lunatic.

Yet everything seemed to point in that direction. Half the porch appeared corroded, as if doused in acid. There were more questions than answers. To say the least, Jack was unsettled, knowing he had been sleeping over top of whatever was going on a mere foot below his crusty ol' tinglin' ass.

A strangely familiar feeling of anxiety crept over him. It was the same feeling that had been present when he awoke. It was something of a dream, remnants of a nightmare—or was it more? He wondered if the anxiety came from something that he had sensed while asleep. The thought was hardly consoling.

"Step back an' relax," he whispered aloud. "There's a reason for everything."

Jack looked out over the swamp. He then moved toward the steps and descended. He looked down at the ground. There was not much to see. The earth between the steps and water was barren. A lifetime of heading up and down the porch steps trampled asunder anything that hoped to live. He strained to see signs of footprints, signs of kids or pranksters. There was nothing but smooth hard-packed sand. Rain had washed away anything left behind.

Jack's focus returned to the scattered salt, and the bag dislodged from the banister. It had been only a few feet from his head while he slept. He walked around to the end of the porch where the rocker sat, and flinched when a field mouse darted before him. He studied the ground with care, and found another piece of the puzzle—deer tracks. They were too deep and plentiful for the rain to wash them entirely away.

"Thank god, at least somethin' around here finally adds up," Jack concluded aloud. He continued to talk to himself. "Roaming deer found the bag of salt... tried to get at it, tried to *lick* it... knocked it off the railing.... And that sent the whole mess flying across the floor."

17

From within a cloud of confused non-sensible thoughts emerged this single logical realization. It made perfectly good sense. It was something he could understand. It was the first thing that brought balance to his sanity. It was a reckoning that pleased him.

"Whoa!"

Jack jumped backward. A stirring near his feet startled him. It was much larger than a field mouse. Within fractions of a second, he realized he had spooked a couple of water snakes. Their dark markings made them nearly invisible in the shadows. He was startled more by the rustle and sense of movement than by actually seeing the reptiles. He watched them slither to higher ground. To his surprise, farther up the yard, he saw two more good-sized snakes moving through the grass, and then another, and another. He stood motionless, taking in the unusual sight.

Jack would have considered himself lucky to see a couple of snakes, but this felt nothing like *luck*. Not when six or seven appeared in the yard. That was more indicative of being spooked, or driven out of the marsh onto higher ground. He thought of the jumping fish. It was unsettling to witness such an odd event, even more so when added to the mystery of his dead dog. He watched the snakes slither slowly across the yard and head for water on the other side. He was waiting for a *"two plus two makes four"* answer. It did not come.

As soon as the snakes were out of sight, Jack walked over to the water's edge and looked into the shallows. Bones. The brighter the light of day, the more they came into view. It was a graveyard. The bones were as plentiful as muck. Jack was way past youthful desires to frolic in the shallows. And so for years, pretty much everything Scrub dragged home, Jack tossed into the swamp. For that matter, even he dragged stuff home—roadkill. It all went into the shallows. It all became fish bait. Little fish cleaned up the bones, bigger fish cleaned up the little fish, and he cleaned up the bigger fish. Highway to freezer; it was the circle of life.

# 3

*"Cory Ballard.* Yeah.... I'm doing good. Who've I got here? Harold Sweeny? Christ almighty, didn't even recognize your voice. Been too long. How you doing? Yeah? Really.... Great.... Great.... Good.... How's business? Good. So, why's a busy man like you calling me? Yeah? Don't worry... no, don't worry, no problem. What d'you got?"

Cory gave the caller his undivided attention. His brow shriveled in a way that formed a number of pronounced crosshatches.

"And what is it that makes this so weird? Really.... Huh.... Hmm.... Yeah, that is kind of strange. Huh. Ooooo, I like the sound of that. Well, you know I'm always interested.... No, no, I'm interested. I like that stuff; you know that. I only hesitated because it's a long-ass drive up to Houghton Lake, and you know I don't get paid squat for writing this crap. Costs more in gas than I'll ever get paid.

"Yeah.... Well, don't forget I also say, it's more about entertainment than income. Yeah.... Dinner? Well, now that clearly ups the ante. What? Hell no, I can't get up there today. No, no way. I'll need at least three or four days to finish up work down here. Harold. Trust me. The world isn't going to change in three or four days. Yeah....

"Look, let me finish what I got going here. I'll try and drive up Friday. I can't make it any sooner than that. We'll do dinner and take it from there, but I'm going to hold you to that dinner. You're buying, bud. You get to write it off. Yeah. Okay. Yeah. All right, how long you at the office? Okay, I'll see you Friday. I'll call you before I head up. Yeah. Okay. See you. All right, Harold. Yeah. See you then."

Cory tossed the cell back onto his desk. He leaned back in his chair. His chin rested squarely upon his thumb while he stared empty-eyed at the phone. The call was certainly intriguing, certainly enough to ignite his curiosity.

"Hmm."

# 4

Derrek pulled out a joint, lit it, and took a hit. He looked down at his feet, let out the smoke, and shook his head.

"Pete. Tell me something. Is there a reason we been sitting out here this long? We caught, *you caught*, one fish. A nice walleye, I admit, but still one fish. I haven't caught anything."

"Yeah. Sure. The beer's still cold."

"Ah. Of course. I should've thought of that. The beer's still cold."

Pete pointed a finger at Derrek.

"You probably thought it had something to do with the kind of fishing that involves hooks an' worms, and casting lures out into the wide-open waters. No sir, this is all about fishing through frigid ice-filled waters and bringing up brewskis from the depths of a busted-up Styrofoam cooler."

Derrek took another hit. He offered the joint to Pete.

"Really?"

"Really," said Pete as he helped himself to a hit and passed the joint back.

"Who knew?"

"There ya go," said Pete as he touched his head with a can of sweaty cold beer in a salute to Derrek.

"All bullshittin' aside, Pete, can you remember the last time we fished Dead Stream and got anything? What's with this place? I mean, how long has it been? A year... two?"

"Long time."

Derrek took another hit. He held the joint over the side of the boat and flicked it, knocking ash into the water. He exhaled.

"I keep wantin' to come back here because I remember how good it used to be. I dunno. I've tried crawlers, stickbait, spinners, Curley Tails, Rapalas, prayers, and sacrifice—the only thing left is a stick of dynamite. I give up. Ain't worth it anymore. From now on, it's Houghton or Higgins. This place sucks."

Pete started laughing uncontrollably.

"Dynamite?" he continued to laugh. "I think you just scared the shit out of the fish."

"Huh?"

"They're offering you a sacrifice."

"Huh?"

"Your rod moved." Pete nodded toward Derrek's pole. "I think ya finally got something."

Derrek turned away from Pete to watch his rod. It quivered.

"I'll be damned."

He picked up the pole and snapped it.

"Here, hold this."

Derrek passed the joint to Pete, and then started cranking the reel.

"Ya get it?"

"Ahh. I think. Yup. Ah.... Shit. I lost it. No, maybe not. I dunno. I can feel a little drag. Feels more like weeds than a fish."

"Feels more like weed?" blurted out Pete as he lost it to laughter, which sent Derrek into a laughing fit as well.

"Weee-eee-eds. I said wee-eeds, you dumb ass."

"Reel it in, you idiot," said Pete. "It's probably the only one you'll get today."

Derrek started reeling faster and faster. He and Pete watched as a nice-sized perch surfaced. Derrek lifted it out of the water.

"What the hell?"

"Oh, man. That's nasty," said Pete.

The two men studied the fish in a moment of silence.

"Are we smokin' bad weed, or does that thing look half-digested? Oh, man. That's just gross," said Derrek.

"If it's the weed, then we're both having the same hallucination. I don't think it's the weed, man. Is that, like, bubbling or what?" Pete studied the fish. "This is really messin' with my head. Unhook it an' toss it back in."

"Bullshit. You unhook it an' toss it back in."

21

"Hey, you caught it, not me. I ain't touchin' it."

"I ain't touchin' it," said Derrek, now starting to laugh. "I don't know what it's got, but I ain't touching anything that slimy and bubbling."

"I think it got spermed. Here." Pete handed Derrek a pair of wire cutters. "Cut it loose."

Derrek couldn't stop laughing. "You are such an ass. Quit bogarting that joint. Give it to me."

Pete handed Derrek the joint. He took one final hit off it and flicked it into the water.

"What do you think happens when a fish eats that?"

Pete was starting to convulse. "They pass up the brownies, but a wee-ee-eed wor-rrm...." He couldn't finish the sentence.

Derrek was howling. He grasped the wire cutters, clipped the fishing line, and let the fish drop. He leaned over the boat and watched it disappear into the depths.

"You just wasted a good leader," protested Pete.

"Don't even mention the word *wasted*, okay? It's unhealthy. Look at that. The bubbles are coming to the surface." Derrek leaned over the boat and watched the water. "I can't believe it. I wait all day to catch a fish and that's what I get? Bubbling slime? Ya gotta be kidding me. What the hell was that?"

"Keep looking at your reflection, and then the fish won't look bad," said Pete as he rolled his head back and let loose.

Derrek looked at Pete.

"Screw dynamiting fish. I need to blow *your* ass outta this boat. You're seriously losing it, man."

Derrek grabbed the line and rigged another lure. He cast the line. The two settled down and sat in silence a moment before Derrek spoke again.

"You ever see anything like that before?"

"Nope."

"I wonder if that's why we aren't catchin' fish. Maybe they got a disease or something."

"Could be," said Pete. "But it would have to be a two-year disease. I'm thinking it's those lampreys. I'll bet one of 'em latched onto that poor sonovabitch an' sucked right through it."

"Definitely. Can you imagine dying like that? Rolling your eyeballs around and watching something suck your guts out?"

"Well, preferably not my guts," quipped Pete.

Derrek totally lost it. He was laughing too hard to catch his breath. It was contagious and Pete fell in step. The two were gagging and convulsing. They turned away from each other in order to break out of their fit of laughter, in order to draw in their senses and a breath of air.

"Oh, god. Shut up," said Derrek. He attempted to focus on something that would keep him from a relapse. "What got me was that slimy look... and what about that bubbling? Looked like somebody dumped soda— Hey! I got another one."

Derrek started reeling.

"Oh, yeah. That's more like it. This baby's got some fight in it."

The two watched the pole spring up and down as the fish ran with the line.

"C'mon, you little devil. Shit! I lost it. Damn it."

Derrek continued to reel, but much slower. He snapped the pole, trying to feel out the fish.

"Still on the line?" asked Pete.

"I don't know. Feels like the last one. Feels like weeds."

"We already been down that road."

"Ya think?"

Both men looked over the side of the boat, more out of curiosity than anything else.

"Look at all them little bubbles. That's weird," said Derrek.

"Nah, seaweed does that all the time. Something disturbs the seaweed and the bubbles come up. Pull that fish up."

Derrek did as Pete suggested. The fish surfaced but showed no signs of life. Derrek lifted it out of the water. He just let it hang as he studied it.

"Is that thing dead?" he asked.

"Huh. Damned if I know. Sure looks like it."

"Why would it be dead? I don't get it. Does that have bubbles on it too?"

The two stared at the fish. It never flopped once.

"Got me," said Pete. "Oh, well. You got an iron gut. Unhook it and throw it in the cooler."

"Yeah, right. Maybe *your* cooler."

Derrek swung the fish toward Pete's head. Pete ducked back and forth.

"Hey! Stop it!"

"I thought you wanted to eat it."

"Knock that shit off. Stop it."

"Yeah, see. You can serve it up, but you can't *eat* it. Ya wuss." Derrek swung the fish back into reach and grabbed it firmly with one hand. He looked at Pete with an expression of torture.

Pete started laughing. He knew the look all too well. Derrek had stuck himself with the hook.

"That smart a little? That'll teach you for picking on me."

"Sonovabitch b-b-burns."

It was an odd thing to say, and it caught Pete off guard.

"Okay. We ain't that fried yet."

"Ouch. Ouch, *ouch*."

Pete frowned as Derrek began shaking his hand violently.

"You okay?"

Derrek never answered Pete. Instead, he leaned over and stuck his hand deep into the water. He began swishing his arm about. A second later, his body shuddered and Derrek toppled overboard. Without thought, Pete reached in to rescue him.

# 5

Jack McGrath steered his truck over toward the shoulder of the highway. He slowed the vehicle as he began wondering about having the strength to load any kind of weight into the pickup box. At first, from a distance, he only noticed what he correctly assumed to be a dead deer lying on the side of the road. However, upon arriving at the scene, he soon realized that a massive red stain covered the highway. A result of the blood and guts of a good many animals. Scrub would have gone nuts sniffing it all out, peeling it all off the road, but Scrub no longer sat in the passenger seat. Jack had not gotten used to it, but he was learning to live with it.

"Mercy me, what a mess."

Jack had never seen so much roadkill in one spot at one time ever. The first thing that came to mind was some sort of failed road-crossing migration, like a large safe of ducks and ducklings. The only problem was the assortment. It was not just ducks. Even when smeared flat as pancakes, you would never mistake flat snakes for flat ducks. He was not sure what had happened, but it proved to be his best find ever.

Jack shut off the engine and climbed out of the pickup. He continued to make note of the assorted roadkill as he walked toward the back of his truck, sliding his hand along the upper edge of the box until reaching the tailgate. There he stopped and looked down at the carcass of interest. It was a fresh kill—no bloating, no vultures, few flies, but....

What Jack saw next was unexpected and deeply troubling. Any disenchantment about his inability to manhandle the doe onto the bed of the truck disappeared the instant his focus zeroed in on the animal's forelegs. The flesh was stripped nearly clean off the bone. It was as if the animal stumbled into a vat of acid and jumped backward, but had no means by which to cleanse itself. To say the sight was distressing was an understatement, not only because it felt as if he were back standing over the

25

remains of Scrub, but also because he was standing over the same wretched-looking mess a good *five miles from home.*

The notion that this vile affliction might be endemic, that it might be pervasive in the area, made him shudder. As if by unseen trickery, everything Jack threw into the shallows beyond his porch turned up stripped clean of meat. It happened fast—overnight fast. Yet, he had neither seen nor heard anything on the news about these ghoulish feats occurring anywhere else. He had figured they were confined to the waters surrounding his cabin. What lay before him now changed all he had assumed.

Just as he had done with Scrub, Jack eased himself down close to the carcass. He noted what little bone was visible appeared white. Unusually white. Just as it had been with Scrub. It was a telltale sign. A clue. He leaned over and sniffed the air about the forelegs. It had a notable biting odor, a scent he recognized at once. Yet, there was more. He inhaled deeper. He closed his eyes. There was the faintest underlying scent of chlorine. Bleach.

Jack refused to believe that some demented soul stopped in the middle of nowhere to catch and torture a deer. The idea was absolutely absurd. Besides, who would delight in torturing snakes and ducks, and the rest of whatever ended up smeared across the road?

Instead, Jack found himself dreading the possibility of something else, something horrific, something yet unknown to the public, something yet unseen lurking within the countless acres of watery quietude. On the surface, the half-submerged landscape was a place of peace, a place where the buzz of insects and the cries of birds were the only disturbance.

The flooding and the swamp both possessed a good deal of ground that rarely felt the press of a man's foot. There were yet expanses seen only by those who dared venture into the area with a small boat, or pass over it in a private plane. Kids trapped in the back seats of cars that raced along its edges might catch a glimpse. A few die-hards might stop briefly to scale a viewing tower and enjoy the experience of mosquito mayhem and annual bird migrations.

Here was a place remote enough to conceal all manner of things. Within the cramped stands of cedar and deciduous forest, or below the surface of coffee-colored flows that floated mats of sphagnum and sedges, unseen worlds thrived.

To the faint-hearted, one hardly need mention suspicions of something strange prowling about these inaccessible water-saturated spaces, something disagreeable, something to be found out and feared. It was a fear shared only by folks unlike himself. Until now.

Jack groaned as he attempted to stand back up. Working to straighten his spine, his mind also twisted and turned. He tried to make sense of what was taking place. It was no different from before. It was perplexing. It was frustrating to feel too stupid to see the truth of it.

Jack looked off the shoulder of the highway. It was mostly standing water, dark, saturated with shades of sepia. He noted the close proximity of the doe's forelegs to the water that bordered the side of the road. He sensed it was some sort of clue. He considered the mess of guts in the road, and thought of the snakes slithering across his yard the night Scrub died. He remembered thinking that they had been driven to higher ground, much like what might have happened here.

Jack's gaze moved upward and out across the flooding. His eyes followed an open shallow flow that meandered into the distance as it washed slowly in and around the thickets of tall shrubs. He thought of the gas and oil wells. He knew those were only in Dead Stream Swamp and not this area.

Jack had yet to figure out what happened to Scrub, and he had no idea what happened to this doe, but if this wasn't due to the drilling operations, then he had just lost his culprit, the target of all his heated anger and disgust. If drilling rigs could not move themselves around the swamp, then their half-dissolved victims could not either.

This had to be something that either flowed within the water or moved about of its own volition. It was clear to him at once that anything flowing in the water would not scale the steps to his porch and attack Scrub. All thoughts that remained were anything but comforting.

Jack desperately wanted to haul the carcass home with him. He needed it for an experiment of sorts, and in his younger years, he would have hopped out onto the road, grabbed the animal, and tossed it into the bed of his truck without hesitation. Not anymore. When one reached his late seventies, one also reached a new set of realities. Nothing got tossed. You might grunt, you might wrangle or wrestle, but back pain made the rules, and nothing got tossed impulsively... ever. Especially dead deer.

Jack let out a breath as he looked westward into the sun through a filter of leaves. It was weak. It was dropping below the crest of treetops, its burning yellows leaning evermore to oranges while turning green leaves into a tapestry of black-speckled silhouettes. The air was cooling and unstill.

A lone car approached. Jack could hear the change of its whine, the sound of its tires lowering pitch as they spun slower in their race along the pavement. The vehicle slowed to a crawl, and for a moment, he thought it was going to stop.

Jack endeavored to identify the driver, to see if the face was familiar, but between tinted glass and a setting sun shining in his face, recognition was impossible. It mattered little. Times had changed. Too many familiar faces were dead and gone; now faces were most often new and strange. Jack watched the vehicle accelerate and speed away.

"Ahh. Screw it."

Jack made a couple of passes back and forth across the road, peeling dead animals off the pavement. He dropped them into buckets kept solely for that purpose. He placed the buckets into the truck, took a final look at the dead doe, and moved to climb back into the cab. He reseated himself and stared at the sun over his left shoulder. The mutter of unformed words escaped his mouth. He shook his head.

Jack wanted to say he did not have time to wrestle with a deer, and that he did not want to get dirty, that it was getting late, when the truth of it was he could not man-up anymore. His gaze shifted to his side mirror. No cars were approaching. He put the truck into gear and stepped on the gas. He watched the deer's reflection in his mirror as it retreated from view. He looked at the white boney forelegs as long as he dared, until it became prudent to keep both his eyes and the truck on the road ahead.

## 6

Cory eased off the gas. His ever-present sensibility prompted him to allow the SUV to throttle back from the posted highway speed. Far ahead, that hypnotic point of singularity formed by intersecting lines of asphalt and faded white and yellow stripes was lost to the distraction of a lone vehicle parked along the shoulder. Cory slowed to make sense of the anomaly coming into view, waiting for it to emerge from the early evening shadows. He understood better than most how all things amiss offered some degree of intrigue.

In short time, Cory perceived a man standing behind a truck. Seconds later, he determined the stranger was looking down at what appeared to be a body sprawled across the side of the road. The road itself was a mess. As he closed in, he could make out the red stain of blood reaching from one side of the road to the other. It was everywhere. He sensed the familiar feeling of his morbid curiosity about to overtake him. Aside from one quick glance into his rearview mirror, his eyes were riveted, sopping up every minute detail. As he drove slowly past, an old man stood his ground, twisting around to stare back at him bluntly with a grizzled and unflinching face.

It was a dead deer.

29

# 7

One by one, Jack lifted out the five-gallon pails stuffed full of roadkill. He carried the pails down the north side yard and around to the back of the house. He set them down upon that narrow strip of land separating porch from water's edge. Jack looked out across the motionless black water. Shadows were filling the coves and inlets. He studied them for any sign of disturbance, but the swamp was still.

"I know you're out there, you devil. Humph."

Jack reached down and grabbed the leg of a raccoon. He yanked it out of the bucket and tossed it into the water about six feet from shore. He tossed a second coon about four feet out. He dropped a woodchuck into the water about two feet from the bank. He carefully placed a flattened turtle half in, half out, of the water. He situated the remaining two woodchucks on the dirt bank about three feet from the water's edge.

Jack's final move was decidedly more bizarre. He walked around to the south side yard and entered his shed. He returned carrying a steel-wire rabbit cage. He set the cage down on the bank and specifically positioned it with the woodchucks and a line of salt to one side, and the water to the other.

"Water, turtle, cage, salt, woodchucks, in that order," said Jack aloud as he pointed to each.

Satisfied, Jack pushed three dead ducks through the open cage door. He then closed the door and double-checked it to assure himself that it was secure. The only thing that remained in the pails was a dead skunk. He grabbed it by its tail and tossed it some twenty feet out across the shallows. Instinctively, he smelled his fingers. Nasty. The skunk toss seemed rude as the following splash disrupted the peace and tranquility of the perpetually unbothered environment.

"Okay. That oughta do it."

Jack stepped back from the water's edge after giving himself a 'thumbs up'. Soon after, he walked back up to his truck to fetch five bags of rock salt. His first thought was of weight.

He dragged a bag off the bed. He did not stop its fall. He knew better. He only guided it to the ground. Gauging the pain in his back, he carried the first bag down to the water. He upended the forty-pound bag and tore off a corner. He poured the contents on top of the already existing white line where it paralleled the water's edge.

Jack poured with care, making sure to widen the existing line, to give it more height, and to cover any gaps where the ground showed through. Using the salt line, he ensured the separation of roadkill. The caged ducks and turtle remained on the waterside of the salt line whereas the woodchucks did not. They rested on the cabin side of the salt line. He emptied all five bags along the same line. It looked substantial.

Jack climbed the porch steps. He stopped at the screen door and reached up to unscrew a bulb out of the porch light fixture. He reached into his pocket and pulled out a fresh bulb. He fitted it into the fixture. After that, he went into the house and washed his hands.

Jack grabbed a filet of fish from the freezer chest and thawed it out in the microwave. He walked it out onto the porch and placed it on a grill. As Jack occupied himself with grilling dinner, the last remnants of sunlight dissipated amid the darkening shadows and emerging mists. By the time that he finished picking through the fish bones, scrounging for something sweet, and settling back into his rocker to light a pipe, darkness was in full measure.

Jack had not turned on any lights, not one in the cabin and not the fresh bulb fitted aside the back door. Only the creak of his rocker on the porch planks disturbed the night. In days past, his voice carried gently across the swamp nightly as he spoke his thoughts aloud to Scrub. He missed that furry cuss. He missed Scrub's devotion and restless personality. The pain of his loss was worst during the late evening hours, when sitting alone.

Jack was on his own. The discomfort of loneliness brought him to contemplate his own death, the deaths of those around him, and the ever-clearer indications that the end of his world was drawing near. As his thoughts meandered, he subconsciously studied the shadows. He studied the marshes more by memory

31

than sight as he turned his head this way and that to zero in on the murmur of invisible creatures. There were once good times about this place... or maybe not.

Jack thought about his daughter. Wanting to see her about killed him. He would not tell her that. He did not wish to burden her. He smiled as he passed time thinking of her while puffing on his pipe. He fed the current of cherry-scented smoke that wafted along the bottom of the porch ceiling. It formed a rainless cloud that hovered overhead until he nodded off to sleep.

Jack's eyes next opened long after his pipe went cold, long after the sweet-smelling cloud was pushed away by the heavy and uncomfortably cool air that awakened him. He sat up, cleared his throat, and tapped his pipe on the banister. He stood up to work out the stiffness and peer into the darkness. It was then that he saw something abnormal. It was unlike anything he had ever witnessed in fifty years of living in the swamp. He stood still, his eyes wide open and unblinking.

"Mercy me. What the hell is that?" he asked in a barely audible voice.

A good ways out from the cabin shore, deep into the flooding, Jack observed an eerie glow. It was a strange silent blue light. Jack figured he was witnessing some form of bioluminescence. From this distance, the glow was distinct as it bled into the mists that hovered above the water's surface.

"So is that what the face of the devil looks like?" he asked in a whisper.

Jack watched the phenomenon for the better part of an hour. During that time, the soft blue luminescence moved from north to south, flowing with the water at a nearly imperceptible pace. He noticed that the light was not uniform in brightness. Some areas appeared to glow with more intensity than others. As a whole, the glow appeared to come and go, sometimes in pulses, and sometimes in waves. It was most hypnotic and made Jack's eyes grow heavy.

After half an hour of standing for a better look, Jack sat back down in the rocker, but remained focused on the soft blue spectacle as it drifted in his direction. It was mesmerizing. It was exceptionally peaceful and, not surprisingly, he was once more sleeping soundly in his rocker.

Hours later, Jack awoke with a start. The air carried the scent of acid. The scent was burned into his memory. In spite of the rocker-induced pain, he sat straight up and wasted little time getting to his feet. He looked down at the bank. He looked for the carcasses. He rubbed his eyes and looked again.

"Goddamnit. Ya fell asleep? Ya fell asleep? Are you nuts?"

Jack reprimanded himself aloud. He was truly annoyed. In spite of all his efforts to get a handle on what lurked in the swamp, he had fallen asleep. The curses continued as he stepped briskly across the porch and down the steps. He walked along the water's edge directly to the cage.

It was the first time ever that Jack experienced this kind of fear. It was a hair-standing sensation that tightened every muscle in his body. He looked out across the shadows and into the mists that covered the flat, motionless, obscured waters. He felt wary of something watching him. It was also the first time he distrusted his surroundings in the backwaters. Jack looked down at the cage. Inside, nothing remained but white bleached bones, strips of tissue, and soiled feathers. Inside the ring of salt laid the dead woodchuck. It was untouched.

# 8

By the time Denny arrived at the Higgins Lake Road public landing, only the last hint of daylight remained. The warm rays of oranges and reds had long since dropped away to leave little more than a murky bluish-gray glow over the river. He and Marki climbed out of the truck.

Marki went around to the driver's side and climbed into the driver's seat while her husband walked back to the boat and unchained it from the trailer. He unhooked the bow from the winch cable, and grabbed the coil of bowline.  In the glow of the pickup's utility lights, Denny double-checked everything.

"Okay, Marki!  Back 'er up."

Marki twisted about to watch out the back window as she eased the boat down the landing.  The boat floated off the trailer.  At Denny's signal, she pulled the trailer out of the water, and drove the truck to the edge of the gravel lot to park it.

The thick and shadowy perimeter of trees unnerved Marki.  She glanced through the trees.  She looked over her shoulder more than once while hurrying toward her husband.  She wasted no time scampering back to the boat.  As soon as she climbed in, Denny fired up the motor and they headed into the frail headwaters of the Muskegon River.

Marki always felt secure in the boat.  It was like a little floating fortress that remained out of reach and unbreachable by the fearful things unseen within the thickets and underbrush that easily spooked her.

As Denny and Marki cruised into the darkness, they applied insect repellent, checked their lights, sorted out fishing gear, and settled back to enjoy hot coffee.  They motored quietly past the last houses on the south bank where they watched the inviting glow and warmth of little square patches of window light.  It made the damp night air feel chilly.

Marki pulled up her zipper and raised her collar as they passed a familiar channel to the left that accessed a neighborhood of homes marking the last trace of development.  They soon approached the first of seven gentle bends in the river as it meandered into the far-reaching expanses of sphagnum, reeds, and grasses.

"How far are we going in tonight?" asked Marki as she rubbed her arms and shrugged.

"Not too far.  I was thinking maybe to Dead Stream or a little past.  I always like fishing just below the confluence.  Well, I should say I always used to like fishing there.  Nowadays doesn't seem like there's any good place to fish."

"Why don't we go down to those small bayous?  We haven't been there in a while."

"We can, but for now let's see how it goes at Dead Stream."

They reached Dead Stream and anchored. Denny grabbed Marki's rod and released the lure. He adjusted the slipknot on the cork popper for six inches of depth, untwisted the leader, and handed the rod to Marki.

"Here. That should do ya."

"Did you put a crawler on there?"

"Dang it, Marki. When are you going to start hookin' your own crawlers?"

"Never. Stick a lure on there, and I won't have to," sniped Marki.

"And you won't catch anything."

"I won't catch anything anyhow."

"Now, that's an attitude."

"Well, you always gotta get on me about hooking crawlers," complained Marki. "You know I hate doing that. I'm not going to change."

Denny hooked a crawler and handed the rod back to Marki.

"Here. Hand me my Thermos."

Denny unscrewed the top and unplugged the container. Fresh air enhanced the aroma of hot coffee. He poured a cup and sipped it as he watched his wife cast into the shadows. She was right about one thing. They were not about to catch anything.

Denny set his cup aside, picked up his rod, and tossed in a line. Together, they listened to the *pop-pop-pop* of cork poppers as they jerked them across the water. Denny swapped the crawlers out for Rapalas and side darters in hopes of improving their luck. They fitted a number of different glowworms, wigs 'n jigs, and wobblers, but to no avail.

"Nothing's biting," complained Marki.

"I'm tellin' ya, Marki. I don't think this has anything to do with *nothin's biting*. I don't think there's anything around here that can bite. I swear to god, there *are* no fish."

"Well, you shouldn't be surprised. That's what everybody's been sayin'. The fishin's terrible. So, what d'ya wanna do?"

35

"Uhhh. Well.... I guess we might as well go down closer to the floodin'. We can go down to the bayous like you said. I don't know, can't be worse than this. We still got plenty of coffee. What d'ya think?"

"Yeah. I thought we should've gone there in the first place. The bayous always pan out."

"I suppose. Hindsight's twenty-twenty, but at least we know. I sure didn't want to motor all the way down to the bayous just to find out all the fish were up here."

Denny pulled up anchor and the two wound their way around one bend after another as the river wrapped back and forth through the swamp. Just as they came upon the first bayou, Marki noticed something a short way downstream.

"What's that, Denny? Do you see it down there?"

Denny looked up. There was just enough moonlight to form a silhouette.

"Looks like a boat. Must be we got company. I think maybe I'll drop anchor here. Best we keep our distance and give 'em their space."

Denny and Marki began casting anew, but as before, their efforts were in vain. Marki's curiosity was now stronger than her hopes for catching non-existent fish.

"Denny, don't you think it's odd that we haven't heard a word or seen a light from that boat? I mean, nothing—nothing at all."

Denny continued to reel in his line, but looked in the direction of the boat. Once his lure was out of the water, he set the rod down in the boat and strained to see in the darkness. He said nothing.

"I won—"

"Shhh."

Denny turned his head and closed his eyes. He listened with intent. He then looked at Marki.

"Dang it, I can't hear a thing. I think you may be right. Something's odd, that's for sure."

"You think it broke loose from a dock?"

"What dock?"

"You know, those houses, like the big one at the channel."

"That wouldn't make much sense to me. I don't know, I'm wonderin' if something's wrong. I can't quite make it out. I can't see it. Boat's just a bit too far."

"You wanna go look?"

"Yeah, maybe we better."

Denny pulled up the anchor and let the boat drift. In the darkness, there was little to be seen, and nothing to be heard except for the drone of insects. The current carried them closer. Their eyes had long since adjusted to the darkness, so without the need of a flashlight, once they closed in, it was easy to see that the boat was empty. It had snagged at a sharp bend in the river.

"Grab a hold, Marki."

Marki did as told, and Denny lashed the boats together. He then climbed into the other boat.

"Hand me one of those flashlights."

Denny took the flashlight from Marki and triggered a harsh beam of light that shot across the boat. He began scouring the surroundings. Marki grabbed a second flashlight and did likewise. They flooded the reeds and grasses on both sides of the river with beams of bright white light.

"You see anything?" she asked.

"Nothing."

"So what d'ya think?"

"I don't know. No idea. Just doesn't make sense. A boat that worked loose from a dock wouldn't be full of gear. If the owners knew it was full of gear, they would've chased it down quick. It wouldn't be sitting here. Dang me! Look at this."

"What?"

"There's a couple o' Shimano reels on carbon rods sittin' here." Denny focused the flashlight on the equipment. "Dang. Symetre 2500... the other one's a 3000. Marki, these rods are St. Croix Legends. We're talking three hundred bucks a pop or

37

more. There's like two grand worth of equipment just laying here."

"Denny."

"What?"

"What are you doing?"

"What do you mean, what am I doing? What d'you think I'm doing? I'm drooling."

"Yeah, well you're droolin' over stuff that doesn't belong to you."

"Marki, I love ya, sweetheart, but you know, right now, you're freezin' a wet dream."

"Really?"

"Really."

"And what were you dreaming about, Denny? Stealing 'em?"

"Just never mind. A guy can dream, can't he?"

"Well, return to the nightmare of reality for a moment and tell me. Do you think they fell out of the boat or what?"

Denny thought a moment.

"I don't know what to think. There's two sets of rods an' tackle bags... two coolers, two nets. I'm sayin' there were two people in this boat. But then you gotta ask, how do two people fall out of a boat... and do what? Drown? Two people? I mean, most fishermen know how to tread a little water. The river's not that deep, and you're not gonna drown in cattails. Of course, who knows how far this boat drifted? In fact, this boat may have drifted all the way down here from Houghton Lake."

Denny turned the beam of light onto the rods a second time.

"These guys are rigged for day fishing. They weren't fishing out here tonight with those lures."

"Is there anything in those tackle boxes with a name on it?"

"That's what I was just lookin' for. Oh, man, look at this stuff. Wild River lighted tackle bags. Are you kidding me? That's another two hundred bucks a bag. These guys must be loaded."

Denny continued rummaging through the gear when Marki interrupted him.

38

"Hey, Denny. What's that?"

Denny stopped sifting through gear to look up at Marki. She was staring away, staring upstream.

"What's what?"

"Turn your light off."

Marki turned her flashlight off at the same time as Denny. He fumbled to turn off the tackle bag light.

"Do you see that?"

"See what?"

"Over there... where we were fishing before."

"I don't see anything."

"Just keep watching. Do you see that blue glow?"

"Blue glow?"

"Yeah, see it?"

"I need a minute for my eyes to adjust."

"Do you see it?"

"Uh.... Yeah, I do now."

Denny and Marki sat quietly in the boats and studied the pronounced blue glow that outlined the river upstream.

"What is that?" asked Marki.

"Damned if I know."

"Isn't that right where we were fishing?"

"Yeah, pretty much."

"Looks like it's pulsating."

Denny watched the fluctuations and waves of luminescence move across the water.

"That's kind of spooky," said Marki.

"Must be some kind of algae."

"Ya think?"

"I don't' know. What else could it be? Never seen it before." Denny switched his flashlight back on and went back to searching the boat. "There's gotta be something in here."

39

Denny began opening the side pouches on the bag. He spotted a piece of paper. He unfolded it and studied the print.

"Hey, I got something. I think."

"What is it?"

"A receipt. It's faded but I can still make it out. Says, Bill and Joes Sport and Tackle Shop, Lansing, Michigan. The name is... Derrek Charney, 1122 Bria... Briar... I can't make out the address."

He looked up at Marki.

"Derrek Charney, probably from Lansing."

"Anything else?"

Denny started opening and rifling through the plastic trays in the other tackle bag.

"This guy's got a really nice selection of poppers. He's making his own. Nope, I don't see anything else with a name or any paperwork."

"What're you gonna do with the boat? Tow it back?"

"Uhh. Better leave it. Yeah. Better leave it here, so that the sheriff's department knows where to look in case there was some kind of accident. I can't believe two guys fell overboard. It must have been somethin' else."

Marki leaned over the boat. Her face hovered inches above the water as she focused her flashlight's beam down into the depths. She struggled to see anything of worth.

"I doubt you'll find anything down there. This boat may have floated forever before coming to rest."

"What is that?" asked Marki.

"What?"

"Pull up that stringer. My eyes must be playing tricks on me."

"What do you see?" asked Denny as he reached for the stringer and pulled it upward.

Out from the water emerged what appeared to be the remains of an enormous walleye's head followed by a body that eroded to little more than scraps of flesh with bones sticking outward like quills on a pissed-off porcupine.

"What the hell is that?" he said aloud.

Denny and Marki sat in silence, staring at the dripping mess suspended before their flashlights.

"Must be the fish made a meal out of it." said Marki.

"Either this boat has been out here for a lot longer than we think, or we got piranha around here.

Suddenly an ear-splitting smack shattered the stillness of the night, causing Marki to scream involuntarily. She nearly leapt into the abandoned boat to get next to Denny. She was halfway there before she realized what had happened.

"Damn it! Damn them fish."

Denny howled.

"Getting' a little nervous, are we?"

"Shut up."

Every time Denny looked at Marki, he laughed harder.

"I said, shut up. Shut up, Denny."

"Sorry. Sorry." He slowly settled himself. "Marki, I swear, the timing couldn't have been better. I don't know how big that baby was, but it sure hit the water hard. Dang, that was one big-ass fish. Now, why can't we catch one of those?"

Denny was still laughing.

"I think I've had enough for tonight, Denny."

Marki eased back into her own boat. She turned off her flashlight.

"Yeah, me too. Bad enough we can't catch anything, but being taunted by something that big is the last straw."

Denny let loose the stringer and watched the bony remains sink below the surface.

"Shall we head back?"

"Yeah. You got cell service?"

Marki produced her phone and turned it on.

"No."

Denny moved his flashlight beam back along the boat planks and stopped at a cooler. He stepped toward it and opened it up. He reached in and grabbed a beer.

"Warm.... This boat has been out in the sun for a long time. Maybe all day, or even a couple of days. Huh, that's strange. Oh, well. Reach up there and untie us, will you?"

Marki moved to unlash their boat as Denny climbed back aboard and sat down. He started the motor, and pointed the bow upstream.

"I can't believe I'm pulling away from an abandoned boat filled full of the very best in Christmas gifts."

"I can appreciate the temptation. But I'm happier to know that I married an honest fisherman. Christ surrounded himself with honest fishermen."

"Yeah, whatever."

Within five minutes, Denny and Marki were back at the mouth of the bayou. As they looked across the shadowy surface of water and vegetation, they again saw the bluish glow. This time it was at the far end of the bayou.

"That is truly bizarre," said Denny. "I've never seen anything like that before. Hmm."

Denny eased off the throttle, holding the boat steady in the stream, as he stared across the bayou to study the apparition-like phenomenon.

"Creepy is more like it. C'mon, Denny. I'm ready to go back."

"Okay.... I wonder what the hell *is* that. I've never even heard of anything that glows blue in the swamp."

"Denny. C'mon. Let's go. What're you gonna do when we get back?"

"What time did your cell say?"

"About three, three-thirty, three-seventeen to be exact."

"Well.... It'll probably be four-thirty or five by the time we get back home. I'll call it in first thing after getting a little shuteye. Say seven or eight."

"What if someone back there needs help? You don't think we should call as soon as we get back?"

"Marki, we fished the bayou for an hour, and there wasn't a sign of life around that boat the entire time. I checked the beer in that cooler, and it was piss-warm. That boat's been there for who knows how long. Hell, it may've been there for a week for all I know. A few more hours isn't gonna make a damn bit of difference."

## 9

Six a.m. was the middle of the day for Jack McGrath. It was plenty late enough to drive over and see the sheriff in Roscommon. He had spent enough time mulling things over, and this morning, he was nothing less than a man with a mission. He was unsure about how to present his concerns, and equally worried about being dismissed as an old fart with a failing mind. Yet to say nothing was cowardice. It was unthinkable. He would take whatever snickering was in store.

Jack drove east on West Houghton to Denton, turned left onto North Roscommon Road, and followed it to the corner of South Second, where he pulled over and parked. He got out of his car and walked up to the front door of the station. He peered through the glass, pulled on the handle, and entered.

"Is the sheriff in? I need to see the sheriff."

"I'm sorry, sir, the sheriff isn't available. Is there something I can do for you?"

"No, I need to see the sheriff. It's important."

"I'm sorry, sir, I would have to screen your request and see if I can be of help before I break into the sheriff's schedule."

"Who're you?"

"I'm Undersheriff Paul Carlton, and I would be very happy to serve you if I can."

"Fine. I stopped in 'cause somethin's goin' on in the Dead Stream Swamp that you guys need to know about."

"May I get your name?"

"Jack McGrath."

"So, what's goin' on in Dead Stream Swamp, Mr. McGrath? What is it that we need to know about?"

Jack went on to tell the undersheriff about how he awoke to find the remains of his dog on the porch. He told the undersheriff about the snakes and rodents scampering away from the water. He told him about seeing bones of all sorts along the banks and in the marshes. He told him about the acrid odor in the air and large patches of dead vegetation. He told him about seeing lights in the shallows at night. He told him about the deer with the de-fleshed forelegs and the bloodstained highway. He told him about the ducks in the rabbit cage. He told him every detail he could recall.

Undersheriff Carlton listened politely. He then focused on Jack's dead dog. At first, Jack answered the officer's questions. Then the questioning seemed to focus entirely on events surrounding his dog's death. Jack sensed that the officer was moving in the direction of animal cruelty, and that set him off. His frustration was heating up his temper, and that raised both the pitch and volume of his voice.

"That dog was my best friend for fourteen years an' I don't need no condescendin' arrogant sonovabitch tellin' me I was cruel or torturin' it, or whatever the hell you're insinuatin'."

"Now hold on, Mr. McGrath. Just calm down. Gettin' fired up and cussin' ain't gonna get anybody anywhere."

"Maybe not. But tellin' it straight ain't getting anybody anywhere either. All I did was waste a good mornin', not to mention getting pissed. You know what? I'll promise ya this much. Shit's gonna hit the fan around here, an' you mark my words, young man, you'll be rememberin' my cussin' on *that* day."

Sheriff Cooper stood up from his desk and stepped over to his office door. He peered into the station to observe a man who was clearly agitated. He watched as the old-timer finally stood up and stormed out, swearing under his breath like a true sailor. He chuckled. His amusement ended when his desk phone rang.

"Yeah, Charlie.... Huh.... Did you get their names? Yeah. What was the guy's name? Derrek Charney.... Name's new to me. Yeah. Listen, get ahold of Quinn. Yeah, he was just out that way lookin' into the Hamilton case.... Yeah. Okay, yeah, keep me updated."

# 10

Cory walked into the Little Boots Country Diner. He had not been up to Houghton Lake in a couple of years and so stood momentarily in the entrance to freshen his memory and enjoy the comfort of an old haunt. His glance swept around the familiar red-curtained windows and matching red and gray vinyl booths, but halted when he spotted a couple of old friends seated at a window table facing the street. He stepped away from the door and headed in their direction.

"Bill —Greg, how you guys doing?"

"Cory! Sonovagun. What're you doin' here?"

"Came by to see Harold Sweeny. I don't know if you guys know him; he owns the *County Chronicle*. He's an old friend, invited me up for dinner and drinks. Mind if I join you? You're not leaving right yet, I hope?"

"Can't stay but a couple more minutes," said Bill. "Gotta work. But for now, hell yeah, have a seat."

"Cory, this here's Jimmy."

"Jimmy," repeated Cory as he offered his hand. "You guys waking up or winding down?"

"Ah, we been out fishin' on the flooding," said Bill. "Took the boat up into the swamp. Don't ask us why. Finally decided it'd be more fun goin' back to town an' eatin' breakfast."

"How's that?"

45

"I'm tellin' ya, Cory. Fishin's become a lost sport around here," said Greg. "I can remember when we used to get bored of catching fish. Now we only talk about gettin' bored."

"Yeah," said Jimmy. "Reminds me of old times when this guy walked into a bar down the street for a beer after a long day of fishin'. Bartender asks him how he fared. Guy says he did good, caught a hundred or two an' the bartender starts laughing his ass off.

*"What are ya, Irish? Never in a million years."*

Guy gets all bent an' says, "You callin' me a liar?"

Bartender says, *"Hell, no. But I got a ten spot that says ya didn't."*

*"You're on."*

The fisherman opens his side bag, pulls out a couple of perch, and slaps 'em on the bar.

"I told ya a hundred or two an' there's the two. *Ten bucks.*"

The four broke out in polite laughter. Bill interrupted.

"I'm not sure the joke's that funny anymore. Seems like all we ever get is two... if that."

"Yeah, an' then ya gotta ask, two what?" said Jimmy.

"Well, if it's Roadkill Ralph, could be two snakes or two squirrels."

Laughter circled the table. This time for real.

"Yeah, two anything that's flat an' half-baked on the tarmac," said Jimmy.

"Roadkill Ralph?" asked Cory, clearly feeling out of the loop. "What's that all about?"

"Ahh, he's some old geezer that's been runnin' up an' down the highway as of late throwin' roadkill into the back of his truck," said Greg. "He's been doin' it enough that the town's taken notice an' made him the butt of a lot o' jokes. Ya know, like maybe he's plannin' on openin' a restaurant. *If it's floatin' or bloatin', get it at the Houghton."*

Everybody chuckled.

"I'll be damned," said Cory energetically. "I think I saw that guy last night on the way up here. He was driving an old brown pickup. I saw him just standing there, staring down at a deer carcass."

Cory's friends exploded into knowing laughter.

"Yeah. That's him. Yeah, you got it. Hey, you should've pulled over an' given him a hand."

"I don't think so. He looked like a pretty ornery old cuss. Christ almighty, he stared my ass right down."

"Hey, we're laughin' but he's the only fool in the county catchin' anything," said Jimmy.

"Amen," the others agreed.

"To Roadkill Ralph, the ornery ol' cuss." Jimmy raised his coffee cup to toast.

"Oh, c'mon, guys," said Cory in an honest state of doubt. "Fishing can't be *that* bad. I don't think I ever once came back from the flooding or the swamp without a bucket-load of dinner."

"Ain't that the truth," said Greg. "Always been that way... since before I could walk. Always was, right up 'til about—I dunno—maybe three years ago when it started slowin' down. And now, shit... ya can't catch a fish if your life depends on it."

"You guys are bullshitting me."

"Nope. We're not," grumbled the men in unison.

"C'mon.... You're pulling my leg, right? You're kidding me. That place is fishing mecca," said Cory.

"Wish we were," said Bill.

"Honest to god, cross your fingers, and all that horseshit."

"Honest to god, cross my fingers, an' all that horseshit," said Bill.

"Wow," said Cory with an expression of disbelief. "So what's with that?"

"Who knows? You remember Ray Staggs?"

"Barely. Haven't seen him in years. Didn't he have uh... the bait shop? Lyman's or Last Resort, or something like that?"

"Right guy, wrong place. He owns the bait shop right there at the 127 exit, just east of it on the north side of 55. You know

47

where all the gas stations are, across the street from all the fast food joints."

"Yeah, I know where you're sayin'."

"Go talk to Ray. I promise ya, he'll tell ya a couple of bizarre stories about fishing in the swamp. An' he's one of the few around here who ain't Irish."

"Anybody looking into it?" asked Cory.

"Not so far. Least not that I've heard. State's outta money. I can tell ya this much. One more year of this shit, an' we can kiss ass good-bye to whatever's left of tourism. People come here to fish. And there ain't no fish—just fish stories. And with that, guys, I gotta go—work time."

Bill pushed back his chair and stood up. He picked his check up off the table. He called out as he waved it.

"Betsy."

"Hey, it's good seeing you again, Bill."

"Yeah, same here, Cory. Let's see if we can get together an' grab a beer before ya head back down." Bill studied Cory a moment. "I'm tryin' to remember... *Lansing?*"

"Grand Rapids."

"Oh, yeah, that's right. I knew it was somewhere around there. Let's try for that beer."

"Absolutely. Take care."

"Cory, sorry man, but Jimmy an' I gotta go as well."

"Hey, no problem. I know about the working world, remember it all too well. It's good seeing you, Greg. Nice meeting you, Jimmy."

"Likewise. Maybe Greg an' I can join you an' Bill for that beer."

"That'd be great. You guys drive careful."

"Will do."

Cory watched his old high-school buddies leave the restaurant. It was a bittersweet feeling. He missed them. He missed a good many faces and places of his childhood. On the other hand, Houghton Lake meant risking a life of poverty, and he was not equipped to take the gamble. He had no regrets. Had he stayed, it would have been a life of scrounging. He looked at his watch and ordered breakfast.

## 11

Cristina nodded her head knowingly.

"Mom... mom.... Yes. I know. I will. Yes, mother. I'm here now. Yes. Hold on, hold on a minute."

Cristina slowed the car as she approached an old weathered wooden sign barely attached to a badly tilted, grayed, and split cedar post. Cristina stared at the base of the post and questioned her long-held belief that white cedar did not rot. It looked rotted to her. Long streaks of stain rose to spots where once shiny nails affixed a plank that read 'McGrath' if one took the time to make it out. The letters were like ghosts of times long passed, but whether better times or even good times, she was uncertain.

Cristina vaguely remembered those days. There were glimpses of sunlit memories, hints of a time when life was lived in the peace and safety of isolation and ignorance. It was a time when there was nothing but mom, dad, Geeter, and herself.

"Yes, I'm still on the phone. Yes.... The place looks terrible; what did you expect? I barely got into the driveway. Dad needs to trim it back. I know. I know. Yes, I know. Mom, I know.

"Good grief, mother. You and dad have been divorced for fifty years, and I swear the two of you are the only ones who don't know it. You're right. I don't understand. I'll never understand. It's a wonder I'm only slightly screwed up. Yes, I'll tell him. I will. I promise. Yes. Okay. I'll call you back. Yes. I'll call you back later. Bye. Bye. Mom... mom... bye.... Mom... good-bye, I'll call you later."

Cristina disconnected. She grimaced as the branches of the trees scraped along the sides of her car. She figured after this she would need to have her car polished at best, painted at worst. She was relieved to see the opening up ahead that marked an end to her poor car's torturous arrival.

Cristina parked the vehicle. She was dismayed to see that her father's truck was gone. She climbed out of her car, closed the door, and took a moment to stretch her back as she stared at the cabin. The poor appearance of the cabin quickly disheartened her. Her mother would be no happier. The place was in a sad state of repair. Old and broken, as was her dad.

Cristina then did what she had done all the years she visited her father. She walked down the north side yard toward the back of the house.

"Scrub! ...Scrub!"

Instinctively, Cristina called out for her dad's dog, who generally came running up to greet her. The dog was nowhere to be seen, but that often meant it was in the boat with her father.

To the best of Cristina's recollection, nobody had ever entered or exited the front door of the cabin. Everybody always went around back fully expecting to see her father sitting in his rocker fiddling with something, or simply blowing smoke rings in the quiet backwater air.

What broke habit today was a highly visible ring of what looked to be rock salt or something of the kind spread on the ground to form a ring, a perimeter that appeared to encircle the house. Cristina tried to follow the path by sight, bending over and looking under the structure.

Unlike the houses of her childhood friends, hers was built on stilts—large white cedar posts. Her mother used to say it helped keep the snakes out. Her father said it was to keep the house dry, not from rising water, but from the humidity of the swamp. The occasional breeze could circulate freely underneath the structure. Truth be known, the whole house was made out of white cedar. It simply would not rot, and that made it well suited for life in the half-submerged surroundings.

Cristina crossed over the barrier and walked its inner periphery. As she rounded the corner of the house, she spied her father's boat tied to the dock. She looked at the back of his home, which had a full-length porch that offered a view of the shallows. Her fingers danced lightly along the banister as she passed toward the porch steps and scaled them.

To Cristina's right as she crossed the porch was her father's rocker. It rested where it had always been, where it should always be. Its creaking reminded her as much of him as the sound of his voice. It sat there motionless like a waiting dog. She reached for the kitchen door, stopping only to turn partially and take a final look out across the backwater. The isolation unnerved her. She wondered if she was just getting old. She stepped across the threshold and pulled the door shut behind her, sealing out the disturbing.

Inside the kitchen, Cristina looked around to assure herself that nothing was amiss. Seeing that everything was as it should be, she was free to worry only about her dad's dinner. She wondered what she might cook up for a meal. She promptly walked over to the freezer chest and flipped open the lid. She was amazed to find it nearly empty.

This was more than just worrisome for Christina. She knew that the freezer was always full—*always*. Something had to be going on, something out of the ordinary. Maybe her father was ill. The man was a fisherman to the core and the chest was always full. Maybe for some reason, he was not getting out. Cristina turned away from the freezer and faced the dishes in the kitchen sink.

"I guess I got here none too soon."

When finished cleaning up her father's mess, Cristina crossed the kitchen and reached for the pencil and paper that permanently rested alongside the old dial phone. She jotted down a note to let her father know she had arrived and was now heading for town. She signed the note 'with love' and stepped back out onto the porch. She cupped her hands about her mouth and hollered through the maze of trees standing tall in motionless water.

51

"Scrub!"

She listened.

"Scrub!"

Cristina called out a couple more times but to no avail. She knew her father often took Scrub with him when going to town. There was no point in hollering for the sake of hollering.

Cristina's hundred-and-fifty-mile journey had taken just over three hours and left her hungry. Being that her dad was nowhere to be found, she decided now was a perfect time to grab breakfast. After eating, she would pick up a few groceries and make her father a decent dinner. She knew he would be grateful. Having someone wait on him hand and foot was a rare experience in his life. It was a change of pace that she knew her father fully appreciated. Nobody ever made him a meal.

Cristina stepped away from the door. She stood against the porch banister and looked out across the water for Scrub one final time. She immediately got a whiff of something nasty in the air. She noticed a slight disturbance on the surface of the water. It was similar to the way pop in a glass bubbles lightly after the fizz has settled down. It was a curious thing. It was odd.

Cristina now turned her attention to the bank where a second item of curiosity caught her attention. It was a cage that she barely glimpsed when arriving. She had paid it no mind, but now from where she stood on the porch, she could see there was some material or bedding inside. She knew it to be one of her father's rabbit or chicken cages.

Moving to leave, Cristina descended the steps, but could not dismiss her curiosity about the cage. She detoured the few paces necessary to see its contents up close. A nearer inspection revealed something that appeared to be the rotted remains of a bird or maybe more. It was a mat of feather and bones. At least one flat-billed skull was visible in the tangle of debris. It appeared to be that of a duck. It had a particularly irritating odor that caused Cristina to whisper under her breath.

"Yuck."

It was a puzzling sight until Cristina determined her father might have brought the cage to water's edge for cleaning. That made perfect sense—certainly more sense than the white ring of salt or whatever it was that encircled the house.

Cristina wondered what mysterious activity her dad was up to. Her eyes followed the line of milky white chunks that passed by her feet. Baffled, she bent down to touch a crystal with her index finger. She stuck out her tongue to taste her finger.

"Yup. Salt. Just what I thought. A *ring* of salt. Geez, what's with that, dad? You into witchcraft or something?"

Cristina straightened up and stepped along the white line of demarcation as it led her back to the front of the house. As she crossed the front yard and moved toward her car, she looked deep into the flooded woods. She felt oddly unsettled and watched warily for any hint of movement.

The surroundings remained eerily silent, and Cristina wasted no time climbing back into her car. She closed the door and sat a moment, twisting her head as she looked out the windows. She half expected something to lunge at her from the mysterious mixture of swamp water and grasses. She felt the hair on her arms rise.

Cristina glanced down at the buttons on the door panel. She hit the lock button and the sound of clicking door locks brought needed relief. She had never done that before. The doors always locked automatically at precisely twenty miles an hour.

"I've been away too long, dad. The place is creeping me out. Imagine that."

Inside, outside, the silence was the same except one felt comforting while the other anything but. Cristina turned the key and brought the Taurus to life. She shifted it into reverse. She looked out across the swamp one last time before releasing the brake and steering the car back onto the driveway.

## 12

"Cri?"

Cristina turned toward the voice that summoned her. She saw a man sitting alone at a window booth. It took her a moment to recognize this person out of context.

"I know you, but I can't remember...."

"Cory Ballard."

"Oh, yes. That's right, Cory. What are you doing in Houghton Lake?"

"I was about to ask you the same thing. I nearly fell over when I saw you walk in. I wasn't sure if I remembered your name correctly or not. I remember it was unusual."

"You remembered correctly. It's Cristina Walker, but my friends call me Cri. I'm here visiting my dad, and you?"

"Listen, I don't want to be obnoxious, but I'd love to buy you breakfast or at least a coffee if you have time. I'm sitting alone, and running into you this far from home has to be an omen of some sort. Would you care to join me?"

Cory stumbled, "Oh, I'm sorry. Duh. You're probably meeting somebody. Idiot that I am, I wasn't thinking."

Within milliseconds, Cristina summed up this man. The initial assessment was not one of appearances—that was yet to come. It was not one of like or dislike, she did not really know him. It was one of safety. Her instinctive opinion of this man, long before she realized it, was that he seemed safe. Then came the pleasure of his appearance and the resonance of his voice.

"Ahhh... actually, I'm not meeting anybody, but whether or not this is an omen, I don't know. I'll join you only if I pay for my own."

"Great." Cory stood up from the booth. "Please, have a seat. I just ordered."

Cristina walked over toward Cory's booth. A waitress followed close behind with pad and pencil in hand.

"Hi, my name is Betsy. Do you need a menu?"

"No, thank you. Couple of eggs scrambled, crisp bacon, and wheat toast if you have it."

"Anything to drink?"

"Coffee and a water with no ice."

"Got it. I'll bring your orders out together."

"Thank you."

Another server approached with a clean placemat, a cup, and a pot of coffee that she moved to pour.

"Mmmm. Good," said Cristina as she savored the hot brew.

"So, you said you're up here visiting your dad?"

"I am. I try to get up here at least a couple of times a year."

"A good daughter."

"I wish. Twice a year doesn't make me a good daughter. It's more complicated than that. He's getting on in years." Cristina took a breath. "I worry about him."

"Is he in bad health?"

"No, I don't think so. It's just the subtle signs of aging. It's the small things that clue you in. Like pulling off the road and hardly being able to get to the cabin because everything is so overgrown. He isn't attacking life the way he used to. The cabin's in disrepair, showing its age just like dad."

"Happens to us all."

"I know, but I just feel like something's changed. I opened up his freezer this morning and it was almost empty. I know this will really sound stupid, but I can't tell you how upsetting that was for me. My dad lives to fish, sunup to sunset. I've never seen the freezer that low. If he's not fishing, I know he's not feeling well, but he's not the type to tell me if anything is wrong."

"Maybe it's not as bad as you think. Maybe it's something else."

"What do you mean? Like what?"

"Well, oddly enough, I was just having coffee with a couple of old high-school buddies and they were crying about the lack of fish this year. Apparently, the fishing's terrible."

55

"Is that true? Really? Geez, do I appreciate you sharing *that*. Far back as I can remember, dad's freezer has always been full. Never seen it even close to empty. Honestly, I was beginning to think the worst. If that's the case, then all I'm facing is a tragic fishing story. White-knuckled fisherman's campfire horror for sure, but at least I, as the *'good daughter'*, can ease up on the worry and guilt. Again, thank you for that.

"So... enough about me. What about you? Why are you in Houghton?"

"I was invited up by an old friend to have dinner and drinks—quasi-business. It happens every couple of years. Whereas I'm retired, he owns the *Roscommon County Chronicle*—the local newspaper. It's easier for me to come see him than vice versa."

"So, you're just up for the night?"

"Oh, maybe a day or two. I haven't decided. But tell me. You say you're visiting your dad. Did you live here? Did you grow up here? Because, I don't remember...."

"No. I left when I was around three or four. Long time ago. My folks divorced. Well, I think they divorced. I'm not so sure anymore. Anyhow, I went with mom, and she ended up moving to Grand Rapids. She told me she couldn't do the Detroit thing—too much of a country girl. Dad stayed."

"You know, you and I've met up a couple of times through—"

"Rudy," Cristina injected.

"Yeah. That's it. Rudy Van Domelen."

"He's a nurse over at Magdalen."

"Right. Is that how you know him?"

"Uh-huh. We've worked the same floor for years together. Rudy's a great guy. Took his wife's death hard."

"Hoo-boy. Isn't that the truth?"

"How do you know Rudy?"

"We were in the service together. Rudy's the guy that talked me into moving down to Grand Rapids when I was discharged. So, I assume you're also in the medical profession."

"Uh-huh. A nurse, like Rudy. When my mother left my dad, she wanted to get as far away as possible, but being wary of big-city life, she was compelled to protect me. Soooo... she rented an old farmhouse in the middle of nowhere, in the middle of these massive fields that the landlord leased out. As far back as I can remember, it was pretty much me and mom, and not much else.

"You could probably say that I was the focus of her life."

"Probably?"

"Yeah." Cristina laughed. "She had me reading by the time I was three. School was my church, education my religion, and textbooks my bible. Believe me, I got good grades.

"Anyway, mom worked at Magdalen in the accounting department. She used her connections to get me on a floor as a PCA, you know, a nurse's helper. And from there, I went for registered nurse. I suppose it gets old like everything else, but it gives me a good life. I've wanted for nothing."

"That's great."

"Okay. You know about me, now what about you?"

"Jesus, I'm just sitting here laughing to myself as I listen to you talk about your mother making sure you knew how to read and write. I have to say, it must be something about a Houghton Lake mother. I went through the *'flip pages or flip burgers: your choice'* the whole of my childhood.

"On the other hand, credit given where credit due. If not for mom, I might've done a whole lot worse. I did okay in high school, but like most kids around here, college was out of the question." Cory stopped, and with a stern look, pointed at Cristina. "To make sure we understand each other, it wasn't due to a lack of brains on my part."

"Of course not," said Cristina with a taunting laugh.

"Hey, you wouldn't know. You didn't grow up here. Work around here is non-existent. Same with money. There is none. There's no possible way my folks could have sent me to college. And I certainly couldn't afford it.

"My best option was to go into the service. And that's what I did. Didn't give it a second thought. Best move I ever made. Learned aircraft electronics and avionics system repair. Rudy said, 'Cory, come to Grand Rapids, there's all kinds of work'. He was right. Couple of days after my discharge, I landed a great job that utilized me for everything I learned, and I spent most of my life there."

"How long were you in the service?"

"Twelve years, three tours."

"Who did you work for when you got out?"

"Krandor Industries."

"What do they do?"

"They're into the design and manufacture of aerospace instrumentation. I worked there for twenty-eight years before the recession downsized them. A number of us old-timers accepted incentives to take an early out. You know—severance packages. No hard feelings on my part. They were generous. I mean, we really got good deals, but the idea that any of us old farts would again see gainful employment was nonsense. No one hires you at our age. So I got into other things, and here I am."

"So, what are *other things*? What do you do now?"

"How about we leave answering that to another time? I always get a little gun shy when asked that question."

"Really? Well, don't let me make you uncomfortable. I've read a lot of books about undercover agents and I understand. I know one when I see one. It's okay, really. Your secret's safe with me."

Cory laughed, "I assure you. It's nothing so glamorous."

Cory and Cristina moved through a number of subjects, and it was clear that they enjoyed each other. They did not rush breakfast, but it became obvious that they were stretching their first meeting. Cory decided to bring it to a close, and moved to pick up her bill.

"No."

"Please, I really would like to. You saved me from eating alone and the view from my side of the booth was great."

"I'll take the compliment *and* the check. Please."

"Very well. I wouldn't want to ruin a good thing."

Cristina waited for Cory to cash out. Cory, in turn, held the door for her as they stepped outside.

"Any chance I could persuade you to join me for lunch tomorrow and maybe afterward go look at some bones?"

Cristina gave him an expression every bit as apprehensive as he would have expected.

"Bones?" she asked.

"Yup. Bones. And then I'll tell you a little more about exactly what I do."

"Bones. Oh, boy. I mean, I don't know a woman alive who could pass up such an appealing offer. Quite seductive in a sort of demented way."

"Great. How about we meet here tomorrow—say... noonish. And I invited you, so I buy. No argument, please. Don't ruin a good thing."

"Against my better judgment, I'll try. No promises, though. I'm here to see my dad. As for buying my lunch... maybe, maybe not."

"Equality of the sexes. I get it. I can do that. So... I'll be here. If you make it, wonderful. If not, I understand. I have to say that either way, it's been a pleasure, Cri. I never would've expected to run into you of all people up here in Houghton Lake. What're the odds?"

"Small world, you have to admit."

"Okay, then. Against better judgment, I'll see you tomorrow—maybe."

"Maybe."

Cory walked Cristina to her car. He opened the door for her.

"Thank you for inviting me to your table."

"No problem. My lucky day."

"Bye."

Cristina pulled the door shut and smiled at him through the window. She fired up the car.

"Bye."

She didn't hear his voice; she read his lips. His smile said enough. She smiled back and pulled away.

# 13

"Deb?"

"What?"

"Can you hear me?"

"Yes."

"Hey, I'm gonna take Cinder down to the swamp for some training. That okay?"

"Okay, but don't come back late. Remember, we're meeting Dave and Linda at five for drinks at the Long Branch."

"Okay."

"What time is it now?"

"Ahhh, about three. I'll be back by four-thirty."

"Make sure you are. Give yourself enough time to get cleaned up."

"I will. All right, I'll be back in a little while."

Aaron looked down at his black lab.

"C'mon, boy. Let's go have some fun."

Cinder was as bright as they come, and Aaron knew his dog understood exactly what was happening. The dog was beside himself with anticipation, and straining to control himself. He sat and wiggled from head to tail, waiting for Aaron to open the back door.

Aaron pulled the door wide and Cinder nearly knocked him over as he bolted for the yard. The dog made a straight line for the truck. He darted back and forth behind the tailgate, barking and beckoning Aaron to hurry up.

"I'm coming, ya dolt."

Aaron walked into his garage and lifted a yellow plastic milk crate off the floor. He pulled it up against his gut and looked over the contents.

"One, two, three, four, five, six, seven, eight."

Aaron accounted for all eight deadfowl trainers. He walked the crate out to the truck and tossed it into the bed. He then dropped the tailgate.

"Go on, get in."

Cinder hardly had to be told. The dog knew the routine and was in mid-air before Aaron could spit out the words. Fifteen minutes later, Aaron arrived at his preferred training spot and parked the pickup. He climbed out of the cab and walked around to the back of the truck.

"Sit."

The dog obeyed. Aaron dropped the gate and dragged the yellow crate across the bed. He lifted it out and began walking across the clearing. About thirty paces from the truck, he dropped the crate to the ground and turned around to look at Cinder, who was watching him with utmost intent.

"Break!"

Cinder jumped down from the truck and took off running around the clearing. The dog was full of energy. He circled Aaron three or four times, running out farther at each pass. Meanwhile, Aaron walked a hundred or more feet from the truck and began tossing his deadfowl trainers into various places. He returned to the truck and summoned Cinder back with a quick blow of a whistle.

The dog approached Aaron directly. At about twenty paces out, Aaron stopped Cinder's approach.

"Sit."

The dog obeyed.

"Look!"

Cinder focused on Aaron, who then gave a command.

"Back!"

Cinder took off at full speed, running away from Aaron in a straight line. He found a trainer, picked it up, and immediately started back toward Aaron at full speed. Aaron watched Cinder and then intentionally stopped the dog from reaching him.

"Sit!"

The dog halted from a full run and dropped at once onto its rear haunches. The dog sat, though bristling with energy. He remained in position twenty paces away from his master. The dog was panting hard, the training bird held firmly in its mouth. Aaron walked the twenty paces to Cinder and commanded him to drop the bird into his hand.

"Out."

Cinder released the bird.

Aaron praised the dog.

"Heel."

The dog walked at Aaron's side back to the truck. Aaron spent most of the hour sending Cinder back to the left, back to the right, and back to center using hand signals. He then went through the 'over' drills, sending Cinder first back two or three hundred feet, and then left or right of his position while far back in the clearing. The dog noted if Aaron raised his arm to the left or the right, and never failed to comprehend his instruction. It was time for a reward.

While Cinder was back chasing down the trainers, Aaron had deftly tossed a couple of the retrieved trainers into the shallows without the dog's knowing. He allowed Cinder to come to him with the last trainer.

"Sit. Good boy. Out."

Cinder simultaneously dropped to his haunches and released the trainer from his jaws. It fell to the ground.

"Place."

Cinder's shoulders unlocked as he dropped down to lie across the trainer.

"Stand."

Cinder stood up.

"Fetch."

Cinder picked the trainer up from the ground.

"Come."

Cinder brought the trainer to Aaron.

"Good boy.  Break."

Cinder ran up to Aaron with his tail wagging, making it clear he was playing a game he liked best.  Aaron gave the dog a couple of treats and then commanded it to heel, to walk alongside him to the water's edge.  Cinder knew he was going for a swim and would be able to cool off after all the running and fetching.

Aaron walked over and picked up the trainer that he instructed Cinder to lie across earlier.  He walked back with it to where Cinder could see him, and then tossed it far across the shallows.  Cinder saw it land with a splash.

"Look."

Cinder turned his back to the water and looked directly at Aaron.

"Sit."

Cinder sat down, but his eyes never swayed from his master.  Aaron then gave the command.

"Back!"

At the same time, he raised his left hand, which instructed Cinder not to go after the trainer that he had seen splash into the water directly in front of him, but to head off in a different direction to retrieve a trainer that he had not seen.  The dog would rely solely on direction from Aaron, who remained on shore.

Cinder dove into the shallows and started swimming away to the left.  He streaked across the water as if he were participating in a canine poker run.  Aaron pressed him on.

"Back!"

But Cinder slowed.  Cinder went under.

Aaron knew his dog as well as he knew his wife.  He realized instantly, instinctively, that something was very wrong.  He did not know what had just happened, but he knew Cinder would drown within seconds if he did not rescue him.  He never gave it a second thought.

Aaron charged the water and dove in to save his buddy.

## 14

Cristina succumbed to taking one last look at Cory standing in the parking lot before she pulled out of Little Boots to head down West Houghton Lake Drive. Now, she thought only about stocking up on groceries for her father and so made her way to Glen's Market. All joking aside, Cory's comments about the fishing being dismal, and a possible explanation for the nearly empty freezer, had gone a long way toward easing her concerns. She would still ask her father about it to be certain.

Cristina took her time at Glen's. She spent as much time thinking about Cory as she did selecting groceries. He was pleasant, and she felt good about their serendipitous encounter. He was still on her mind when she exited Glen's, but even thoughts of Cory proved no match for thoughts of her favorite gift shops coming into view.

Cristina understood she was supposed to be in Houghton Lake to visit her father, and the idea of shopping risked being a guilt-trip in the making. The guilt should have been almost unbearable—should have been. Almost. But the child in her refused to be denied. The shops beckoned and she obliged. She stopped at every door just 'for a peek' into the string of shops that lined West Houghton Lake Drive.

Needless to say, by the time Cristina turned to plow through the overgrowth of her father's drive, it was late. She felt like that teenager who continued to drink because she was already too drunk to hide the fact. She cringed at the thought of the note she placed next to the phone saying she would be back shortly.

It was pushing five by the time she pulled up in the yard. She saw her father's truck parked there, and the sight of it only increased her guilt. It would have been so sweet if she had arrived home first.

Cristina's desire to return unnoticed prompted her to realize that Scrub had not come racing across the yard to announce that company had arrived. Immediately, her hopes rose at the possibility they were out fishing and unaware of how late she had returned.

Cristina turned the car off and grabbed the groceries. She started across the yard with arms full, stepped across the perimeter of salt, and followed it as it circled around the cabin leading her to the back of the house.

"Shoot."

Cristina let out a hint of her dismay upon seeing her father's boat tied up to the dock. He was home. Immediately thereafter, she saw a swing set sitting in the shallows about fifteen feet out from the shore. The swings were dangling about six inches above the surface of the water. A length of yellow line stretched through the air from a bucket attached to the frame of the swing set back to the porch banister, where it was tied close to the steps.

A frown of confusion crossed her face. She could not help but chuckle as she wondered what he was up to now. No doubt, a story of interest was close at hand. However, any thought to ask vanished the instant she saw him sitting in a haze at the far end of the porch as he rocked slowly in his chair. He was smoking his pipe.

"Hello, dad. Forgive me," she whined. "I'm sorry I took so long. I honestly thought I'd be back in an hour or so, but I ran into a friend from Grand Rapids. Can you believe that? He insisted on buying me breakfast and—"

"Cri," her father interrupted.

"Yes."

"It's fine. No explanations. Actually, I drove up to Roscommon this mornin' on business, came back, and fished most o' the day. Just got back to the cabin myself. If you'd been back earlier, you'd a been sittin' alone anyhow," he lied.

He understood his daughter would have felt terrible to know he had waited most of the day for her arrival, and he did not want to see her upset for any reason.

"Catch anything?"

"Mercy me, don't ask."

65

"Yeah, I heard the fishing's been terrible."

"Terrible doesn't begin to describe it. In all my years, I've never seen anything like it. I think I'm down to five filets in the ice box."

"Yes, I noticed the freezer was empty. I thought maybe you were sick and not getting out."

"No, I'm plenty fine, an' gettin' out all the time for whatever that's worth."

"Well, I brought home some steaks."

"Steaks! Mercy, I can't remember the last time I had steak. Well... actually I can. I think it was the last time ya came visitin'. Bless you, honey. I must say, it's nice to see ya, Cri. You're a wonderful sight for sore eyes."

"I guess that means you're hungry."

"There might be some of that in there as well. I wish you'd've come to see me before goin' after groceries. It ain't right you payin' for those steaks an' cookin' to boot. Makes me feel useless, dependent, ya know? To be clear, I pay for food, and I won't take no for an answer."

"That's just plain silly. Don't worry about it. I make a good living, dad. Did you see my note? You know, I stopped by earlier, but the truck was gone. Scrub didn't come when I called, so I figured you took him into town. Which reminds me. Where is Scrub? I haven't seen him since I arrived. He's usually always in the yard when he hears someone coming up the drive."

Jack pulled the pipe out of his mouth. He leaned forward and tapped it on the banister. He did not look at Cristina.

"Scrub died, honey."

Cristina was crushed.

"Ohhh, dad. No. I'm so sorry. Ohhh, don't tell me. He was such a sweet thing."

"Yeah, he was. But we all gotta go sometime. That's just the way it is. I woke up one mornin' an' he had passed. Just lyin' there on the porch alongside me. Never made a sound. I don't even wanna talk about it. I miss him, an' it depresses me thinkin' about it."

"Well, no wonder. It makes me feel bad, and you're the one who lived with him. I'm so sorry."

"Me too, Cri. But it's passed. It's done. Anyhow, I'm sorry I missed ya this mornin'. I wouldn't've minded goin' into town."

Cristina had no desire to dwell on or drag her father back through memories of Scrub's passing. She gladly changed the subject.

"Maybe, I can run you in tomorrow. If not, the day after for sure."

"Mercy me, sweetheart, ya don't need to be runnin' me into town. I was there this morning. It was more about goin' to town with my baby."

"Baby? Oh, please."

"I mean it. You'll always be my baby."

"Whatever, dad, whatever. So.... Tell me, you feeling okay? Is everything all right?"

"Best I know. Let's face it, I can't remember what feelin' great was like, so I can't imagine feelin' any better now."

"You're too funny. You have to understand, dad, I have *never* seen that freezer so empty. I was thinking, what's with this? I was worried that maybe you were under the weather. For you not to be fishing is like me not out shopping. I'd have to be on my deathbed."

"Put that way, I can see your point, but I'm fine. Been fishin' plenty, just got nothin' to show for it. Fishin's terrible."

"You care if I grill these steaks inside? Oh, forget that. I bought a can of bug spray. I'll just soak in it. Would you do me a favor and fire up the grill while I make us a salad?"

"Sure."

"Make lots of smoke. I hate those darned mosquitos."

"Will do."

Cristina finished tossing the salad and picked up a plate with two handsome-looking slabs of deep red meat. She descended the steps and placed the meat on the grill. It flashed up. Cristina waited for the sizzle to simmer down as she seared the first side.

Her dad came walking up to look over her shoulder. She flipped the two steaks. He kissed her affectionately on the side of her head.

"I'm thinkin' whereas I might've been hungry before, now I'm famished. Mercy me, that's some mighty good-smellin' steak."

"When was the last time you ate?"

"Yesterday. Why would ya ask me that?"

"Because there's no food in this place," Cristina scolded.

"I just told ya, sweetheart, there's no fish in the backwaters."

"Geez, dad, there's a lot more to life than just eating fish. There's no eggs or bacon, no bread, the cupboards are bare. I mean, really?"

"Well, I would've gone to the store, but there was no point once ya called t' say you were comin' up. Figured I'd wait to see what ya planned on cookin' me."

"I see, your little slave. Here, have some non-fish for a change—enjoy. Salt it... and put some salad on your plate."

"Just so ya know; I *have* been eatin' non-fish. They sell them whole cooked chickens at Glen's. Actually, they're not too bad. Not as good as fresh pan-fried fish by a long shot, but they'll do in a pinch. That is, if ya don't mind all that salmonella crap."

"Don't get me going on that," said Cristina. "I swear to god, we're ruining the planet. I can remember grabbing chickens on the farm. We never even heard of salmonella."

"Yeah, an' if I wanted a fish all I had to do was reach in the water an' grab one. Hasn't been that way for a long time either. Chickens aren't the same, fishing ain't the same."

"Cory was telling me, it might be the lampreys. Are they killing everything off? I thought the state set up house on Dead Stream to reduce their numbers." said Cristina.

"I'm surprised ya even remember that. They were workin' on it, but got cut short when the station burnt down. Heard they moved the research up somewhere around Cheboygan, ya know, 'cause of lamprey migrations along the inland waterway. Never saw 'em again 'round here."

68

"Huh. Makes sense I guess *or not*. Did the Muskegon River suddenly stop flowing all the way across the state? What's the inland waterway, forty miles? What's that in comparison? Zip."

"Cristina?"

"Yeah."

"How's your mother doin'? She gettin' by okay?"

"Oh, Geez. I was supposed to tell you that she said hello. She's doing fine. Don't tell her I forgot." Cristina looked at her dad with an expression of stupidity. "What am I saying? You guys don't even speak. I must be losing it. You want some more salad or anything?"

"No thanks, honey, I'm good. It was great. Everything tasted fantastic. You're a chef extraordinaire. She seein' anybody?"

"Oh, come on, dad. Are you kidding me? Good lord. That'll be the day. Far as I can tell, you're still the one. For whatever that's worth."

Jack stood up from the table and stretched.

"That's too bad. She's a good woman. I'm gonna fill my pipe. D'you mind?"

"Of course not. I'll be out as soon as I clean up. Would you like a cup of coffee?"

"If ya like. Listen, don' get too fussy about the mess. I got the rest of my life to clean the kitchen. Jus' bring the coffee an' sit with me. I much prefer it."

"Okay, go. Go."

Cristina watched her father as he stepped out onto the porch. He sat down in the rocker and filled his pipe. The aroma of cherry-flavored smoke drifted gently past the screen door. The scent worked its way into the kitchen. Cristina placed the last dish into the soapy water and stepped outside with two mugs of coffee. She parted the smoke that hung suspended in the evening air.

"Dad, I want to ask you something."

"What's that, sweetheart?

69

"I know it's none of my business, but so much time has passed, and now that you and mom are getting up there in years, and there's no hard feelings.... I was wondering.... I mean, you don't have to answer—"

"Cri."

"Yes?"

"Just ask the question, honey."

"Okay." Cristina paused. "I want to know exactly why you and mom got divorced. I mean, I don't—"

"What makes ya think we're divorced?"

Cristina was stunned. She just stared at her father as her mind raced.

"Are you telling me that you and mom *aren't* divorced?"

"I'm tellin' ya it was so long ago, I can't remember."

"Ohhh. Ohhh. You are *cruel*, father."

Jack started laughing. "I'll bet your mother told ya that."

"Mother never says anything. I'm pretty sure she still cares a great deal for you. I can hear it in her voice whenever she asks about you. You should've heard her on the phone when I arrived. I mean... I mean....

"I know you also care for her, dad. The thing is, I'm fifty years old, and I still don't get it between you two. All I do get is a sense of emptiness, you know, like a big part of my life was missing. Was it all because of Geeter? Was it all about Geeter?"

Cristina knew in her heart that nothing her father could say would fill the void that represented so much of her adolescent years. She also knew that she would never stop asking herself the same questions repeatedly, trying to make sense of it. She was a middle-aged woman and still she needed to hear it from her father. She needed to be sure that he would not mention some exceptionally small detail. Something that had somehow gotten by her during all those years of longing. Some sort of key that magically unlocked all the understanding in one big swoosh.

"It was *all* about Geeter. But the pain wasn't his fault, just like the sufferin' wasn't your fault. An' it wasn't just you who suffered, Cri. We all suffered. We all suffered terrible. I can't explain it. It was just meant to be. Fate. God's plan. Destiny. A stroke o' bad luck. Call it what ya will, but it destroyed us as a family. The sad thing was we didn't come apart because of a lack of love, Cri. We came apart because of too much love, too much concern."

"That's a funny way of putting it, dad. You know, a little explanation would go a long way right about now. I mean, I'd really like to know what that.... I want to know exactly what you mean by that."

"Sweetheart...." Jack let out a long breath. "Mercy me. That's a bit harder to explain than ya might think. I guess I'd have to say that after your brother drowned, your mother couldn't bring herself to believe anything other than it bein' my fault—"

"But, dad, you told me you weren't even there when it happened. How could it be your fault?"

"Well... in a way it was my fault because I moved us off the farm. Ya have to understand, I lived to fish an' hunt. Farmin'...not so much. Farmin' was so competitive, an' so prone to the whims of weather an' markets, I just didn't much care for it."

"Is that when you started driving the truck?"

"More or less. I bought the dump truck cheap to haul in some fill for a low spot that was in the middle of my field. It never stayed dry, and it never stayed the same size. I was always gettin' my tractor stuck in that damned misery pit every time I got near it with a plow.

"Anyhow, some of the neighbors knew I'd been haulin' in fill an' so paid me to do the same for them. There's so much low land in these parts needin' fillin' that it was easy to make some really good money on the side. I decided it was worth my while to trade the truck in for somethin' a little larger an' more reliable.

"One day, a guy named Paul Cousins calls me up an' asks if I could maybe haul some top soil over to a parcel where he was buildin' a cottage on Houghton Lake. He was willin' to pay some good money, so I said sure. Thing was, Paul Cousins was a developer an' before I knew it I was haulin' top soil from sunup to sunset and makin' damn good money doin' it. Didn't take long before I said to hell with farmin'. I sold the place an' moved out here. But... an' this is a *big* but, your mother didn't like that one bit. In fact, she didn't talk to me for a month."

"Well, dad, can you blame her? This wouldn't have been my first pick for neighborhoods either. I mean, of all places, why did you have to pick the center of a swamp?"

"Sometimes I think it picked me."

"Geez. Leave it to a man to say that."

"Honey, I never gave thought to livin' in a swamp. It's just that I never got a chance to look for a place to live. I didn't have time. The farm sold so fast it caught me completely off guard. But I was desperate to find financin' for newer excavating equipment. So... I jumped on it. Right then an' there, like the snap of a finger, we were homeless."

"Come, on, dad. And so, you just ended up here in the middle of a swamp. No alternatives? Really? Even I can't believe that."

"Maybe ya can't, but that's pretty much the truth of it. Ya see, sweetheart, Paul Cousins asked me if I could find him more top soil for these lots he was developin' an' after havin' lived with the misery pit for years, I knew exactly what he was lookin' for. It was in this swamp. Hell, this was all crap land. Nobody wanted anything to do with it, bein' mostly underwater an' all. But for scrapin' top soil? That was a different story.

"I bought forty acres for next to nothin'. I brought over the excavator an' started diggin' up muck. Dig it from the left, dig it from the right, dig it from the left, dig it from the right, back an' forth, back an' forth. Each time I'd haul out my diggings, I'd have to move the excavator farther in an' so I'd pile dirt up in the center to keep me up out of the water. That's how the drive got formed with those trenches runnin' along the sides. You know, just like those drainage ditches on the side of the road. When I'd gone in as far as I could, I went back to the road an' started diggin' out the basin.

"Well, at that time, my most pressin' problem, besides findin' a place to keep your mother, was findin' a place to keep my equipment an' supplies. Everything was either too expensive or too far away. And so after spendin' months of lookin' at all the dead cedar logs lying around here where I was excavatin', I began thinkin' about collectin' an' cuttin' some up, an' makin' posts that I could drive into the ground. I figured I could fashion myself a storage shed for tools an' stuff. I'd build it on a platform atop those cedar posts an' keep everything off the ground an' out of the wet.

"Well, I got to workin' on it, and in no time I had a nice little shed, dry an' secure. Next thing I knew, a change here, a change there, an' I had an office. It didn't take long before I dragged in a cot an' began sleepin' over when I was workin' long days.

"It was at that point, things were gettin' difficult for everybody. Your mom an' me were livin' in the basement of your Aunt Carol's place, that is, if I wasn't sleepin' in the shed an'—"

"I remember that. I must have been about three or four years old."

"You were. You were three an' Geeter was seven. An' your Aunt Carol was an angel, God bless her, puttin' up with us an' you kids, but livin' as a family in the basement was no way to go. At that time all I could think about was gettin' outta there an' into our own place. Even something temporary was fine.

"One day, I was sittin' here in the office an' realized that the quickest way to do that without spendin' a lot of money was to add on a room or two to the office an' make it somewhat livable... just for the time bein'. Just until we found a place. Once winter set in, business would slow down an' I'd be free to find us a home. And so that's what I did. When I wasn't haulin' fill, I was buildin'. Didn't cost me much an' after about six weeks I had a couple of bedrooms, a bathroom, an' a kitchen. It was a small cabin for sure, but it was private an' paid for."

"And that's when we moved in?"

"Well, *moved in* is a bit generous. It was more like dragged in. Your mom was none too happy about the *shed*. That's what she called it 'til the day she left. When I first brought her up the drive between those two water-filled trenches, she broke down an' cried."

73

"I know it's not funny. I shouldn't laugh. I can just see mom's face…. Poor woman."

"Well, let's just say us guys an' you gals see things differently. Where I saw great fishin', your mother saw great isolation an' fear."

"My god, dad. How could you blame her? What woman wouldn't?"

"I suppose, I can see it now, but not back then. I thought she was just overreacting."

"Overreacting? Oh, lord…." Cristina wiped her brow. "So, then what happened?"

"Well, for a short while, she settled down a bit, not much ya gotta understand, but just enough that I was goin' to bed every night with a belly full of the freshest, best-tastin' fish imaginable. I was startin' to believe she might come around, but that ended the day I was out on a job an' got a call over the radio to go home. There was an emergency. The deputy would only say that Geeter was in a bad way."

Jack McGrath suddenly convulsed. It was a single unexpected heave of his chest and a flash of tears across his eyes just before they lowered. Cristina was fully taken aback. She was shocked.

"Dad…? Are you all right? Gosh, I didn't mean to upset you. We don't have to talk about this. I'm so sorry. I don't know why I'm so nosey. I'm so sorry. I didn't realize—"

Jack choked back a long-buried emotion. He caught his breath. He looked back at Cristina and smiled.

"No, no. You're fine. Ya have a right to know these things. It was the cause of much grief for ya as a child. I know that. It's just that I generally keep most of my thoughts about Geeter at a safe distance."

"I don't want to see you upset, dad. We don't have to do this."

"I'm fine, Cristina." Jack took a deep breath and then continued with a tightened throat. "Anyhow… I was sayin' that the deputy gave me a call to go home, an' I did. I was drivin' the dump truck an' I remember pullin' up in the yard, an' lookin' down from the cab at your mom standin' there. She never took her eyes off of me."

74

Jack stopped a moment to rein in his emotions. He was in a place he hadn't visited for a long time.

"Dad."

"It's okay. It's okay. I'll be fine."

"We don—"

"It's okay."

Cristina arose from her chair. She stepped over to the back door, and reaching inside, she flipped the switch to turn on the porch light. She wanted to give her father some room, a moment to regain his composure without the feel of her breathing down his neck. She sat back down.

"I was sayin' it was about two in the afternoon. The summer sun was shining down an' she was wearin' this light-blue summer dress. She was holdin' your hand an' just starin' at me...." Jack stopped. He looked away from Cristina as he spoke guardedly. "Her eyes an' face were so red from cryin' she looked like she'd got sunburned. I got down outta the cab an' walked over to her. I asked her what happened. I knew right then an' there that I didn't wanna know."

Jack halted.

"Your mother never said a word."

Jack never looked at Cristina. She watched him wipe his face with the sleeve of his shirt. She was terribly uncomfortable, but understood it was best to be silent. It seemed best to let her father's emotions flow. He continued.

"She walked past me with you in tow an' climbed into the pickup. I watched her drive away an' that was pretty much the last I ever saw of you or your mother for many years to come. She never spoke to me again until you grew older an' began askin' 'bout me.

"I knew from family that she had moved down Grand Rapids way. Now an' then I would get word on how she was faring—how you were doin'. I paid the price, Cristina. I lost my son. I lost my wife. And I lost you."

"You could have come to see me."

"I know that's what ya think, an' rightfully so, but in my eyes that was impossible. It was more than impossible. It would've been cruel."

"Cruel! *Cruel?* What could be crueler than leaving me to cry for a father all those years? Geez," Cristina protested.

"I know how ya felt. I know that's how ya see it, sweetheart. I cried for you as well, but ya have to understand that your mother believed I was fully responsible for Geeter's death. Cri... that was something she had to believe. It's somethin' I wanted her to believe. You see, it's like ya said, I wasn't home when Geeter drowned. Your mother was. I didn't want her to question her bein' a good mother. She was a wonderful mother.

"I hope ya can understand that the best thing I could ever do for your mother, to make up for what happened to our son, was to let her hate me. The idea of me comin' around to take off with you would've been nothin' short of heartless. It was best I stay up here far removed from the two of ya. I don't expect you to fully understand, Cristina. It's all in the past. It's all in the past, an' your mother an' me, well, our lives are spent. We're just waitin' around for the inevitable."

"I know she still loves you. Well, I guess you would call it love."

"Time has a way of burying pain," said Jack. "You don't forget much, ya just think about the bad times less than the good."

Cristina looked out across the shallows now lacking definition, lacking depth, now lost to nightfall. All that was visible was obscure. All that was bright showed dark. Sights were supplanted by sounds. Sounds that blended in the blackness of night to create the eons-old rhythm of the swamp—the voices, the conversations of unseen creatures, the incessant hum, the mysterious throbbing of nature's nighttime heart.

"What was that?"

"Huh?"

"What was that?"

"What was what?"

"Didn't you hear that? That wail or cry or whatever?"

"Sweetheart, I got old-man ears.  Most everything escapes me."

"You're lucky.  You should feel my arms.  My hair is standing up.  What the heck kind of light bulb is in that socket?  How can you see anything with that?  You get that out of a fridge or something?"

Jack chuckled.

"Tell me what you heard.  What'd it sound like?"

"Sounded like torture to me.  I don't know.  It reminded me of a coyote, but it wasn't that."

"Probably an' owl or fox callin'."

"Sounded like it was a long ways off.  Better that than something creeping around here.  I don't ever remember getting spooked like this when I was a kid."

"When you were a child, you were naïve."

"What does *that* mean?  Am I *supposed* to be worrying about something?"

Jack offered no answer, and Cristina waited long enough.

"A bear?"

Jack shook his head.  "Ain't no bear."

"Okay, dad, now you're creeping me out.  What're you talking about?  What's out there?  Wolves?  I heard the wolves are making a comeback."

"Don't know, sweetheart.  Don't know."

"Dad, does this have something to do with the ring of salt?"

"Yeah, somewhat.  This summer's been bad for snakes an' vermin.  Never seen so many.  Salt seems to keep 'em away.

"Yeah?" said Cristina with apprehension.  "And what's with the swing set?  And the cage full of bones?"

Jack sat in silence, drawing on his pipe, staring out into the nothingness as the dim porch light snagged trails of a million insects buzzing about in circular amber streaks.  He exhaled a plume of smoke.  It drifted toward Cristina.  He took a deep breath.

"There's something out there, Cri.  I don't know what it is, but it ain't kind."

## 15

"May I help you?"

"Yeah, Cory Ballard to see Harold Sweeny."

"One moment."

The woman disappeared from the foyer. Moments later, a nearly bald, heavy-set man, in an open-collar white dress shirt came barreling through the doorway. He threw out a hand to shake and an arm to toss around Cory's shoulder.

"Mr. Ballard—good to see ya."

"That it is, you old fart."

"Mary, hit the lights and go home. We've been here way too late. Your husband's going to think we're having an affair."

Mary started laughing. Harold turned to Cory.

"I was thinking about dinner at Limberlost's. How's that sound?"

"Can't do better'n that."

"There ya go. You want to ride with me or drive yourself?"

"Ahh.... Let me follow you, Harold. I'm staying at the Beach Front, just up the street."

"Perfect. See you in five."

Harold waited for Cory at the restaurant's front door. They walked in together and took a table on the deck. It was a perfect summer evening that presented a great sunset casting warm hues across the waters of Houghton Lake. The waitress brought a couple of drinks and took orders as the two men got past the small talk and catch-up.

Harold was just about to plunge into an explanation for dragging Cory up to Houghton Lake when two choice-cut steaks were set before them. The aroma settled Harold's impatience.

"Oh, now, that's a steak, eh, Cory?"

Cory sucked in a deep whiff of perfectly grilled meat. He began salivating at once.

"A light dusting of salt and nothing more."

"There ya go. Dive in while I do the talking."

Cory picked up his silverware. His ears were for Harold, but his eyes and all else were devoted to his plate. He took in a morsel of the steak and, amid the rush of flavor, looked up to acknowledge as much to Harold, who was breaking into a sermon.

"Cory... I haven't got time to dawdle, you know the paper must get out and all that, so let me get right to the point. I know I teased you about some weird-ass stuff going on in the swamp. Let's face it. I know you're into all that spooky-ass shit, aliens, and you know—"

"Put's meat on the table. Just never this good."

"There ya go. I hear ya. I'm all about putting meat on the table. *Especially* if it tastes like this. Jesus, this is good. Point is... Right now, I'm the closest thing around here to an investigative reporter. Unfortunately, I have to concede that the pinnacle of my investigative career focused on the ingredients of Mrs. Johnson's award-winning carrot cake at the county fair a decade or two back or some shit like that. You get my meaning?"

Cory couldn't help but laugh. He knew Harold was no fool. The man took pleasure in underselling himself.

"I gotta be honest, Cory. Trying to make a buck with a paper nowadays in light of the Internet and all that horseshit is goddamned near impossible. If it wasn't for old folks needing a place to stick obits, the only obituary would be that of the *County Chronicle*. My life's work, my life's savings are wrapped up in this place, and I'm watching it slip through my fingers. The economy is killing me, Cory.

"These stories about the swamp, no matter how small, no matter how trivial, no matter how pathetically stupid, could very well translate into some badly needed cash for the paper. All I gotta do is be able to break the news and lead 'em on.

"Cory, I'm not gonna bullshit ya. I need you, man. I need you in the worst possible way. If you'd be willing to work with me, be willing to let the *Chronicle* break the stories, I'd pass on everything I can to get you the leads out there.

79

"I work close with the sheriff's department. I got an in. I know for a fact, I got a doozy of a lead right now. I can go ahead and print it, but I know I'd just be cutting off my nose to spite my face. I'm thinking there's a lot more money to make if we can work this together—build it up and draw it out.

"I can help you keep the rights to your story. I can help make sure nobody else picks it up without paying for pics and all of that. So I just wanna know... are you at all interested?"

"Harold, if it's any kind of weird, I'm interested. If I can do anything to give you a hand, I'm in. I got a soft spot for small presses; you know that. That's how I got into all this."

"Oh, thank you, lord!" Harold threw his hands up and praised the heavens. "Let me buy you another drink. Hold on." Harold signaled their server.

Cory started laughing. He liked Harold... no, it was more than that. There was nothing pretentious about the man. Harold spit it out just the way he saw it. There was no sugarcoating, no beating around the bush, no bullshitting. Even Harold's personal life was all about the facts, nothing but the facts. The man plunged back into his commentary.

"I'll tell ya, Cory, I was sitting at my desk bemoaning the fact that I didn't have an investigative reporter, and just thinking about the money to be lost.... Shit! I thought, Cory Ballard. If anybody can keep me in the game, it's gotta be Cory. You're the only person I know who's good at writing crap for the tabloids. Well, I don't exactly mean crap. I mean... ahh. I don't know, Cory. What d'you call that stuff? Fiction?"

Cory set his fork down. He was laughing aloud. He took a sip of his drink.

"I assure you, Harold, it's not fiction. You wouldn't believe the stuff people swear to. Last year, I interviewed a woman who made a thirty-foot sweater for a tree. It had sleeves where the branches stuck out. It made perfect sense once you understood that the tree told her it was cold. All kinds of people swear they communicate with their plants. You tell me, Harold. What kind of person would turn their back on a freezing tree? Like I said, not fiction. Just the facts. *Unbelievable* facts."

Harold stopped chewing his food. He sat across from Cory and just stared. It was as if he saw God.

"Cory. It was like an angel of mercy was singing medleys in my ear. I about dropped to my knees. I folded my hands and said a little prayer—*'Get his ass in here now. I mean, right now'*. And here ya are. A miracle, Cory. A miracle. Who says angels don't exist? You ever write about angels?"

"Angels are big."

"There ya go. I knew it. Cory, you're my angel. You're big. You see, here's the thing. I don't want no polished *New York Times* editorial piece on the odd events in Dead Stream Swamp. I want a fucking ridiculous over-the-top headline that sells fucking papers. I want my front page to say, *DEAD STREAM SWAMP MONSTER EATS HALF OF FUCKING HOUGHTON LAKE!* D'you get what I'm saying? I want crap. I want ridiculous over-the-top bullshit that sells papers to the dyslexic. You can do that, right? Please, please tell me you can do that, Cory."

"Harold... I'll have you know that I just made a killing on a breaking story titled *'Century-Old Baby Alive in Backyard Bathtub Shrine'*. Destined to be a classic, you watch. It might be my ticket to meaningful retirement."

Harold again stared at Cory. He was speechless. The potential for profit was written all over the man's face. He shook his head and whispered, "Unbeeelieeeevable. And people believe that shit. Was it true?"

"Well, the lady I interviewed thought it was."

"What d'you think?"

"I thought it was a dead thing wrapped in a blanket."

Harold looked at Cory. "What does that mean?"

"I don't know. You tell me."

Harold tilted his head, unsure of how to take Cory's answer. He started snickering and then passed into a fit of laughter.

81

"You're killing me, man. You're too much."

"Well, I call it factual entertainment. Don't forget about the facts."

"Exactly! Look—I don't wanna spend a month driving around getting firsthand accounts from little old ladies in order to build a book, okay? I want something that's fast, short, and sweet. I want something that hits hard and leaves the reader suffering to get the next edition. And believe me, around here, there's going to be no end to wanting the next edition. Everybody's bored to death. What better than a good swamp monster mystery? I got no competition on this one. D'you know what I'm sayin'?"

"Absolutely," said Cory "So why don't you fill me in on these reports? What d'you got here? One on the two dead fishermen. Something about a crazy guy's dead dog. And what was the one you mentioned on the phone?"

"The Hamilton place. The dead cows."

"Oh, yeah, the dead cows."

"That just happened. In fact, it's fresh enough you can probably still get pics and everything."

"What about the crazy guy with the dead dog?" asked Cory.

"Well, we absolutely wanna get the story, but he's an old-timer. I'm not sure if he's got both oars in the water or not. I heard he made quite a scene over at the sheriff's department. They said he was nuts."

"Hey, Harold, Harold, my good man, there *is* no better source than a crazy person. Crazy is good. And the fishermen?"

"Yeah, a couple of guys out of Lansing. My contact at the sheriff's department is a guy named Toby Quinn. We go back a long ways. He's the Roscommon detective sergeant. You'll be meeting him soon enough. He can fill ya in on the details. That's already sizzlin' hot.

"But for now, I need ya to get over and check out the Hamilton place. The dead cows. We gotta hurry on that one. Quinn says word's getting out. You won't need to do anything but talk to Hamilton and take some pics. There's nothing more to it, but it's a story I can push out now, and I need to get something out *now*. I need to get this thing started."

"There wasn't anything coming out of Houghton Lake on the feeds, so you're still on top. I'm sure it's yours to break," said Cory.

"Oh, *please* make it so. I'm seeing something like *'Dead Stream Swamp Monster Ravages Cattle'*. Maybe we fit in a subtitle that says *'Nothing left but bleached white bones; farmer scared shitless'*. You know, something like that. What d'ya think?"

"I like it. ...Over the top—lots of intrigue. I'd tweak it a little to say *'Dead Stream Swamp Monster Drops Daisy'*. That way the first impression might be a woman's involved instead of a cow."

"In my life that was the same thing."

Cory drew a blank. And then nearly choked on his steak while laughing.

"Oh, yeah. I forgot you were once married."

"I didn't."

Cory settled down.

"Well, you get what I'm saying. Bones white as milk. The whole swamp monster aspect should draw in most of the UFO and alien cults. You can never have enough monster. *'Louisiana Lady Gives Birth to Twenty-Pound Monster'*. *'Third-Grader Takes Monster Dump; Classmates Stunned.'* You can't go wrong with monster headings."

"There ya go! I love it. Now, like I said, you keep all rights to your stuff. I don't even want to go down that road. Just gimme the breaking news. I know you work with other tabloids, and if you need any help getting the story out, lemme know. I got a zillion contacts. I know I can peddle it and make us both some cash."

"Harold, let's get this first piece out and we'll go from there."

"Great. Listen, while you're working on that article, I got another lead that may tie in. Friend of mine, Donny Simpson, he volunteers for the DNR, the Wildlife an' Game Service, stuff like that. He gives me a call wondering if I heard anything about fish dying off. I say, not particularly, and ask why. He says, he was checking on his fish traps, and when he pulled them up, something like ten or fifteen of the nets were full of dead fish. Not just your usual dead fish, but perfectly stripped white bones. No *shit*, I'm thinking."

Harold looked at Cory and nodded his head knowingly.

"Weird enough for you?"

"Getting better all the time, Harold. You said his name was Donny Simpson?"

"Yeah. I've known him for a long time. I'll get you a meeting with him tomorrow, say lunchtime. That work for you?"

"I'll be at the Hamilton place."

"Oh, yeah. Well, we'll work it out."

"Sounds good. What did you say that crazy man's name was?"

"McGrath. Jack McGrath."

"Got it."

Cory jotted down the name on his napkin.

"Hey, I just wanna say thanks for working with me, Cory. I wish I could tell ya what it means to me. You're a blessing, a blessing come true."

"Only until you get to know me."

"What the hell are you talking about? I've known you forever."

"I suppose. But, seriously, it's not a big deal. Sounds like fun, and hopefully we make a few bucks to boot. And hey, let's not forget about the steak. I got a great steak out of it."

"I'm glad you enjoyed it."

"And the drinks," noted Cory.

"And the drinks," repeated Harold.

"I'll see you tomorrow."

"Okay. Talk to you later. Drive careful. Good seeing you again. I'm glad you came up."

"Same here, Harold. I'll be in touch."

84

## 16

"Hey, you made it. How's your dad?" asked Cory.

"Good, I guess," replied Cristina. "Seems to be okay. I told him about running into you while I was making him dinner. He *insisted* I join you for lunch. It bugs him that I'm not married—no hidden message there."

"None heard. You can look over the menu or take my word, the house burger is outstanding."

"I'll take your word. I'm too tired to read a menu."

"Sorry to hear that," said Cory.

"It's not your fault. You just have to understand, morning to dad is that time before the sun rises. Once it crests over the horizon, he calls it midday. So if you plan on making breakfast for my dad you best be on your feet by four-thirty."

"I'm an early riser, but four-thirty? That's a stretch even for me."

"It might have been bearable if I'd managed to get some sleep beforehand, but I swear to god, every little noise had me tossing and turning. I always remembered the swamp as a place where the drone of frogs and crickets or whatever lulled me to sleep like one of those oscillating fans."

"And you'd be right."

"You'd think. But that was *not* the case. No sir. It was a night full of godawful–I don't know what to call it—howls, cries."

Cory and Cristina halted their conversation once the server approached. They placed their orders and continued.

"Howls, cries.... Must be you got some coyotes around your place."

"Well, that's what I thought at first, but it wasn't that."

"Okay, what'd it sound like?" asked Cory.

"Without exaggeration, it sounded like the world was coming to an end one creature at a time."

"Wow. Bad night, indeed. You prone to nightmares?"

"Only when I'm sleeping. I don't think I made it that far last night."

"Well... what'd your dad say about it?"

"Are you kidding? His ears are so bad, he can't hear the half of it. In fact, worrying about him only added to the problem."

"How's that?"

"For starters, while I'm freaking out from all the weird sounds I'm hearing, he's outside on the porch sleeping in his rocker. Then if things aren't weird enough, dad dragged a swing set into the water right in front of the cabin. And it doesn't end there. He's been pouring a ring of salt around the house. You think maybe that's a bit odd? I asked what was with the salt, and he said, *'It keeps away the snakes'*. I didn't press him on the swing set."

"Mmmm. I don' think so," said Cory.

"You don't think what?"

"I doubt a ring of salt will stop a snake. Slugs and snails for sure, worms most likely, toads, frogs, maybe, but a snake? I don't know."

"Well, he said snakes and vermin to be exact, but he said something else that freaked me right out. He stared into the darkness and said *'There's something out there, Cri. I don't know what it is, but it ain't kind'*. Take it from me, that makes for the world's worst bedtime story."

Cory laughed. "That really is funny. I know we got bear around here for sure. There's been rumors about wolves migrating down here from the U.P., but nothing confirmed. As for coyotes... they've been around here for as far back as I can remember. They make a hell of a racket at night."

"Yeah, but I know what coyotes sound like. We have lots of them down at the farm. When the rabbit population gets out of hand, they come trotting in on the sly and clean 'em out. They usually have that yip-yip-yip sound before the cry. You know what I mean?"

"Absolutely. You're dead on."

"Well, there was no yip-yip-yip last night. Well, I mean, there was some, but for the most part, I could tell the coyotes from the rest. This was something else."

"Maybe you got owls around your place."

"That's what dad said. I don't know."

"You know, come to think of it. There's been a growing problem with feral dogs. It's a big deal in Detroit. Have you ever heard a pack of dogs howling at night?" asked Cory.

"I have no idea."

"I guarantee you, it'll stand your hair on end. It's worse than wolves, and every bit as unsettling as coyotes."

"Well, whatever it was, I can tell you this, it kept shivers running down my spine all night long."

"So, tell me. In view of all these swamp mysteries, are you an adventurous sort?"

"Based on how little sleep I got last night, I'd have to say no. Why?"

"Well, yesterday I invited you to go along with me and look at some bones. I gotta go visit a guy named Ben Hamilton. He's got a farm that borders the Dead Stream Swamp. Apparently things are also going bump in the night over at his place. Only those bumps cost him a few head of cattle. That's what I'm off to investigate. You game?"

"That's a little unsettling."

"So it's a yes?"

"Oh, that's how you took that? Mmm. Sure, why not... *in spite of better judgment.*"

"You just told me your whole night was unsettling. This sounds dull by comparison. Don't you think?"

"Does it matter what I think?"

"Of course, it matters. I don't want you to say no."

The comment left Cristina smiling. They finished with lunch and climbed into Cory's Blazer. They headed north out of Houghton Lake on 127 to Pine Road and then north and west along 104. They were bordering swampland.

"So, you did say that if I lunched with you today, I would see bones. But you also said you would tell me what you do now that you're retired."

"I also told you that I was a little gun shy about answering that question."

"And I said that I have read plenty of spy novels so your secret is safe with me."

"Ha, ha. Yeah, you *did* say that."

"I'm not sure what's going to be more intriguing, the bones or you."

"The bones."

"Honestly? Do I have to get on my knees to find out something about you or what? Right now, I'm headed into a swamp with a serial killer."

"All right, all right. Let's see. We were talking about our mothers leaning on us to read, and like you, reading and writing came easy for me. In the service, I got to know this guy who headed up the base newspaper. I was intrigued and expressed an interest in what he did. He told me to come in and help anytime. You see, most of the staff were volunteers. So, I helped around the shop with printing and collating, or bindery. Whatever was needed. I enjoyed it all.

"One day, I wrote an article about the magnificence of a place called Amalfi. They read it, loved it, printed it, and I was hooked. I began writing articles on current events, historical pieces, travel tips, and anything else that was needed. It got under my skin, and I never strayed too far from playing with it.

"When Krandor downsized, I thought a lot about getting a job, or doing the things that made life worth living. I decided to enjoy myself for a while and write without time restraint or pressure. So that's what I do now when I feel up to it."

"So, you write books?"

"Nope. Nothing so glamorous. I do write fiction of sorts, but not books."

"Well, what then, fiction as in short stories?"

"Shorter."

"What's shorter than a short story? Newspaper articles? But you said fiction."

"I said fiction of sorts."

"Fiction of sorts.... I give up. What does that mean?"

"Well.... My last notable piece was titled, *Century-Old Baby Alive in Backyard Bathtub Shrine.*"

Cri went silent. Her mind raced to determine if he was joking or serious.

"You're kidding me, right?"

"Hey, I got nearly five hundred bucks for that masterpiece. Most people write books and go in debt."

This time, Cristina broke out in laughter.

"You write for the tabloids, the rag sheets?"

"More or less. Tabloids might even be a little lofty, but yes, I do."

"That's insane. So, are you here visiting or writing some kind of travelogue— Wait a minute! We're going to look at bones! You're writing something crazy for bored shoppers in check-out lanes."

"Bingo. You're onto me. In fact, I have a friend who owns the *Roscommon County Chronicle.* He called me with a tip on a story he wanted me to chase down. He thought I'd be interested in making a few bucks, and so invited me up for drinks and dinner. You know, hash over old times with a sprinkle of nine to five."

"I can't believe anything around here could possibly warrant *story* status."

"Yeah, I hear you."

"So?"

"So what?"

"So, you're not going to tell me? I know it has something to do with bones."

"Hey, trade secrets. We come from the same breed of moms. For all I know, you might be a part-time reporter yourself."

"Oh, *puh-lease.* My brain couldn't plunk down a creative thought if my very life depended on it."

"You expect me to believe that?"

"Believe it. Bet on it."

"Well, in that case.... Understand, I'm giving you the benefit of the doubt. I hope I won't live to regret it."

"Trust me, Cory. Your cash-worthy secret is safe with me."

"All right. But know I'm taking you at your word."

"My word is good."

"I see. Well, you're right. What we have here is a peculiar issue with bones. Now that's all I'm going to say except that bones always translate into bucks. Oh, and also that we've arrived."

Cory turned onto a drive that led up to an old farmhouse amid pastures covered in cattle and mud. He parked the car between the house and one of the barns. A man appeared and strolled toward them. Cory climbed out of the truck.

"Mr. Hamilton?"

"That's right, and you are?"

"Cory, Cory Ballard."

The men shook hands.

"Mr. Hamilton, I don't wish to bother you, but Harold Sweeny over at the *County Chronicle* asked me to swing by and investigate an incident involving some dead cattle."

"Who?"

"Harold Sweeny, over at the *County Chronicle*."

"Can't say I know him."

"I believe that. Harold's no celeb. But I'm sure you've heard of the *Roscommon County Chronicle*."

"Yeah, I know the paper."

"Harold owns it. He picks up on stuff for the paper by listening to the scanners. I'm sure he picked up on a call you made to the sheriff's patrol. Say, Ben, this is my secretary, Cristina Walker. I asked her to ride along. She's real good at picking up on details, if you know what I mean. Her daddy lived his whole life in the swamp."

"Really. What's his name?"

"Ja—"

"Whoops!" Cory interrupted Cristina. "I forgot my stupid cell phone in the truck. I need it to take pics. I'll be right back."

Cristina watched Cory run off.

"You were about to say your father's name was...."

Cristina turned back to face Mr. Hamilton. "Jack McGrath."

"Uhhhhhh.... Jack McGrath. I know that name. That goes way back. Wasn't he in the excavatin' business?"

"Yes, he was. Good memory. I'm impressed."

"He used to run the swamp for fill. I remember him doin' some work for my dad ages ago. He must be gettin' up there in years."

"Seventy-seven," said Cristina.

"Seventy-seven. No kidding."

Cory came trotting back.

"Okay, now I'm ready."

"So what would ya like to know?" asked Ben.

"Just tell me in your own words what happened or what's happening. Cristina takes the notes, and I take the pics unless that's a problem."

"No. No problem. That's fine. But I think you should walk down to the marsh with me to fully appreciate what I'm gonna tell ya."

"Yeah, that's fine. Cristina?"

"Sure, why not."

Ben started to lead them across the pasture.

"Ya see that opening in the tree line at the far side of the pasture? That's where we're headed. The cows have beat a path through there that they've used for as far back as I can remember."

"Where's it go?" asked Cory.

"Leads to the water's edge. It's not stagnant. The cows prefer it to the trough. Cristina?"

"Yes."

"See that low area along the tree line—to the left?"

"Yes."

"If I'm not mistaken, your dad filled that area years ago." Mr. Hamilton pondered his comment. "Boy, that must've been maybe thirty, thirty-five years ago. He was digging out top soil from back in those woods."

"I wouldn't know. Like you said, it was a long time ago."

91

"Yes, ma'am. That it was. Ah, damn it. Excuse my French, Cristina. I'm so used to wearing these boots that I wasn't thinking about you folks wearin' shoes an' this starts getting real muddy just a short ways up. The ground up ahead is close to water level, an' the cows trample it into quite a slurry, especially if it's been raining. They like to wallow in it to ward off the flies.

"Tell you what. Ya really need to see the bones, so how about we go back up to the barn? I'll give you both a pair of boots an' you can go in and see for yourself. You don't really need me to tag along, but it'd be a shame to come all the way out here and not see those bones. They're a sight to behold."

"Oh, trust me. We'll be seeing bones. I want pictures. Bones are brow-raisers."

The three turned about and headed for the barn.

"So, Ben, why don't you tell me what happened? Take your time. The more details the better."

"Sorry to say, there's not much in the way of details. Not much to tell because I really don't know what to say. I took a count of head, which I do regularly. I have a small enough herd to make that possible, and I came up two short. Needless to say, I counted over an' still two short. Next mornin', I take another count and I come up three short. One, two, or three makes no difference. Comin' up short two days in a row is enough for me to go lookin'.

"Obviously, I can see across the pasture, so first place I'd check would be the swamp or the path leadin' there. The cows use that walk day in day out, and it's the only place I can't see from the barn. Knowin' that they usually take water down at the swamp was what brought me to realize that the herd was congregating around the water trough. That wasn't earth shatterin' or anything, but it was a bit odd. Like I say, they prefer the swamp.

"Anyhow, I make it down to the water an' I'm tellin' ya, I see the damndest thing ever—piles of bones. Turned out to be three piles of perfectly cleaned, white-as-my-ass cow bones. Never seen anything like it... ever. I didn't know what to make of it. I didn't have a clue.

92

"So, I called the sheriff's department.  Who the hell else would ya call?  I mean, I knew they wouldn't be able to do anything but take down a report, but I needed the report for proof of loss, you know, for a tax write-off.  And that's about it.  There's nothin' else I can say."

"You have any trouble around here with predators?  You know, wolves, coyotes... bear."

"Oh, bears aren't strangers around here, but certainly nothin' to be considered a nuisance or trouble of any kind.  Wolves and coyotes would be more of a concern.  I've heard the coyotes at night, but that's it.  Never seen a wolf, at least not that I can remember."

"Did you hear or see anything you'd consider unusual as of late?"

"Nothing.  Like I said, I took my mornin' head count and came up short.  That was it."

"Not much to go on."

"Wait'll ya see the bones."

Cory and Cristina followed Ben into the barn and laughed about his sizable assortment of knee boots.  Finding the right size was no problem.  Without exception, a thick coat of dried gray mud covered every pair.

"Ready?" asked Cory.

"I guess.  But let's not stay too long.  I got a taste of what the mosquitoes and flies are like down there."

"Would you rather wait here?  I won't be but a few minutes."

"No.  I'll walk down with you, but don't plan on dawdling."

"Fair enough," Cory laughed.  "I just need a minute to pop off a couple of pics and we'll be out of there."

"Let's do it."

Cory and Cristina left Ben to his work and crossed the open pasture.  In short time, the forest canopy closed in to swallow them.  It didn't take much longer before they encountered what appeared to be an uninviting road that looked like a river of blackstrap molasses frozen in a hard boil.

"I guess that's where cows like to wallow."

"I wish I was a cow and could fully appreciate it."

"How you doing?"

"I'm trying to keep these boots from being sucked off my feet."

"I think that's the water right up there. Looks like that's where the path ends."

"If I fall over in this stuff, you're gonna wish you didn't know me."

"Thanks for the warning. I must ask. Do I, or do I not, come to your rescue?"

"You come to my rescue, and you say nothing about my foul mouth ever... to anybody."

"Understood."

"What's that?" asked Cristina.

"What?"

"Right there. The white stuff. Looks like the bones he was talking about."

"C'mon."

"Cory?"

"Yeah."

"What's that smell?"

"Yeah, I was just getting around to wondering that myself. You probably got a lot better nose than me."

"What *is* that?"

Cory's chest expanded as he took in a deep breath of the swamp air.

"Smells acidic." He took another breath. "You ever smell muriatic acid? You know, cleaned with it, anything like that? You ever smell battery acid?"

"I don't think so."

"It has a sharp, biting odor. It's a smell all to its own. It gets in your nostrils and makes you want to pinch them. You wouldn't like it. I promise. Wow. Will you look at that?"

Cory pulled out his cell phone and activated the camera.

"They really are white," said Cristina.

"Yeah... *click*... he wasn't... *click*... bullshitting... *click*... about that.  Those are the cleanest picked bones I've ever seen."...*Click.*

Cory lowered his cell phone.  He stooped low alongside the water and stared into it to view the skeleton up close.

"Huh."

"What?"

There's something really wrong here."

"What do you mean?" asked Cristina.

"I know a couple of guys who strip and clean bones to sell them, carve them, or make jewelry.  I'm telling you right now.  It takes a lot of work to get bones that clean.  A lot of work and a lot of hydrogen peroxide.

"What I'm saying is that bones that lay around on the ground for a couple of months will clean up quite nicely, especially if the sun bleaches them.  Between the birds and bugs, there's no leftovers.  Bones left in water take a lot longer or don't clean up at all.  I mean, fish will pick them clean but the amount of time to get them white like this—I can't venture to guess.  Maybe never.

"According to what I understand these cows haven't been dead a week.  How could their bones be this clean?"

"I don't know."

"Neither do I.  Huh.  That is strange."

"Can we go back?  Please?  These mosquitos are bleeding me dry."

"Yeah, they're bad.  C'mon, let's get out of here."

Cory and Cristina started slogging their way back through the mud and made for Ben Hamilton's barn.  He greeted them upon arrival.

"Well, I take it ya got your pictures."

"Yeah, I got them.  You weren't kidding about them being bleached white.  What's with that?"

"My exact thoughts."

"How long did you say the animals were dead?"

"Can't say positively.  Can say that I first came up short on my count last Thursday, that'd be five days.  After the second day,

95

I went lookin'. That was four days ago. So... at least five days, but I'd bet my paycheck they weren't dead more'n six. Countin' heads is my morning ritual, like sayin' prayers."

"Yeah. Say, there was something else I wanted to ask you. What the hell was it? Uhhhhh.... Oh, yeah. Did you happen to notice the smell down there by the water?"

"Yeah. It comes an' goes. Been gettin' worse as of late. Depends a lot on the wind. I sense maybe you're from these parts. If so, then ya know there's gotta be dozens of oil an' gas wells out in the swamp.

"Sometimes ya get that nasty-smellin' stuff, you know that hydrogen sulfide or whatever stinking up the place. Kind of a rotten egg smell. This smells different, but it's just as nasty. I'm thinking, it's probably from the same place. It's worse down by the water. But then, ya know, the air can get really still in the thickets an' them odors can be slow to move on once they settle in."

Cory nodded. "Yeah, I know what you're saying. Well, Ben, it's been a pleasure. I appreciate you letting us walk your land and giving us what you know. I think we got all we need. So, that being the case, we'll say our goodbyes and thanks."

"You're welcome. I'll take the boots back up to the barn. You folks drive safe."

"Thanks."

"Bye," said Cristina.

Cory and Cristina climbed back into the Blazer and headed for town.

"So, what did you make of that? Does it compare to a century-old baby found in a bathtub shrine?" asked Cristina.

"Mmmmmm. Dead cattle... bleached-white bones... bug-infested swamp... unusual odors.... I'm thinking it's working its way up the chart. Yeah, yeah. It's working its way up. If I can work in a monster, or a ghost, or an alien. Then it's the real deal."

"Prit-tee juicy tabloid fodder, huh?"

"Yes, ma'am. Could be. Can I buy you a coffee or something in town?"

96

"Oh, I appreciate the offer, but no can do."

"Not even a quick cup?"

"No. I want to get back to my dad's place. I want to be sure I make supper before he does. Like I said, the man gets up at three, eats breakfast at four, lunch at eight, and dinner at two. Besides, yesterday, I was gone all day, and I know he was sitting around waiting for me."

"Well, in that case, I just want to say that I truly enjoyed your company, and I hope I'll see you again before you head back home."

"I'd like that. Hanging with you isn't exactly run of the mill. By the way, did I have a good time? I'm scratching so bad, I'm not sure. I guess you had better tell me. Did I have a good time?"

"You had a *great* time. In tabloid terms, you trekked a treacherous trail, you battled bug-infested swamps; you even investigated the great white-bone mystery. You gotta believe me, Cri, it would've cost you at least ten bucks for a ticket to see a movie like that."

Cristina sat still with an *'are you for real'* expression on her face.

"What? You don't believe me?"

"I don't believe *you* is precisely what I was thinking."

"Cristina, the life of a tabloid adventurer isn't for everyone. I understand. And I don't want you to think you've failed in any way, or are any less of a person. Considering...."

"Considering?"

"Well, if seeing me again hinges on your less than favorable account of what was a truly exhilarating experience... well, then... we weren't meant to be."

"Geez. I see why Harold Sweeny pays you. Listen, if we could just be serious. I enjoyed my day with you, but dad comes first."

"Of course."

"Give me a call. I can't wait to see what a second date is like."

"It only gets better. I promise. Now, you take care."

Cory and Cristina parted again at the front door of Little Boots. Cristina watched Cory's Blazer pull away. She got into her car and headed for her dad's place.

# Dead Stream Swamp
# Monster Bones Daisy

**By Cory Ballard**

Roscommon Co., Mi. The recent discovery of three skeletons stripped clean of flesh and bleached white along the wooded perimeter of the Dead Stream Swamp has many locals locking doors at night.

According to longtime dairy farmer Mr. Benjamin Hamilton, the only thing that remains of his three prized milkers are bones. Three piles of perfectly clean bones that appeared almost overnight.

"How can three 1500 pound animals vanish overnight?" asked Mr. Hamilton.

Was it aliens? Was it the work of some demonic cult? Satanists? Or was it the leftovers from some yet unknown monster lurking within the shadowy thickets and water-glazed lowlands that border his pasture?

The dark backwaters of Reedsburg Dam seep across 30,000 acres of dense, waterlogged, frightening terrain that would spook the bravest biker gang…

Cory looked up from the morning paper and glanced out the window as he sipped his coffee. The parking lot was mostly empty so when the older green pickup pulled into the Little Boots Country Diner parking lot, Cory was reasonably sure it was Donny Simpson.

Cory watched the front door. When the young man stepped inside, Cory raised his hand. The man nodded and walked his way.

"Donny Simpson?"

"Yah, man. You're Harold's friend?"

"I am. Cory Ballard."

The men shook hands and Donny took a seat at the booth.

"I appreciate you taking time to see me."

"Hey, man, my pleasure. Harold paid me twenty bucks for my time, so I'm happy. It isn't like I got a lot to say."

"Well, I'm just going to take a few notes if you don't mind."

"Not at all, man. Go for it."

"So you live around here?"

"Yah. Just down the street by Federal and Desoto."

"Lived here most of your life?"

"All twenty-four years. Born here."

"And, you're a fisherman. Spend a lot of time in the flooding or swamp?"

"Oh, hell, yah. I do most my fishing on Houghton, but I know the flooding and Dead Stream pretty well."

"Now, according to Harold, you work for the DNR."

"No, no, no, man. I volunteer. They call when they need help taking samples. Sometimes it's water, sometimes soil, other times fish."

"Well, Donny, why don't you tell me something 'bout these traps full of bones?"

"Sure. Ahh.... There ain't a whole lot to tell. NatureEco, who is subcontracted by the DNR, asked me to help with a marking program above Reedsburg Dam. I had to check ten nets daily for a two-week period. Anything caught had to be tagged. It was a one-time deal. They paid me two hundred bucks."

"Do you know why they were being marked?"

"Yah, mortality."

"Mortality?"

"Yah, man, you know. Everybody's complaining about how bad fishing's got. They're looking into it."

"Interesting. What do you think about it?"

"About what?"

"The fishing?"

"Oh, man, it's just terrible. That's why I spend most of my time on the lakes, either Houghton or Higgins."

"So tell me about the bones."

"Sure. Ahh.... I was supposed to check a set of nets twice a day for fourteen days. A total of twenty-eight times. That's ten nets or two hundred and eighty nettings. Something like fifteen or sixteen of those nets were full o' bones. And I mean bones. Nothing but bones and scales."

"Did you report it to the DNR?"

"Of course. I didn't have much choice. I found a couple of tags as well."

"What'd they say?"

"I wouldn't know, man. I just fill out a form and turn it in."

"What d'you make of it?"

Donny hesitated and then looked at Cory as if sizing him up.

"What I made of it was simple. It was creepier 'an hell. The strangest thing I've ever seen. The first time I saw it, it freaked me right out. Same for the second an' third. After that I started paying close attention to my surroundings."

"In what way?"

"I don't know. I was spooked. I watched what was in the water. I kept an eye on the thickets. I mean, what does something like that?"

"And.... Did you notice anything?"

"Mmm. No man, not really. I did notice that the vegetation around those nets was dying off. That was kind of weird. Like whatever killed the fish, killed the reeds an' stuff."

"So, were those nets all in the same area?"

"Yah, 'bout halfway up Dead Stream."

"You notice anything else? Anything at all?"

"Like what?"

"Oh, like bones along the shore or funny smells."

"Wow. Now that is crazy. I never saw any bones along the shore, but I do remember a couple of times smelling something weird."

"Weird in what way?"

"Ahhhh... I don't know, man. Kind of a chemical smell."

"Strong smell?"

"No. Just something in the air."

"Can you describe it?"

"Mmmm... not really. It was like an industrial smell."

"Anything else?"

"No.... That was all there was to it. It probably spooked me because I was way up in Dead Stream. You know what I'm sayin'? I was alone and my imagination was getting the best of me. Stupid. I know. But there it is."

"No, not stupid. If it'll make you feel better, you aren't alone on that count. Been a few bizarre occurrences lately."

"Like what?"

"Donny, I really can't say, but a lot of bones have been turning up, and you're not the only one to smell strange smells. So, I'm just saying, don't be too hard on yourself about getting spooked. D'you know if anybody else was working with you or if they might have run into the same thing, you know, dead fish and stuff?"

"No, man. No idea at all. I just go where I'm told, fill out the forms, and turn 'em in."

"Good enough. That's it, Donny, it's been a pleasure. I thank you. Harold thanks you, and I gotta go. You said Harold already paid you."

"Yah."

"Great. Well, then, have yourself a good day. And thanks again."

Cory extended his hand, and after shaking with Donny, slid out of the booth. Donny followed him out the front door and they went their separate ways.

## 18

"Let me see."

"Hang on...."

"Hurry up, I want to see."

"Okay.... There you go."

Cory spun the laptop around so that the screen faced Cristina. He got up from his seat and moved across the booth to sit next to her. Cristina was keenly aware of his approach. It pleased her to know that, given the choice, he elected to be close.

"So this is it. *'Skeletons Scream Existence of Dead Stream Swamp Monster, by Cory Ballard'.* Wowwww."

"I can tell you're impressed."

"Indeed. I take it you've got a following?"

"Oh yeah, for at least a couple of hours. People suck this stuff right up. The main thing is that the article got picked up in Madison, Wisconsin. Look here."

Cory went back to the search engine results and brought up another posting.

"Looky there, *The Jackson Gazette.*"

"What can I say? Are there more?"

"Ah, let's see.... I'll do a search on skeletons and.... We got recent—*holy shit*, what is this?"

"What? What do you see?"

"You got to be kidding me. Look at this. Bones for sale. Look, Houghton Lake, Michigan. Well, that really pisses me off."

"That pisses you off?"

"Hell, yes, that pisses me off. I'm trying to stir up rumor and speculation. You know, sensationalism for the supernaturally inclined. I can't have some bimbo out there selling bones to the general public like they were Girl Scout cookies. Takes all the mystery out of it. What *rotten* luck. I wonder how old this posting is. Let's see.... Posted the 17th. That's a month ago."

Cory leaned back away from the laptop. He was lost in thought.

"So what are you thinking? Somebody else may be responsible for these bones?"

"I'm thinking somebody unknown to us might be behind the whole bleached-bone fiasco."

"You think they killed the cows?"

"I don't know. That seems a stretch. But one thing I've learned in this line of work is that there are a whole bunch of crazies out there."

"What are you going to do?"

"I'm not sure yet. Let me look at this site a minute."

Cory leaned forward and read the website with renewed vigor.

"Anything?"

"Mmmmm... mostly he just lists the variety of bones he has for sale. Claims they're all excellent specimens. He does have *cow* bones. That's interesting.... He's got pictures. His collections can be—Oh yes, baby! Here's what I'm looking for—can be seen at the Great Escape flea market on the corner of Old 27 and Birch every Thursday through the end of September. He goes by... *Boneman ?!*"

Cory looked at Cristina, his face in twisted contortion.

"What's that look for?"

"*Boneman?* Seriously? The guy does enough business to go by *Boneman?* I can't believe I'm reading this crap. My article just got hammered. Mmmm. On the other hand, well... maybe not. What I need to do... is get an interview with this guy."

"Does he give a phone number? We could look him up. I'll bet he's a story all by himself. Boneman. You never know."

"Oh, Cristina, how I love an optimist. Let's see... no phone number. He does give a PO Box address. Hold on a minute...."

Cory picked up his cell phone and punched in some numbers.

"Harold—Cory Ballard. Good, good. Say, question.... You know anybody over at the post office who can tell me the owner of PO Box 103? Great. Yeah. Great. Give me a call back as soon

103

as you got something, okay? Yeah. Yeah. All right, talk to you later. Wait! Harold! Hang on. One other thing. You know anything about the Great Escape flea market on the corner of Old 27 and Birch? ...Okay, just wondering. Call me if you get something. That's fine. Talk to you later."

Cory looked at Cristina.

"And?"

"Harold says he always knows somebody. Says he knows the gal who's the mail sorter and stuffs the boxes. She works part-time so he's not sure if she's there now or not. He's going to call over and let me know."

"What about the flea market?"

"Never heard of it. Says they pop up around here like pimples at Hershey's."

"Oh, nice image. Geez. So, if he finds out who it is, then what?"

"Then I plan on checking the guy out. You have to know your competition. Right?"

"So, on top of everything else, you're a stalker."

"I prefer to think of myself as insatiably curious. It's a healthy trait, a sign of a youthful mind."

"I'll remember that the next time I listen to gossip."

"You want to go with me?"

"To the flea market?"

"Yeah. Today's Thursday. It may be fun. Isn't too far away. Up there toward Higgins Lake. Let's see... according to my good buddy Google it's only... 10.3 miles from Little Boots to the Great Escape. ETA 12 minutes. Twenty if I get gas first. What do you say?"

"Why not?"

Cory and Cristina paid the bill, exited the restaurant, and walked toward Cory's SUV.

"Here, let me get that." Cory reached for the door.

"Wow. Old school."

"To the core. I suffered through the whole women's lib thing. Almost got my ass kicked for opening a door once."

Cory walked around and climbed into the driver's seat. He started down the road.

"Don't hold a grudge. Historically we've been relegated to sex and servitude. So we got a little carried away. Big deal. How do you *not* get drunk on freedom from repression?"

"You did say that you moved away from here at an early age, right?"

"Yeah. I think I was three or four. Why?" asked Cristina.

"Just making sure it wasn't *you* who tried to kick my ass."

"Probably should have been, but no, it wasn't me."

"Yay."

"Not to change the subject, although I am happy to do so, I've been noticing how many for-sale signs are around this place. It seems like every other cottage or business is up for sale."

"I'd say you're probably right. All they have is fishing and tourism, and if the fishing's getting as bad as everyone claims, there's going to be a whole lot more signs going up."

"Too bad," Cristina lamented.

"Okay. Old 27. We go right."

Cory and Cristina ceased chatting as the seemingly limitless waters of Houghton Lake passed by to their right. The open expanse of blue made it impossible not to be captivated. The spell broke when the scenery on their left changed.

"As much as I like the view of the lake, this stretch creeps me out so bad, I can hardly stand it," said Cristina.

"The flooding?"

"I call it a swamp."

"Well, to be truthful, this is a floodplain. The real swamp lies farther to the north and west."

"You do understand you're lecturing a gal whose dad lives in the middle of your so-called swamp."

"Just saying."

"If you're a naturalist or a fisherman, it's heaven. I get it. But for a city gal, it's nothing short of snake-infested quicksand and nightmares."

"Hmm. I may have to buy you a new pair of waders."

"Over my dead body."

"Put that thought on hold. I think we've arrived."

Cory slowed the SUV as he came up on the crossroad.

"That's definitely a flea market. I'll park over there."

The Blazer veered off the road to enter a gravel parking lot populated with an excess of pickup trucks covered in a similar topcoat of cream-colored dust. The same dust falling out of a cloud now overtook Cory and Cristina from behind. It prompted them to wait out its passing before cracking open the doors. They stepped out of the Blazer and began strolling toward the stalls. They took their time walking from one end of the market to the other.

"So much for bones. I didn't see anything," said Cory as he turned to look back and scan the stalls.

"I didn't see anything," said Cristina. "What now?"

"Now, I ask. I think I'll ask that guy over there selling the car parts."

Cristina followed Cory.

"Howdy."

"Good afternoon, folks. How can I help ya?"

"Well, I wish I could tell you that I'm in the market for some of your parts here—give you a little business, but to be honest, I need something else."

"An' what's that?"

Cory extended his hand. "My name is Cory Ballard, and this is my friend, Cristina Walker."

"Pleased to meet ya both."

"Same here. Say, we drove up from Grand Rapids hoping to find a gent who goes by Boneman. I'm a part-time scout leader and we use bones to help our boy scouts identify signs of nature in the woods. You wouldn't by chance know the guy, would you, or where I might find him?"

"You know, I'm a newbie 'round here. I've only set up four or five times so I don't know the guy personally. But ya don't soon forget a vendor pedalin' bones. I've always seen him set up over there alongside that guy with all the tractor parts an' tools." The vendor pointed away from the road. "All those guys haul trailers. They all set up on the back lane where they can work outta their trailers or unload an' load back up within a few feet of where they set up. I'll bet dollars t' donuts the tractor guy knows him."

"Thanks. I appreciate it. The scouts appreciate it."

"No problem. Have a good one."

Cory and Cristina left the car-parts vendor and made their way to the parked trailers at the back of the grounds. They zoomed in on the tractor-parts stall. Cory glanced down at Cristina, who was fidgeting with her hands. He started laughing.

"What are you doing?"

"How do you make that scout's sign of honor? You know, the three fingers, thou shalt not lie and all that."

"Very funny."

"I knew there was a dark side to you. It was just a matter of time."

"Hey, how you doing?" Cory called ahead.

"Not bad fer an ol'-timer. And yerselves?"

"Doing good. Making the best of a beautiful day."

"That it is. Somethin' I can do fer ya?"

"Well, we hope so. I'm Cory Ballard, this here is my friend, Cristina. We're from down Grand Rapids way and we work with the scouts. We came up here looking for the Boneman. The guy who sells auto parts up there next to the road thought you might know him. Any chance of that being right?"

"Ahh, yes an' no. He does normally set up next t' me here. Let's say, more times than not. An' we do get t' talkin' now an' then, but he keeps t' himself mostly. He's not what ya'd call sociable. I gotta say, at my age not much impresses me, but that guy has a collection of bones that'd be the envy of any museum.

"In fact, it's almost ghoulish. But the guy does a damn good business with people like yerselves comin' from all over. I'm guessin' he wants t' keep his sources an' suppliers private so as t' avoid competition. Can't say I blame him. Either that or he's got his own secret process fer strippin' an' bleachin' them bones an' he don't wanna be asked any questions."

"You know what time he sets up?"

"Oh, first thing as a rule. He ain't here today. We shut the market down 'round three. He'd've been set up at seven if he were to be here."

"You don't know his name by chance."

"Nope. Like I said, he's an unsociable sort. I definitely remember introducin' myself at the beginnin' of the season. He shook my hand, said please' to meet ya, an' didn't return a name. I took the hint."

"Well, sir. I do appreciate your time and patience. Hope business goes good."

"I appreciate that. Have yerself a good day, an' if ya care fer some fresh fruit, my wife's got a stand up there by the road. The peaches are t' die fer."

"We'll keep it in mind."

Cory and Cristina took their leave.

"Hey!" hollered the vendor across the lot.

They turned to look back.

"I just remembered. There was a guy who must've known him 'cause when he saw him he yelled out Glover or Glovern or something like that."

The man raised his arms in a *for whatever that's worth* gesture.

"Thanks, we'll look into it," said Cory.

"Soon as he buys me a peach," quipped Cristina at the top of her lungs, at which point everyone laughed.

They turned away from the vendor. Cory looked at Cristina.

"And for what do I owe you the pleasure?"

"For being such good company on your quest to get the scoop at any cost."

"The price being a peach?"

"The price being a peach."

"A small price to pay."

Christina steered Cory toward the peach stand where he was obligated to buy her two splendid-looking pieces of fruit. She wasted no time biting into the first and devoured it by the time they walked back to the truck.

"That good, huh?"

"Excellent. You should have bought one for yourself."

"What can I say? I spent my life savings on two peaches for you."

"That was soooo sweet. I'm giving the other one to my dad."

"I spent my life savings on your *dad*?"

"You spent half your life savings on my peach, and the other half trying to woo me. And you did *good*. Really, you did."

Cory walked Christina around to the passenger side of the Blazer and opened her door.

He then climbed in and started the truck. He reached out to grab the gearshift when a sharp rap caused Cristina to let out a muffled scream. She lurched toward Cory, who instinctively looked in her direction. Cristina was pulling against the seat belt and leaning over toward Cory as both of them assessed the stranger pressed up against the window. He was an unshaven and rough-looking thirtyish type. Cory rolled the window down a fraction. He nodded at the man.

"I heard ya askin' 'bout the Boneman."

"Yeah?"

"I know where ya can find him."

"Come around to my side."

Cory rolled the passenger-side window up.

"He scared the daylights out of me," whispered Cristina.

Cory smiled at her as he rolled his window down. He turned to greet the stranger.

"You know the Boneman?"

109

"Yeah, I've worked for him. I know where ya can find him, but ya gotta make it worth my while."

"Fair enough, what's worth your while?"

"What's it worth to ya?"

"Hey, buddy, let's get this straight. I'm leaving. I ain't got time to be screwing around playing games. I'll find the Boneman with or without you. Give me your price and make it quick."

"Twenty."

"And what do I get for twenty?"

"His name an' address."

Cory reached for his wallet. He pulled out a twenty and sandwiched it between his fingers. He then grabbed his notepad and pen. The twenty was clearly visible to the stranger as Cory turned toward the window.

"What's his name?"

"Ahh, the twenty?"

"Give me the name—I give you the twenty—you give me his address."

"The name's Carl Gloven."

Cory handed him the twenty.

"And where can I find Mr. Gloven?"

"He's got a place west of the flooding, just south of Haymarsh Creek, at the end of East Walker Road. But that ain't where you're gonna find him."

"What d' you mean?"

"I'll tell ya where ya can find him an' a whole lot more for another twenty."

"What makes you think I need to know more than his name and address?"

"Nothin' at all, unless ya give me another twenty. Then it's obvious."

"You're smarter than you look."

Cory reached into his back pocket a second time and withdrew another twenty-dollar bill. He handed it to the stranger.

"Carl lives in a brown an' black trailer at the end of East Walker Road. Ya can't miss it. It's the last drive an' there's a lot of shit lying 'round the yard. Where the road ends there's a trail that goes back into the swamp. It's got a gate an' a bunch of signs that say 'no trespassin' an' 'keep out' an' shit. If ya follow that trail to its end, you'll come across one of them old aluminum Airstream trailers an' a few other storage trailers. That's where he spends most of his time."

"You mean to clean bones?"

"Yeah. Don't get caught back there. Carl'd soon shoot ya as look at ya. Ain't nothin' nice about him. He's a real prick."

"So why are you so generous with the information? You're not worried?"

"The sonovabitch owes me. He runs off an' hides every time I go over to collect. Ya can't trust a thing he says. The man lies through his teeth. I aim to get my money one way or another."

"Fair enough. Well, I guess our business is finished. I thank you for the information."

Cory rolled up his window and nodded as the man backed away from the truck. Cory put the Blazer in gear and started back for Little Boots.

"That guy gave me the creeps."

"Yup."

They steered away from talk of bones and the Boneman and chatted lightly about other interests until Cory abruptly changed the subject.

"I better grab some gas here at the Fast Stop. I was going to do it on the way out. Just be a minute."

Cory pulled into the gas station and jumped out of the truck. From the safety of her seat inside, Cristina studied him without fear of getting caught. She found it amusing that he so easily captured her attention. He was well mannered and intelligent. He was just rough enough around the edges to give him that essence of unpredictability, that certain male appeal. On top of it all, she

111

found him physically attractive, a real bonus. He was fortunate to have aged well.

The ring of Cory's cell phone stifled Cristina's musings. She took a liberty.

"Hello, this is Cristina Walker answering Cory Ballard's phone. ...Yes, he is. Hold on a minute."

Cristina leaned over and tapped the horn. Cory's face appeared outside the driver's door window. She showed him the phone. He opened the door.

"Thanks." He grabbed the phone. "Cory, here. ...Yeah. ...Okay. ...Yeah. ...Is that right? ...Oh. Okay. ...Ahh, I'm on my way back from the flea market. No, nothing. He didn't show. ...Yeah. All right, talk to you later."

Cory tossed the phone onto his seat and closed the door. He finished pumping gas, took his receipt, and climbed back into the truck.

"That was Harold."

"Oh. What'd he have to say?"

"He said his lady friend was there but that she couldn't tell him who the PO Box belonged to because it could get her into a lot of trouble. She said he hasn't been in lately, but generally stops in every day a little after nine when the doors open. She said Harold could probably get a good look at him then. She also said that he hasn't had the box all that long and gets a ton of mail. A lot of it ends up in the trash—and you gotta love this—she says most of the mail in the trash bin has the name Carl Gloven on it."

"You wasted your money."

"Not even close."

"How's that?"

"She proved that guy was straight with us. And if he told the truth about his name and address, he probably told us the truth about the Airstream at the end of the trail. I would've spent a hundred bucks in gas easy traipsing around looking for his hideout. Trust me, I did good. Really good."

## 19

# DNR Contractor Traps Skeletons Swimming in Dead Stream Swamp

### By Cory Ballard

Roscommon Co., Mi. A longtime resident of Houghton Lake reported netting dozens of fish skeletons. How the DNR nets ended up filled with skeletons of dead fish is just one more swamp mystery quickly blamed on the Dead Stream Swamp Monster.

Donny Simpson knows the area well and routinely volunteers his services for DNR wildlife projects. When asked to study fish catches in the Dead Stream Swamp for purposes of research, he never gave it a second thought.

Now, Mr. Simpson never stops thinking.

"Never in my life have I ever seen anything like it. It made my hair stand on end." So said a badly shaken...

"Mr. Ballard?"

"Yeah, you must be Jerry."

"I am."

The man sniffed. Cory rose slightly off his chair and accepted Jerry's gesture to shake hands. The man blinked with much effort as if suffering from itchy eyes or allergies. His eyelids were red and swollen. Jerry flagged down a waitress and called out for a cup of coffee before pulling out a chair to sit. Cory wasted no time getting to the point.

"So.... Your phone call has me intrigued, Jerry. What information could you possibly have that is *priceless* to me?"

"Let's just say those articles you wrote about skeletons, swamp monsters, and alien invasions may be a whole lot closer to the truth than you think. Ya know what I'm sayin'?"

"Okay. A man with an open mind. I like that. You got my attention. What do you got?"

"It's gonna cost ya a thousand bucks."

"Whoa! Jerry. Too much attention. A thousand bucks? Yesterday, it was twenty for a tip, today it's a thousand? Trust me, I don't make that kind of money writing articles for the tabloids—not even close."

"You will with what I know. In fact, you'll be writing a lot more articles," he sniffed.

"That may be well and so, but I'm not about to shell out a grand on information that I already have, or for something that turns out to be useless."

"I understand. Completely. So this is how it works. For two hundred an' fifty bucks, I give ya some insight. For five hundred, I give ya the gist of what I got. For everything I know, it's gonna cost a grand."

"I don't think so, Jerry. Two hundred and fifty bucks for insight is pretty steep. I can get that stuff free from a priest."

Cory focused on the man's repetitious blinking.

"Sir, the reason I know what I know is because people think I'm an uneducated idiot. They're right about one thing. I'm uneducated. But they're badly mistaken when they think I'm an idiot. I sought you out because I'm an opportunist. Right now, this is an easy way for me to make a buck. Ya know what I'm sayin'?

"You're workin' for the *Roscommon County Chronicle*. For me to make a bigger buck, I only need go to another paper like the *Detroit News*, or an Internet news feed. You already whet the world's appetite about Dead Stream swamp monsters; now I'm ready to feed it. Yes or no. Your choice."

"My choice is to keep from going broke."

"Yes or no?" He sniffed.

"I'll give you sixty bucks for a tip. I'll pay more fast if your story warrants it. And for the record, I don't just work for the *County Chronicle*, and I don't just keep a grand in my wallet. I'd have to go to a bank to get that kind of money."

"Hundred an' fifty."

"Sixty bucks. Take it or leave it. Yes or no. Your choice."

"Fine, sixty bucks. Hand it over."

Cory pulled his wallet and unfolded it. He removed three twenty-dollar bills and handed them to Jerry.

"This better be good."

"This is better'n good. You're gonna kiss my ass even after payin' me a grand."

"So you say. Let's hear it. What've you got?"

"I worked maintenance in a facility that was involved in genetic research relevant to the swamp. I overheard a great deal. I saw a great deal. I think it may be the reason for all these rumors about a swamp monster."

"And?"

"And what I'm sayin' is now you're at five hundred. Yes or no? Your choice."

"Are you serious?"

"Yes or no?" He sniffed as before.

"I got two hundred bucks in my wallet. Say something sweet and it's yours."

"I know the facility like the back of my hand, and I'm sayin' something escaped."

"Shit." Cory studied Jerry's face. Begrudgingly, he pulled his wallet back out. He handed Jerry his last two hundred dollars. "Now what?"

"Now it's expensive. A thousand bucks."

"That's a lot of money, Jerry."

"Yeah, well, I'm givin' ya a lot o' story."

"That's a chunk of change."

"Call it a leap of faith. Tell ya what; I'll make a deal with ya. You give me the money, an' I'll give ya my word. If it doesn't end up in print, I'll return half. Five hundred bucks back in your pocket."

Cory sat and studied Jerry's blinking as Jerry sat and returned Cory's stare. Jerry was waiting for an answer. He had room to be patient.

"You're a hard man, Jerry. Being in print doesn't make it profitable. A thousand bucks. Christ almighty. You ever hear of highway robbery? Let me make a call."

Cory grabbed his cell.

"Hey, Harold—Cory... good, good. Listen. I'm sitting with a guy who says he's got enough info to blow this whole swamp monster thing wide open. Story of the century kind of thing, but it's going to cost a thousand bucks. How bad d'you want to know what he's got? Yeah. Jerry. ...don't know." Cory turned to Jerry. "What's your last name?"

"Jerry."

"Ahh, yeah, Harold. I don't think we're going to get that at this point. No, what he's said is that he worked at a facility involved with genetic research and he thinks something escaped. I'm taking it to mean something abnormal. So what do you want to do? Personally, I'm not jumping to pull a grand out of my pocket. I don't have advertising revenue to fall back on. Yeah. Okay. Will do."

Cory turned off the cell and turned to look at Jerry.

"Okay. You got your five hundred, but a grand is out of the question. If Harold isn't going to pay a grand, I sure as hell can't. He pays me. He'll go seven-fifty tops. That's it. Your call. And for that price it better be good, I mean, really good."

"You know I could just go to Detroit."

"You could, but I've been in the business for a long time, and I doubt Detroit's going to pay a grand for anything that's not front page. What you got is front page here in Houghton Lake. Here's where the money is. Your call."

"How do I know I can trust you for all seven-fifty?"

116

"Call it a leap of faith. I'm already out two-sixty."

"Fine. Seven-fifty it is. You might wanna start takin' notes or something."

"Really?"

Cory pulled out his tablet. He adjusted his pencil lead.

"Okay, hot-shot. We're ready as ready's going to get. Speak your mind, buddy, and don't be bashful on my account."

"I don't know if you're from around here or not—"

"I grew up here."

"When did you leave?"

"Thirty-some years ago. I joined the service. What the hell's that got to do with anything?"

"It's too far back. That's way too far back. Things have changed. Maybe stories around here still prick your ears, maybe not. I don't know. What ya need to know is this. Some eight or maybe nine years back, sea lampreys were discovered up north movin' around Mullett Lake. And—"

"Sea lampreys? Oh, Jesus. Don't tell me this is another sea lamprey story. Man, that's been played to death. You're going to have to do a whole lot better'n that, Jerry. In fact, if that's all you got, I want my two-sixty back."

"Hey, relax, man. I told ya this was gonna be good, but ya gotta let me finish. You're payin' *me* to talk, remember?"

"All right. All right. Point taken. Proceed. So, tell me, what have lampreys gotta do with this?"

"Shortly after showin' up in Mullett, they'd moved along the Indian River and were spotted in Burt Lake. Folks said lampreys were migrating south from Cheboygan along the Black River toward Black Lake. Likewise, folks feared they would soon turn up in Crooked and Pickerel Lakes.

"What was really disturbing about these finds was an indication that these lampreys no longer seemed to be swimmin' back to Lake Huron for mating, but instead remained in the lakes. There was a concern that these fish were now fully established, fully sustaining themselves on fish in the inland lakes an' waterways.

117

Pretty scary stuff if ya like to cater to fishermen. Ya know what I'm sayin'?"

"What d'you do for a living, Jerry?"

"I'm a maintenance man. I do anything from clean out a plugged toilet to hookin' up four-forty. Why? Ya thinkin' that makes me stupid... somebody who doesn't know what he's talkin' about?"

In spite of Jerry's blinking and sniffing, his expression was stern.

"Not at all. Quite the opposite in fact. As scarce as jobs are around here, my first thought was you must be pretty sharp to have held on to yours."

"Well, I don't know 'bout you, but there was no college in my future, an' there's no trade schools or apprenticeships when there's no business. You do what ya can with what ya got—the reason I'm here. I've got information an' I'm workin' with what I got."

"Hey, I've been there. I know exactly where you're coming from. And besides, I like an honest man. Keep going, Jerry. I'm not bored yet."

If Jerry had been getting defensive and irritated, he settled down. You could hear it in his voice as he continued.

"What I was about to say... is that the only thing around these parts that brings in money is catering to sportsmen. Fishermen an' hunters. It's not that they're big money, it's more like they're the only money. So when lampreys were discovered in the flooding, in the backwaters of the Reedsburg Dam, it was like the whole town got broadsided by the news.

"Nobody's ever gonna know how the hell they got here. Probably hitched a ride on a fishin' boat that was trailered down from the inland waterway, or maybe across from Lake Huron. Maybe some idiot was using the larvae for bait. Who knows? Who cares? What I do know is that everybody was predictin' our fisheries gettin' wiped out by them blood-sucking bastards.

"One day, rumor had it that the Great Lakes Aquatics Commission, the Lakes and Fisheries Canada, the DNR, along with a bunch of universities and private firms were going to put up money to figure out how to wipe these things out. That was like *best news* ever. Not just here, but all across the northern part of the state.

"The name of one company in particular was ARL Inc.— Aquatic Research Laboratories."

"Never heard of it."

"Neither has anybody else. I know about it because that's where I worked," he sniffed.

"Really?"

"Really. I told you this would be worth your money. Ya ever hear of cone shell snails?"

"I couldn't tell you. Probably not."

"Suffice it to say that they are poisonous as hell. I heard one drop of venom from a cone snail could kill twenty people. We're talkin' about a fricking snail in a pretty shell. The kind that people pick up off the beach. Ya know what I'm sayin'?

"Lucky for you, I know that ARL had a warehouse full of tanks filled with the most godawful shit you ever heard of. Hundreds of things like them cone shell snails, things that are unbelievably poisonous. They had pufferfish, stonefish, boxfish, an' stargazers. Ya ever hear of a bobbit worm?"

"No."

"Believe me, it's disgusting. It's just the most disgustin' thing I've ever seen. These worms can grow to be ten feet long. They love warm shallow water. They lie buried in the sand with just their heads stickin' out. They lunge at whatever swims past them and drag it to its grave. Their jaws are like steel traps... so strong that they cut fish clean in half. On top of that, they've got these toxic bristles along their bodies that can cause permanent nerve damage to anything that touches them.

"There were all kinds of nasty-ass creatures in those tanks. They had these things called ragworms that were like three feet long and made your skin crawl. But ARL wasn't just about poisonous animals. It was also about genetically creating shit from the DNA of those things."

"Jerry, you gotta forgive me for asking, but how the hell does a maintenance man come to know all this stuff? You know, *genetically creating shit* and all of that?"

Jerry looked at Cory with a mixed expression of amusement and disdain. He pulled out a handkerchief and blew his sinuses clean. He wiped his already red nose, back and forth, back and forth, and blinked.

"You know, Cory, I once watched a documentary that stated if you were to lock up a smart kid in a closet for four years while the rest of the world went to college, an' then let him out the day they graduated, he would most likely be just as successful as the graduates. Let's face it, you either got brains, or you don't. Ya know what I'm sayin'?"

"Actually, I do."

"School doesn't fix stupid. But I'll tell you, when it comes to stupid, I learned early that the best way to get smart is to get stupid. Play dumb, play ignorant, and ask a lot o' questions. I'm taken for a toilet-scrubbin' fool who can't possibly grasp the science of genetics an' so the researchers are tickled pink to pump up their egos by showering me with all their knowledge, and laughing without worry of me understanding any of it.

"So, they ran their mouths, an' I learned that they were usin' these creatures as buildin' blocks for something that would search the river an' lake bottoms for lampreys an' kill 'em."

"Okay. Jerry... you weren't bullshitting. This is compelling stuff. I got to give it to you. It doesn't get much better. But I'm dealing with dead cows and such. Are you saying ARL created a super snail or something that can take down a cow? Something that's living or swimming around in Dead Stream Swamp? Something that can kill people?"

Jerry raised his eyebrows. For a brief moment, he did not blink.

"I have no idea."

"Bummer. So, then what? Did they come up with something? Did they hatch a monster? What's ARL doing now?"

"ARL is history. The place burned down—"

"Burned down? Really?" Cory interrupted. "Gone?"

"Yeah. Burned down. Gone. And I'm thinkin' that's where your problem begins."

"You're killing me, Jerry. Talk man."

"ARL went up like a dried log pile. It went through a chain of unforeseen events that took it right out."

"D'you know what happened?"

"Yeah, pretty much. The place used a lot of juice. Primarily for tank heaters. If I remember correctly, ARL had a dedicated feed for a six-hundred-amp service. Some dude named Larry Wellington, aka *unlucky Larry*, was a contract electrician. The guy touched something he shouldn't have. He, along with part of the service panel, got vaporized on the spot. My understanding is that the panel suffered heavy damage. The explosion set off the fire alarms, which notified the fire department. It also activated the overhead sprinklers, an' that's where things took a turn for the worse, if that's even possible.

"Ya see, those tanks had twenty-four-hundred-watt heaters because most of the specimens came from tropical regions an' needed to stay warm durin' Michigan winters in order to survive. They also needed to bring these tanks up to temperature fast when called for. Normally, the tank heaters only come on individually, ya know, one here an' one there, as needed. Nobody ever gave thought to what'd happen if the fire sprinklers were activated, which is to say, drown everything, includin' the tanks, with a continuous spray of cold water. Well, what happened was all the tank heaters kicked in at once.

"There were forty-eight one-thousand-gallon tanks, each with a twenty-four-hundred-watt heater. They figured it added up to nearly five-hundred continuous amps of juice that immediately overloaded the wiring. The breakers should've tripped instantly, but they didn't because they were fried. The investigators determined the damage done to the service panel in the initial explosion caused the breakers to fuse, to fail. They were welded closed or whatever. They never tripped, the wiring turned red hot like a giant toaster. Wasn't long after that an' the walls and anything else close by went up in a blaze of glory.

121

"Of course, you can't burn down fish tanks full of water. They just sit there. Ya'd think they'd get too warm an' kill off anything inside, an' maybe they did, but then again... maybe they didn't. Ya see, the fire sprinklers kept showerin' cool water across the tanks. So, be it life, or be it death, the outcome would be based on water temperature after a battle between the cold-water sprinklers on one side, and the fire an' tank heaters on the other. Question is... did the water get too hot... too cold... or did it stay just right to keep them critters alive? Ya get what I'm sayin'?"

Jerry stopped talking and let Cory ponder the outcome.

"Seems to me if they all died, you'd've had a crap load of dead fish stinking up the place."

"We did, thanks to a large containment that was designed to collect accidental overspills. It was full of dead fish."

"There you go."

"So you'd think. And if it was as simple as that, I wouldn't be here hittin' you up for a grand," he sniffed.

"So what're you saying?"

"I'm sayin' that the containment might've been a red herring."

"Go on."

"The containment had never before been used to control an accidental spill. But it was routinely used to cleanse the rows of tanks by submersing them simultaneously in a bath. That was the most efficient way to prevent cross-contamination of specimens or to stamp out diseases and parasites when projects were started or completed.

"The containment had a drain that remained closed by default, and *had* to be opened manually to drain the sterilization bath. The cleansing bath process was always well manned an' monitored. The bath water was monitored for toxicity or environmental hazards before being drained. The entire process was performed step-by-step following documented quality-control procedures."

"Nice to know."

"Yep. So, after the fire, I was called in to assess the damage. I entered the tanks facility, and between fire sprinklers an' the

122

fire department hosing everything down, the tanks had all overflowed. But the overflow was captured within the containment walls as designed, or so it seemed. Ya see, the tanks had all overflowed, but the spillover hadn't reached the top of the containment wall. There was a lot of dead stuff both inside an' outside of the tanks, but everything was within the containment.

"Believe me, there were plenty of jokes flying around about these livin' nightmares gettin' out into the swamp. Laughter aside, my fears were eased by knowin' that most of the stuff in the tanks could only live in warm saltwater environments. Anyhow, I went about my business cleanin' up whatever died in the tanks or in the containment and that was that. End of story. Look for a new job."

"And then?" asked Cory.

"It was only after all these rumors began to surface about fish disappearing, and then having read the articles you wrote about carcasses an' bleached bones turnin' up around the swamp.... Well, that brought home all those memories of the horrible shit in them tanks.

"I had always been consoled by knowin' nothin' had left the containment. It did its job. That was until your article about the fish skeletons in the nets. That reminded me of when I was lookin' into the bottom of the containment an' seeing all those deadly animals around the drain grating. I didn't think much of them clustering around the drain at the time because it was the deepest part of the containment, and I believed they were lookin' for a place to escape or hide from the fire overhead. That would've made sense. I mean, the containment tank was meant to contain things. The drain was never opened. Ya know what I'm sayin'?

"On the other hand, it's a different explanation that has kept me up at night. And that's why I was prompted to find you," he sniffed.

"And what explanation is that?"

"What if they were sucked into the drain? Ya see, everybody— including me, made an assumption that the containment did its job and kept the spillover from the tanks in check. But what if it didn't?"

"What d'you mean?"

"I mean, when we ran cleansing baths, we always opened the valves manually. Always. The reason we did this is because there was an automatic system, but it wasn't designed to drain the containment. For environmental protection, it was designed to contain as much spillover as possible. So it would kick in, drain... say a quarter of the tank max, and then close the valves. It was designed to repeat this hi-low range in order to keep as much bad shit in the containment housing as possible. In order to fully drain the containment, we had to physically open the drain and keep it in the open position."

"So, you're saying—"

"I'm sayin' that the auto system may have drained the tank repeatedly, but nobody realized it. Everything we worried about was lying dead in the bottom of the containment. Amid all the confusion, the tank appeared nearly full, and nobody gave thought to the overflow havin' set off the auto-drain. There were no records. There was nothing left in that place that would raise suspicion. The very last thing anybody would've imagined was the drain being opened automatically because no one ever thought about a flood from the *fire sprinklers*."

"Nobody but you."

"The only reason it occurred to me was because I just happened to remember seein' all the shit lyin' dead around the drain. I'm sayin' maybe they weren't lookin' for a place to hide, but instead got sucked toward the drain by the current of passing water."

"Speaking of current. I thought you said the wiring burned up. What makes you think the pumps even worked?"

"Now, that, Mr. Ballard, is the million dollar question. I don't. I asked myself the same question. But being that I was maintenance, what I did know was this. All the power for the heaters came from overhead feeds. Ceiling drops. That was because having two-forty so close to water required a disconnect at each tank for changing out heaters. On the other hand, power for the pump passed through conduit buried in the concrete floor. The overhead feeds would have burned first for sure, but power in the floor might never have burned. Water soaked concrete would stay cool. The feeds inside would have been more likely to short out from flooding than burn up from fire. It was just a question of how long the mains held up."

"Humph. Makes sense. And we'll never know."

"And we'll never know."

The two men studied each other as they considered the odds. Jerry went on to speak.

"Not that I need to add any additional fear to this nightmare, but I keep reminding myself that the sea lamprey was a fish that had to go from freshwater to the saltwater of the sea. It's been that way since the time of dinosaurs... until the past couple of years when they decided to screw the sea and stay in Lake Huron, which has no salt. And now they don't even go to Lake Huron. They stay put in the freshwater of Mullett and Burt Lakes. Ya get what I'm sayin'? How can they do that?"

"So. What you're sayin' is that you think it's highly possible the larvae or eggs of these animals made it through the drain and into the Dead Stream Swamp, and then adapted?"

"Adapted? Hardly. How 'bout puttin' larvae and eggs aside, and imagining what made its way outta the tanks, through the drain, an' into the Dead Sea Swamp was some genetic crap cooked up by the researchers at ARL. Something that may no longer need to live in saltwater to survive. Something that planet earth has never seen before. Something like that."

"Jesus, Jerry. No shit."

Cory's attention was solidly within Jerry's grip.

"No shit is right. Now, you see why I'm here."

"I do. Damn."

"Anyway, I'm sayin' that the whole county is totally freaked out by an alleged swamp monster of some sort. I'm sayin' I got seven hundred an' fifty bucks that says nobody's put together a better story than the one I just gave you. It's in your hands now."

"Yes, it is. And I'm thinking it's worth every penny. Even if it's all bullshit, I can work with it. You're about as close to bringing aliens into the story as it gets. Everybody wants aliens. Now....

You do understand that I'll have to check your story against whatever facts I dig up."

"Absolutely," he sniffed.

"Why don't you give me your last name?"

"For now, I'd rather not. I don't need to spend my nights lookin' over my shoulder for the ARL nazis. But if you get into ARL's personnel records there were only two maintenance men. The other dude was a lot older. Might even be retired by now. I would much rather have ARL thinkin' it was you who put two an' two together."

"That's a lot o' two an' two."

"Yeah, but that's what you do, right?"

"Fair enough, but back to last names.... Can you give me the names of any scientists, or technicians, or employees, anybody in general that might be able to give me any additional information?"

Jerry's face scrunched up. His blinking seemed out of control.

"Ahh, yeah, I can do that. Let's see, there's Jim Johnson. Uhhhh, Fred Biller, Bill, ah, William Dorskey, Tammy Tagart. They were all scientists. I'm not sure about Tammy. She might have been a technician."

"She sounds perfect. Not too high in the pecking order. Hopefully, a gal with a conscience. She's the one I need to get to. Tagart is the last name?"

"Yeah. Ahhh... if I remember correctly.... Tammy said she'd finally got a job at Morrison Medical in Traverse City. Far as I know, she moved there."

"What would a marine biologist do at Morrison Medical?"

"I assume it was meant to be a temporary job. I imagine she's qualified to do lab work or something like that. But for all I know, she may be in Florida or California by now. I have no idea."

"Mmmm." Cory murmured as he finished jotting his notes and closed his tablet. "Well, Jerry. This is all very interesting. You sure you won't give me your last name?"

"I'm sticking my neck out here."

"Has to go on a check."

"Cash."

"Suit yourself, Mr. Doe. Cash it is. Listen, for what it's worth, if I could've afforded a grand for the info, I'd a given it to you. Having said it, let's go see Harold. He's got the purse."

## 20

## Did Mad Scientists
## Doom Dead Stream Swamp?

**By Cory Ballard**

Roscommon Co., Mi. On the assurance of anonymity, a former employee of Aquatics Research Laboratories suggested that the flood of bones and associated deaths in and around Dead Stream Swamp may be the direct result of maniacal minds.

According to the source, ARL employed a number of scientists who were researching a host of extremely toxic life forms. These hellish creatures, best left to nightmares, lived in holding tanks at the facility. ARL used their DNA in hopes of creating the ultimate killing machine.

A drop of venom could wipe out...

"Can I help you?"

"Yeah, I'm looking for Ray Staggs. Is he around?"

The clerk glanced around the shop.

"He must be in back. I'll get him."

Cory turned away from the counter and wandered along an aisle of fishing rods. One in particular that touted carbon construction grabbed his attention. He began muttering under his breath.

"Eight hundred dollars? *Jesus.* Whatever happened to bamboo poles? I'm in the wrong business."

Cory was still muttering to himself when a man with wispy trails of near colorless brown hair walked into the showroom from somewhere in back. Cory spotted his approach, but struggled to recognize him.

"How can I help—wait.... Do I know you? You look awfully familiar...."

Whereas the features had changed, the speech had not. If nothing else resurrected a memory of his old classmate, the man's slow manner of speech sufficed.

"Cory Ballard."

Cory held out his hand. Ray took it with a firm grip.

"Cory... Ballard.... No.... High school Cory Ballard? Oh, for heaven's sake."

"One and the same."

"Obviously, you didn't stick around Houghton Lake. I don't think I've seen you since high school."

"Nope. Can't say I did."

"So, up here visiting family or friends?"

"That and business. In fact, that's why I came by your place. You got a minute?"

"Oh... for an old schoolmate? Yeah.... I guess. What's up?"

"Couple days ago, I ran into Bill Peterson and Greg Morrell—"

"Oh, yeah...."

"They told me to stop in and see you. Said they do a lot of business here."

"Yeah.... Bill and Greg like to fish. They come around a fair amount."

"Well, we were sitting around having coffee, and the guys really got into this rant about how bad the fishing is around Dead Stream Swamp and the flooding.

"Just so happened, I was looking into matters somewhat related, and they suggested I stop by your place and look you up. They pressed me to get your opinion, said you'd give me a real good

128

idea of what they were talking about. I was hoping they gave me good advice, and that you might have a minute or two to fill me in."

"What do you do now, Cory?" asked Ray in his long, drawn-out manner.

"Nothing. I'm retired. Do a little writing when I'm in the mood. I probably should get back into fishing, but then by the sounds of it, maybe not. So tell me, Ray. Is it really as bad as they make it out to be?"

"Worse."

"Seriously."

"Oh, yeah. Been bad for a while now."

"Ray, they're telling me you can sit out in the swamp all damn day and come home empty handed. I'll be honest. I'm having a tough time swallowing that."

"Empty handed? No.... I wouldn't say empty handed. You'll catch something.... But not much.... It's killing us.... Right now, the store's only in business because there's fishermen out there still blaming themselves, or their choice of bait. But... they're slowly starting to suspect.

"Business began dropping off the season before last. That was the first time since I bought the place. It wasn't good. But... it was great compared to last season, which was terrible. And this year? Oh, brother, this season put me solid in the red. I've sold bait here for better'n thirty years, and I've never seen anything like it."

"And why do you think that is?"

Ray gave Cory a peculiar look. He hesitated.

"Honestly.... I don't know. I will say there's been a real sense of uneasiness in the backwater. It's like sitting in a boat, looking around the swamp, and thinking the axe is gonna fall. It's like thinking somebody's watching you from behind. I can't explain it, but I can see it in the faces of the regulars. I can hear it in their voices an' stories. Something ain't right and the locals know it. We all do."

"What kind of stories, Ray? Can you give me an idea?"

"Oh.... Lemme see.... Well... the one I hear that upsets people the most, the one I seem to hear about every other day has to do with reeling in dead fish. I said you won't come home empty handed, but that doesn't mean you'll catch a fish worth eating.

"Customers come in and say that they were hooking into fish that gave 'em a good fight only to be netted and found dead. Not once, but three or four or five times in a row. Sometimes the fish would come up half-missing, half-digested, or mutilated or something.

"Lot of guys got spooked, afraid of the water. Lot of 'em moved to different fishing beds or avoided the swamp altogether, preferring to fish Houghton or Higgins. If they stayed in Houghton, it wouldn't be so bad, but when they start heading north to Higgins, I lose business. One thing is for sure: they aren't about to eat anything caught down here that's netted dead or half-wasted."

"Huh. Interesting. What else?"

"Oh.... I've had a number of customers complain about getting their hands burned by fish when they grabbed hold of 'em. There's talk of bones littering the shores, and patches of dead vegetation in the shallows—strange noises and whatnot. Heard a few stories of guys getting really sick. Talk spreads fast, and stories are shared. The locals pass 'em around, and sooner or later they get told here at the cash register. I've heard 'em all. And... they may be inflated or exaggerated, fisherman tales no doubt, but.... I'm telling you one thing for sure—there's always an element of truth. Something's way outta whack.

"And now... with rumors of cows and whatnot dying around the swamp.... Locals are grumbling more and more about something poisonous in the water. I don't know.... But... if it was a chemical spill, the oil and gas companies aren't saying a thing. All I know is that if this keeps up much longer, I won't be in business to worry about it one way or the other. I told the wife, maybe it's time to move to Florida."

"So how far down are we talking, Ray? Fishing-wise. Give me an idea, a percentage, say ten, twenty, thirty percent down or what?"

"Oh... hell.... I don't know.... Maybe, fifty, sixty.... Actually, it could be worse than that. It's gotten gradually worse over the past few years. But... this year it's way down. It's still good in the lake, just not the backwaters. But that's where a lot o' folks fish."

"Unbelievable."

"Yup.... If I've heard that once, I've heard it a thousand times. It's all anybody can say."

"Well, I owe you. Thank you for your time, Ray. I gotta run, but uhh... for what it's worth, Bill, Greg, and I are going to try and get together for a brew before I head back down to GR. I'll let you know when. Love to have you join us."

"Hey.... I'd like that. Give me a call. It's been a while since I've seen Bill and Greg in the store. Do me a favor; tell 'em I said hi."

"Will do. See you later, Ray."

Cory left the bait shop with a mix of feelings, but now, for the first time, they shifted toward ominous.

## 21

Cory parked his Blazer in front of Tammy Tagart's house. He and Cristina sat and chatted while they waited for her return.

"So, tell me something about your father. Are the two of you close?"

"Mmmm. That's a tough one. I don't know if we'd ever think of ourselves as close. We've lived the majority of our lives apart. And I don't mean on different streets. I think a better word would be *fond*. I'm very fond of him. He's strange in a way. Or maybe he's just eccentric, or maybe he's just old and too independent for his own good. Maybe I just find him interesting. I don't know. I suppose he'll always be a mystery that for me will remain unsolved. Whatever it is, it's safe to say I'm fond of him."

"So, he wasn't a part of your life at all?"

"Nope. Not until I was twenty-six. That was the year I got married. Apparently, he and my mother had come to some agreement and he walked me down the aisle."

"Wow. You hadn't seen him before that?"

"Nope."

"Did you resent it?"

"Resent what? That I never saw him until my wedding, or that I never saw him until my wedding?"

"I guess that would be both."

"Okay. I would say that not seeing him until I got married was just status quo for my life. I outgrew most of the *what was the matter with me torture.* The question occupied too much of my younger years and it just got old. I stopped thinking about it.

"As for not seeing him until my wedding? No.... I didn't resent it. Not really. I think I was too stunned, or too self-conscious, or fearful that this stranger would somehow trash my wedding. The only thing I might have resented was how his presence seemed to overshadow everything about the wedding. But then that was only in my mind. Nine out of the ten guests who saw him walk me down the aisle had no idea who he was. Of course, you have to appreciate the humor. Twenty years later, my husband left me, and wouldn't you know it, my dad is still here. And lives to support me through thick and thin. Go figure."

"You never told me what his—"

"Wait. Wait. There she is," Cristina interrupted Cory.

Cory spun around in his seat to watch the woman pull into her driveway.

"Give her a minute to get inside and then we'll go up."

As they exited the truck, Cory gave Cristina instructions on how to handle the introductions. He wanted to let her approach Ms. Tagart in order to keep the woman's concerns to a minimum.

Cristina stepped up onto the porch and knocked. A woman of about forty opened the door a crack and peeked out. Her features were concealed by shadows.

"Tammy Tagart?"

"Yes."

"Ms. Tagart, my name is Cristina Walker, and this is my colleague, Cory Ballard. I'm very sorry to disturb you, but we're investigating some odd events surrounding the Dead Stream Swamp over in Houghton Lake, which has led us to you. We were hoping that you might be willing to offer us a moment of your time to answer some questions. Would you mind?"

"Who are you with?"

Cory leaned in toward the open door and flashed his open wallet.

"We're investigative reporters working for the *Roscommon County Chronicle*. I'm sure you're familiar with the paper."

"Yes, I am. Odd events? What kind of odd events?"

"May we come in?" asked Cristina.

"No. I'm sorry. I don't know you."

"No problem. We understand. Tell me, Ms. Tagart, is there a coffee shop nearby where we could sit, a place where you'd feel comfortable? A place where I could buy you coffee in return for your time?"

The woman didn't immediately respond. Her eyes were darting back and forth as she studied both Cristina and Cory.

"What odd events?"

Cory spoke up. "Ms. Tagart, there's something very peculiar going on in and around Dead Stream Swamp. We don't know exactly what's happening, but we think it might have something to do with ARL. You're the only employee we found who still lives within driving distance of Houghton Lake. To make a long story short, we drove out in hopes of meeting you personally. It would mean a great deal to us if you'd be willing to answer a few questions. Nothing more."

"ARL? They've been closed for years. Place burned down."

"Yeah, we know."

The woman pulled the front door open. Cory and Christina got their first look at her. She was wearing a pants outfit that was appropriate for professional work. Her facial features appeared plain, but not unattractive.

"I can't imagine anybody wishing to do me harm would know the first thing about ARL. You might as well come in."

"Thank you."

The woman's home was small and clean. There were numerous pictures of younger people, children, or nieces and nephews. She led them into the kitchen and motioned them to sit at the table. It did not appear that she was married.

"Coffee? It's fresh. Timed for when I get home."

"Please."

"Sounds great."

"Go ahead and have a seat."

The woman retrieved three mugs from a cabinet and set them on the kitchen table. She poured coffee, pulled out a chair, and sat down across from Cory and Cristina.

"So what could I possibly know about ARL that is of interest to the two of you?"

"Maybe nothing, but that's what we're here to find out," said Cory.

"How'd you get my name?"

"Jerry, the maintenance man."

"Oh! Jerry McFarlen." The woman's face lit up. "Great guy. I liked Jerry. He was a lot smarter than people made him out to be."

"Yeah, I found that out firsthand. Apparently, the feeling's mutual. Jerry suggested we talk to you."

Cory lied, but he was intent on making Tammy feel comfortable. He wanted her to believe she was among friends. He was also delighted to get Jerry's last name.

"Well, what is it you want to know?"

Cory took over.

"To start, let me just say that Jerry gave us an overall picture of the ARL's last days, the fire and all. He explained the cause, the cleanup, he told us about the tanks, and all the stuff inside. But we need to understand more about what went on at ARL. We think there may be a connection between past activities at ARL and what's now happening in the Dead Stream Swamp. We're hoping you can give us an idea of what ARL was trying to accomplish before it burned down."

"I see.... I guess I don't see any harm in that. I mean, there was nothing secretive about what we were doing. We had to submit the usual paperwork in order to obtain grants. I'm sure everything is in the public records."

"I'm sure you're right, Ms. Tagart. But I'd really love to have you just tell us in your own words—*what went on at ARL.* What was the mission?"

"Ahhh... let me see.... I assume Jerry already informed you that we were researching a more efficient means of targeting and eradicating sea lamprey."

"More or less, he did. Yes."

"Okay, then I would start by saying that an association was formed by a number of public and private institutions to pool resources and address the threat. At first the project was manned by whatever scientists or technicians were available or willing to volunteer services. But as things scaled up, the government made additional staff available as best they could, considering budget constraints. In the beginning, the operation was being populated by people that possessed sometimes more, but oftentimes less of the needed skills and experience.

"For example, over at Fort Grayling there was a small contingent of experts that were assigned to keep base personnel up to date on the latest developments in chemical and biological warfare, among other things. The government requested assistance from the Grayling staff because of their database on biological poisons. Also, did I fail to mention they came for free, and that free was always a big deal?"

Cory chuckled, "Makes sense, I guess."

"Point is, we were trying to think outside the box. We were looking for alternatives to mass applications of rotenone or piscicides. We wanted a more efficient lampricide than Bayluscide or TFM, which can wreak havoc with trout and other non-target species. For example, tadpoles are ten to fifteen times more sensitive to TFM than sea lamprey larvae. TFM is also toxic to humans and has no antidote.

"So aside from collateral damage to non-target species, you have to deal with all of the chemical regulations governing storage, transportation, application, and notifications. And then there's all the training involved with hazardous materials. There are issues with contaminating drinking water, and the list just goes on and on.

"Believe me, there were plenty of reasons to continue the search for lampricides that were more practical, more economical, and better suited for targeting. We strove to eradicate lampreys entirely, instead of just holding them in check.

"Between the Grayling database that covered every venom, toxin, or poison known to man, the DNR with its volumes of research and understanding of current methods for controlling sea lampreys, and genetic scientists with the Fish and Wildlife

Service, who studied lamprey immune systems, we were off to a reasonably good start. All parties set off working together as best they could. But it didn't take long after delving into the project before the organization determined there was a void in the level of needed expertise. We realized that void would be best filled by scientists who understood cloning, molecular biology, genetic engineering, and like fields of study. And that is where Aquatic Research Laboratories, or ARL, came into the picture."

"Soooo... you did what at ARL? Genetics?"

"No, no, no. My degree's in marine biology. It was my background in invertebrate zoology, specifically cnidariology and malacology among other things that made me attractive to ARL. I also studied ichthyology and worked a number of years in various fisheries and medical research labs. At ARL, my job was to monitor the health of our specimens. That's how I met Jerry. He helped me scrub a lot of tanks during our time together. When you're rubbing elbows in gunge, you tend to become good friends or not."

"Do you know what direction ARL was taking at the time of the fire, before the facility was destroyed?"

"You mean, like how were they approaching the problem?"

"Precisely."

"Ahhh, pretty much. In essence, they were looking for aquatic specimens that shared certain qualities. They were looking for creatures that preferred to live within the sand of a river or lakebed. They wanted creatures that were aggressive. They wanted creatures that were highly toxic or venomous—"

"Like a bobbit worm?"

"Yes, exactly," said Ms. Tagart with an expression of surprise. "Jerry must have told you about that. He claimed they gave him nightmares."

"He said as much."

"Bobbit worms are good examples. They stay buried beneath the sand. They are aggressive, and reasonably poisonous, but not nearly as venomous as other things like a number of snails belonging to the *Conus* genus. Still, what they lack in toxicity they more than make up for in their devastating striking ability.

"Now *Conus geographus*, which is rather darkly nicknamed the cigarette snail because it's said that once poisoned, a person only has enough time to smoke a cigarette before dying, they're nasty. They possess these tiny barbs by which they inject a neurotoxin that has a multitude of compounds, each attacking a different part of the nervous system. The venom has so many compounds in its makeup that so far it has been impossible to manufacture an effective antidote.

"Another animal that we invested a lot of time studying was *Chironex fleckeri*, or as it is more commonly called, the box jellyfish. Deadly beyond belief. But even more important, it thrives in oxygen-depleted waters. That would be Dead Stream Swamp. All of the branches, the tree limbs, all of the wood lying beneath the slow-moving swamp water depletes oxygen as it decays.

"I'll be the first to tell you that we had a pretty impressive collection of scary stuff in the facility. Certainly on par with any zoo in the state that has a herpetarium or serpentarium."

"Do you know what the others were up to?"

"Well, you understand I'm not a toxicologist per se, or a geneticist."

"I understand, and I'm only interested in your speculation. A guess is fine."

"I really can't say. I focused on my own work. I can't speak for individuals, but as a team, our objective was to develop a genetically altered or designed life form that had a voracious appetite for ammocoetes. It had to be a life form that had no interest in anything but ammocoetes, and therefore presented no danger to anything but ammocoetes."

"What the hell are—what'd you call them?"

"Ammocoetes?"

"Yeah. Those."

"Sea lamprey larvae. Let me give you a little background about sea lamprey. You might find this interesting. Sea lampreys are an invasive species of parasitic fish here in the Great Lakes that first entered Lake Ontario in the eighteen-thirties. Niagara Falls prevented them from entering the rest of the Great Lakes until the late eighteen-hundreds, early nineteen-hundreds. After that the Welland Canal, which bypasses the falls, was improved, and subsequently opened the door to the sea lamprey invasion. Within twenty years, all four remaining lakes were invaded.

137

"I say that matter-of-factly. But to give you an idea of the impact, an idea of the devastation to the native fish populations that followed, you have to know this: Before the invasion—if I remember correctly—the U.S. and Canadian harvest of lake trout totaled fifteen million pounds annually.

"At the time of the explosion of sea lamprey in the nineteen-forties, the harvest dropped to about three hundred thousand pounds. That equals two percent of the original harvests before the species invaded. At the same time, eighty-five percent of fish not killed by sea lamprey were scarred with lamprey attack wounds. We're talking near total annihilation of lake trout, just one native species in the Great Lakes that was under attack.

"Right now, lamprey are held at bay by lampricides and larvicides that attack the fish when they're in their larval stage. In this cycle of growth they live in the sand of streams where the water is about eight to ten inches deep. Poisons that sink to the bottom are used as well as traps and low-head barriers, but a single female can lay up to a hundred thousand eggs. You simply cannot let your guard down because the Great Lakes provide a perfect spawning environment, and the fish have no natural enemy to hold them in check.

"Now you also have to understand that aside from saving the environment from an insidious invader, there is also a great deal of money to be had for any industry that develops an effective means of eradication with less collateral damage and regulatory oversight. Current methods are good, but where there's money to be made there's incentive to cash in. The threat is overwhelming, but then so would be the financial reward."

"I can see that. Especially something on such a large scale."

"Especially when the federal government foots much of the bill. You have the government supporting private industry with staffing, logistics, and research and development grants. And you have private industry looking at the problem from the latest perspectives of science.

"ARL looked at the problem from the perspective of genetically engineering a life form that had traits taken from those marine animals that I mentioned. They concurred that attacking the larvae was still the best approach.

"You see, sea lamprey spend the first four or five years of their lives as huge worm-like larvae, six to eight inches in length, but they stay put. After that, they morph into fish and swim away, which makes them far more difficult to eradicate. Extermination has to take place while the larvae are still in the sand. Do you understand?"

"Yeah."

"Now going back to something like *Conus geographus*, which is most commonly known as the cone shell snail, and something you've seen many times in nautical knick-knacks—these little devils prefer to bury themselves in the sand in exactly the same way. They spend their time moving about slow as molasses, searching out worms among other things. They're also quite aggressive. They stay buried and leave just their antennae protruding to sense movement in the water. They more or less harpoon their prey. Death is instant.

"ARL viewed the DNA of creatures like these as ideal building blocks for something that would get the job done. It's because ammocoetes spend so much time in this larvae state, living in the sand, that ARL believed it could effectively eradicate the population. It just needed a good aggressive, poisonous sand-sifter or bottom-dweller that found them tasty."

"Hmm." Cory was hanging on to Tammy's every word. No more so than Cristina, although she remained silent.

"So now that I've told you my secrets, I trust you'll be equally generous in telling me yours. What does all this have to do with Dead Stream Swamp?"

Cory and Cristina looked at each other. They were each wondering how the *monster* theory would be accepted.

"Taking it a step at a time, I'd begin by saying something appears to be killing off all the fish in the swamp. All of Houghton Lake is talking about the damage this is causing their economy. Word's gotten out and business is off big time."

"Well, there's a lot of things that can cause a fish kill. An acute toxic event, like say... pesticides for crops comes right to mind. Just consider what happened at Clear Lake in Minnesota. Nearly three hundred thousand fish were killed when they sprayed for mosquitos using a pesticide that contained permethrin. A million fish were wiped out in Louisiana after crop spraying with an insecticide."

"I can understand why you'd think that. The problem is nobody's ever heard of a pesticide or insecticide killing cattle and leaving nothing behind but tatters of flesh and bleached white bones."

It was apparent that Cory's comment caught Tammy off guard. Her eyes revealed the way in which her mind was racing through inner calculations.

"Cattle?"

"And possibly humans."

"What?" she whispered.

"Yeah. It's looking that way. We're fast coming to the conclusion that all these events are linked by a single cause. Everything is connected to the swamp. The question begging to be asked is whether it's something or some *thing* that's in the swamp."

Tammy Tagart lowered her head and looked upward across her brow at Cory.

"When you say some *thing* in the swamp, you're implying some *living thing,* some *invasive* thing in the swamp?"

"I'm implying once you rule out pranksters, pesticides, insecticides, lampricides, oil and gas field effluents... options for what can kill a cow start getting scarce."

"You're thinking ARL created a freak of nature that's out there foraging? I don't believe that for a second. When you take into account all of the public wariness over anything that smacks of making Frankensteins, you can imagine the steps taken to prevent those types of horrors."

"Were you there when Jerry was cleaning up the tanks?"

"Of course. Nobody but me was allowed anywhere near the tanks. I'm the only person who knew the toxicity of the specimens that were lying about. Nobody was allowed into the containment until I called it clear of danger. That also included Jerry, but he was the first person to enter the tank facility after me."

"Okay. If you were there, then let me tell you what Jerry saw, and the reason why he came to me."

Cory went on to relay all that Jerry had told him, and about Jerry's deep concerns about what might have escaped the containment via an automatic drain monitor.

"What I'm asking is this. Do you think it's possible that something genetically modified might've escaped through the drain, or do you think it's possible for something to be created from whatever genetic material might've drained out of the facility?" Cory started laughing. "I guess your expression says it all."

"I don't wish to be rude, Mr. Ballard, but that is such a farfetched possibility.... I mean, the odds would have to be in the trillions-to-one category. First, the *thing* would have to disregard its base genetic code, its DNA structure that only knows how to produce saltwater species. It then would have to somehow work out a scheme for living in freshwater.

"Next, it being the only member of its species, numero unero, it would have to survive any old ordinary bacteria, and later, fish that come along wanting to eat it for the hell of it. Not to mention a number of cold hard winters. I mean, how many years has it been since ARL burned down? Four? Five? And then there's the feat of reproduction. Need I go on? I'm sorry, Mr. Ballard, but the odds are improbable to say the least."

"What month did ARL burn down?"

"June."

"Warm."

"Not a chance. Even if it did, it would have to make it through winter."

"And there's no way something might've cracked the code of life during the hot days of June and August, put on a little weight, and burrowed down deep enough into the peat to find enough warmth in all that decaying matter to survive a winter? A lot of other things do."

"No way. Impossible. We can't make life in the best of conditions—*in the laboratory.* And we're guiding the progress."

"Maybe the laboratory's your problem. Maybe it's too sterile an environment. I did a little research, and discovered that cedar swamps, like Dead Stream, are the most nutrient rich of all swamps. Maybe Dead Stream provided the collective cocktail of raw ingredients needed, you know, building blocks to start the clock of life for Frankenstein with fins."

"That's a whole lot more *maybe* than you can possibly imagine." Tammy shook her head in dismissal. "Not a chance. Well, I guess anything is possible, maybe we can talk to the dead, but the likelihood is probably something near zero-point-zero infinitum."

"Ms. Tagart—"

"Call me Tammy."

"Thank you. Tammy, I want you to know that I understand your skepticism. And I also want to say thank you very much for being generous with both your time and your knowledge. I'd like to ask if you'd mind us getting back to you with questions as they come up. Your background and expertise would be a great resource for us."

"Anytime. In fact, now that you have my curiosity soaring, I hope to hear from you as you progress with the investigation. Please keep me informed. It's intriguing."

The three laughed, finished their coffee, and said their goodbyes. Back in the Blazer, Cory and Cristina beamed with satisfaction as Cory looked over his notes and they discussed the wealth of information Tammy Tagart provided. Between the two of them, Cory rounded out and clarified all that he had written.

"Now what?" asked Cristina.

"Are you bored?"

"No, I'm having fun, but it's starting to rain. I don't want to be cooped up in the cabin all day. I don't have anything there to entertain me. Well, I mean, dad's there, but—don't give me that look— you know what I mean."

Cory laughed. He started the Blazer and flipped on the defrosters to clear the fog building on the widows.

"Are you feeling brave?"

"Why? I know, I probably shouldn't ask."

"I'm thinking about paying our good friend Gloven a visit."

"Uhhhhh...."

"Sit in the cabin... visit Gloven.... Sit in the cabin... visit Gloven...."

"I'm not sure which would be worse. Do you think it's safe?"

"I'll make it safe."

Cory reached over and opened the glove compartment.

"Holy crap! Is that a gun?" inquired Cristina in disbelief. "You have a gun?"

"I take it you don't belong to the NRA."

## 22

"Stinky white bones monster party? What're you talking about?" asked Angela.

"Yeah, tonight. Everybody's goin'. You should come. It'll be great. Kyle's goin'. Ted's goin'. Pat an' Pam, Sally, Jim an' Nono, Al an' Debbie are goin'. Nancy, Steve, Bill Carsen, Andy an' Natalie, they're all going. I'm tellin' ya, Angie, it's gonna be fun."

"What time?"

"It probably won't get started until around eleven. We want it to be dark, besides Og an' Rickie, and Ted, they don't get outta work 'til after nine. You gotta go, Angie. See if you can talk Sladjana into goin'."

"You're such a douche, Zack. You got the hots for Sladjana."

"Well, you gotta admit, she *is* cute."

"Yeah, well it's your job to work it, dude, not mine."

"You're a heartless bitch, Angie."

"Look, Zack, I can't make any promises. I can't not go to my cousin's birthday party. I'll talk to Tripper. Maybe we can drive out afterward. Why don't you give him a call and tell him how to get there?"

"I'll do that. Try an' make it. We got all kinds of booze. Og's gonna bring all the unsold pizza, so plenty of eats. Don't forget, you have to wear a mask. Costumes if you want, but everybody wears a mask. A word of caution... don't get one of those that when ya wear it, you can't drink. You know what I mean?"

"Yeah, I know what you mean. Call Tripper, okay?"

"Will do. See you there."

"Bye. And, Zack...."

"Yeah?"

"I'll call Sladjana."

"Yes! I owe ya."

"You do. Big time. Bye."

143

## 23

## Dead Stream Swamp Mysteries Prove to Be Anything but Dead

### By Cory Ballard

Roscommon Co., Mi. Lansing residents and longtime friends Derrek Charney and Peter Brownstone are officially listed as missing according to the Roscommon and Easton County authorities.

"Baffling," said Roscommon Co. Undersheriff Paul Carlton. He agreed it was as if a spaceship swept them off the face of the earth. Dennis and Marki Lehman found the boat registered to Mr. Charney abandoned in Dead Stream Swamp last Friday night.

Sources remain puzzled by yet another account of a mysterious blue light in the waters of the swamp. According to the Lehmans, a "blue glow" in the water moved about in close proximity to Charney's abandoned boat.

Foul play is suspected. Investigators concluded that the chances of two experienced adult anglers drowning in the shallow waters of that area in Dead Stream Swamp are virtually impossible. It was also determined....

Cory slowed the Blazer to a stop. He had reached the end of East Walker Road, the end of the road that marked the beginning of a two-lane trail not often traveled and barely visible.

"What are you thinking?" asked Cristina.

"One, I'm thinking that the path goes due east and that takes us directly into Dead Stream Swamp. Two, I'm thinking that's one bad-looking sky. The rain's got me wondering whether or not this trail gets mushy, and if the truck can handle it. And three, I'm thinking in spite of all that, I'd *really* like to know what's back there."

"Not that you'd ask, but I'm thinking we're nuts; correction, you are nuts."

Cory turned to look at Cristina and began laughing.

"I know that feeling!" he exclaimed. "Trust me, it isn't that bad yet. Gloven or somebody's been using this trail, so it can't be all that terrible."

"I was more focused on what I might not want to find back *there*. But as long as you brought it up, maybe we should wait until it stops raining."

"They're talking rain for the next three days. Even if it stops, it would take a week to dry out."

"In other words, downpour or not, you're still planning on driving back there."

"Well, I thought I'd ease my way back in, but if you're opposed to it, we'll call it quits and I'll bring you back home."

"And then you'll come back and ease your way in, downpour or not."

"Something like that."

"So, I'm either the party-pooper or the party-pooper."

"Or the aspiring investigative reporter—the tabloid adventurer."

"The tabloid adventurer, yeah, right. Geez. You're impossible. Hey, I got an idea. Why not step out of this Indiana Jones moment and see if the trail shows up on Google maps? Maybe we can see where this adventure ends up."

"Mmmmm. Good idea but...."

Cory picked up his cell. He studied it for a few seconds.

"I'm not getting any service here. Nope. Didn't think so. Try yours."

Cristina fiddled with her phone.

"Great. Why am I not surprised?"

"Well, this is a massive swamp, Cristina. They say it's one of the largest cedar swamps in the country. There's nothing out here except gas wells and snakes. What's the point of putting up cell towers?"

"The point is it makes me feel better. What if we get stuck back there? We can't even call out."

145

"I guess that's true, but Gloven must be driving in and out all the time. Remember, Harold told me that the lady at the post office said Gloven arrived every morning to check his PO Box. Trail can't be that bad."

"She also said he hasn't showed for a week. I'll bet *he's* probably stuck. Worse yet, what if we run into him?"

"We say, 'Hi, we're city slickers wanting to see the swamp, and unsure if we're on a county road or private property. But as long as we're here, would you like us to pull you out?'"

"And if he says, 'Geez, I thought all the no trespassing signs on the gate would have been a clue'."

"Then we high-tail it. He isn't going to catch us. He's stuck." Cory looked over at Cristina. "Seriously, I doubt he's even around."

"You doubt? Okay. And why do you say that?"

"I waited for him at the post office this morning, and he didn't show. This is the height of flea market season. He's probably on the road with his bone-trailer."

"And if he's home, and it's private property, and he pulls out a knife or a gun?"

Cory looked at Cristina with an expression of puzzlement.

"You know what I think?"

"What?"

"I think maybe you should be the one writing for the tabloids. I'm beginning to think you're a natural. I can see it now. *Horrifying Gnarly, Knife-wielding Boneman Emerges from Swamp to Attack Helpless Woman in Stuck Truck.*"

"Maybe you *should* take me home."

"Seriously?"

"Would you please just drive? Geez. Go. Go. Drive."

Cristina flipped her hands impatiently, signaling Cory to move forward. He laughed as he put the Blazer into gear and steered the vehicle cautiously past the gate and into the brush. The rain continued to beat down on the roof of the truck.

"For what it's worth. I wouldn't bet on this being private property. Could very well be state land and the signs are just bullshit."

"Whatever. How far back do you think we have to go?"

"Can't be too far. A couple thousand feet. Swamp can't be more'n a half mile in."

"I hope you're right. It's starting to rain awfully hard."

"Yeah, but the road bed feels pretty firm. I think we'll be okay as long as it doesn't flood over."

"Wonderful."

Cristina grew quiet. She was preoccupied with the terrain and searching for any hint of trouble. Between the numerous no-trespassing signs and the haunting details of dead, twisted, broken-down trees slowly disappearing into the thick of reeds and marsh grasses, she was too uncomfortable to engage in conversation. She especially didn't want to distract Cory from his driving.

"You're quite the trooper, Cristina. I'm impressed."

"Don't be. I'm plenty nervous. I always err on the side of caution."

"That's not a bad thing. It means you got brains."

"Brains? Really? Right now, I question that."

"Well, at least you got a sense of humor."

Cory brought the Blazer to a halt. The trail stretched out before them some two or three hundred feet as it cut across low flat ground covered with reeds and open patches of water that butted up tight against the sides of the trail.

"Now that frightens me, Cory. That is really narrow. Will we stay on the road? I really think we should turn back."

"Turn back? Whew, I don't think so. Easier said than done. I would have to back all the way out. That's a pain in the ass, and the best way to get us stuck. This can't go on much farther, Cristina. The swamp has to be just ahead."

"Cory, I beg to differ. Look around. How much more swamp can you get us into?"

"What I mean to say, is that the trail has to end soon and there has to be a place for vehicles to turn around. Believe me, Cristina, people don't back out of here. No way. I'm saying a little bit farther and we'll see a turnaround. Obviously, Gloven has to do it."

Cristina let out a long breath of resignation.

"Whatever."

Cory piloted the Blazer slowly along the narrow strip of land that divided the waters. He wasn't an idiot. He understood that Cristina was right to be nervous. The swamp was an unsettling place at times, even for the experienced. Cory moved forward with care, and eventually scaled an incline that lifted them above the waters of worry.

In short time, the underbrush fell away to expose a small open area of ground thinly covered in tall grass. Trees ringed the clearing. Looking through car windows shedding the downpour, they saw an old Airstream travel trailer at the far side of the clearing. They also saw a truck and enclosed trailer parked alongside it. Cory stopped the truck.

"I wonder if that's the bone-trailer."

"Okay, losing it. I thought you said he was on the road traveling?"

"I said it seemed probable."

"Well, it wasn't probable. Remember what that freak at the flea market said? Don't get caught back here. So what are we doing?"

"What we're doing is pulling ahead so I can turn around—."

"Thank you, Lord."

"—and leave as soon as I see if he's at home."

Cristina was too upset to comment. She could not believe Cory would consider such a thing. She sat in stunned silence as he pulled the truck into the opening and followed a turnaround that passed right by the Airstream almost close enough to touch it. Cristina slowly slid down into her seat. She shrunk away from the door window. She fully expected to see a face peer out from the darkness behind the trailer windows. Cory stopped the Blazer.

"That's strange."

"What is strange? Why are you stopping?"

"Look at the front door. It's open. Who would leave their front door open to a pouring rain?"

"A lunatic."

"Or... a person in need of help."

148

"Oh, god, I should've known. Now, you're a good Samaritan?"

"Well, not really."

"Don't tell me you're thinking about going in there."

"Not at the moment. I think I'll just sit out the rain for a bit. See if it clears."

"Then you're going in."

"We'll see."

"What am I doing here?" Cristina rolled her eyes. She was anxious. "Cory! Honk your horn. Maybe he's sleeping."

"Good idea."

Cory did as Cristina suggested. After three attempts, it was clear nobody was asleep inside. There was nothing to do but sit and talk as the rain moved through cycles of intensity. The light conversation did little to relax Cristina. She never stopped studying her surroundings.

"The rain is easing up."

"Not by much," protested Cristina.

"Yeah, it is. I think we're done with rain. This is drizzle. Low-cloud drizzle. The guts of a grounded cloud slobbering all over the place."

Cory reached around behind the seat.

"What are you doing?"

"I'm going for a walk. But first, I'm putting on these waders. Here, I got a pair for you."

"I'm not putting on any waders. No *thank you*."

"Suit yourself. You can wait in the truck."

"You're going to make me wait in the truck by myself?"

"No. You decided that on your own. I brought you waders."

"You are so considerate," Cristina whispered loudly.

Cristina snapped the waders from Cory's hand. She struggled to climb into them while seated in the truck to stay dry.

"How do they fit?"

Cristina did not answer but instead gave Cory an *'are you kidding me'* expression.

"Just a show of concern." Cory grinned. "C'mon. Let's see if Gloven is alive or dead."

"Ohh, shut up."

Cristina stayed close behind as Cory bolted toward the half-open camper door. She watched warily in all directions as he hollered inside.

"Hello! Hello! Anybody home? Mr. Gloven? Hello!"

Cory turned about to scan the clearing. There was too much mist to define anything clearly within the ring of trees.

"Now what?"

"Now, I'm going inside."

"You can't do that," blurted Cristina, still whispering loudly. "What if he shows up and finds you poking around inside his trailer? After all that horn-honking, he's probably on his way back right now."

"I'll just tell him his front door was open and I thought he might be in need of help."

"Help explaining his no-trespassing signs? I'll wait outside."

"That's fine."

Cory entered the trailer. Cristina followed until his frame disappeared into shadows beyond the open door. Once confident no one was about to jump out at him, she became more nervous about what was behind her in the opening. She turned her back toward the trailer door and hardly dared to blink.

"Hurry up, Cory. Cory?"

"Yeah."

"Hurry up."

It was just then that the sky unleashed a fresh torrent of rain. It was a heavy downpour. Instinctively, Cristina stepped up into the trailer. She purposely left the door open so she could watch outside.

"Can it get any more miserable?" asked Cristina quietly to herself.

"Well, he ain't inside," said Cory as he walked back to the door.

"I thought you said no more rain."

"Yeah, I guess I was wrong. Here."

"What's this?"

Cristina knew what it was. What she meant was *'What am I supposed to do with this?'*

"Put it on."

"What for?"

"So you don't get wet."

"Believe me, I can handle whatever wet there is between me and the truck."

"The truck? We aren't going to the truck. Let me rephrase that. I'm not going to the truck."

"Oh, geez. Where are you going now?"

"Investigating."

"Of course. Investigating. *Investigating,*" Cristina repeated as she slipped into the raincoat. She shook her head. "Lead the way, Cory."

Cory was laughing as he stepped out into the rain. He made straight for the enclosed trailer hitched to Gloven's truck. He began to fiddle with the door latch.

"I really don't think we should be poking around like this. He could show up at any minute. What are you going to do if he shows up, Cory?"

Cory swung the door open.

"*Christ almighty.* Get a load of that."

The two stood transfixed by the shelves of bones. They were all bleached white and sorted in boxes, baskets, and milk crates. Cory stepped into the trailer. Cristina did likewise in order to get out of the rain, but instead of looking over the bones, she stood guard, staring through the downpour at the perimeter of trees, watching for anything that might suddenly appear. She remained anxious as Cory continued to pick through the assortments. He pulled out his cell phone and began snapping pictures.

151

Abruptly, he lowered the phone and raised his head upward. He started sniffing.

"Do you smell that?"

"Smell what? That stink?"

"Yeah. Damn. That *is* nasty."

"I smelled it as soon as we stepped out of the truck."

"Really?"

"You didn't?"

"I guess not. I just now got a good whiff of it."

"What do you think it is?" asked Cristina.

"Not sure. Smells putrid. Maybe something he uses to clean these bones. You know, a cleaner of some kind, something like that."

Cory stepped close behind Cristina and peered outside. For a brief moment, the two stood side by side searching the surroundings in silence. Finally, Cory raised his arm and pointed at a row of trailers. One was a dump-trailer, one was a flat bed, and the remaining three were enclosed.

"I wonder what Gloven's got stashed in those?"

"I'm sure we're about to find out."

"You want to wait here?"

"No, I don't want to wait here. Are you kidding? All I want to do is get the heck out of here. This place gives me the creeps."

"All right, let's go."

"Thank god."

Cory stepped off the bed of the trailer.

"Here, give me your hand."

Cristina did as asked and stepped down with care. Cory put his arm around her shoulder.

"C'mon."

"Where're we going?"

"Right there to that trailer. Where were you going?"

"Very funny."

"Boy, you sure are jittery."

152

"Any sane person would be. You don't just go traipsing in and out of other people's homes and belongings."

"True."

Cory more or less ignored Cristina's concerns as he focused on the handle to the next enclosed trailer. He released the latch and pulled the door open.

"Holy shit," he exclaimed as he spun around and stepped away.

"Oh, my god...."

Cristina moved back a few steps and then turned away from the open door with an expression of revulsion.

"Ugh. What is that?" she asked.

Cory grabbed his handkerchief and placed it over his nose. He stepped up into trailer.

"Now we know where the smell comes from."

"What *is* that?"

"Beetles."

"Beetles? You mean like bugs? Beetles like bugs? What kind of person is this guy?"

"No, no. These are those flesh-eating beetles. You know. What do they call them, ahh.... Demest... Dermest, ahh... I can't remember. Carrion beetles, that's it. Carrion beetles. Taxidermists and people who work with bones for carving and stuff use them to strip bones clean of flesh. They're really efficient. Couple of days on the dinner table and those bones are clean as a whistle."

"You think this is cool? Really?"

"Yeah, actually it is if you can appreciate what they do and how they're used. That's why you see all those propane tanks. Gloven has to keep these beetles warm all winter. Whew. It's plenty warm in here now."

"It's really nasty in there right now."

"You're such a wuss, Cristina. C'mon. Get in here. You'll like this."

"I don't think so."

"C'mon. Look at all these bones. They're getting picked clean by these little devils."

"Cory... the smell makes me want to vomit. You look at them all you want. I'll stand out here and drown. Thank you."

"Oh, all right. Have it your way. You don't know what you're missing."

Cory climbed out of the trailer and closed the door.

"Let's see what's in the next two."

Cory opened up the second trailer and it also was filled with glass aquariums full of bones and beetles. The third trailer was different. It had a row of large, heavy-duty, wheeled, plastic garbage bins lined up along the right side of the trailer end to end. Rolled out and nailed to the opposite wall of the trailer was a six-foot-high length of chain-link fence. A number of exceptionally white bones were hooked with bent dry-cleaning hangers and dangling randomly from the wire links.

"What is all this?"

"A bleaching room. Took a minute for me to place that smell. These tanks are filled with hydrogen peroxide. Gloven takes the bones that've been stripped by the bugs and soaks them in these tanks. It bleaches them white, at which point he hangs them up on that chain link fence to dry."

"Who does stuff like this?"

"Hey, don't forget what we found. The man's got quite the Internet business going and remember those guys at the flea market said people come from all over waiting for him to show up. Sounds to me like the guy's making pretty good money. In Houghton Lake, that says something."

"What a career."

"Hey, if you got the stomach for it... why not?"

"Oh, please. I'll bet the guy smells just like those bugs."

"I'll bet he smells like greenbacks."

"You're hopeless, Cory. So, can we leave now? Have you seen enough?"

"Well, as long as we've gotten this far...."

"And you're in no hurry to go back...."

"And, I'm in no hurry to get back.... I say we follow this trail into the woods toward the swamp and see what we find."

Cory did not want to know what Cristina was thinking as she glared at him. She turned away and looked along the trail. She shook her head, said nothing, and started walking into the downpour.

"Hold on. Wait for me."

Cory and Cristina walked with heads low to keep the rain out of their faces. Cristina's head twisted back and forth beneath the hood of her raincoat. She fully anticipated somebody or some *thing* jumping out to take them by surprise. Cory focused on the path itself. The trail was well traveled and clearly visible as it crossed the clearing. The path remained nicely maintained as it passed into the periphery of trees.

"It looks as if Mr. Gloven has gone to a lot of trouble widening and dressing this trail. He's been using a drag to keep vegetation down."

"How come there's so many bones?"

"Funny you should say that. I was just thinking the same thing."

Cristina watched Cory bend over and pull a bone out of the mud. He rolled it and flipped it in his hands. The rain was washing it clean. Having satisfied his curiosity, he tossed it back onto the trail.

"Broken. These are all bone fragments. Either he has been driving over discarded bones and breaking them up, or he's been discarding broken bones and driving over them."

"That's a lot of fragments."

"He's probably using them to hold the road bed together, to firm it up, I would imagine."

"Look how many are up there. It's like the whole road is paved in bones."

Cory placed his hand across his brow like a visor. Shielding his eyes from the downpour, he looked up and ahead into the distance along the trail.

"Jesus.... You got that right."

Cory could hear the nervousness in Cristina's voice. He did not blame her. Not that he would ever admit it, but even he found the road of bones an unsettling scene. The farther into the woods they walked, the worse it got.

Cristina stopped. Cory's attention sharpened.

"What's the matter?" He glanced around. "You see something?"

"Can you smell it?"

Cory sniffed the air.

"Smell what?" He sniffed again. "Yeah, I guess. I smell something."

Cristina turned her head, all the while sniffing the air.

"That's the same smell that was around those cows at the Hamilton place. Can't you smell it? It smells like chemicals and rotting fish or something. Makes your nose tingle."

Cristina pinched her nose and rubbed it a time or two.

"Fortunately, my sniffer isn't quite as good as yours."

"Fortunately for who? I don't think your sniffer works at all."

"You're being mean."

"You're not the one suffering."

"C'mon, let's walk a little farther."

"Now I know you can't smell anything."

"C'mon."

"Why would you want to go any farther?" Cristina spread her hands out before her. "It's pouring. We're starting to wade in mud and bones, the smell's godawful—"

"I want to know what I'm looking at up there over the hill."

Cristina hushed. She shielded her eyes from the rain, and stood alongside Cory staring into the distance.

"Can you make it out?" asked Cory.

"Looks like the top of a shed or something."

"Yeah. Right in the middle of the road. Must be the trail ends at the shed or turns before it. C'mon. A little farther and we go back. I just want to know what that is."

"Well, let's hurry up. If I don't puke from the smell, I'll puke from my nerves."

"Okay. I don't blame you. I'm about ready to get out of here myself. Let's go up, take a quick look, and call it quits. It's not that far. Let's just see what it is, and then we'll head back to the Blazer."

"Fine. Let's do it and go."

They continued forward, but in a short time their advance halted unexpectedly.

"Huh. I guess the trail's going to end here. The rising water is calling the shots."

"Oh, my god. Look at all these bones. There's got to be thousands," said Cristina in disbelief.

"See the center of the trail?" Cory raised his arm and pointed forward. "It's still above water. I'm going to follow it to the other side. See where the ground goes high again? I just want to get to that rise and take a picture of the shed or whatever it is, and I'll be back. I think you should stay here. You aren't going to like wading through that water anyhow."

"If you think I'm waiting here alone, you're dreaming, pal. Go. I'll follow."

"Okay. If you want. But watch your step."

Cory started along the narrow center strip of the trail that stood proud in comparison to the tire tracks that had now disappeared below the surface of the floodwaters. The center strip would soon follow, but Cory only needed a minute or two to get some photos.

"Let's go."

Cory took off, walking at a quick pace along the narrow raised line of earth and crushed bones. After he and Cristina walked across the flooded trail and reached the high ground, he found himself standing before a ghoulish setting. The two halted and stood astonished by the scene before them. Beyond the crest, the trail sloped slightly downward. It ended at a wide dock that extended into the shallows. At the end of the dock stood the shed that Cory had spied from the trail.

"Cory, this makes my hair stand up. I won't sleep for a week."

157

"Yeah, it's weird. Cattle. There must be forty or fifty skeletons. All cattle. No wonder this thing had a taste for Hamilton's cows."

"That smell. Now do you smell it? Whew, it's really getting strong."

"Looks to me like somebody was paying Mr. Gloven to dump cattle on his property. Probably diseased animals that couldn't go to slaughter. Huh."

Cory started walking slowly toward the dock. It was now easier to see the shed through the falling rain.

"What do you suppose that is?" asked Cristina

"Tool shed, I imagine. Why would anybody want a dock at water level?" he asked. "Actually, it's more underwater than not right now. Why would anybody need a dock that wide?"

Cory's attention turned to a garden tractor that was protruding up through the dock planks. The tractor would have been laying on its side half submerged had it not been hung up on the dock supports.

"That tractor got dragged down through the dock by its trailer. He must have overloaded it. Dock couldn't take the weight. He's lucky the engine's still above the waterline. I don't envy him. It's going to take some doing to lift that puppy back up onto the dock."

"Look at all the skeletons in the water," said Cristina.

Cory noticed a cow's skeleton draped over the trailer, which was underwater.

"Yeah. You know what I think?" muttered Cory mostly to himself.

"What?"

"I think our man Gloven was loading the wagon with carcasses and hauling them out onto that dock. He made it wide enough to turn the tractor about and dump his load into those nets for the fish, or whatever, to clean the bones. He just didn't make it strong enough to handle the weight."

Cristina followed Cory as he stepped closer to the dock. He was staring at the far end of the dock where the shed stood. The structure was deeper, but not much wider than an outhouse. He wondered if in fact it once served as such. The door was open.

Back on the trail, he hadn't noticed the door was open because of the rain and mists, and because it had swung out to face him edge on. He pulled out his camera.

"Now, I get it."

"Get what?" said a remarkably quiet Cristina.

"I'm thinking our man Gloven may not know that Hamilton's cows are dead, but he sure knows what happened to them. I think Gloven got out of the buying hydrogen peroxide and beetles business in order to team up with the swamp monster. A road of bones from the shallows to his trailers. All for free. Just fish them out of the pond. Haul out the nets, dump them into the wagon, and sell them on the Internet. Smart. I wonder if he's raising piranha. That would be brilliant. It would explain everything."

Cory raised his cell phone and worked to keep it dry while composing a picture of the nets full of bones.

*Click... click... click.*

"Cory!" Cristina let out a shriek at the same time she grabbed ahold of Cory's arm. She nearly climbed on top of him.

"Christ almighty! What are you do—"

"Did you see that?"

"You scared the ever-loving crap out of me."

"Did you see that?"

"See what? I didn't see anything."

"It's in the water!"

"What's in the— Hey! Where you going?"

Cristina did not answer. She bolted back along the half-submerged trail, splashing water high and wide in retreat. Cory's eyes followed her only briefly until he digested what she said. He turned to focus his attention on the water.

This time Cory was spooked. He studied the water that surrounded the dock. He studied the water that was creeping across the trail behind him. He did not see anything, but he chose to give Cristina the benefit of the doubt. He raised his camera and took a couple of pictures of the shed, the fallen tractor, and the bones that littered the banks. He put the camera back into

159

his pocket and took off running as if something was breathing down his neck. Churning water as he sprinted back along the flooded trail, Cory reached the safety of high ground where Cristina was waiting.

"What was that all about?" he asked while trying to catch his breath.

"You didn't see it?"

"See what?"

"I don't know what it was. It was in the water."

"Well, what the hell did it look like?"

"I don't know."

"What do you mean you don't know? I thought you said you saw it."

"I saw something."

"What? What? What did you see for crying out loud?"

Cristina went silent. Cory understood at once that he was yelling. He had gotten aggressive.

"Forgive me. I didn't mean to yell. I apologize. You gave me quite a scare back there. I'm overloaded with adrenaline."

"It's okay. I apologize for losing it. I didn't mean to panic and run. I didn't mean to leave you standing out there alone."

"Well, don't worry about that. I lived. But I'd like to know what you saw. What the hell scared you so bad? I mean, you were booking, lady."

"I don't know what I saw. It wasn't like I saw a fish or something. It was more like a wave, no more like a swell. It was like the water itself moved. Like it shifted. The first time I thought it was an illusion, you know, something I dreamed up. But the second time.... No way. I saw it. It scared the shit out of me—pardon my language—and I was out of there. I wasn't looking back."

"Yeah, I noticed."

"Sorry."

"It's okay."

"You know what, Cory? It's starting to get dark out here, and that smell is making me sick. It's getting stronger. It's time for me to get out of here. I'm going back to the truck with or without you."

"Hold on, I'm going too."

"Walk fast."

## 24

To Cristina's relief, she and Cory emerged from the wooded trail and entered the better light of the clearing. The rain had eased up, backing off to a drizzle. They glanced at the trailer and noted no one appeared to have returned while they were poking about back in the swamp. They climbed out of the waders, out of the weather, and into the security of the Blazer.

"Feeling better?"

"A little. I'll feel a lot better when we get out of here."

Cory started up the truck. He flipped on the windshield wipers and put it into gear. He swung the vehicle around in a large circle and headed back in the direction they came. He entered the periphery of trees and followed the trail back through the woods. He drove slowly until reaching the incline that from this direction overlooked the long flat stretch of low ground. This time, instead of being bordered by water, the trail was completely submerged. There was no sign of the path until it appeared on the opposite high ground.

"Shit." Cory swore under his breath.

He hardly dared look in Cristina's direction, for he knew that this would not make her happy in the least. He glanced her way and saw her sitting upright, leaning fully forward to study the flooded ground beyond the dash. She was visibly tense, but said nothing at first, which only made it worse for Cory.

"Will you be able to drive through that?"

"Thank you for not starting out with *I told ya so*."

161

Cristina looked hard at Cory. "It wants to fall right off my lip."

"I have no doubt, but it didn't. That's all that matters. You just might be the perfect woman."

"Don't get your hopes up, cowboy. What do you plan on doing now?"

"Well…. I'm sure we could probably make it across, but I know once I drive off this bank, I probably won't be able to reverse back up it. So… it's going to be straight ahead, all or nothing. What concerns me is that I can't see where the roadbed is. I remember it was really narrow, and if I drive off it, we're sunk—literally."

"What happens if we wait? Will the water go down?"

"I wish I knew. It will either continue to rise as the swamp fills, or it'll drop as fast as it rose once the wash passes through. In this part of the swamp, which way it goes, I can't say."

"I vote we wait a while and see what it does. It's getting too dark to see the road under the water. Believe me, I definitely will not be the perfect woman if we get stuck in there, and I have to walk out of this place in the dark. I will be genuinely pissed. I say we lock the doors and wait it out."

"Point taken. I just don't want to get into any trouble. Your dad didn't say what time you have to be in, did he? I mean, you don't have to be in by dark or anything like that, do you?"

Cristina looked at Cory and wasn't sure if he was joking or not. Finally, she saw the faintest glint in his eye.

"Right."

They both started laughing.

"Lock the doors."

"Doors are locked."

The comforting sound of the locks engaging around the Blazer eased much of Cristina's uneasiness. She began to relax and talk freely. They were lost to playful conversation when the last of an overcast day's dim light disappeared altogether. On cloud-covered nights, the swamp was so starved for light, the black scraped the skin.

Cory let Cristina do most of the talking. It kept her mind in a better state. He was content to listen. After a while, he retrieved his cell phone and began studying the photos he had captured earlier at the dock. He passed through them one after another, back and forth, stopping to zoom in as far as he could and pan across the images.

"What's the matter?" asked Cristina.

"Huh?"

"I said, what's the matter?"

"Why are you asking me that?"

"Why? Because at one point I was having a conversation with you, and then it was more like I was talking to you, and now it's more like I'm talking to myself. I caught on when I specifically asked if you were listening to me, and all I got back was a mumble."

Cory looked up from his phone. He grimaced.

"You're right. I'm sorry. I didn't mean to be rude, but I want to ask you something."

"What?"

"You remember that shed on the end of the dock?"

"Yeah. Why?"

"Well.... In that split second after you scared the ever-loving shit out of me, and just prior to me running for my life, I snapped off a couple of shots of that shed. I just now zoomed in on it, and I want you to tell me, what does this look like to you?"

Cory handed Cristina his phone.

"Where're you looking?"

"Right there." He pointed with his finger. "In the center. The door to the shed is open. I'm zoomed in on it."

Cristina stared at the image. Cory watched as her eyes rose from the screen and turned to look at him.

"I know you're gonna tell me that's not what it looks like."

"What's it look like to you?"

"It looks like the picture is blurry. Could be anything."

"Really?"

"It could be anything, Cory. You're looking inside the shed and it's dark and shadowy. There a lot of stuff in there like tools and whatever."

"Well, what about this one?"

Cory swiped the screen. He spread his finger across the phone to zoom in on the second image. Cristina studied it intently and then turned to Cory.

"That picture isn't any better. It's still too blurry to say—"

"To say what?"

"You know what."

"Say it."

"Why?"

"I want to hear you say it. I want to know I'm not kidding myself."

"You tell me what you think it is."

"I think it's a human skeleton in clothes sitting up against the wall looking right at us."

"Oh, god."

Cristina was suddenly aware of the darkness. Cory could sense her anxiety. She quieted and began looking out the side and rear windows, which were heavily fogged. Cory understood.

"Can't see anything. Here, I'll roll down the windows for a minute to clear the—"

"Don't!"

"What?"

"I said don't. If you want to clear the widows, start the truck and turn on the stupid defrosters."

"Are you *that* frightened?"

"Can we not go there? Let's just say I don't want to sit in a car full of mosquitos."

"I can buy that."

Cory fired up the Blazer and turned on the defrosters.

"Can you see anything? Can you see if the water's gone down or not?"

"Let's see."

Cory switched on the headlights. He waited for the fog to clear off the windshield.

"The drive is still covered with water. It looks deeper from here, but I really can't tell without going out to look."

"Are you *crazy?!*"

"Cristina.... What do you think is out there?"

Cristina was dumbfounded with disbelief.

"You just showed me the skeleton of dead person. I don't know what's out there, but it had no problem killing cows and who knows what else—people."

"How did this turn into '*it*' with such conviction?"

"All right, *they*."

Cory started laughing.

"Cristina... I need to go look. I'm not going more than twenty feet. You can leave the headlights on. You can lock the doors behind me. I won't ever be out of your sight."

Cory immediately opened his door.

"Cory!"

"Relax. Lock the doors behind me."

Cory closed the door and heard the locks click. He looked around the clearing. He immediately noticed the strong acrid smell. He knocked on the window.

"Hey, unlock the doors. I need to get my waders out the back."

The door locks released. Cory opened the hatch, sat on the bed, and slipped his waders back on.

"Okay, I'll just be a few feet in front of the truck. Just give me a minute and I'll be back."

"I'm locking the doors."

"That's fine."

Cory stood up and slammed the hatch closed. He heard the locks engage. He walked toward the bank and carefully eased his way down the muddy slope. He was not about to drive into a flood without knowing precisely how deep the water was over the trail.

165

Cory began wading through the flow. In the beams of the headlights, he carefully felt out the ground, moving forward one slow step at a time. When Cory reached the center of the flooded stretch, he felt confident the ground was solid enough for his Blazer to make a pass. He searched out the shoulder of the trail by stepping about and checking for the fall-off with his foot. He could feel that the trail, built up with fill, had shoulders steep enough to be an issue if he drove over the edge.

As Cory turned to head back toward Cristina, he looked out across the swamp and noticed a faint blue glow in the distance. He stopped to study it, but the headlights splashed too much light around for him to see clearly.

"Cristina!"

Cory waved his arms in the air. He called out again.

"Cristina!"

Cristina responded on the second call with a muffled response, most likely from behind a window barely cracked open.

"What?"

"Turn off the headlights. I'm trying to see something."

"Turn off the headlights?" asked Cristina with concern.

"Yeah, just turn them off for a minute so I can see in the dark."

Anything seen disappeared within a dense black that engulfed all. Cory stood motionless in the shin-deep water. He waited for his eyes to adjust. Slowly, his night vision came into play and the pale blue luminescence came back into view. It was closer.

Cory turned to look behind him, beyond the other side of the road. It was only black and featureless. Confident nothing strange was at his back, he looked forward and watched as the luminescence grew brighter and closer. It was drifting with the current in his direction. Cory walked back to the Blazer. The doors unlocked.

"You're going to have to do me a favor."

"What?"

"I need you to drive the truck."

"Where?" asked Cristina with suspicious alarm.

166

"Partway across, just following along the trail."

"Through the water? I can't do that."

"Sure you can. I'll guide you. The problem is this. The shoulders are steep. They don't fall away far or anything like that. It's just that they're steep, and I can't tell where they are beneath the water. Do you remember how narrow the trail was when we came across? I need you to take the wheel and ease the truck down the bank and along the road. I'll be in front of you telling you which way to turn so that we stay on the trail. Simple as that."

"And what if I say no?"

"It's going to be a long three or four days waiting for the water to go down. Not that I would mind...."

"Oh, shut up."

"That a girl."

"Last date. Ever."

"Ouch."

Cristina stepped out of the Blazer and walked around the front, staying in the light of the headlamps. She met Cory at the driver's door and he helped her in.

"Okay. Listen, you can keep the windows up and doors locked. All you have to do is watch my hands, and I will direct you. Don't make any sharp turns, just drift easy one way or the other as I say. Okay?"

"Okay."

"Good. Now, do me a favor and hand me the flashlight out of the glove box."

"You want the gun too?"

"No. I don't have any batteries for the gun. The flashlight should do it."

"Figures."

Cristina handed Cory the flashlight as asked and he shut the door. Cristina locked the doors, but rolled down her window. Cory turned on the flashlight and then looked back up at her.

"Okay, put it in gear, and keep your eyes on me. The worst part will be easing your way down the bank. After that, it's a piece of cake and you only need to go partway across. I'll drive it up the other bank. Okay?"

"Okay."

Cristina rolled up her window. Cory walked forward and stepped into the light of the headlamps. He stepped carefully down the bank and into the water. He motioned Cristina forward.

"That a girl. Easy. Easy. Keep coming. You're doing fine. Keep going. Come on, keep going...."

Cory had directed Cristina to the halfway point when he noticed a shift in the water. It felt like the push or pull of current. He immediately looked down and pointed his flashlight toward his feet. He saw nothing, but he could feel the pressure against his legs. He moved the flashlight about and carefully studied the water surrounding his waders. He did not see anything beneath the surface, but he wanted to choke on the strong acrid odor.

The sensation unnerved Cory. He instantly recalled Cristina carrying on about the shifting water, and about not seeing anything but a wave of sorts. He felt his skin tighten. He sent the flashlight beam out across the water and swung it in a circle around him. At the same time, he continued to beckon Cristina forward. He turned to assess the distance to the opposite bank.

Cory looked back into the water at his feet. He saw nothing whatsoever, but it was clear that the water was rising up his legs. He assumed the trail dipped at this spot, but as he walked toward the opposite bank, the dip only seemed to get deeper. Instinctively, he sensed something was not right. Growing anxious, he flashed the light wildly back and forth in a circle about him. He moved his legs and sensed the water felt thick.

"Fuck this."

Cory headed toward the Blazer. He had his fill. It felt like he was dragging his legs through a light syrup or oil. Cory did not want Cristina to get out of the truck, so he headed toward the passenger-side door. He noticed the water was right at the bottom edge. Once he heard the locks release, he opened it and climbed in.

"What's the matter?" asked Cristina.

"I don't know, just go. Just go straight. And when I tell you to hit it, give it some gas so we can shoot up the opposite bank."

"Can't you do this?"

"No. There's no way to change places without one of us getting out of the truck. And that isn't going to happen. Now pay attention. When I say hit it, hit it. Are you ready...? Hit it!"

Cristina stepped on the gas, but instead of the Blazer shooting forward, it snapped sideways.

"Whoa!"

Cory let out a yell, but Cristina had the good sense to brake, even before he called out.

"What happened?" she asked. "Why did it do that?"

Cory did not answer. His mind was racing for an explanation. He figured Cristina must have stepped too hard on the gas, but his gut knew that was not the case. She had done exactly what he wished.

Something else was going on. His mind was racing for answers when she interrupted his thoughts.

"What is that, Cory?"

"What?"

Cory looked away from the wash of headlights and toward Cristina who was looking out the driver's side window.

"What is that?" she repeated.

The two of them stared out the window.

"Hold on."

Cory reached up and twisted the headlight switch. At first, the world went black, but within seconds, it returned from the darkness to be awash in a vivid blue luminescence.

"Oh-my-god. What is *that*?" asked Cristina.

"Not a clue. Never seen anything like it."

"It's everywhere."

"It's everywhere there's water."

Cory searched the high ground both in front of and behind the Blazer. Those spaces remained dark. The blue glow only spread across the surface of the floodwaters now slowly flowing past them. It stretched as far as they could see through the thickets and woods.

"Cory?"

"Yeah?"

"Look at your waders."

Cory looked down at his waders. From his shins on down, parts of his legs were also glowing blue. A faint luminescence emanated from the puddle surrounding his boots on the floorboard.

"I wouldn't touch that."

"No argument here."

Cory twisted the headlight switch back to ON, and the world of blue luminescence both inside and out disappeared.

"Wow. That was different. Do you think it's safe to have that stuff inside the car?"

"Nothing's getting through these waders. Listen, let's just worry about getting this truck straightened out without driving off the shoulder and that's not going to be easy. You have to do exactly what I say."

"Nope. I'm climbing in back. You're driving."

This time Cory did not argue. Cristina put the Blazer into park, and worked her way across the console. She fell purposely into the back seat, after which, Cory, taking utmost caution, eased the waders off his legs. He then twisted himself about until he was able to drop into the driver's seat.

"All right, here we go."

Cory put the truck into gear and carefully eased it forward and backward as he felt out the drop of the shoulder. He quickly aligned the Blazer back to the trail until it faced the opposite bank square on. He started forward.

As he closed in on the opposite bank, he stepped harder on the gas pedal and immediately noted the lack of traction. At once, he thought of the syrup-like feel about his legs when he stood in the water. He pressed on, applying more gas and fighting the truck's tendency to drift sideways. He gained most of the needed speed by the time he reached the opposite bank, but the Blazer nearly halted as its wheels spun in the greasy mud of the opposite bank.

"What the hell?"

"Are you going to make it?"

"This thing should fly up this hill. It's like I'm in slime or something."

Cory poured on the gas and the engine roared as the tires began flinging mud and dirt in all directions. The Blazer began drifting dangerously sideways, wanting to slide back down the bank. Cory spun the wheel to compensate.

"C'mon, baby. You can do it. C'mon. C'mon. Dig. C'mon, dig, dig."

The tires dug themselves deep until finding hardpack below the rain-soaked soil. Cory held the steering wheel locked to the right. The front tires grabbed a hold, and snapped the front end around into a more favorable attack. The truck lurched forward to scale the bank and reach safety on the high ground. Cory stopped the Blazer and let out a deep sigh.

"You okay?" asked Cristina.

"Yeah. I'm okay. I'm just confused. I'm not sure what that was all about. When I was standing in the water, I felt something sweep by my legs. It felt like I was standing in syrup or oil. You know, something thicker than water. It's like the truck was bogged down in the same shit."

"Well, we're out of it now. Let's just get the hell out of here. Okay?"

"Yeah, good idea. Just one last thing."

"Oh, for god's sake, Cory. What now? Can we please just go? It's not that hard. Just step on the gas and go that way."

"This'll just take a second."

Cory opened the truck door and stepped out.

"Really? You're going out there?"

"Yeah. Why don't you climb up front? I'm going back to have one last look. I'm going to see if I can snap a picture of that blue glow or whatever so someone can tell me what it is."

"I'm not climbing up front with that stuff. What do you need a picture for? Just tell them you saw a blue glow."

"I could, but you know what they say, a picture's worth a thousand words, and they sell like words never will. I'll be right back."

Cory reached into the truck for his cell phone. As he started back toward the flooded road, he noticed the glow covered the side of his truck, including the wheels and tires. He raised his cell and snapped a picture.

"Shit."

Cory swiped his cell screen and turned off the flash that had burned out all the detail and any sign of the blue glow. He looked back to take a second shot, but either the glow was gone, or the flash screwed up his eyes.

"Unless the flash affected the bacteria," he thought aloud.

Disappointed, Cory walked back the thirty or so feet to the bank. There was no hint of blue light in the near vicinity. He looked back at the taillights shining his way. There was too much light. He could still see it in the distance where its mottled appearance wavered within the woods.

"Oh, well. Take the picture, Cory," he said to himself.

Cory snapped off a couple of pictures in each direction and then headed back to the SUV. Once inside, he called the images back up and reviewed them.

"What do you see?"

"Nothing. Absolutely nothing. Just black. Every one. Just black. The glow's too faint to photograph. You wouldn't think so, would you? Sure seemed plenty enough bright."

He set the cell phone on the center console and put the Blazer into drive. He started back down the trail toward the road. They said nothing more until passing the no trespassing signs on the metal gate. Once on the road, tensions eased.

"So, you have no idea what all that blue glow was?"

"Not a clue. Never seen anything like it. Whatever glows blue like that must be some sort of bacteria or algae. The currents must be stirring it up. Has to be an awful lot of it to cover the surface of that much water." Cory fell momentarily into his thoughts. "It would make a lot of sense if there's some sort of bacteria that's killing everything."

"Last I heard, you thought it was piranha. You honestly think bacteria could kill those fishermen and those cows that fast?"

"I thought you were a nurse."

"I am a nurse."

"Well, then, you know all about botulism, right? I just read an article that said a new strain's been developed that's so deadly, for the first time ever, the scientific community will not release the details until an antidote is developed. They said if a human breathes just thirteen billionths of a gram, he's dead. One spoonful in the water supply can take out an entire metropolis. Yeah, I think bacteria can take down a cow. A really big one, in fact."

"And you think botulism glows?"

"I have no idea. I didn't say it was botulism. Maybe it is piranha. That wouldn't necessarily be a bad thing. Piranha are big in the world of tabloids. I'm just sayin' that events as of late have been mighty strange, and what I saw out there was also mighty strange. That's a number of mighty stranges."

"So what do you plan to do now?"

"I'm not sure. Maybe have another talk with our new acquaintance, Tammy."


## 25


"So what d'ya think?"

"I don't know, Tripper. It's awful late."

"C'mon, Angie. It's too early to call it a night."

"It's been raining half the night."

"So what. Zack said Kyle towed his camper out there. He said they've got a bonfire goin'. Everybody's there. It'll be a good time."

"When did you talk to Zack?"

"He texted me. There's no cell service out there."

"I don't know, Tripper."

"C'mon, Angie. Let's drive out. We'll see the gang, have a couple of drinks, enjoy a little *us* time."

"All right. But if it's raining out there or everybody's slobbering drunk, then we come back. I don't wanna deal with a bunch of horny-ass dudes groping at me all night."

"Fair enough."

Tripper and Angie left the birthday party and drove out toward the swamp. Tripper was familiar with their destination. He had been there many times before to drink and fish with the guys. It was way back in the swamp and isolated beyond worry of disturbing neighbors or hassling cops.

The rain had passed, but heavy mists shrouded the woods. The headlights looked like horizontal cones as they pierced the fog-bound trail.

"Great night for a monster party."

"Who came up with that name? *The stinky white bones swamp monster party?*"

"Who knows? One of the guys. They've all been talkin' about the rumors goin' around. You know, all the stuff turnin' up dead, an' all the bones everybody's finding around the backwater."

"Trip!"

"What?"

"You're not going to drive through that, are you?"

"What... that water?"

"Yeah. Is that safe? I don't want to be gettin' stuck out here."

"Geez, Angie. Little tense or what? I go *muddin'* with this beast. That little bit of water ain't nothin' for this thing."

"Yeah, whatever."

"Relax. Watch."

Tripper stopped the pickup and engaged the four-wheel lock. He started the truck forward. They entered the water.

"Piece of cake."

Angie did not share Tripper's confidence. While he focused on his truck's awesome handling on the flooded trail, Angie was looking out the side windows into the water-covered mists.

"What's that?"

"What's what?"

"That. Over there."

Tripper glanced out Angie's passenger-side window.

"I don't see anything."

"Tripper look. Everything's glowing blue. Look."

Tripper stopped the truck midway across the standing water. He leaned over to look out Angie's window.

"Do you see it?"

"Umm."

He switched off the truck lights.

"What're you doing?!"

"I wanted to get a better look. Wow. That's really cool. It's everywhere. Look, it's all the way around us."

"What is it?"

"Hell if I know. But it's pretty."

Tripper and Angie grew silent as they sat and absorbed the vision of bioluminescence.

"You think I can get a picture of that?" asked Angie.

"I doubt it. I don't think it's bright enough."

"I wanna try."

"Go ahead. Roll down your window. You're gonna wanna turn off your flash or you'll never pick up the glow. It's too faint."

Angie reset the flash settings on her cell phone. She then rolled down the window and leaned out, only to retreat almost immediately.

"Oh, god! What's that smell? It's like vinegar or something."

She turned her head sideways, took a deep breath, and leaned back out through the window. Quickly, she snapped three or four pictures. Her lungs nearly exploded as she pulled herself back into the truck. Tripper rolled up her window as she called her images back up. A pronounced frown said it all.

"Anything?"

"Nothing."

"I didn't think that was gonna work. You're using a cell phone. You need a good camera to pick that—"

A blood-curdling scream echoed through the woods. Angie jumped back from the window and grabbed Tripper's arm with both of her hands. She was trying to move his arm between her and the window.

"What the hell was that?" she asked.

"Damned if I know," said Tripper.

The two sat perfectly still and listened. They heard nothing other than the rumble of the truck.

"Let's go, Tripper. I didn't like the sound of that at all."

Tripper stepped on the gas and the truck started moving through the water. It found high ground, and a few minutes later, they came up on four parked vehicles. Tripper pulled up alongside and shut off the engine.

"I thought you said everybody was here."

"That's what Zack said."

"Tripper, really? That's Zack's car. That's Kyle's car. Isn't that Tim what's his face's car? You know...."

"Tim Wayland."

"Yeah. Who's the fourth car belong to?"

"I dunno."

"I'm the only girl. I don't belong here, Trip."

"Fine. We won't stay. But as long as we're here, we might as well stop in and say hello and maybe have a beer."

"Trip."

176

"Geez, Angie. We drove all the way out here. What's fifteen minutes to have a beer? C'mon."

"You got fifteen minutes and we go. Fifteen minutes. I have no intention of sitting around with a bunch of drunk, horny assholes talkin' shit to me."

"Oh, my god, Angie. Gimme a break."

"Tripper! You don't have to deal with it. Where're we goin'?"

"Not very far. There's a path through the woods down to the water."

"I thought you said Kyle was bringing a camper."

"I can only tell ya what Zack said. Maybe he decided to bring his tent."

"What? Pitch a tent for one night in the rain. I doubt it."

"I dunno, Angie. I'm just tellin' ya what Zack told me. Can we please just go? We're gonna be leavin' in a few minutes anyhow. You're gettin' your way."

Tripper stepped out of the truck. He waited for Angie to step outside and come around to where he stood. She opened her door, but paid close attention to the surrounding woods before stepping out.

"What are you doing?"

"Nothing. Quit hurrying me."

Once out of the truck, Angie slammed the door shut and wasted no time racing to Tripper's side. He started down the trail. She grabbed his arm and held on tight. It made him feel good. He enjoyed having her trust.

"What do you think that scream was?"

"I have no idea. Maybe it didn't like the way you're always bitching at me."

"Very funny, you ass."

Tripper and Angie both started laughing. They could hear the music echoing through the woods, and after a short distance, could see light working its way through the thickets.

"There they are."

"Tripper?"

"Yeah."

"What on earth is that smell? It makes my nose run."

"I don't know, babe."

"Doesn't that bother you? It kinda burns."

"Yeah, a little bit. Somebody's probably dumping industrial waste illegally. C'mon, pay attention or you're gonna trip."

Tripper led Angie to the camp. There was no camper; there was no tent. There was only a large canopy like those used for high school open houses in the backyard. It was pitched at the water's edge.

"Hey, we made it!"

At the same time Tripper blurted out notice of his arrival, subconsciously he was processing the odd silence in the camp. He fixed on body-like forms beneath blankets under the canopy.

There was no response. The radio was blaring away, but that was the only sound. It was an eerily singular sound. It was jarring. It was almost embarrassing to hear it playing so loudly in the stillness of the night.

Angie said nothing. She stood alongside Tripper, content to let him call the shots. He started laughing.

"What's so funny?"

"Don't you see what they're doin'? Them sons-of-bitches are settin' us up for a scare."

"Why?"

"What d'ya mean, why? C'mon, Angie, everybody's drinkin'... *swamp monster party....* I'd be doin' the same thing."

Tripper started scanning the woods and thickets for a flicker of light or a sign that would give away their position.

"It ain't gonna happen, guys!"

"Where d'you think they are?"

"Close enough to watch us, but far enough away so we can't hear 'em laughin' their asses off."

Tripper walked forward on guard. He was fully anticipating something about to jump out at him. He left Angie behind as he stepped beneath the canopy and looked down the forms concealed under the blankets. Just then, out of nowhere came a second hair-raising scream that nearly buckled his knees. He cowered as his mind grappled with the shock. A second later, Tripper realized Angie screamed. He turned around just in time to see her bolting straight for him. His immediate thought was that his buddies had got her good. He started to laugh.

"Jesus, Angie! You scared the crap outta me. What're you doin'?"

Angie wasted no time reaching out for Tripper's arm. She latched on to it and then positioned him between her and something unseen.

"It was a snake. It was huge. Oh, my god. I thought I was dead."

"A snake?"

"It was huge, Tripper. It was like ten feet long."

"I doubt it."

"I don't care. I don't care."

"It's just the guys runnin' shit on ya, girl."

"This is bullshit, Tripper. Do what you gotta do. I'm waiting in the truck."

"Chill, Angie.... Chill. Settle down, sweetheart. Besides, the way you scare, you ain't goin' back to the truck alone an' you know it."

Tripper turned away from Angie and reached down to grab a corner of the blanket spread out beneath the canopy. He whipped it away. Four half-fleshed skeletons immediately came into view.

"Whoa!" Tripper stumbled back. "Goddamn, does that stink or what? See, what'd I tell ya? It's the guys. Look at this. Unbelievable."

"Ohhhh. That's disgusting. That's just nasty."

"There's your smell. This is what you were supposed to scream about. Not some stupid fake snake."

Tripper walked up to the corpses and stooped down to study them.

"Wow. These things are great. I wonder where they got 'em from. They're incredible. You should see these up close, Angie.

They got all the bones an' tendons—man, these things stink. No wonder we could smell it halfway through the woods."

"What's all over 'em?"

"Slime. Probably somethin' Og got from the pizza shop. Used oil or grease or somethin'."

"God, that smell is terrible," complained Angie. "Doesn't that irritate your sinuses? It's making me sick."

Tripper stood back up and walked out from under the canopy. He looked into the woods.

"Hey, guys! Gags up! C'mon, let's have a beer. I gotta bring Angie back in a few minutes. She saw a snake! Party's over for me. C'mon!"

Tripper was smiling. He fully expected to get a response, most likely an explosion of laughter. He got nothing.

"C'mon, guys! I haven't got that much time. Hey! I'm drinkin' your beer!"

Tripper walked over to a cooler and grabbed a cold beer. He popped it open and took a hefty gulp.

"Ahhhhhhh."

"You want a beer, Angie?"

"Hardly."

"Hey! C'mon! Angie's making me drink alone! Drinkin' alone is no fun!"

Tripper listened but there was no response.

"Where are they?" asked Angie.

"I dunno. I'm thinkin' maybe they went wanderin'."

"Wanderin'?" Where would they wander? Who would want to wander out here? You guys are all nuts."

"Well.... Wherever. The party probably cleared out because of the rain. Everything's too wet, so Zack an' Kyle an' the rest of the guys took off into the woods. They probably gave up on us."

"What would they do that for?"

"No reason, just horsin' around. You know, drinkin' and bullshittin'. Why do you girls go from one mall shop to another

180

all day long? That don't make any sense at all, but you keep right on doin' it."

"Hardly the same. So, they're wandering and we're doing what?"

"Oh, baby.... Ease up. We're gonna head back, cuz that makes Angie happy."

"Well, Tripper, I'm not trying to be a bitch, but nobody's here."

"Oh, somebody's here, Angie. They're here someplace, but never mind.... C'mon. What Angie wants, Angie gets. Let's go."

Tripper tossed his half-full can of beer down next to the cooler. He turned away from the corpses and started back into the woods. Angie was fast on his heels. He turned to look back one last time and hollered.

"We're outta here!"

They continued along the path.

"What are you doin', Angie?"

"I don't wanna run into another one of those snakes."

"Really?"

"Don't worry about what I'm doin'. Just hit your key and turn on the truck lights so we got some light."

"Yes, ma'am. Your wish is my command. Whatever you say."


## 26


Cory looked at his watch. It was ten to nine. It was time to head out for Little Boots where he was supposed to meet Cristina and Tammy Tagart for breakfast.

Cory stepped outside his motel room and was about to pull open the door to the Blazer when he happened to glance down along the bottom of his rocker panels. Something seemed amiss, so he stepped back from his truck. He leaned over slightly sideways as he attempted to view the rocker panel from a different angle.

Finally, he squatted alongside it. He ran his fingers along the body. To his chagrin, he noticed the paint was peeling off.

"Christ almighty. You'd think for thirty-five thousand dollars I could get something with paint that lasts more than a couple of years. I don't believe it."

The more Cory studied the paint, and the more he realized the damage, the more he stewed. It appeared as if the paint dulled along much of the lower half of the SUV.

"How did I not notice that before?"

Mentally, Cory was trying to remember if he had received any recall notices for bad paint when he realized he was running late. He looked at his watch. He had to go. He jumped into the truck and departed for Little Boots.

After Cory pulled in and parked at Little Boots, he hopped out of the Blazer and hustled into the restaurant. He saw Cristina and Tammy already seated at a window booth. Cristina waved for his attention. He walked toward them.

"Good morning, ladies."

"I'd say 'good morning' back, but I'm wondering if you got any sleep. After that little escapade around Gloven's place, I could see you huddled beneath the faint glow of a desk lamp, sitting at your laptop, writing the *National Enquirer* magnum opus."

"I really am that good, but to be honest, other than making notes worthy of a Nobel, I got plenty of sleep. It's just I was walking in and thinking about.... I noticed all the—"

Cory stopped midsentence and turned around to face the direction of his truck. He could only see it in his mind, but what he saw made some kind of sense. He looked back at Cristina and Tammy.

"I'm thinking that I know what we're dealing with here. In fact, I'm almost certain of it."

"You worked this out before coffee?"

Cristina's humor sailed over Cory's head, as he pieced together his thoughts.

"We gotta be dealing with some kind of chemical spill. It's the only thing that adds up. It's something that poisoned the cows and killed the hunter. It's something with properties that makes it glow in the dark, and it is corrosive enough to bleach the bones we've found.

"*And...* I might add, as of this morning, peel the paint off my truck. What didn't get peeled is as dull as banana skin. I gotta tell you, that pisses me off. That Blazer's only two years old. Christ, I'm still making payments, and now I have to repaint it?

"But... at least it adds up. It all adds up. That's why we always smell the acrid odor around those bones. It's gotta be something that has leaked out of the gas wells that are spread all over the swamp. That has to be it."

"You think?" asked Cristina. "No piranha, no botulism?"

"No. Chemicals are the only thing I know of that can peel paint off a car. Makes a lot more sense than new life or genetic mutations roaming about unleashed."

"I couldn't agree with you more. So, do you still need me?" asked Tammy.

Cory looked at her and smiled.

"Of course we do. Breakfast wouldn't be the same without you. Besides who drives all the way down here from Traverse City just to drive back?"

Cory, Cristina, and Tammy managed to eat breakfast without mentioning a single word about the swamp or its monsters. The conversation was more personal, revealing something of their lives and personalities. Through stories of common experiences and humorous recollections, they laughed their way through the Little Boots breakfast special. It was only in closing, during coffee that talk turned to the swamp and mysterious disappearances. As if by cue, the ring of Cory's cell phone interrupted their conversation.

"Hey, Harold. What's up? Yeah.... You gotta be kidding me.... Oh, man, this is going to blow sky high.... Yeah. What's the address? Jesus, that's right by Gloven's place. Yeah.... I'll get right on it.... Yep. See you."

183

Cory set his phone down on the table, but never took his eyes off Cristina.

"What?" she asked.

"The game's changed big time."

"What do you mean?"

"We aren't talking disappearances anymore. We got three dead kids."

"Oh, no!" Cristina whispered as she brought her hand up to cover her mouth. Her eyes opened wide. "My god, *you're kidding*."

"I wish I was. That was Harold. He just got a call from Toby. Said Toby's on his way there now and expecting us. Harold's hot to get the story first."

"How'd they die?" asked Cristina.

"Playing. Playing in the swamp." Cory looked at Tammy. "What d'you think, Tammy? Interested in getting a firsthand look?"

"Actually, it feels kind of rude or callous to say yes. I'm a little embarrassed to admit it, but I'm really curious. I'm already here in Houghton Lake, so why not?"

"Did they say anything about the cause of death? Anything about a chemical spill or...." asked Cristina, her voice trailing off.

"Harold didn't say."

"This does not sound good," said Cristina.

"I agree. C'mon, ladies, we gotta go."


## 27


Cory drove up the driveway. He took a moment to sort out the sight before him. The yard looked every bit a crime scene with a parked ambulance, an unmarked sheriff's patrol car, two state trooper vehicles, three Denton Police squad cars, and three volunteer firemen trucks. The vehicles appeared to compete for *most visible*, having lights that flash annoyingly from every side, top, and bottom. There were also a number of other cars. Some appeared to belong to family members, who were standing in plain view, lost in tears. Some belonged to relatives and friends, who were consoling the family. Cory turned away to face Cristina and Tammy.

"The state boys are here, so they may get a little persnickety about us showing up. Just let me speak first and follow my lead. Let's go."

Cory climbed out of the SUV and waited for Cristina and Tammy to do likewise. The three headed toward the house. Cory took note of the state trooper now looking him over. The trooper started in their direction.

"May I help you, sir?"

"Yes, sir. Name's Cory Ballard. Investigative reporter, this is my assistant, Cristina Walker, and this is Tammy Tagart from Morrison Medical. Detective Sergeant Quinn has given us clearance to take the story for Harold Sweeny and the *Roscommon County Chronicle*. Ms. Tagart is a marine biologist who specializes in toxicology. She's here to assess the possibility of biological or chemical poisoning. That being in light of some other deaths occurring recently under suspicious circumstances here in the vicinity."

All the while Cory was spewing, he flashed his quasi reporter credentials. The trooper looked at his pass briefly and nodded for the three to pass. Once out of earshot, Cory turned to the women.

"Now we get to that ambulance before it leaves."

Cory picked up the pace and zeroed in on one of the medics. His credentials were still flashing about in the air.

"Excuse me, sir!"

The man, mildly startled, turned around and looked at Cory with an expression of surprise.

"Cory Ballard, reporter for the *Roscommon County Chronicle*. This is Ms. Tagart, a specialist in toxicology from Morrison Medical, and my assistant, Cristina Walker. Ms. Tagart would like to have a moment to observe the injuries to the children before you head out. It won't take but a second of your time, sir."

"Wow. You guys don't waste any time, do ya?"

"Can't afford to, sir. There've been some similar incidents in the past few days. If we can help get to the bottom of it, we may save the lives of the next victims." Cory did not skip a beat. "Can you tell us the presumed cause of death?"

"Not a clue. I thought maybe you were gonna tell me."

"Do you mind if I take a quick look at the bodies?" asked Tammy.

"Uhhh. Where's the family?" The medic saw his partner still speaking to the trooper. The family was moving back into the house. "I'm not sure if that's appropriate. Don't you guys normally do that at the morgue?"

"As a rule, yeah. But it'd be helpful to understand what we're up against before we head back into the swamp. I'm sure you understand," said Cory.

"You're going into the swamp? I don't think I'd be doing that."

"Why?"

"I've been hearing talk that there's something back in there."

Cory started laughing.

"Folks been saying there's something back in there since campers first sat around a fire."

"Maybe so, but this isn't the stuff they were talkin' about around campfires. Lemme show you."

The medic escorted all three around to the back of the ambulance. He glanced around the truck toward the house for assurance and then opened one of the doors and reached inside. He flipped a sheet off of the legs of a young girl. Cory immediately pulled out a camera.

"Hey, you can't do that."

"Actually, as long as I am working for Ms. Tagart and Morrison Medical, I really can. We need a couple of pics for reference."

"You're not lying to me, are you? I could lose my job over this."

"Look, Ms. Tagart's going to have a hundred pics by tomorrow. What's one or two a day early? How about forty bucks for you to turn your head? You didn't see a thing."

The medic studied Cory.

"Fine. Make it quick, but turn off the flash."

"Will do."

Cory took a couple of quick pics. The medic pulled the sheet back over the girl's legs.

"What about the other two?"

"One boy looks the same. The other boy's completely covered with burns and lesions or whatever. He was found floatin' in the water. These two were on shore. Looked like they might've started runnin' for home. Probably to get help for the one we pulled from the water. Or just runnin' for their lives out of fear."

The medic threw back a sheet covering one of the boys' bodies. Severe blistering was visible on both legs below the knees. There was a notable amount of raw skinless meat. The flesh, stripped from the toes, left little more than bones and nails. The anklebones were skinless, protruding, and clearly visible.

Cory turned to Tammy. "Any ideas?"

"I'm not sure. What we've got here is significant tissue damage. These are third-degree acid or alkali burns. In fact, I would assume by the depth of the damage that we're dealing with an exceptionally potent alkali. Acid burns don't usually penetrate tissue to these depths."

Cory turned to the medic.

"Did you go into the water by any chance?"

"No. That's strictly the responsibility of the sheriff's department. We stay on shore."

"But you saw them go in?"

"Yeah."

"How were they dressed?"

"The usual. Protective gear. I mean, in this case they also had to wear waders. Why?"

"Just curious. It seems there was something in the water, and I wondered if they were exposed or made mention of any discomfort or the like. Did they smell any unusual odors or anything?"

187

"You mean besides the way these corpses smell?"

"I noticed it the minute he pulled the doors open," said Cristina to Cory.

"I thought that was disinfectant or something inside the ambulance," said Tammy.

"Yeah, it would be a smell just like that, only a hell of a lot stronger. It would irritate your sinuses."

"Nope. Nobody's said anything so far. I didn't treat anybody. But they're pretty well protected when they handle people that die from unusual circumstances. They wear facemasks, gloves, and everything. The whole nine—" The ambulance driver hesitated. "Wait a minute.... You know, now that you mention it, I did hear talk about bad odors. In fact, I believe they were told to don gas masks."

"Interesting." Cory pulled the sheet back across to cover the boy's legs. "Any idea how long they've been dead?"

"We think between three or four hours. At least according to the mother, that was about how much time passed before she decided to go lookin' for 'em. But I'm not so sure she's telling the truth. Things don't add up."

"Really? Why's that?"

"Well, these wounds are definitely life threatening, and may very well have led to death, but not in the space of three or four hours. It seems odd that all three kids would've died that quickly. Based on anything I've ever seen, those bodies would've had to have been dead a lot longer than that. Unless something besides the wounds led to their death."

"Like a poison, or something of that nature?"

"Yeah, exactly. I mean, we've had emergencies where people had limbs ripped off. We've had people covered with third-degree burns, skin damage as bad as or even worse than this, but they didn't die that fast.

"I suppose anything's possible. It's possible all three children died of shock. Hard to believe. Maybe the kid in the water. He probably drowned. But the other two only showed wounds on their legs. Nowhere else. Wounds like these kill by infection, but that occurs over the course of days or weeks not hours."

"To the best of my knowledge, the only thing around here poisonous enough to possibly kill you is a Massasauga rattler," said Tammy. "And I've never heard of anyone dying from one in these parts."

"Don't get me wrong," said the medic. "I'm not making any insinuations, but I could just as easily say that Mrs. Palmer had a breakdown, poisoned her three kids, threw acid on 'em, but seein' it didn't work as anticipated, she dragged them to the swamp and then called authorities.

"I seriously doubt that's what happened, but it's entirely plausible from what I've seen. But... I give her the benefit of the doubt. She just lost her three children and has completely lost it herself. Fact is, it's not a snake, Mrs. Palmer is not a murderer, and nobody has the faintest frickin' idea of what happened." The medic closed the back doors of the ambulance. "To be honest, I was *really* hopin' you guys were gonna tell me what happened."

"I wish I could," said Tammy. "I'm sorry."

"What now?" asked Cristina.

"We need to go into the swamp and take a look around," said Tammy.

"Okay," said Cory, who then turned toward the medic. "Listen, thanks for your assistance, uhhh...."

"Noah."

"Noah. I appreciate your help. Here's a couple of twenties. We're going to head into the swamp and look around. Thanks again."

The call of the state trooper interrupted the three as they started for the path that entered the woods.

"Hey! Where you folks going?"

"Uh... sir, as I said on the way in, Ms. Tagart is with Morrison Medical and she'd like to search the area for signs of toxins."

"That's a crime scene—"

"It's okay, officer. I'll take responsibility for escorting all three there an' back."

189

The three turned to see a gentleman dressed casually, but wearing a wind jacket that had *Roscommon Co. Sheriff Department* embroidered across the breast pocket. The man walked into their midst. The trooper said nothing, but nodded his approval. The man smiled as he extended his hand.

"Detective Sergeant Toby Quinn. Harold Sweeny said to expect you folks. I'm your escort."

"Perfect timing," said Cristina as she noted how the man squirmed in his clothes. He was constantly straightening his collar, straightening his jacket, adjusting his tie. It was as if everything about him had to be perfect. The four swapped introductions.

"So, what've you got in mind? Go back and look around?"

"Yeah, if that's okay." said Cory. "Ms. Tagart's expertise is in marine biology, marine toxins among other things."

With that, the four began their trek along a path that would lead them back through the woods toward the swamp shallows. Five minutes later, they came upon the scene. Outlines made by yellow spray paint marked the trail. The detective sergeant spoke up.

"This is where we found two of the bodies. The first outline is that of the youngest boy. It seems he made it the farthest. Next was the girl. The oldest boy was found floating face down in the water... over there by the reeds."

The four walked up to the water's edge.

"You can see that it's not all that deep. Maybe a foot an' a half at the most in the area where we found him."

"And he was the one completely covered in lesions?" asked Tammy.

"Yes, ma'am. The other two showed tissue damage up to about their knees."

Tammy looked around and nodded.

"That same wretched smell is in the air. It's not as strong, but I can still smell it," said Cristina.

Tammy turned to face Officer Quinn.

"Officer, what do you think happened here?"

"We don't have a clue. No idea at all. We're waiting for the autopsies."

"What do you think happened, Tammy?" asked Cory.

"Hard to say."

"Take a guess."

"A guess? Well.... If I were to take a guess...." Tammy looked around. "Understand that I am going to paint a possible scenario that is completely unrealistic."

"Go for it."

"Please do," said the detective sergeant. "At this point, we're all ears. I've never seen anything like it. Nobody has. Throw out your craziest thoughts. I don't care what you say. Anything's better than nothing."

"You gotta know, I'm going to feel like an idiot the minute I open my mouth."

"Spit it out, Tammy. Out of all of us, you'll sound the least stupid. I'm still toying with aliens."

Everybody laughed.

"Well, the only afflictions other than acid or alkali burns that I have ever seen resembling what we have here were the result of Ebola or cutaneous anthrax. But the key word here is 'resemble'. The fact is, I've never seen tissue damage or lesions this extensive without being the result of an industrial accident.

"Also, we could assume that the boy in the water was overcome first and collapsed, possibly causing the other two to come to his rescue, only to find themselves in trouble, at which point they tried to escape the water and race home for help. The fact that they didn't make it... the fact that they died so quickly and show the same type of leg wounds leads me to speculate they were envenomed."

"What does that mean?" asked Cristina.

"It means they may have been poisoned by a venom that either was splashed or spread on them, or injected like a snake bite. The tissue damage up the legs is comparable to the height of the water on two of the victims, and covers the entire body of the third who was found floating or fully submerged."

"But you said no chance of some kind of snake. Maybe a water snake?"

"A snake is out of the question. Nothing natural to these parts could inflict wounds that extensive in so short of a time. Snake venom would take days or even weeks to cause that wide an area of damage. You wouldn't see that degree of severity for days. It has to be some sort of chemical, some agent in the water.

"We need to look for something corrosive that can break down tissue at an alarming rate but at the same time is highly toxic. It would have to be both. The problem is how can something that corrosive maintain its pH extremes in a lake of neutral swamp water? Doesn't make sense. None of it makes sense.

"But if I'm correct, the autopsies will show they have toxin in their blood. Probably a neurotoxin. That would account for the children dying so quickly. They barely got out of the water. So what we need to find out is what kind of corrosive substance is also a potent neurotoxin."

"Well, then, it's up to you, Tammy. Can we leave it to you?" asked Cory.

"Ahh, yeah, I'm happy to look into it for you. Actually, I'd be curious to know myself."

"Great. Do you need to see anything else around here?"

Tammy scoured the area.

"No, I think I'm good."

"All right. Let me just take a couple of more shots of the area and...."

*Click... click... click.*

"That should do. Let's head back."

During the walk back, Tammy was notably quiet. Cory and Cristina both noticed, but Cory was first to make mention of her silence.

"You seem to be grinding the mental gears pretty hard."

Tammy raised her eyes to look at Cory.

192

"I suppose I am. If I were to state the obvious, I would say that anytime the discussion turns to neurotoxins, we get uncomfortably close to my days at ARL. That is what you folks originally came to see me about. Correct?"

"No, not true. Also, not obvious. We did come to see you about ARL, but we had no idea why. You brought up neurotoxins."

"Yes, I did."

## 28

### Swamp Monster Party
### Crashed by Swamp Monster
### Four Found Dead

#### By Cory Ballard

Roscommon Co., Mi. It was supposed to be a good time for all. An old-style grasser on the banks of Dead Stream Swamp. But something went terribly wrong in the thick fog that cloaked the Saturday night celebration.

Billed as the 'Stinky White Bones Swamp Monster Party', invitations went out to everyone. Everyone human, that is.

Nobody knows what showed up that night to crash the festivities. The only witnesses are dead. Whatever it was, it left nothing behind but coolers half filled with beer, good tunes on the radio, and the slime-covered skeletal remains of four close friends dressed in monster attire.

According to authorities....

"Morning, dad."

"Good mornin'."

"Did you eat?"

"Been waitin' for you, baby."

"Give me a minute to wash up, and I'll make us some breakfast."

"Take your time. Did you read your friend's article in yesterday's paper?"

Cristina started laughing. "No. Am I going to be embarrassed by association?"

"The man has a sense of flair. I'll give him that."

"That might be an understatement."

"Good. We can use a little flair around here. Get a few folks off their dead asses."

Cristina halted her trek to the bathroom.

"Ahhh. All right, if you say so. How are *you* doing this morning?"

"So-so."

Cristina dropped her head and eyed her father suspiciously.

"Everything okay, dad?"

"Somethin' got into the chicken coup. Killed a bunch of 'em."

"Fox?"

"I wish it was a fox. Nasty ass smell in there. I know that smell, but I'll be damned if I can figure out what it is, or how *whatever* it is got in. I keep that coop sealed up tighter'n a drum. Did ya hear anything last night?"

"Sorry. I slept like a rock. Made up for the night before."

"Yeah, I usually sleep light, but these ears are gettin' so bad...."

Jack's voiced trailed off as he shook his head in disgust.

"Don't tell me there's no eggs. You always have fresh, so I didn't buy any at the store."

"We're okay. I salvaged a few, but I'm gonna have t' get me a few more chickens. There's a couple of pounds of pepper bacon in the fridge. I had a cravin' for it, so I went into town while you were out yesterday havin' lunch with that newspaper fella."

"His name is Cory."

"Cory."

"Okay, then we should be fine for breakfast."

"You like this guy, Cory?"

"Yes, I do. But then, I like a good many guys. So let's not read anything into that."

"Fair enough. Shouldn't be nosey anyhow. So, you're positive them young ears didn't hear anything last night? Anything at all?"

"Not a thing, dad. Sorry. But I gotta say you sure know how to make a fifty-year-old woman feel like a kid."

"You are a kid, an' I wish I had your kid ears instead of the joys of old age. Cri, I'm goin' back out to have another quick look around the coop if ya don't mind."

"No, I don't mind. Go. I need a few minutes to shower and brush my teeth."

"Give us a yell when breakfast is on. I won't keep ya waitin'."

"Go, go."

Cristina showered and emerged fresh and spirited. She was humming to herself as she slid pans back and forth across the stove. The aroma of breakfast cooking filled the air. She stepped over to the kitchen door and hollered through the screen.

"Dad! Time to eat! Come on!"

Cristina noted the partially submerged swing set now had a bucket hanging from it. A rope passed through a pulley hooked to the top rail from where a swing chain attached. She wiped the frown of curiosity off her face the second her father rounded the corner of the porch. She backed away from the door as he entered. The two sat down at the kitchen table.

It was a limited opportunity to study her father. He was not always talkative, but his presence fulfilled her. She was past being a young woman and yet she still needed something from him. He was filling a void that had been created forty-some years ago. It would have been easier to hate this man and walk away from the memories of a fatherless upbringing. But she was inexplicably drawn to him. She could feel his affection for her.

"You find anything in the coop?"

He looked up from his plate to meet her eyes.

195

"The only thing in the coop is a rotten smell," said Jack as he cut into his egg with a fork. He stabbed the bleeding yoke with a piece of bread and then looked up at his daughter. "Cri, I need to ask a favor of ya."

"What's that?"

"I need ya to run toward town with me. I gotta pick something up. It's not real heavy, but it's awkward. You got time, or are ya booked?"

"Booked? Now, that's funny, dad."

"Well, I don' know. You said ya had a good time with Cory. I thought maybe the two of ya might've made plans for the day."

"Well, you thought wrong. When do you want to go?"

"Sooner the better. Let's leave the dishes 'til later."

"Oh. Okay. What do we have to pick up?"

"I can't say."

"Why not? Is it a gift for me?" Cristina cooed.

Jack laughed. "No, it ain't a gift for ya. But I'll probably have to buy you one after ya help me."

"What does that mean?"

"Oh, you'll find out soon enough."

"That settles it. I don't want anything to do with this."

"Sure ya do. Your curiosity is already killin' ya. I could even say that you're gonna hate me afterward, and you'll still do it."

"You are either way too smart or way too obnoxious for your own good."

They laughed and chatted while breakfasting, but Cristina made no attempt to inquire about the swing set or the bucket. It was as inexplicable as it was outrageous to see, and evidently, nothing her father wished to discuss, or it would have been explained long before now. Instead, Jack pushed away his plate and waited for Cristina to finish, at which point he backed away from the table and held the kitchen door open for her.

Cristina walked across the porch and started down the steps. She stopped to look at a new row of bags standing in line along the narrow strip of land.

"What did you do, buy more salt?"

"Yeah."

"Dad, how much salt did you buy? Geez. You know this stuff is going to kill off anything that grows for years."

"Yeah, I know it. The thought troubles me, but I got priorities."

Cristina turned on the step to look up at her father.

"Priorities? I'm not asking any questions, *but know* this all looks really weird from where I stand. The ring of salt, the swing set, the roadkill, and the cage. I know you well enough to understand you don't do anything without clear reason. I know you're not losing your mind, so what's this all about? You honestly expect me to believe that all this salt is to stop snakes from getting into the house? I haven't seen a snake around since I arrived. In fact, I haven't seen anything crawling around here period."

"I know. And that may be a bad sign in itself. Hear me out a second," said Jack as he angled his head to sort out his thoughts. For a moment his mouth hung open. "Understand this, Cri. As of late, snakes an' stuff don't just stumble or slither across the property matter-of-factly. When they show up, they show up all at once. And when it happens, I can live with it, because I'm gettin' used to it. But I promise, it'll scare the bejesus outta *you*. Now, come on. We gotta go."

Cristina studied her father as he walked away. She was somewhat annoyed, but mostly perplexed as she looked back down at the ring of salt. She looked back up and, obedient as a child, she followed her father across the yard. She continued to consider him from behind. He was no fool, but he was saying foolish things, or at least hiding the truth about whatever he was up to. And yet, he was right about one thing. Confronting a bunch of snakes coming up out of the swamp would be more than enough to make her lose it.

"Cri, let's take the pickup."

"Okay."

Cristina climbed into the passenger side of Jack's pickup. Her father drove the back roads, twice stopping to pick up roadkill before merging onto the highway. Instead of conversing, they listened to the morning news. Cristina was lost in visions described by the announcer of a young man who saved a young girl from a house fire. He had been badly burned in the process.

Cristina looked over at her dad. He was so rough around the edges. She wondered if he would have charged into a burning house to save her when she was a child. She wondered if he loved her enough to do it now that she was an old lady. She tried to imagine facing the searing heat, when the braking of the truck abruptly snuffed out her daydream.

"What's the matter?" she asked.

"We gotta stop."

"For what?"

"That deer."

"What deer?"

"The one we're about to steal from the vultures."

Cristina sat up straight to look out the windows.

"You mean that *dead deer* lying there?!"

"Yup."

"Dad. What... what.... What are you doing? What on earth do you want with a dead deer?"

"You'll see in time."

"Dad.... *Please* tell me you're not losing your mind, because any rational person would wonder. It's like one thing after another. The cage, the swing set, the salt, and now we're picking up dead deer off the road? Dead deer? Really, dad. This is why you brought me out here?" Cristina shook her head. "That thing can't be pretty."

"Yeah, ha, ha." Cristina's father let out a robust laugh.

It was unexpected, and Cristina spun around to look at him. It was the first time in many years that she heard him laugh in that manner. It heartened her. It gave her a break.

"I can only imagine what's goin' through your head, Cri. Take heart in knowin' I'm not crazy yet. But, I promise you this. If I were to tell ya what I was up to, you'd most certainly think I had lost my mind. It's better just to go along with my peculiarities, call 'em eccentricities. Us old farts are supposed to be full of 'em."

"Yeah. Okay, dad. If you say so, but it doesn't help much."

Jack had already pulled off onto the shoulder of the road and now backed up the truck. He stopped, threw it into park, and climbed out. Cristina did likewise.

"How we going to get *that* into the truck?" she asked as she threw her hands up in a gesture of futility.

Jack dropped the tailgate and grabbed a couple pairs of gloves off the bed. He handed one pair to Cristina.

"Simple. We pick it up an' pull it onto the bed of the truck."

Cristina looked at the bloated corpse.

"Oh, god, dad. That's disgusting. Look at the flies.... What do you want with a dead deer? Especially that one? Geez."

"Mercy me, Cristina. Quit your whinin' an' grab its hind legs."

"Oh, dad, no way. That thing is nasty."

"Come on, Cri. Grab hold."

"Really?"

Unhappily resigned, Cristina reached and took firm hold of the animal's hind legs.

"Oh, god, that stinks," complained Cristina as she turned her head away.

"Okay, now lift its legs up so we can roll it onto its back. That a girl. Now, climb up on the bed."

"Oh, god."

Cristina did as she was told, always feeling like the child.

"All right, now hang on to these hoofs so I can get up there."

Jack climbed up onto the bed of the truck and then took a fresh hold of the animal.

"All right. Now step over here alongside me."

Again, Cristina did as told.

"Are ya ready? We're gonna just drag it up onto the tailgate and then we'll pull it onto the bed. Okay?"

"Whatever you say, dad. But if I vomit, it's your fault. I'm tellin' you, this is plain disgusting."

"True. Just a note... we'll still have to unload it."

"*You* still have to unload it. Just push it off the back of the truck. You don't need me for that."

"Ha, ha, ha. Pull!"

Together Cristina and her father yanked hard on the animal, lifting it up and across the tailgate. Maggots were dropping from the carcass and wiggling about on the road and the tailgate. With some effort, they dragged it fully onto the bed. Jack jumped out of the box and offered Cristina his hand. She hopped out and he closed the tailgate. They tossed their gloves back into the box, and climbed back into the cab. Jack fired up the truck and eased it back onto the highway.

"You need anything from town?"

"Yeah, I'm thinking a new life, but I'll settle for a shower."

Jack laughed heartily for the third time. It was obvious he was having a good time at her expense. In spite of the revolting chore, the sound of his laughter made it bearable for Cristina. She shook her head in mild exasperation and tried to fight off a grin. Truth was, she'd probably walk through hell with him.

"You've lost your mind, dad."

"Maybe so."

"Just don't be telling me we're having that thing for dinner. I don't want to hear anything about you coming up with a way to serve roadkill. That would be just like you. Why do I always have to feel like I'm fourteen around you?"

Jack continued to laugh, probably more than he had in a year. The sound flooded into Cristina's heart.

Her father turned his truck onto the drive and plowed through the overgrowth with indifference. The branches slapped the windows and squealed in protest.

"Do you think maybe it's time to cut back the branches or what?"

"It's time."

"I'm thinking that's better spent time than collecting rotting deer."

Jacked stopped the truck and shut it off. They climbed out.

"Wait here, honey. I gotta get a wheelbarrow outta the shed. I'll be right back."

Cristina watched her father walk across the yard to the shed. As he disappeared, she looked at the wretched carcass in the truck bed. It made her squeamish. She looked away upon hearing the squeak of the wheelbarrow wheel. Her father followed his wheelbarrow out of the shed and down the ramp, but instead of continuing on to the truck, he set the wheelbarrow down and walked around behind the chicken coop. When he came back into view, he was shaking his head. It was obvious he was troubled.

"Come on, honey."

Jack positioned the wheelbarrow at the rear of the truck, and then dropped the gate. Cristina put her gloves back on and reached for the animal's hind legs.

"Atta girl. Okay, let's drag it off."

Together they pulled the animal across the bed, off the gate, and into the wheelbarrow.

"Thanks."

"You need anything else?"

"We're just about done. Don't take those gloves off just yet."

"This isn't girl fun, dad."

"I know. Just follow me."

Cristina did as instructed, and followed her father around the salt perimeter to the back yard. She stopped as he maneuvered the wheelbarrow between the ring of salt and the water's edge. He dumped the carcass onto the bank. The forelegs ended up in the water. He took a deep breath and stared at it.

"I hope you're not planning on leaving that right there."

"I'm not."

"Good. Wouldn't take much of that to stink the whole place up."

"I'm thinking it won't be around that long."

"What are you going to do with it?"

"Fish bait. I'm gonna use it for fish bait. They'll nibble it to nothin' in no time. Maybe get some fish back in the shallows. Gotta do something."

"Well, I'm just telling you now. I brought a book to read on the porch, and if I gotta smell that thing, I'm going back to Grand Rapids to read it."

"If it gets to stinkin' that bad, I'll be goin' back with ya. We can surprise your mother."

"Deal."

"Wait here while I grab some waders."

Once again, Cristina obliged her father. She waited and watched as he walked to the shed. Shortly after entering, he stepped out with two sets of waders draped over his arms. Cristina's eyes narrowed at the sight of *two* sets of waders. She started shaking her head along with her index finger, signaling her objection.

"No, no, no."

"Here, put these on."

"For what?"

"C'mon, sweetheart. Just put 'em on."

"Where exactly are we going that I need waders?"

"To the swing set."

"What do you need me to go to the swing set for?"

"I need you to help me drape this deer across the swings."

"Okay. That's it, Pops. I've had enough. Enough."

Cristina threw down the waders and scaled the porch steps. She dropped into her father's rocker, and began rocking with purpose. Her father called from the water's edge.

"C'mon, Cri, don't be a panty-waist."

"Panty-waist! Dad, you want to drape a dead deer over swings in two feet of water! No. I stand corrected. It's worse. You want me to hug a dead, rotting, maggot-infested deer and drape it over swings in two feet of water. I've seen a lot of fishing lures up here, but I've never seen one that looked like a dead deer."

This time Jack keeled over with laughter. He choked on his breath. Tears came to his eyes.

"Sweetheart, you said it yourself. I don't do anything without clear reason. This ain't any different. I just don't wanna go about tryin' to explain what this is all about, because if I do, it's like I said before, you'll think I'm nuts. What I am is too old an' worthless to get this deer on those swings without wastin' a week's time an' ruinin' what's left of my back. So, just give me a hand, sweetheart."

Cristina jumped up out of the rocker.

"You're right. It's not you. I'm the one who's crazy. I can't even say I'm senile. I'm just crazy, crazier than you. I have to be."

Reluctantly, Cristina descended the porch steps to stand once again alongside her father and the dead animal.

"And we're doing this how?"

"Only one way. Like you said, we hug it. We carry it out an' try to get it draped over the swings."

As Cristina surmised, it was a job far, far easier said than done. Trying to lift and pass a hundred pounds of dead, rotting, bloated, soaked, and slippery flesh through two flailing swings while standing in knee-deep water was no small feat. Cristina was smeared in crushed maggots, and as soon as she fulfilled her father's request, she high-tailed it out of the water. She dropped the waders on the bank and sped up the back porch to disappear beyond the screen door of the cabin. Jack hollered after her.

"Hey, you should see this, Cri. The fish are already goin' crazy over the maggots." He started laughing. "Ya made my day, Cristina. I didn't catch what ya said to me, honey, but I don't think I ever so much appreciated bein' deaf 'til now. Hey, ya earned that gift, sweetheart."

## 29

Cory looked around. There was a single supervisor giving orders to a large group of what looked to be high-school students or young adults. He was attempting to direct the search party into position along the shallows. It was raining.

"This is *not* going to be good. This search site is way too close to both Gloven's place and where those kids died."

"What can you do?" asked Cristina.

"On the whole, nothing. According to Quinn, the organizers have dozens of these small search parties spread out all over the swamp. You might bring one to their senses, but the search operation overall is fully underway. I promise you this. If we don't end up with ten more bodies by the end of the day, it'll be a miracle of God, and nothing less."

"So we just sit?"

"What do you want me to say, Cristina? It's a free country, and right now it's a free country full of idiots. I drove out here because I know that this is too close to Gloven's place. This could get really ugly. I mean, look at those girls over there. They're wearing tennis shoes for Christ's sake. Nobody should be allowed anywhere near the water without chest high waders at a minimum. They're on a mission to find missing people without a clue of what they're getting into. It's like going to the North Pole because the ice is free. Insanity."

"You wouldn't catch me wandering about this place. No way."

Cory reached for the door handle.

"Yeah, but you're one of the few who has an idea of what we're up against. Oh, well, I guess I should go up there and see if I can talk some sense into whoever's running the show. I mean, that's pretty much the reason I came here."

"What are you going to say... or do?"

"I'm going to try and tell him politely that he's got his head up his ass. I'm going to try and dissuade the idiot from sending anybody into the shallows. You joining me or what?"

"How can I not? This ought to be interesting. Grab the umbrella."

Cory opened the rear door of the Blazer and picked up the umbrella from the floor. He walked around and opened up Cristina's door. As soon as she stepped out and under the umbrella, she looked directly into his eyes.

"You smell that?"

Cory was caught off guard by the question, but instantly understood its significance. He started sniffing the air.

"You smell it?" she asked again.

"Yeah, unfortunately this time I do. Things are getting worse by the minute. C'mon, we have to move."

They walked quickly toward the man directing the search party.

"Excuse me, sir."

The man turned to face the two of them standing huddled beneath the umbrella. He didn't respond. He appeared to be in his mid-thirties, and bothered by having to take a moment of his time to figure out who they were. He wore a look of superiority that inferred he didn't believe anybody standing under an umbrella was up to the task at hand.

Cory and Cristina did not fit in with the teenagers that were horsing around on the shore and impatient to take off through the rain. Unlike the kids, they weren't about to charge forward into the shallows and search for anything, missing friends or otherwise.

"I'm sorry to both—"

"Make it quick. We're getting underway."

Cory did not appreciate the man's rudeness or his arrogance.

"All right, I'll make it quick. You're out of your goddamned head sending these kids into those shallows. You have no idea what you're getting yourself into, and if you get as many of those kids back out as you send in, it'll be the luckiest day of your life. I'm telling you to call off this search. Do you understand what I'm sayin'? Call off the search. Someone's going to die."

"What?" The man clearly was taken aback. "And who the hell are you people? And who the hell are you to talk to me like that?"

"Jesus, man. It doesn't make a rat's ass bit of difference who we are. It matters that you don't do the stupidest thing in your life and send anybody into those shallows. A half dozen people have died or gone missing in this area. It's dangerous."

"What's dangerous?"

Cory knew this was where things would fall apart, and he would start sounding like an idiot. At least having Cristina at his side kept him from looking like a murderous idiot.

"What's dangerous?" asked the man a second time.

"If we knew *what* was dangerous, we wouldn't be having this conversation. All we know is that there is something in that swamp, something in those shallows, in those marshes, that's killing animals and people alike. We're expending a great deal of energy trying to locate it."

"To locate what?"

"Sir, I thought I made myself clear. We don't know what it is. We do know it's dangerous. We believe it's the reason for the recent spate of deaths and disappearances. It's the reason you're out here with a search party."

"Look, you people gotta do better'n that. I have no idea who you folks are or where you come from. What I do know is that I've lived here my whole life an' there ain't anything dangerous whatsoever in this swamp except for possibly bear, and we're makin' way too much noise for their liking. Now if you'll excuse me, I've got a couple of missing kids to find. And that's bad enough. Maybe you should expend your energy on that tragedy."

"What kids?"

"The ones that turned up missing last night from the Reedsburg Dam campground. Now if you'll leave me be."

The man turned away and began barking out orders.

"What a jerk," said Cristina.

"Mmm, well... not really. You gotta understand from his side of the fence, we're the ones who come across as misinformed intruders. Most of these guys have lived or fished these waters

206

their whole lives. To them it's a place where you go to get away from monsters, a place of peace and tranquility."

"I thought he was kind of a prick."

"Well, maybe, but then we barged in on him just as he gave word to start the search. He's got a lot on his plate, and wasn't expecting or needing the distraction. What I want to know is what kids was he talking about. What kids?"

"I wonder if my cell will get out to Harold?"

Cory swiped the screen of his cell. He punched numbers. While he waited for a connection he looked at Cristina and frowned.

"What are you doing?" Cory's attention shifted to the phone. "Harold? Harold? Can you hear me? Yeah. Hey, listen. Do you know anything about kids missing from the campground down at Reedsburg Dam? Any issues down there? Harold? Harold?"

Cory looked back at his cell.

"No service. Figures." He looked back at Cristina. "What are you doing?"

"Can't you tell that smell is getting stronger?"

Cristina had raised her face and was sniffing the air. Cory inhaled more deeply.

"I can smell it, but it's obvious I don't have *your* nose."

"Trust me, it's getting stronger."

"What way's the wind blowing?"

Just then, Cory and Cristina snapped their heads to the left as a horrific scream, first from one, and then two young women broke the stillness. Cory bolted out from under the umbrella in a dead run. Cristina followed in pursuit.

Cory pushed his way through the thickets and came up behind the search leader who was torn between reaching the two women and making sense of what he saw. Others were now appearing as they closed their ranks to investigate the disturbance. Cory could hear the gasps as they caught the first glimpse of two bodies floating in the rain-disturbed shallows.

Cory sprinted along the water's edge.

"Don't go in the water! Stay out of the water! Stay out of the water!"

Cory saw the leader charging toward the bodies floating in the shallows. In the back of Cory's mind, he wanted to see the man dive in to rescue the already doomed, but his heart prevailed. Instead, he ran along the shore at full speed.

His eyes darted in all directions. He was frantically looking for any sign of movement, any sign of disturbance or evidence of something alien in the shallows. He plowed through the thickets until his lungs burned. He reached out with his hands and plowed full force into the search leader, knocking him off his feet. Both men flew through the air and landed painfully hard on the branch and root-covered ground. The man looked at Cory in a state of shocked confusion.

"Don't go in the water," Cory gasped. He was panting hard and barely able to speak. He had the man pinned to the ground. "Don't go into the water.... You'll die."

The man laid there in stunned silence. He was not afraid. He was confused. He was full of questions, but unsure of which one he should ask first.

"Don't go in the water."

No sooner had Cory given his advice, when a ruckus broke out on shore and a boy charged into the shallows. Cory turned away from the supervisor who still laid on the ground.

"No! No! Stay out of the water!" Cory ran over to where the teenagers gathered near the water. "Get back! Get back from the water!"

Cory never looked at the second boy who entered the shallows. He knew the outcome. He was determined to stop a mass plunge by unsuspecting victims. He ran to place himself between horror-struck kids who placed bravery and honor above all else, and two dead classmates just out of arm's reach. He bent over and strained to catch his breath. He stood up and looked at them.

"It's too late. You can't save either one. You go into the water— you die. Simple as that. You go in, you die!"

The teenagers went silent. The look of shock was evident in all their faces.

"It's over. I understand you want to help. You're brave, but there's nothing you can do. You go in, you die."

Cristina was running in his direction.

"Are you all right?" she asked as she pulled him in under the umbrella.

Cory said nothing. He succeeded in stopping the crowd from plunging to their deaths. Now he was watching the search leader who had picked himself up with what little dignity remained. The man went to the aid of the girls who had been screaming. Cory placed his arm around Cristina and moved her in the direction of the man.

"I want to hear what's being said."

The girls were so unnerved that between fits of crying and fear, they were having a hard time speaking coherently. The man finally calmed them down enough to get a sensible account of what had taken place. Cory and Cristina listened with intent.

"Joey saw something... in the water—"

"Yeah, he was hollerin' that he thought he'd found something."

"He was callin' for help."

"We went runnin' in his direction from this side an'—"

"Jonnie and Kurt came from the other direction."

"We saw Joey go right down. His hands went out like this, and he just went over face-first into the water."

"Jonnie and Kurt ran into the water to help him and I saw Jonnie go down. Kurt stopped to turn around and made it back to shore and then fell right there. That last guy, Chris Cramer, I didn't see him go in. I just know who he is."

The girl pointed at Kurt's body lying face down on the ground just feet beyond the water's edge. In a sudden wave of silence, the leader looked, the crowd looked, and so did Cory and Cristina. Between the dead boy on the bank, and three more floating in the shallows, everything about the scene was horrifying.

"We didn't know what to do."

"We didn't dare enter the water. Not after that guy started screaming to stay out."

The girl pointed at Cory. The man turned to see Cory and Cristina standing under the umbrella watching him. His expression said it all. He would never be able to wish away their warning. The man would live with this the rest of his life.

The search leader had heard enough. He began yelling in both directions to call off the search. He kept yelling to pass the word, to call off the search and stay back from the water. He ordered everyone to get back, and stay back from the water. He ordered everyone back to their cars until the police arrived.

The gathered youth said little, and only in whispers and hushed nervous tones. They walked solemnly back to their vehicles and waited inside or stood around in small groups and talked. Cory and Cristina did the same.

"I saw the regret in his eyes," said Cristina as they walked.

"I'm sure of it. I feel bad for him."

Once Cory and Cristina reached the Blazer and climbed inside, Cory searched for his cell.

"What now?"

"Right now, I'm going to try to give Toby a heads up."

Cory couldn't get a voice connection, but did manage a text message that let Toby know where in the swamp he and Cristina were located.

"Is he coming?"

"Yeah. He'll be here in about fifteen minutes. Listen, I want to go back out and get some pictures, and maybe ask some of those kids if they know anything about what happened at the Reedsburg campground. You should stay in the truck and dry out. Do you mind?"

"No, not at all. Take your time."

Cory looked at Cristina. He leaned in her direction and kissed her lightly on the hair covering her ear.

"Thanks."

Cory stepped out of the Blazer to await the detective sergeant's arrival. Cristina watched him wander off and begin snapping pictures with his cell. She watched him head over to where the kids were standing by their cars.

Cory pulled out his wallet, and quickly flashed his reporter credentials. The high school kids flocked around him. They were young and thrilled to have their pictures taken for the paper. It was easy to talk to them now that he had earned their respect by tackling their leader and saving the man's life. He had become a small-time hero of sorts.

Cory had seen everything that they had seen here in the swamp. But he was curious about something else.

"So tell me. Any of you guys know what went down at the Reedsburg Dam? You know anything at all about the kids that went missing?"

The kids were all speaking on top of each other, forcing Cory to seek out the clearest voices amid the confusion.

"Just what we've been hearing, word of mouth."

"Tell me what you've been hearing."

"There's two stories."

"There's more than two stories."

"Well, there all kinds of stories, but there's only *two* main stories."

On that point, the crowd fell into agreement.

"And what would those be, who can tell me?"

A boy spoke out loudly, and overshadowed a girl who first stepped forward to respond.

"They were kidnapped yesterday!"

"Kidnapped?" asked Cory.

"There's been sightings of a blue van driving around the campground for the last couple of weeks," said the girl. "They're sayin' right now, that two girls may have been kidnapped. They've got announcements on the radio and TV. They're asking everybody to keep an eye open for a blue van and to report it to the authorities."

"I think it's the Dead Stream monster!" yelled another.

"Yeah!" a chorus erupted.

"What do you know about the Dead Stream monster?"

211

"It stalks people at night," said one.

"It's invisible," said another.

"It likes naked women."

"Oh, my god! It's standing right in front of me," said Cory, as he stared at the boy who made the off-color remark. The crowd of teenagers was too respectful of the tragedy to go crazy, but snickered in as subdued a manner as could be mustered.

Sirens once heard in the distance were now closing in. Cory, along with the others, turned to look, and so caught the first glimpse of flashing lights through the trees.

"Thanks, kids, I gotta go."

The horror of the situation escalated once the line of police and emergency vehicles paraded into the already congested clearing. The kids stood somber as they watched the sheriff's personnel and medics begin to remove the bodies. As expected, friends closest to the victims cried the hardest. Others came to their aid. It was a lesson in life that the teenagers barely understood.

Cory walked toward the water at first sight of Detective Quinn's arrival. A couple of officers, indifferent to his credentials, stopped him at once and ordered him back. Rather than push it, he kept his distance, took pictures, and wandered farther down along the bank looking for anything of interest. After discussions with the other officers, Cristina watched Detective Quinn walk toward Cory. The detective was adjusting the cuffs of his jacket. The two remained in place conversing until the emergency personnel recovered the final body. At that point, Toby returned with Cory to the SUV.

"Hello, Cristina."

"Hi, Toby. How are you?"

"I'm good, but I have to say this stuff is getting me down."

"I can only imagine."

"Well, I'm heading back to the station. Not much else can be done around here. Not much else can be done about anything until we get reports back from the autopsies. I'll see you folks later."

Quinn headed for his cruiser, and Cory climbed back into the Blazer. He started up the truck, but was obviously deep in thought. Cristina watched as he slowly turned to look at her. His expression was one of puzzlement.

"They were all wearing waders and rubber gloves, which is standard procedure when handling corpses. I wonder what would have happened if they had touched those boys with bare hands?"

"What do you mean?"

Cory stared through Cristina as he thought aloud.

"I wonder if their skin would've burned or if they would've gotten a rash or reaction of some sort. Makes you wonder."

"Did you get a look at the bodies? Did they look anything like those Palmer kids?"

"I couldn't tell. The three floating in the shallows were too far out. The one on the shore looked normal, but then it's been raining hard enough to wash the shit out of anything."

"Mmm." Cristina nodded her understanding.

"You know, Cristina, while I was out there walking along the bank of those shallows and getting soaked, I started thinking that the one person who might have a handle on some of this is your old man."

"My dad?"

"Yeah. I been thinking you said that he's lived his whole life in this swamp. I wonder if he knows something. I wonder if he's ever seen anything strange. You said he was out fishing all the time. He must be as tuned in to the swamp as anybody. I wanna know what he was doing with that swing set. Tell me again."

"I have no idea. I came home the other day and there it was sitting in the water. He must've dragged it in by himself. I didn't ask him why, because if he wanted me to know, he would've told me. He had plenty of time to do it."

"How far out did he drag it?"

"I don't know. Maybe ten or fifteen steps."

"And then he takes you to fetch roadkill. A deer no less, and you two string this thing up across the swings."

"Yup."

"But he didn't say why. You have no idea why?"

"No. And I wasn't about to ask. I figured he would've explained something that bizarre if he wanted me to know. He always says everything that gets tossed into the shallows is fish bait."

"You do realize that there isn't much difference between throwing in dead cattle or dead deer."

Cristina said nothing. She looked at Cory and mulled over the implications.

"Was there anything else besides the swing set, or anything about the swing set that was... I don't know, different?"

"Ahhh... not really. He had a bucket strung to a pulley that was hooked at the top. The dock line or anchor line–you know that yellow stuff that floats in the water, you know like for ski ropes—"

"I know what you mean."

"That was tied to the bucket, and the rope reached back to the porch where he tied it off to the banister. I have no idea what he was doing with the bucket. To be honest, I helped him with the deer carcass as he asked, but I wasn't any too happy about it. I gave him a piece of my mind and went back into the cabin. I took it for one more of his eccentric amusements. All I cared about was that it didn't end up on my plate."

"But he told you there was something in the swamp that wasn't nice."

"Uh-huh. Yup. '...an' it ain't kind'. He said that the night I first got here."

"You see, that's what's been sticking in the back of my head— 'an' it ain't kind'. He said it ain't kind. What did he mean by that? What's all that bullshit with the salt?"

"And the cage."

"And the cage," Cory repeated. "And you said something about his dog dying?"

"Yeah. I really felt bad for him. That must have hurt. He said he found Scrub dead on the porch when he woke up. He nailed Scrub's tag to the floor alongside his rocker. Said Scrub and that tag had laid at his feet for fourteen years. The tag made him feel good when he smoked his pipe and looked down at it."

"I suppose it's no different than looking at a photograph of your wife or kid."

"I guess," said Cristina. "Makes sense. It was just the two of them for a long, long time. Dad said he isn't about to get another dog."

"How did the dog die?"

Cristina frowned.

"You know... dad never really told me. He just said he woke up and found Scrub dead on the porch. He said he didn't want to talk about it."

Cory's mind finally put together a puzzle that was embarrassingly simple. He sat in the Blazer and stared at Cristina. He looked to be in shock.

"Why are you looking at me like that?"

"His dog died on the porch?"

"Yeah. So what?"

"Your last name is Walker. Cristina Walker."

"Yes."

"Sonovabitch. I don't believe it."

"You don't believe what?"

"Walker is your married name."

"Yeah. Why wouldn't you believe that?"

"Oh, for Christ's sake. Cristina, what's your maiden name?"

"McGrath."

"Christ almighty. *McGrath?!* I don't believe it. I *don't* believe it."

Cory's face fell forward. He closed his eyes and shook his head.

"There a problem with that? Oh, geez! Don't tell me. We're first cousins or something."

"Cristina. Is Jack McGrath your father?"

"Yes."

"Jesus jenny. I don't believe it," Cory whispered to himself. He looked over to Cristina. "Do you know that it was your father who

215

*first* went to the authorities and reported something strange going on in the swamp? They laughed him out of the place. He found his dog dead on the porch half-digested or rotted away in the space of hours. He never told you about any of that?"

"No. He never said a word other than Scrub had died. He made it very clear; he did not want to discuss it. He said it depressed him."

"He probably didn't want you to think he was crazy. Can't blame him for that. Everybody else did. Listen, do me a favor and don't mention any of this to your dad. I don't want to upset him. I'm sure he'll fill you in when he's ready. If now was the time, he would have done it to explain stringing that deer up across the swings. Let's just keep this between us, okay?"

"Okay. But what's the deer got to do with this?"

"Don't you see? He's baiting. But not for fish. He's looking to catch a monster. *'Something's out there and it ain't kind'.* Cristina... your old man's fishing for a monster."

## 30

"Ah, shit. It's startin' to drizzle."

"For cripes sakes, Jim. Ya got them hundred dollar fancy-ass waders an' you're complaining about drizzle. You are kidding, right?"

"Waders are meant for water coming up, not down."

"Oh, c'mon, it ain't that bad yet. If it rains, we'll call it a night."

Bob eased his pickup cautiously through the trees.

"Are ya sure we're still on a gas road?" asked Jim.

"I'm thinkin' this hasn't been road for quite some time."

"Okay then, two-track, trail, whatever."

Jim strained to assess the ground across which Bob was driving.

216

"I'm not sure if the trail goes in this far or not. I was back in this area a couple of weeks ago. Trouble is, when it's nighttime nothin' looks the same. We should be comin' up to water just ahead."

"Just don't drive us into any quicksand," said Jim.

"Quicksand? What the hell are you talkin' about? There ain't any quicksand around here. This ain't a bog, you idiot. It's a swamp."

"Meaning what?"

"Meaning, how long you lived here? This ground is flooded. You know that. It's hard."

"No, it's *supposed* to be hard. It started out hard. And right now, you wouldn't know any of that by looking at it."

"Maybe so, but…. There's the water."

Bob stopped the truck. He left it running so the headlights would not drain the battery. Both men climbed out and grabbed their waders from the box. They worked their way into the gear.

"What's that smell?" asked Jim.

"No idea. Ya ready to go?"

"Yeah."

Jim fastened the clasp on his waders and reached for his raincoat.

"Got your gun?"

"Do now."

"Don't forget your flashlight."

"Bo, I swear to god, you're worse than my wife."

"How would ya know that? I never slept with ya."

"*Shee-yut-up.*" Jim drew out the syllables to express his revulsion.

Bob laughed aloud. "Let's leave the flashlights off for a couple of minutes after I kill the headlights, okay? I want my eyes to adjust."

"All right."

Bob reached across the driver's seat and grabbed hold of the ignition keys. He shut off the engine and then the truck's lights. A brief silence followed.

217

"I can't even see my stupid nose," said Jim.

"Cloud cover. No stars. Nothin' but drizzle."

"Lord. It's dark out here."

"Dark an' quiet."

"Dark, quiet, an' smelly," Jim complained.

"You sound like one of those EPA tree huggers."

"Oh, and you think it smells good out here? The place smells like an industrial cesspool. Why did you decide to hunt here?"

"Hey, I didn't smell anything when I was out here yesterday."

"And now?"

"And now it smells like hell."

"Thank you for that."

The two men remained fixed in position, awaiting something to take shape.

"I don't think we're gonna see anything without the flashlights," said Jim.

"I don't know. Give it a minute. I can see something. What's that over there?"

"Seriously? Like I would know where you're looking," said Jim.

"Straight ahead of the truck. Out over the water. See it?"

"See what?"

"That light. Don't ya see it?"

"I don't see anything. I just smell something nasty," said Jim.

"Straight ahead, over the water. See it? It's real faint. Kind of a bluish light. Reminds me of those glow-in-the-dark toys we used to play with as kids. Can't you see it out there?"

"Oh, yeah. I'm beginning to see it now. It's taking a while for my eyes to adjust."

"Probably the mist makes it hard to see."

"What d'you suppose that is?" asked Jim.

"Who knows? Probably plankton-like shit. Lot of that stuff glows."

"Huh. I guess. So, what's the plan?"

218

Bob turned on his flashlight. The beam zeroed in on a rise in the distance.

"You see that rise?" he asked.

"Yeah."

"I dumped a couple of bags of carrots an' corn over there. Thought we'd head that way and see what happens."

"Are ya shittin' me, Bo? You wanna wade across all that water now?"

"Why not?"

"I'd think twice about doin' that in the middle of the day, let alone middle of the night."

"What's the difference?"

"The difference is I don't generally fall flat on my ass trippin' over roots an' shit in the middle of the day. Besides what if a bear comes calling and you're way the hell over there?"

"You're not really worried about running into a bear, are ya?"

"Yeah, really I am."

"What is it with you and bears? You honestly think there's bear around here? You're kidding me, right?"

"You know, Bo, for someone who's just explained the intricacies of a swamp versus a bog, you of all people, should understand it's not like we're sittin' in McDonald's."

"Uh-huh."

"That just reminded me, I was reading a DNR report the other day that said hunters pulled something like five hundred bear outta this swamp back in nineteen forty-six."

"Well, for cripes sakes, no wonder you're going on about bears. That's what you get for reading that crap. Nineteen forty-six? That was a century ago."

"I know that. I'm just sayin'."

"Well, you tell me, Jim. What do *you* wanna do? Go home because we might run into a bear, or hunt? We sure ain't shooting any deer standin' in this spot."

"Bo, I have no desire to wade through the shallows. You go right ahead. I'm gonna stay on the high ground and walk that-a-ways."

Jim pointed his flashlight along the water's edge at his left. The light dissolved into the distance.

"I got no problem with that. Lemme check your two-way." Bo triggered his two-way radio and listened to it click on Jim's handset. "Sounds good. All right, I'll be just across the shallow, just over that rise where I dumped the carrots. The whole bank is pretty much surrounded by water so I can't go too far. I'll look for a good place to sit and wait out the deer, and if I need something, I'll get you on the two-way."

"Sounds like a plan. Keep the water out of your waders—don't drown yourself. I don't wanna have to go in there and fish you out."

"Ha! That'll be the day."

Jim stood his ground and kept his flashlight trained on Bob and the surrounding water. He had no desire to see his friend trip as he maneuvered his way through the submerged roots and vegetation. When Bob reached the far side of the shallows, he turned to Jim and waved.

Jim lowered his light away from Bob's eyes. As he swung the beam to his left, he got a final glimpse of Bob turning away to head through the reeds and up the shallow bank of the rise.

Studying the less formidable ground at his feet, Jim began walking carefully through the scrub and trees until he found a place that appeared to have a deer run. He spied a raised root that would make a comfortable seat high enough off the ground to keep his butt dry.

Jim sat back and sucked himself into his raincoat. He worked to evade the damp. He took one last look around and then turned off his flashlight. It was so dark in the mist-enshrouded swamp that he found himself annoyed with Bob's adamancy about poaching this night instead of waiting for things to dry out a bit.

Jim let loose a deep breath. He closed his eyes and occupied himself by mentally working out solutions to the everyday problems of family life. At the same time, he devoted an ear to catching any sound of rustling within the brush.

After about ten minutes, for no reason other than reassurance, Jim opened his eyes and looked around. He was surprised to see the soft blue light emanating from the water over in the direction of the truck. His eyes were now sensitive to light, and so the glow appeared relatively bright. It was exceptionally serene and mesmerizing. He sat motionless, peacefully staring at the cool liquid luminescence.

As Jim stared numbly at the glow, a disturbance in the underbrush grabbed his attention. The commotion intensified and surrounded him like the large swell of a wave. The ruckus reached him from every direction. First, he thought a rafter of turkeys was passing through, but he knew better. Turkeys would not be on the ground this late at night; they would be up in the trees. He quickly ruled out deer. This was not the sound of deer.

Growing anxious, Jim switched on his flashlight. He swept the ground before him. Out of the corner of his eye, he caught a glimpse of what he first assumed were shadows adding movement to a large root. The shock was profound when he fully appreciated how large was the root slithering toward his legs. Leaping up like a scared cat, he was instantly on his feet.

"Ugg. Frickin' eh."

Jim shivered as he imagined a snake of that size crawling across his legs. Frantically, he searched the ground with his light, but as fast as the serpent appeared, it disappeared. Jim snapped his beam of light back and forth in quick succession until he no longer saw any further signs of snakes or unwanted company.

Slowly, Jim twisted around to scrutinize the underbrush with a flood of light. Only when feeling confident that nothing else was slinking about did he settle enough to sit back down. He continued to pay close attention to his surroundings, and when satisfied all seemed well, he extinguished the flashlight.

Jim sat in silence for almost ten minutes before he realized that in spite of his listening effort, he not only heard nothing of nighttime creatures, he heard absolutely nothing at all. He closed his eyes and became obsessed with the silence. He concentrated on sounds. There was none of the normal buzz of swamp life. It was eerily quiet, enough so that the silence held his attention as profoundly as the prior commotion. He blamed the mists for muffling the louder sounds of the swamp, let alone the purr of a million invisible creatures.

Jim was feeling unsettled. He worked to dismiss his uneasiness, blaming it on a restless imagination. He leaned back against the tree and focused on the soothing blue glow. He felt the tension leave his shoulders. At least the silent glow was relaxing.

## 31

When Jim awoke, he snapped upright. His head also snapped. It went left to right and back, repeatedly. His eyes darted in every direction as if he was expecting an attack. He had no recollection of falling asleep. He raced to gain his senses as the echoes of a most horrid scream dissipated in his ears. He was full of adrenaline, and his skin was drawn tight with fright. His mind raced to assess his situation, and once he realized that he was alive and well, his next overriding thought was the well-being of Bob. His hands raced across his belly in search of the two-way.

"Bo. You there? Bo.... Hey, Roberto.... You there...?"

Everything went on hold for Jim as he focused on his two-way. He carefully depressed the button as far as it would travel.

"Bob? Bob, you there?" The first wave of mild concern crept over him. "Bo... don't be screwin' with me, man. You there?"

Nothing. Jim released the button. He laid his head back against the tree. It was possible that Bob had turned off his two-way because deer had strayed in close and he did not want the two-way sounding off to spook them. It was possible.

It was also possible that Jim had not actually heard anything. But it felt like he had. He felt chilled by a sensation that haunted him. Had he been dreaming? He did not think so. His body acted as if he had heard something unsavory. He wanted to believe it was an owl, or a fox—a vixen's call that worked its way into his dream. Whatever it was, the questionable blood-curdling cry was enough to cause his heart to race. He activated the two-way.

"Bo! ...Bob?"

Jim had no recollection of hearing a gunshot. He had no recollection of hearing anything. Even now it was uncomfortably silent. He was growing anxious. His obsession with prowling bears only added to his uneasiness. He listened to the night with full attention. It was inexplicably silent—unnervingly silent. He fought every urge to call Bob again. He did not want to piss him off.

Jim listened intently for ten long minutes, all of which seemed an eternity. He did not hear so much as the crack of a twig. There might have been only silence and blackness had it not been for an insufferable odor. It was that mildly pungent, somewhat acrid smell, which was hard to get out of the sinuses.

Jim raised the cuff of his jacket to look at his watch. It was just shy of three in the morning. With reluctance, he raised the two-way to his mouth.

"Bob.... Do you read me, Bob? Bob? If you're screwin' with me Bo, you're pissin' me off. Ya hear me? Bo? Bo?"

Jim had his fill. He was annoyed. Was the radio working or not? If it was, then he had three possibilities to consider. One, Bob was screwing with him. Two, Bob was in trouble. Or three, and most probable, Bob was sawing logs. It bordered insult to think Bob was in trouble, so Jim was unconcerned. Bob was more than just familiar with the area; he poached it regularly at night.

Jim stood up from the tree root and peered into the dark. Losing contact with Bo was the last straw, and so he decided to walk back to the truck. Between a potentially faulty two-way and this *thing* he had about meandering bears, sitting inside the cab seemed the perfect solution. He was tired, and to his way of thinking, no matter what Bob might think, dozing off out in the open was just plain stupid. Visions of the snake came to mind, which he replaced immediately with visions of the truck. He switched on the flashlight. The light was harsh until his eyes adjusted. He focused on the ground, stepping with care over the roots, and through the thickets, as he made his way back.

When the reflection of the pickup flashed before the beam of light, Jim breathed easier. A couple of hundred feet more and he was standing outside the passenger door. He opened the door. He reached inside and flipped on the headlights. He scoured the shallows one last time. A mist was rising off the pools of water and clouding the view.

Jim turned to look behind. He felt as if something was watching him. The feeling compelled him to climb out of his waders and raincoat quickly. He tossed his gear behind the seat and climbed into the cab. He pulled the door shut. He studied the shadows behind the truck.

Jim reached over and locked the driver's door. He locked his door and then let out a deep breath. He stared into the swath of light beyond the windshield.

"Where the hell are you, Bob? You shithead."

Jim brought the two-way up to his lips.

"Bob.... Bob, can ya hear me, you sonovabitch. Quit fuckin' around and answer me." He waited. "Fine. I'm in the truck. If I don't answer it's because I'll be sleepin'."

Jim sighed. He was disturbed. Too tired to think, he stared mindlessly out the windshield. He had no desire whatsoever to wade through the shallows looking for Bob. He told Bob nighttime was no time to be walking through the water. Too many roots, too much stuff to trip over. He told him. Besides, the whole area smelled obnoxious, and you could not see where it was coming from or what was causing it.

"Screw it."

Jim reached up and flipped off the truck's headlights. He adjusted the seat back to recline. He laid back. He sat motionless, staring out into the swamp as his eyes slowly adjusted to the dark. His eyes perceived light to his side. He knew that peripheral vision always served him better in the dark. With every passing minute, his peripheral vision expanded until his primary vision took over.

Jim grew enraptured by the vision unfolding before his eyes. The darkness had given way to a world of blue light that moved in waves and pulses across the water. His mind stalled; his thoughts hung suspended as he gave in to the soothing sensation. The scene about the shallows was enchanting, unlike anything he had ever experienced.

Jim was not the least bit frightened. He understood that nature was a cornucopia of wondrous things if one only took the time to investigate. He laid his head back on the seat and watched the patterns and rhythms until his eyes grew heavy. The spectacle outside erased his concerns about Bob or anything else. His mind was blank and filled with peace. Nothing could have better prepared him to sleep.

"Sleep tight, Bo."

## 32

Jim grit his teeth while slowly twisting his head around. His neck was painfully stiff from being wedged for hours between the headrest and window. He opened his eyes and saw the pale gray light of dawn passing through windows completely covered with fog, both inside and out. He rubbed the glass. The view improved little.

As soon as Jim was reasonably awake and thinking, he realized Bob had not returned to the truck. Everything about that fact made him uncomfortable. He refused to believe harm had come to Bob, but warranted or not, Bob's absence raised all manner of concern. Red flags were flying in Jim's mind.

Jim opened the truck door so the cooler outside air would hasten clearing sleep from his head. He could feel the hot and cold currents push and pull as they mixed. He rolled his head around to work out what stiffness remained, and then stepped outside to straighten out his legs. He glanced around, but his gaze quickly settled on the rise of ground across the water. It was there that he had last seen Bob. He yelled in that direction.

"Bob!" He listened. "Bob!"

Jim reached back to the truck seat and grabbed the two-way. He pressed the transmit button.

"Bob? ...Bob, can ya hear me? Bob? Are you awake? Bob? Bob?"

Finding himself on perpetual hold, Jim slid his forefinger back and forth across his lips as he contemplated what to do next. The morning was not off to a good start.

"Shit. Well... at least it stopped drizzling."

Like it or not, it was time to hunt Bob down. Jim reached behind the seat, grabbed his waders, and climbed into them. He closed the truck door, and started toward the shore. He was feeling resigned as he stared down at the water. It was black and opaque. Morning light washed across the surface, forming large silvery sheets that reflected a featureless gray sky and the webbing of tree branches like a fluid mirror.

Jim focused on the rise of the opposite bank. He estimated its distance and then disrupted the water's glassy surface with his foot. His waders disappeared into the black. There was no seeing deeper, not until the sun moved overhead, but he knew the swamp walk—shuffle-shuffle-shuffle. Sliding one foot ahead of the next, he moved cautiously forward, feeling out the roots and tangle of dead limbs and vegetation. It was slow going.

About midway, the water approached his waist. He was in no hurry, and proceeded with care.

"Shuffle-shuffle-shuffle, and stay dry, shuffle-shuffle-shuffle, and stay dry," he repeated.

The water slowly receded, dropping below his waist, dropping down to ripple midway on his thighs. Jim looked back up at the rise ahead. It was only about thirty feet away. With care, he continued to navigate the underwater obstacles. The surface of the water displayed its disapproval by cracking into smaller erratic fragments of silvery-mirrored light.

Jim had moved only a short distance farther when he noted the water displayed something else—an unusual phenomenon. An area of about fifteen or twenty square feet before him was effervescing. The spectacle was peculiar, and unlike anything he had ever witnessed. It immediately brought to mind the blue glow he had observed the night before. He had never seen anything like that either.

Jim stood in place wondering whether to walk through the soft fizz. He questioned if the ground had changed in some fashion. He wondered if it had gone soft, if it had turned into quicksand or something full of air and gas. He moved his foot forward cautiously, testing the earth that he could not see.

As he approached the fizz, he understood at once from where the horrible smell emanated.

"Ohhh, lord."

Jim figured there was oil or gas underground. He turned his face away to take his next breath. Even that was not about to prevent the discomfort in his nose. He held his breath, while hurriedly poking around with his foot, testing the firmness of the soil and navigating the roots and obstructions. It was nearly impossible to find a clear path through the underwater debris. He bumped his toes back and forth and finally felt his way across the top of the entanglement. He stopped moving forward, distracted by bubbling that ever so lightly disturbed the water's placid surface.

Inquisitive about the source, Jim strained to see below the surface. The early morning light was intensifying as if to help, but was disappointingly slow. The bubbling broke up the reflective surface and allowed a single ray to reach deep enough to bounce off an object and return a sparkle to the surface. It disappeared and reappeared between surface reflections, but remained pronounced enough to capture his curiosity.

Jim was sidetracked from his mission by this small find. He gasped for another breath and held it. He brought his face down to within inches of the water and studied the flicker below. He had no desire to plunge his arm into the smelly, dark, bubbling water. He glanced about and reached for a branch that had fallen from above to impale the muck. It stood straight up as if waiting for him to happen by.

Jim pulled it free and began poking about the entanglement that trapped the miniature treasure. After a bit of careful prodding, pushing, and pulling, he hooked enough debris to raise the jewel up to the surface. It broke free of the water and revealed itself. A watch still fastened about the boney wrist of a skeleton.

"Frickin' eh!"

The shock was overwhelming.

"Shit!"

Panic drove Jim to let loose of the branch. The watch and bones sank from sight. Instinctively, he sloshed a couple of steps backward. To his benefit, a quick wit suppressed the urge to run through the stained water. He had no desire to go head under next to a skeleton. Simultaneously, he had seen enough of the arm to realize this was a person long dead and not about to give him any trouble. It came as a shock, but nothing more. He was okay. It was only a matter of taking a breath of decent air, and a moment to regain his composure.

"Frickin' eh, that was a rush."

Jim could feel his heart racing. The only thing racing faster was his thoughts. It would have been a bad enough fright in the company of friends, but being alone wading suspiciously through a swamp, wondering what happened to your best friend—that was altogether a different animal. He turned his head away to take another breath. He gave himself a little more time to relax.

Jim built up his confidence by first understanding that a corpse belonging to Bob would look blue and sickly white. It would be ghastly looking and bloated according to every cop show he'd ever seen on TV. And you didn't have to be a forensic expert to know that bones stripped clean of flesh must have been submerged for months or maybe years. Jim believed his assessment to be accurate, because cop shows always depicted events as close to reality as possible.

The shock was wearing off. Emboldened by the facts, Jim stepped closer. He bent over for another look, moving his head from side to side in order to see beneath the surface reflections. The morning light was yet too dim to reveal anything under the water. He no longer saw the reflection of the watch. This time instead of feelings of panic or dread, Jim simply accepted his responsibility to notify the authorities of human bones once he and Bob returned to town. His fears were also somewhat diminished by believing he was about to become a mini-celeb. He would be on the local news by day's end.

There was nothing else to be done here, so his thoughts returned to locating Bob, now more than ever. He was impatient. A smile crept across his face. He wondered if Bob walked over the skeleton last night. Bob was going to lose it when he got a load of this.

Jim began to wonder what he would have done if the body had been Bob's. He entertained himself with inner thoughts of telling the public how his best friend had disappeared and was then discovered drowned the following morning.

"I swear before God and all things holy, *I didn't do it.*"

Jim dismissed any further poisonous thoughts along that line, and moved to step carefully over the remains and make his way to the rise. He looked back once while making his way to shore, and once again after standing on the bank. The skeleton made him feel as though a ghost was keeping tabs on him.

Jim set out walking the length of the rise, some hundred yards along the water's edge until reaching its end. From there, he looked out across another expanse of uninviting sphagnum, sedges, and swamp. It was obvious that there was no place for Bob to continue walking farther, certainly not in the middle of the night, and the realization chilled him. He swallowed hard.

Jim started back along the opposite bank, searching the narrow strip of soggy ground. It occurred to him that, whereas there was no sign of Bob, there were bones lying around everywhere he looked. The place was a natural graveyard. The ever-present odor was getting on his nerves. It filled his sinuses. It irritated his lungs. Even in the light of day, everything about the place was truly unpleasant and disconcerting.

Walking the entire perimeter of the rise, and returning to his start point, Jim took one last look in and around the thickets. He then looked back across the shallows toward the truck. There was no sign of Bob. The sun had risen high enough to burn off the mist and brighten his surroundings. He was confused and nervous. He reached for the two-way. He was beginning to assume the worse even before calling out, but it had to be done. It was his only hope. He applied pressure to the button.

"Bob, do ya read me? Can ya hear me? Listen, click your button if you can hear my voice."

Jim waited. He stared at the collection of holes covering the small two-way speaker. Silence. It was not that he thought there would be a different outcome, but it was more about taking time, time to figure out what he was supposed to do. The idea of going back into town alone did not sit well with him. He was not one to abandon a friend or a stranger for that matter, but it was obvious something had gone wrong. There was only soggy rises and water. Bob was nowhere to be seen standing on the rises. That only left the water.

The thought brought Jim back around to the submerged body, or even more dreadful—the possibility of two submerged bodies. He began to wonder what might have caused the submerged stranger's death. He next wondered if the same thing might have brought harm to Bob. He scrubbed his memory for a clue, but only one thing stood out. That god-awful smell.

It was one thing to find a skeleton of somebody you would never recognize, but if he were to see Bob lying beneath the surface, he would totally lose it. He was not in a frame of mind to start fishing around the shallows looking for his best friend's corpse. Chills ran down Jim's back as he imagined Bob looking up at him from within the sunken leaf-covered branches and roots.

Jim stepped off the bank and carefully gained his footing as he moved back across the shallow and toward the truck. He watched for the fizzing water. The effervescence marked the location of the remains. The swirl of fizz utterly baffled him—so did the biting fumes. Now that the morning light was reasonable, the form of a body was somewhat more visible just ahead of him.

He pinched his nose as he leaned over and looked into the depths. The details of the skeleton were hidden beneath disturbed leaves and rotting vegetation. Only the skull was distinguishable. At least it was not Bob. That realization made him wonder if he had the balls to search for a wallet or some form of identification. He stepped closer.

Jim reached into his waders so he could retrieve his handkerchief. He wadded it up against his nose to alleviate the discomforting smell. He then peered down through the leg-deep water. He stared for however long it took to gather details. He knew better than to disturb the setting. The police would not be happy with that, so he just studied what lay before him.

Jim wondered what happened to the bones wrapped by the wristwatch. He broadened his search. The brighter light of day was beginning to illuminate the bottoms. It was because of that, Jim zeroed in on the hard lines of a gun barrel. It took a few more minutes for him to separate the camouflaged raincoat and waders from the surrounding branches and leaves that littered the bottom and cradled this corpse.

Jim felt a tightness in his neck. He placed his hand below the back of his skull and rolled his head. He removed his hand and noticed that he was shaking. He stared at his hands and then back down at the skull. All the skin on his neck and arms turned to gooseflesh. In one simultaneous rush of deduction, he assembled the fragments of images before him—the gun, the camouflaged waders and raincoat—the truth. Against all possible rational explanations, he was standing over the remains of his closest friend.

Jim's throat closed off. He choked. In a state of horror, he gaped at the white skull looking up at him. Against all instinct, he stepped over the corpse and plowed through the water. He tripped and stumbled repeatedly until nearly falling into the murky shallows. He regained his balance only enough to carry him haphazardly to the bank, where he fell flat on his face, but he was spared the dunking he so tried to avoid.

On shore, Jim raced for the truck. He yanked off his waders, and tossed them into the pickup bed. He jumped into the driver's seat. Before his thoughts could catch up with him, he reached

231

for the key. There was no key. Bob had the keys. The keys were in one of Bob's pockets.

Jim understood his options. Go back into the shallows and rifle through Bob's pockets or walk the many miles back to town. He looked across the water to that place bubbling just above Bob's remains. He shuddered. He struggled to grapple with what he knew. There was nothing there but bones. How could that be? Nothing but bones in hours. Why was his best friend fizzing like a Mentos lying at the bottom of a lake of Coke? The entire incomprehensible mess rattled him to his core.

Jim jumped out of the truck and started running. He felt the pressure of Bob's ghost pushing him to run faster. He followed trampled grass and tire tracks that led him to the trail, which led him to the gas road, which led him to public road. He ran. All the while, he looked back over his shoulder.

Jim ran until it came down to stopping or vomiting, at which point, he dropped to his knees. He pitched forward onto all fours. He allowed himself to slowly collapse to the ground. He closed his eyes and concentrated on his breathing. His chest burned painfully; it heaved; it pitched him up and down. He gulped air. He opened his eyes and looked to his side only to acknowledge a car pulling up.

## 33

"Hello."

"Cory, this is Harold. How ya doin'?"

"Fine. What's up?"

"This is red hot. Toby Quinn just called me. He's been dispatched to the Conner place out on Root Road, you might know it as the end of Robinson Lake Road."

"I remember it. Ends at the swamp."

"Exactly. Address is 1420, borders the Roscommon State Forest."

"What's going on?"

"Guy by the name of Jim Conner just got home. Wife called the deputy saying her husband is hysterical. Said his best friend is dead in the swamp. Said there's nothing left of him but bones. Toby is on his way over there now."

"Bones? Are you kidding me? Christ, I'm so sick of bones that—"

"Hey, don't forget you're the one who said bones are big."

"Sonovabitch, I did say that. Yes. I guess I did. So... Quinn'll let me in?"

"Yeah, he's waitin' for you."

"I'm on my way. I'll get back to you as soon as I got something."

"Great. I'm holding the presses. Hurry up."

Cory pressed the CONTACTS icon on his phone. He pressed the CALL icon.

"Hello."

"Hey, Cri. This is Cory. Say, you said you were a nurse. You ready for another date? You know it won't be boring."

"Oh, geez. What now? I'm afraid to ask."

"Guy's going crazy. Says his best friend's lying at the bottom of the swamp. Says there's nothing left but bones."

"Bones again? Does this not end?"

"You gotta wonder, don't you? So, what d'you say? You interested?"

"Interested? You mean like being offered front row seats in a traveling freak show? That kind of interested?"

"So that's a 'yes'?"

"Your intuition is uncanny. Really, it is. Okay, I'm in. Maybe I can get the guy some meds to settle him down. I'll stop by the pharmacy at Walmart for something over-the-counter."

"Great, but you gotta leave now. Quinn's meeting me, and Harold's holding the presses. I'll be waiting for you in the parking lot."

"I'm leaving now."

233

Cory knew he should have gone to the Conner place straight away. Every minute counted, but if there was any excuse for him to see Cristina again, he'd be giving it every chance. In the meantime, he would arrive at Walmart first, and that would give him time to work up an outline for his newspaper article.

Cory spotted the old brown Ford pickup coming west off 127 almost as soon as it left the exit and started toward the parking lot. He recognized it at once as the truck belonging to Roadkill Ralph, but paid a great deal more attention when it pulled up and parked alongside him. To his surprise, the grizzled face of Roadkill Ralph was looking over at him. The man got out of his truck, and looked across the bed toward his passenger.

Cory's eyes followed Roadkill Ralph's gaze, and he was astonished to see Cristina walking around the back of the truck. She opened Cory's passenger door.

"Hi. Cory, this is my father, Jack McGrath."

"No shit."

"I beg your pardon?"

Cory called out over Cristina's shoulder.

"I'm pleased to meet you, Mr. McGrath."

"Pleasure's mine. How 'bout we dispense with the Mr. McGrath crap an' call me Jack."

"Jack it is."

"I hope ya won't blame Cri for my bein' here. I 'bout had to hogtie her until she quit fightin' me an' agreed t' take me along. I know I'm bargin' in, an' I'm sorry, but I'll get to the point. Cri told me that you put two an' two together an' figured out I was her ol' man. She said you knew about my little outburst at the sheriff's office."

"Jack, fact is I didn't give it a second thought, but I should have. I can tell you that now. Cost me my *gold star detective* pin."

"Yeah, I'll bet that hurt. Listen to me, Cory. I'm mighty interested in what's goin' on around the swamp these days. Especially when it has to do with the—*viola*—body t' bones bit. For too long, there's been things goin' on around here that just ain't natural."

234

"Hallelujah. You got that right. Get in you two, we gotta hustle." Cory wondered what a gold mine of great stories the old man must be. "So, you're Cristina's dad. I about fell over when I figured that out."

"That I am, an' damned proud of it. Don't get to see much of her, but she sure is good to me when she stops by. Does the heart good to see a smilin' face now an' then."

"You need to get out of that swamp, dad."

"Sweetheart, I've lived the whole of my life in that swamp. I'll probably end it there."

"That's what I'm afraid of. By the looks of things that might be sooner than later. You'll end up a pile of bleached bones and nobody will have a clue for half a year. Face it, dad, you're not one to call, and if you don't, I have no idea how you're doing. Nobody does."

"And aside from you, nobody cares. Mercy me, girl, I'm just one old man in a world that presses forward without a care about what's left behind. I was no different when I was young. I didn't give a hoot about the world then, an' the world don't give a hoot about me now."

Cristina looked at Cory.

"Hit him, will you? I don't care how old he his. He needs some sense pounded into him."

Cristina shook her head in exasperation while Cory and Jack had a good laugh.

"Where exactly are we headed?" asked Jack.

"Just up the road. Not far. The Conner place, 1420 Root."

"Root, huh? That'll take ya in pretty deep if you stay with it."

"I don't think we're going in that far. Harold said across from the state forest."

"Oh. It's been a while since I've been out this way. Things sure change."

"How's that?"

"Got houses, buildings. Never used to be anything around here but oil wells an' hauntings."

235

"Hauntings?"

"Oh, you know—trails. We used to follow some of them trails 'til they wound down to paths made by deer an' bear. You'd get so far back in that swamp that you'd get spooked. Ain't a man alive that didn't. You were always haunted by what ya couldn't see. Bear watching ya, wolves watching ya, spirits of the dead watchin' ya, and god only knows what else. We called them old footpaths *hauntings*. After the flooding, some guys called them old two-tracks that disappeared beneath the swamp water 'hauntings'.as well."

"Now that you mention it, I recall hearing that term in my younger years. Ahhh.... I think we're here. This should be it."

A sheriff's patrol car was clearly visible from the road. Cory pulled into the driveway. He drove cautiously toward the house. The place appeared run down. It looked like most other places in the county. A residence owned by an unfortunate with no work, no income. A homeowner who got by however he could, sometimes legally, sometimes not.

Detective Sergeant Quinn suddenly appeared. He was scrunching his shoulders in an attempt to position his jacket. He stepped out from the back door of the house and came walking toward Cory's vehicle. Cory rolled the window down.

"Toby."

"I see Harold got a hold of you."

"Yeah. We got here as fast as we could. Toby, this is Jack McGrath, Cristina's father."

Toby leaned down to look through the window.

"Mr. McGrath," Toby chuckled. "Forgive me, sir. But your reputation precedes you."

"I'm sure that's a fact at the sheriff's department."

They shared a friendly laugh.

"Listen all. I know you wanna ask questions and I'm not gonna tell you not to, but I'm asking that you tread very lightly. The guy's mighty upset. I understand that the alleged missing individual was his best friend, a lifelong buddy."

236

"Have you located the body?" asked Cory.

"Not yet. Officers are en route."

"Have they been warned about exposure to the water?"

"They've been instructed to take all necessary precautions."

"Good. That's good."

"Officer Quinn?" Cristina spoke up. "Do you recall my being a nurse?"

"I do."

"I'd be happy to check your man over if you wish. I brought along some mild sedatives that might be a big help."

"Wonderful. Why don't you follow me back to the house? Settling him down before any more questioning can't hurt. I'm going to ask the two of you to wait out here until I call you in."

"No problem," said Cory.

Cristina got out of Cory's vehicle and walked off with the detective sergeant. They disappeared inside the house, leaving Cory and Jack sitting awkwardly next to each other in momentary silence. Cory made the first effort to break the ice.

"So, Jack, may I ask why such interest in this?"

"You mean, about what's goin' on between you an' my daughter?"

"Oh, Christ, no!" Cory spun around to look at Jack with an expression of outright shock.

"I'm kiddin' ya, Cory. Mercy me, my daughter's fifty years old."

It took Cory a second or two to piece himself back together before he started to laugh. Jack broke into a broad grin.

"You got me. I admit it. You got me good. You kicked my ass clear back to high school. Wow." Cory was still grinning as he shook his head in wonder. "I can't remember the last time I felt nervous in front of a gal's old man."

"No point in startin' now."

"I suppose not. Funny, isn't it? How we grow up too fast to think of ourselves as old. I don't know if our brains ever get it. We daydream about bar fights and kicking ass, and we can't even

237

walk out to the mailbox and back without getting our own asses kicked. Pathetic."

"Every age has its awakening."

"True enough. Anyhow, now that I stopped sweating the shotgun, getting back to my original question. Why such an interest in what's going on here?"

"I don't know that I had a choice. I've lived in or around this swamp the whole of my life. Lived at my current place for near fifty years, ever since Cristina was about three or four. You best believe I know the shallows around my place like the back of my hand. I know 'em well enough to know when somethin's amiss, when somethin's a kilter, when somethin' just plain ain't right."

"In what way? Why d'you say that? What ain't right?"

"Mmmmm. It's like when ya come down with a cold. It starts out with a feelin' that somethin's a little off. Ya say to yourself, I'm okay. I feel okay. You're goin' about your business, but you're thinkin', man, somethin' just don't feel right. It's kinda like that."

"I get what you're saying, Jack, but I need you to be more specific. In what way wasn't it right?"

"Oh, for example.... I've fished these waters far back as I can remember, an' I never recall there ever bein' a time when fish were scarce. Nowadays, I got all I can do to stick somethin' in the freezer. Never seen a year the freezer wasn't filled to the top, an' me not sellin' the remainder to restaurants. Always had more fish than I could eat. Always. Not anymore. Not as of late. No sir-ree. Not as of late."

"What's *as of late*, Jack?"

"Well, it's been getting progressively worse. I think I first noticed fishin' gettin' slow about, oh, mercy, better'n three years back. Yeah, I'd say all of that. Ya gotta understand, it wasn't like somethin' jumped out at me. It was more like a slow realization that the swamp was changin'. Changin' for the worse."

"But, Jack, something's gotta give you that gut feeling. It's like you say when you're coming down with something, you feel great except for the fact you're sneezing. It just hasn't hit. But you're starting to ask yourself, why am I sneezing? What was it that got you to thinking?"

"Well, the absence of fish was the first thing. I guess it really hit home when the amount of fish stashed in my freezer started slowly goin' down. That caught my attention. It was the first sign that I wasn't just imagining things. I could actually see it was gettin' worse. It stuck in the back of my head as I found myself wanderin' farther an' farther out into the swamp tryin' to catch fish. You gotta appreciate, I always fished off the dock. I never needed to get in a boat. For what?

"Then there was this one day. It was a day that I dismissed to the quirks of nature. It wasn't until later as I found myself questioning everything, that it slapped my ass silly and said, *'Wake up, Jack'*."

"Tell me about it."

"Ohhh, it was just an ordinary afternoon like a thousand others when I was out fishin' an' relaxing. On that day, I was a good ways up Dead Stream, near Cole Creek, too far up to see anything of the dam's backwaters. I got to enterin' a pool back in a little secluded area where I dropped anchor and.... And, I don't know how to explain it. I was back there an' all of a sudden it felt like my surroundings shifted. It wasn't somethin' that I could put my finger on. It was subtle, like a gentle pull on the anchor line. I noticed somethin', but I couldn't tell ya what—thought maybe I got a touch of vertigo.

"Anyhow, I just relaxed until the sensation passed. Figured maybe I just turned my head too fast or somethin' like that. So, I just went on fishin'. I was out there for a good hour or two when I spotted this commotion on the water. It was a bit upstream, not too far. I couldn't make out what it was, but I'll tell you this, it reached me fast.

"The fish big an' small were leaping outta the water. It wasn't a random act. It was like the roll of a wave. A tidal wave of leaping fish flyin' straight up out o' the water. I immediately gave thought to something movin' beneath the surface. I know I wasn't too far off the mark, because as the wave of fish passed by so did a rise in the water."

Jack stopped and stared directly at Cory in order to drive his next point home.

"You don't get swells on the surface waters of a swamp... ever. You understand? Never. But I felt the boat rise an' fall in sync with the passin' fish. The water following the swell, the water about my boat was fizzin', almost bubblin' in a way. Between the wave an' the air comin' up, I thought we had a goddamned earthquake. I thought it shook all the air an' gas out of the ground, out of the seaweed. It was the only thing I could figure.

"Trouble was there were other things that didn't figure. Like why was there suddenly so many dead fish floating by. I never caught another fish after that swell. And then I started noticing that fish comin' down from farther upstream were a mess. I mean, a real mess. I mean, they were scum-covered and fizzin'. Lots of them passin' by looked to be half-eaten or half-digested.

"I didn't know what to make of it. Like I said, maybe an earthquake, maybe all the fizzin' and bubbles were some kind of poisonous gas seeping outta the ground. One thing was for sure, the whole place smelled terrible. I thought maybe whatever caused the smell poisoned the fish, making them easy prey for lampreys. Them bastards can devour good fishin' grounds in a day or two, and so I cussed 'em out and let it go. I went home and never thought much about it again.

"That was until I woke up to find my dog, Scrub, dead on my porch. That changed everything. It wasn't just the look of Scrub. It took a bit for me to realize that was how all them fish looked in Dead Stream. It was more the smell that was workin' my brain. It was the smell that drove me to connect the dots. It connected my memories. I realized that same biting smell that was in the air on every occasion that things got weird or confusing to me.

"Later on, I began noticing other things—associations. Like, whenever I smelled that acrid odor, the swamp was quiet. There was hardly a sound whatsoever. You gotta understand, Cory, strangers think Dead Stream Swamp's exactly that... dead. A place no livin' creature cares to venture. A hellish place full of snakes and mysterious creatures that lie in wait. But if they lived in the swamp for any stretch of time, they'd discover it's full of life. Noisy life. Well, at least it used to be. Some places are fine; some are anything but—there's Cri."

Cory looked up. Cristina had stepped out of the house and was signaling them to come.

"I guess this is where it starts," said Cory.

The two men exited Cory's SUV and walked across the yard to join Cristina on the porch. She offered a suggestion.

"Go easy on him, Cory. He's upset. When I walked in, he was physically shakin' from shock. I gave him a couple of sedatives, and he's doing better, but don't get him worked up."

"I won't. I promise."

Cory and Jack followed Cristina into the house to where Detective Sergeant Quinn was standing in the living room. He nodded his approval for them to approach. Cristina spoke up.

"Jim, this is my father, Jack McGrath, and a friend, Cory Ballard. My father has been suspicious about changes in the swamp and very much wants to hear what you have to say. Mr. Ballard is an investigative reporter who has been working for the *County Chronicle* on this case. He would like to ask you a few questions, providing you feel up to it."

"What d'ya mean, workin' on this case?" asked Jim.

"If what you say proves true, then this isn't an isolated incident," said Cory. "Not by a long shot. I've been investigating dead cattle, dead or missing fishermen; we just had three children killed, and four teenagers, another three teenagers, there's talk of two missing girls. And now possibly your friend. You must have seen it on the news."

"You think this is the same thing," asked a bewildered Jim.

"No idea. What I'm trying to say is we've seen enough bizarre goings-on in this swamp to make anything you might tell us, no matter how outrageous, be given the benefit of the doubt. No one's about to call you crazy or a liar. At least nobody in this room."

"Okay. So, what d'ya wanna know?"

"I'm not sure what you've already told Detective Sergeant Quinn about this."

"Not much. He wanted to wait for you."

"I haven't asked him much more than the routine questions I need for my report," said Toby. "Mostly standing back while Ms. Walker got him settled. I thought I'd let you go ahead and ask away while I take notes. If there's anything I need, I'll step in. But understand that if I hear anything that may be self-incriminating, I will have to read him his rights, and we'll be stopping the questions right there."

"Got it." Cory turned toward Jim. "Well, Jim, I'd like to ask a few questions, some of which won't be comforting. You don't have to answer anything that upsets you. D'you understand? I know you've had a rough night, and the last thing I want to do is make things worse for you than they already are."

"Yeah. It's okay. I'm feelin' better now. The pills helped a lot."

"Good." Cory pulled out a small recorder. "Jim Conner, do I have your permission to record my questions and your answers?"

"Sure."

"Would that be a 'yes'?"

"Yes."

"Excellent. Now, tell me, Jim. What's your friend's name, and where do you believe he is at present?"

"Bo. We call him Bo. His real name is Bob or Robert Crandale."

"And where is Bo right now?"

A clear expression of grief moved across Jim Conner's face.

"You don't have to answer. If it's too uncomfortable, we'll pass."

"Nah. It's okay. He's in a shallow. Maybe two or three feet of water. It's way back in the flooding."

"Would you be able to take us back to him? So we can bring the body out?"

"I can take ya there, but there ain't no body."

"D'you mind explaining?"

"I'm saying there's no body—just bones. Bones, waders, and his gun."

242

"Did you see any signs of a struggle? Was the ground or surroundings disrupted in any way?"

"Ya wouldn't be able to tell 'cause he's underwater."

"So, Mr. Crandale was alone when he was in the shallows?"

"Yeah."

"So, why was *Bo* wading through the shallows and you weren't? I thought you guys were together."

"We were."

"But you didn't go into the shallows?

"No."

"Okay. Why don't you tell me what you guys were doing? Why did you split up?"

"We were out driving around. Had a couple of beers and decided to go scouting for places to hunt. You know places to put up tree stands and stuff like that."

Cory listened to Jim and quickly interrupted him, as he turned off his recorder.

"Listen, Jim. Before you go too far, I want you to know that I grew up in these parts, and I have to be straight with you. I never heard of anybody scouting hunting sites in the middle of the night. Drinking beer, hell yes. But scouting tree stands? Now, I have heard of folks poaching deer in the middle of the night, you know, way back in the swamp. Heard that a lot. I'm not saying that's what you were doing. But you just said one of the things I'd find was Bo's gun. I'm not sure why anybody'd need to carry a gun to pick out a tree. Why would two guys split up when they're drinking, or looking for a place to stick a tree stand? The only time guys split up is when they're hunting.

"You gotta be honest with me, Jim. Especially if you expect me, or any of us, to believe a story that might sound really off the wall to begin with. Understand, fact is, the more logical assumption would be an accident... or worse... foul play. That would be easier to believe than some far-fetched yarn. Foul play, Jim. Foul play. You see my point?"

Jim digested Cory's not-so-hidden warning. Cory turned the recorder back on and repositioned it.

"Fine. We were running low on food. Fishin's been for shit. Food stamps go just so far, an' neither one of us can afford to buy meat. Bo's single, but I got mouths to feed."

"Okay. So, you were on the lookout for deer."

"Yeah, I guess ya could think that."

"So, you guys head off to a place in the swamp that you're familiar with and then what?"

"We decided to split up."

"You decided to split up."

"Exactly. Bo wanted to follow a stretch of high ground that snaked northward, but he had to cross the shallows to get to it. I hate wadin' at night. Too easy to trip and fall in. So I stayed back and followed the bank southward. He went one way; I went the other."

"How d'you keep in contact? Cell phones?"

"No, man. Cell phones are too expensive to lose or drop in the drink. Besides, they're worthless once ya get back in there. We've always carried two-ways."

"What kind of range you getting with those?"

"I don't know, maybe half a mile if they're charged up good."

"So.... You boys split up. You hold back and walk south. Bo wades through the shallows and takes a dry bank that snakes northward."

"Yup."

"Then what?"

"Then nothin'. I'm not seeing a thing. In fact, I notice that the swamp is really quiet. I mean, like no sound at all. I probably could've heard a deer browsin' a mile off. I decided to sit down and wait. Trouble is, every time I do that at night, I fall asleep."

"Is that what you did?"

"Yeah. Something startled me and I woke up."

"You know what it was?"

"No. Might have been an owl. Maybe a fox."

"Then what?"

"Then I grabbed my two-way. I didn't know how long I'd been asleep. I tried calling Bo, but no answer. I tried a number of times. I figured he fell asleep."

"So, then what?"

"I got spooked. Not because of Bo, but because I fell asleep out in the open. I got this thing about bears. I know, stupid. What can I say? But, I wasn't about to go to sleep in the open again. So... I checked my watch again, and figured until I heard back from Bo, I'd go back to the truck and sleep."

"What time was that?"

"Ahh. Ten to three. Yeah, ten to three. I remember."

"So, it's ten to three in the morning and you didn't get concerned about Bo not answering you?"

"No, not at all. He knows the swamp, and I figured if there was something wrong, he'd have called me. I figured he didn't wanna give away his position by talking on the two-way. I figured he turned his radio off. Later, I figured the idiot fell asleep like me. Bo never worried about bear."

"What happened after that?"

"That was it. I told him I was heading back toward the truck. I didn't know if he'd hear me or not. I got to the truck and waited. I called him a couple of more times, but didn't get an answer."

"And you didn't think that was odd?"

"Sir, we're out there poachin'. He would've turned off the handset the instant he'd seen a deer or something to keep from spookin' it. To be honest, I climbed into the truck and dozed off before I knew it. It wasn't that big a deal. I mean, I was annoyed that he didn't call me first and say he was turning off his handset, or waiting so long to turn it back on. But Bo's like that. Unless, like I said, he fell asleep."

"And then?"

"And then I woke up and it was morning, early morning, hardly any light. That's when I started thinking, somethin's wrong.

That's when I got nervous. I couldn't imagine Bo sleeping in that late. It wasn't like he was in his bed, you know what I'm sayin'? I tried raising him on the two-way, but nothing. This time I figured it best I start lookin' for him. I climbed out of the truck and hollered five or six times, but he never answered.

"So, I started wadin' across the shallows. That was when I bumped into the skeleton. Scared the piss right outta me, but I didn't think for a minute it was Bo. There was nothing there but bones. I figured that thing must've been down there for months or years. Who the hell knows?

"I couldn't tell much because at first I couldn't see below the surface of the water. Just too dark. So, I just made note of its location and continued on lookin' for Bo. I followed the bank all the way around and realized there was nothing out there but water, and no place to go except back across the shallows to the truck. It was then that I began thinking about that skeleton.

"The second time I got a look, it was brighter outside. That time I saw Bo's gun and waders. I knew it was him. Don't ask me how, I know it sounds insane, but I'm telling ya if you go out there and bring him back, you'll see nothing but bones. But I'm telling ya, it's Bo."

"What did you do at that point? Why didn't you just drive back?"

"Well, once I realized it was Bo, I was so upset, all I wanted to do was get the hell back home. But I didn't have the keys to the truck. Bo did, and I wasn't about to search through his pockets. I thought about it for about a half a second. No way in hell. I dumped the waders and started running. I ran most of the way back, and then some guy picked me up and brought me home. And that's about it."

"Nothing else we should know about?"

"No, man. That's it. Believe me, that's enough."

Cory was satisfied. He looked over to Jack, who had taken in every minute detail, and now spoke up.

"Tell me somethin', Jim. Did ya happen to smell anything odd, or did ya happen to sense the water shift?" Anything like that?"

Jim thought a moment. His eyes narrowed.

246

"Yeah, I sure did. The air smelled weird all night. In fact, it smelled really nasty this morning around Bo's remains. You know like... ahh.... Well, it rather reminded me of ozone, no... maybe acid. I can't remember, but I figured it was connected to the oil wells."

"Anything unusual about the water, like maybe somethin' was swimmin' in it?"

"No. But it was too dark to see anything in the water."

"What about the next mornin' when you waded across the shallow?"

"I didn't see anything swimming in it, but I saw something else that was really strange. The water around Bo was sort of bubbling."

"What d'ya mean? Kind of like soda pop?"

"Yeah, a lot like soda pop. I remember thinkin' about people stickin' Mentos in Coke bottles. And the other thing I should've mentioned was that last night we both saw a blue glow in the water. Don't ask me what it was, I have no idea. But I watched it for some time. It pulsed in waves. I can't describe it. It was sort of like... I don't know. Like... fireflies. That was what it reminded me of. Fireflies. That glowing green. Only this was definitely blue."

Jim went silent.

"That's it for me," said Jack.

Nobody moved to continue the conversation, so Toby stepped forward.

"Okay. Folks, if I could ask you to excuse yourselves so that Mr. Conner and I can finish up some paperwork, we can catch up later."

"Absolutely."

The three excused themselves and stepped outside the Conner home. They had only discussed the Conner incident for a few minutes before Detective Quinn stepped out the back door and headed their way.

"You folks wanna grab lunch?"

"Sounds good to me," said Cory.

Jack looked at Cristina, and then at Cory.

247

"Not to be unsociable, but I got some errands to run.  Cory, would ya mind runnin' Cristina home?"

"Dad! You can't ask him that."

"I'd love to, Jack."

"Great.  Settled.  I'll see ya later."

## 34

"Hey, Toby."

"Glad to see ya made it.  I hate eatin' alone."

Cory signaled the waitress.  He and Cristina joined Toby at his table.  Toby took a sip of his coffee, set the cup down, and shook his head.  He started folding his napkin into perfect halves.  Cory piped up.

"You look way too serious."

Toby looked up.

"This whole swamp thing is really gettin' under my skin.  People are dying or disappearing left an' right.  You can't imagine what life is like at the station.  We're working sunup to sunset.  Everybody's on edge.  I shot my mouth off the other day and told the sheriff, I didn't think sendin' a bunch of happy-go-lucky volunteer searchers into the swamp was the smart thing to do."

"*Really.*  What'd he say?" asked Cristina.

"It pissed him right off.  Said, first off, he wasn't sendin' anybody into a swamp.  Said, secondly, he had no choice in the matter.  The town had a meeting and took it upon themselves to call up volunteers and form the search party.  Said, when a half dozen people turn up missing, and the department can't find any bodies, he doesn't have a leg to stand on.  Said they weren't doing anything illegal, and it wasn't his place to tell them no.  Best he could do was express his concerns about safety and make sure order was maintained."

"Well... from what we saw out there, he had plenty to be concerned about," said Cristina. "That was a disaster waiting to happen. But I thought you were making some progress on the missing persons." Cristina turned to Cory. "Didn't Harold say as much?"

"That's what he told me."

"Harold gets most of what he knows from me, and yes, we have made some progress," said Toby. "In fact, I just got word that the sheriff over in Missaukee County located Aaron Baxter's truck this morning. They dredged the shallows and found—need I say it—the skeletal remains of both him and his dog. The current washed away any clues to his death. We found Crandale right where Jim Conner said he'd be, but same problem. Any clue to what happened was washed away by the current.

"The grasser teens were found shortly after their friends became concerned and drove back out to the party the following evening to look for them. Those kids are going to need some counseling. I got a good look at those remains, and I'm telling you, I don't know what happened there, but honestly, I'm scared shitless to find out. I mean, it was stomach turning. There was hardly anything left of them. What remains we collected are on their way up to state forensics, and may give us our first clue to figuring out what the hell is going on."

"Doesn't sound to me like you're doing all that bad. I'm surprised there's so much complaining going on," said Cristina.

"It doesn't take much to get the public fired up. Especially when they start running scared. The way I see it, the public is using the missing persons issue as leverage to pressure the authorities into getting at the bottom of everything that's been happening for the past year or two. The community is tired of it. They know something's not right. Just too many rumors."

"I suppose."

"The sheriff's getting the brunt of it. You gotta understand, nothing's happening in Houghton Lake, or farther over in Denton or Prudenville. Nobody's going to give those police departments hell, because these incidents have all occurred outside their jurisdiction.

249

"Everything has happened in or around Dead Stream and the flooding so it gets escalated to county jurisdiction, which means the sheriff's department. Therefore, Cooper's getting all the flack. Problem is, these things aren't just happening in Roscommon. They're also happening in Missaukee County, so now we have a multi-county problem and jurisdiction gets escalated once again, this time to the state boys.

"But, whereas the local police can't satisfy the public's thirst for answers, the state police are out of reach. So that leaves the sheriff's department—good ol' Cooper. And he's not in control of anything at this point except calming nerves and taking the heat. He's in a bad place."

"Ouch," said Cristina. "Doesn't sound like fun."

"It's not. Believe me."

The three fell back momentarily to their thoughts. Cristina watched Toby arrange his keys into perfectly spaced rays of a circle centered at the key ring.

"So, where in the swamp were you when I called this morning?" asked Cory.

"Oh, hell. We were way back in on the west side. Right on the county line. Took the gas road back to where it ends at Dead Stream east of Bear Lake. Everybody in that search party headed out in boats. They were going upstream to try and find those fishermen from Lansing. Left me behind, standing alone on the only hard spot of high ground in sight. Your call couldn't have come at a better time. I owe ya."

The three worked on breakfast while taking turns at offering utterly speculative opinions or explanations of what they were up against.

"What *does* the sheriff think is going on?" asked Cory.

"Well, he's not buying into your newspaper articles about swamp monsters, if that's what you're asking."

Everybody laughed.

"Honestly, I don't know what he thinks. He needs answers and I know he's way past desperate. Oh, hell. Speak of the devil."

All discussion came to an abrupt halt when they spotted Sheriff Cooper pulling off the road and into the Little Boots parking lot.

"Uh-oh. I can't see this as being good," said Cory. "You in trouble? Eating eggs at Little Boots instead of donuts at the coffee shop?"

"I guess I'm about to find out."

"You want us to leave?"

"Hell no. The more people on my side of the fence the better."

The three sat not saying a word. Toby arranged the food on his plate, and then looked up at the sound of the door opening. The crackle of a radio transmission announced the sheriff's presence.

"Toby!"

Cory and Cristina turned in the sheriff's direction as he walked up to the table.

"Yes, sir."

"You know Jack McGrath?"

Confusion coursed across Toby's face, while at the same time Cristina and Cory looked at each other in astonishment. Cristina's eyes were big as saucers. Before Detective Sergeant Quinn could answer one way or the other, Cristina spoke up.

"What do you want with Jack McGrath?"

The sheriff looked at Cristina as if she had disrespected his authority.

"I'm sorry, ma'am. The reason for my asking is a sheriff's matter, and I'm not at liberty to discuss it with the public."

The sheriff dismissed Cristina, but she was having none of that.

"I'm sorry as well, sheriff. Jack McGrath is my father, and I would suggest you tell me exactly what you want with him. He's old, ailing, and in my care."

The sheriff went silent. He studied Cristina at length and then turned away from the table.

"Waitress?" The sheriff raised a hand to gain the woman's attention. "Coffee, please." He then turned back to face those at the table. "May I join you?"

251

"Sure."

The group nodded in agreement, and the sheriff pulled up a chair from a nearby table.

"May I ask you your name?"

"Cristina Walker."

"And you, sir?"

"Cory Ballard."

"Cory Ballard. That name rings a bell." The sheriff proceeded cautiously. "Were you folks a part of yesterday's search party?"

"No, not exactly. We were there, but I'm in town to look in on my father."

"And you, Mr. Ballard?"

"I'm in town at the request of Harold Sweeny over at the *County Chronicle*."

The sheriff winced.

"Cory Ballard. *Swamp monsters....* You're a reporter."

"Yeah. Actually, I've been following this case for a while now."

The sheriff appeared both wary and weary.

"An investigative reporter." He looked at Toby. "Detective sergeant, you keep some interesting company." He looked back at Cristina and then spoke. "About twenty minutes after the search got underway, a seventeen-year-old boy went down in knee-deep water. Not so much as a peep. He goes down, and two others rush in to help and die in the process. A fourth, in an act of bravery, runs in to save the others and dies as well. Just like that—four boys dead."

"Yeah, like Cristina said, we were there," said Cory. "Saw the whole thing go down."

"It was very nearly a dozen," said Cristina. "Cory saved the group leader's life by tackling him just as *he* was about to jump into the water. He was one luck—"

"And what was in the water? For the love of god, did anybody see what was in the water?" The sheriff interrupted Cristina. "Did you see anything? Did anybody see anything? Why is it that

252

nobody ever sees anything? How can anything cause this much mayhem and be that much invisible? I don't get it.

"All I'm getting is swamp monster stories. I don't believe in swamp monsters. I don't believe in ghosts or invisible creatures. But I do believe something really insane is going on, and it all started the day your father came into the station ranting about something being in the swamp. And to his credit, he was dead on when he assured us the day would come, we'd remember his saying so.

"It's becoming all too obvious that I've entered this race late; even worse, I may have been responsible in part for some of the deaths that have driven the town to taking matters into their own hands. Not to mention today's fatality."

The sheriff stared directly at Cristina.

"Ma'am, I *do* remember your dad showing up at the station. I *do* remember your father telling us to mark the day. I remember him being agitated and quite adamant about filing a report about a—let me say—a *swamp issue* for lack of a better term. He was so adamant that the ruckus he raised earned my full attention. Let's just say he's got a way with words when his dander gets up."

Cristina smiled.

"Yeah, I'm sure you know," the sheriff continued. "But, I have to tell ya that from my office, listening to what the man was sayin'—I mean, it was so preposterous—we all figured he was off his meds or something of that order. Your father was going on about his dog being dissolved by something that came out of the swamp. He said it was eatin' all the fish.

"I'll be frank. Every person in the place just stood there looking at him. I'm ashamed to say this, but the more insistent he became, the more we started to laugh behind his back. In the end, we just humored him and let him go his way. I mean, I was more concerned about him being behind the wheel of a car than anything he was sayin'.

"You have to understand that the whole county's in an uproar about what's going on in the flooding and Dead Stream Swamp. And it ain't just Roscommon. Damn, Missaukee County, Kalkaska,

Crawford, Clare, they're all watching this and getting real nervous. They're calling me day in and day out for updates. Everybody wants answers, and what've we got?

"What we got is everything from mass poisoning and mass murderers, to monsters and aliens. If you can think it, it's already out there as a rumor of fact."

The sheriff looked specifically at Cory with mild disdain.

"Just making a living, sheriff. I'm in the entertainment business."

"I guess that's one way of looking at it. Point is, I've heard it all, and your father's story was just one more. But it was the *first* one. It's killing me to admit his story actually appears to have a semblance of truth, and for that reason, I didn't waste any time going back into the records to dig up his name.

"This morning, when we finished with our interviews of the search party, two things stood out. One, nobody saw anything. They all heard the screams, which turned out to be those of bystanders, but nobody saw anything. I mean, two girls saw the first three boys go down, and a group of kids saw the last boy go down, but that was it. Nobody saw *anything* in the water. And two, everybody within close distance reported smelling an irritating odor just before or at the same time the boys went down."

"It's true," said Cory. "Cristina smelled it as soon as we arrived. We smelled it in the area where the Palmer children died. We smelled it when we investigated the dead cattle over at Hamilton's."

"Well, I distinctly remember your dad going on about the smell of acid. About his dog being killed with acid. At that time it raised flags that were pointing to animal cruelty. But since then, other residents have complained of blue lights and bad acid, or sometimes bleach-like odors. In fact, a few days back we contacted one of the drilling companies to find out if they were using some new cleaning agent. I've been assured they are not. So, we asked them to look over a few of their rigs just to make sure everything was in order. They did. Everything was fine. No issues.

"Point is... your father isn't soundin' so loony anymore. That's why it would mean a great deal to me and the department if we could talk to him. We want all the information we can get, and nobody can deny he spouted off first. You might say, it's burned into our memories."

Sheriff Cooper looked at Cristina.

"Ma'am, I gotta say, it's a mind-boggling coincidence that I show up here to ask Officer Quinn to drop by your father's place, and find you sitting at his table having lunch. It's either too funny or too scary. But I swear to god, I hope it's an omen for the best."

"Well, I can assure you of one thing, sheriff. My father can act as eccentric as an old man can get, but he's as rational as a calculator. The man isn't on meds, and he isn't crazy. And for what it's worth, he hasn't offered up anything about the swamp other than to say something's out there and it ain't kind. I have no doubt that he believes something's in that swamp."

The sheriff looked around the table. He was reading the truth in their faces.

"And what about you?"

The sheriff immediately sensed a mutual reluctance to dismiss entirely the idea of there being *'something'* in the swamp.

"You believe that, Toby?"

"Sir, something killed the cattle on Ben Hamilton's farm. It takes serious intent to kill just one fifteen-hundred-pound animal let alone three. Hell, the slaughterhouse pops 'em in the head, and they still don't go down. If they'd been poisoned by water, then half the herd would've been killed. But it was just the three. Maybe the rest smelled or sensed danger, I don't know. But nothing explains the animals being reduced to piles of bones in a few days' time. Those animals should've been out there rotting and stinking up the place for a month or more."

"And let's not forget about that odor," added Cristina. "Just like this morning, just like at Gloven's place. Terrible. You didn't want to breathe it for anything."

"Gloven?" The sheriff's eyes locked on to Cristina. "What do you know about Gloven?"

"She doesn't know anything about Gloven," interrupted Cory. "I asked her to join me while I was riding around looking for him."

"We're gonna need to talk about that as well," said the sheriff. "Gloven's on our missing persons list. Nobody's seen anything of him for a week. Why were you looking for Gloven?"

"No reason in particular. Just information in general about sources of bones. But let me show you something that you might find really interesting."

Cory pulled out his cell. He went on to answer the sheriff's question as he fumbled with his phone.

"Gloven was running an Internet business under the name Boneman. I tracked him down to this area, to a flea market called the Great Escape on the corner of Old 27 and Birch. He wasn't there. Some guy who overheard me asking about him approached us, and for a price, gave me Gloven's name, address, and instructions on how to get to his secret processing site. We drove out, saw the site, didn't see Gloven, and came back. That's all I know about Carl Gloven."

"I'll need to get those directions."

"No problem. Follow the trail off the end of East Walker Road. Goes into the swamp just south of Haymarsh Creek. Here, look at this."

Cory handed the sheriff his phone. The sheriff stared at it.

"That's a lot of bones."

"Yeah, it is. But forget those bones. Look at the shed. Zoom in and look inside the shed."

The sheriff drew his fingers across the cell phone screen, and studied the image. His attention shifted from the phone back to Cory.

"Is that what I think it is?"

"Looks like it."

"You saw it?"

"No. I was just taking some shots and happened to be looking them over afterward when I noticed it. Got my attention. I'm curious. I was thinking about heading back out there to have a second look as soon as I got a chance."

"You think that's Gloven?"

"I was wondering, but I wasn't sure until you said he's missing. If I were to put two and two together, I'd say he was on that tractor when it took a plunge through the dock. Could be the man had a fatal encounter with his partner in the bone business. And I don't necessarily mean a human partner. Just saying."

"Can I get a copy of this?"

"Yeah, sure. I'll email it to you."

The sheriff pulled a pad out of his shirt pocket and jotted down a few notes.

"Thanks.... So, getting back to my first nightmare... I'll be boiling in hot water over these last four deaths. I wanna ask all of you one last time. Do you believe there is some *thing* moving about in the backwaters of Reedsburg Dam? Toby?"

"No idea, but I'm not gonna dismiss it."

"Ms. Walker?"

"I'm with Toby. I'm with dad, who's acting out what he thinks."

The sheriff then looked at Cory as if expecting him to be the least likely voice of reason.

"You?"

"I don't know, sheriff. It's killing me." Cory leaned back in his seat, and folded his hands behind his head. "It's hard making poison do what's been going on. Poisons, acids or bases, are diluted by water, especially when there's thousands of acres of it. Any quantity of substance floating by that was concentrated enough to dissolve three cows would set the swamp on fire, so to speak.

"The whole floating chemical thing just gets harder to swallow by the day. Not to mention the timing of where these events occur. It isn't a natural occurrence of events from north to south with the flow of the current. The events appear to move upstream and we all know that nothing floats upstream. It's this movement upstream and downstream that has me so perplexed.

"Unless there's numerous outbreaks or patches of this stuff, north and south, east and west, to wreak havoc whenever-wherever, then all that's left is a singular entity that has the ability to navigate—to swim. Of course, that would make it a *thing*, and god forbid, possibly an *intelligent thing* at that."

"So that would be a yes," stated the sheriff.

Cory threw his hands up and shrugged.

"Sheriff, I've heard enough ridiculously stupid stories to know that everything about this is different. As reluctant as I am to admit it, at this point, I'm left with little choice but to side with Toby and Cristina. I just can't dismiss it."

The sheriff looked down at the table and exhaled. His head moved from side to side in resignation.

"All right. Let's say there is something to what you suspect, what all three of you leave open to chance. People have been complaining about the fishing and telling stories for a while now. But the earliest I heard anything that specifically addressed the idea of something being in the swamp was from old man McGrath. Yet, he never said anything to the two of you about it?"

The sheriff looked at Cory and Cristina. Cory answered first.

"I only just met the man. He touched on it lightly. One thing was for sure, he was definitely looking for answers to something. I got the impression he was searching for a thing. Whatever that means."

"He never said anything to you, Ms. Walker?"

"He said there was something in the swamp that wasn't kind. He didn't elaborate."

"That settles it. I need to talk to McGrath. I need to know if he's seen something or not. Can you bring me to him, Ms. Walker?"

"Yes, I'm sure I can, but that doesn't guarantee he'll be agreeable."

"Understood. Can't say I blame him, but I can only do what I can do. I can apologize. I'm willing to eat crow, and see where it goes from there. Are you free to go? Honestly, after this morning, I haven't got a minute to waste."

"Sure, but Cory's my ride," said Cristina.

The sheriff turned to Cory.

"No problem. Long as I get to stay and listen to what he's got to say. Especially about that swing set."

"Toby, why don't you ride out with me?" asked the sheriff.

The four paid their bills and left Little Boots as a group.


## 35


Cory and Cristina led the way back to her father's cabin. They parked in the front yard and waited for the sheriff and Toby to climb out of the cruiser and catch up. The sheriff's expression was evident as he approached. He was looking at the cabin. Cristina realized at once that all three men were either perplexed or amused by the ring of salt. She cleared the air.

"Yes, it's a ring of salt. Dad believes it keeps the snakes and such away."

"That's a lot of salt," said Toby.

"What exactly is *such*?" asked the sheriff.

"Yeah, we've been wondering the same thing," quipped Cory.

The four walked around the house.

"What the hell.... What is that? A swing set with a—"

"A dead deer. It's a dead deer," interrupted Cristina, again attempting to explain. "I know because I had to help him wrestle that mess across the swings. It was a bitch. Pardon my French."

The four stood on the bank and stared at the partially decomposed remains of the deer carcass.

"Humph," grunted the sheriff. "You're *sure* your old man ain't on meds?"

"I'm sure. He's got his ways, don't always say much, but he ain't crazy."

"I hope not, cuz I'm counting on him for some answers."

"I'm surprised he didn't meet us. His truck's here. The boat's here. That's odd. Huh."

Cristina was at once suspicious. She turned away from the water to glance toward his rocker. As she neared the steps and a view of the porch unobstructed by the banisters, she saw her father lying face down on the porch just before the threshold to the back door. It appeared as though he had attempted to go inside. She let out a scream that startled everyone. The sheriff's hand immediately dropped to his holster.

"Dad? *Dad?!*"

Cristina bolted for the porch steps. She leapt up the steps while the three men went on guard, assessing the surroundings, and trying to make quick sense of what was taking place. As the sheriff and Toby scanned the yard, Cory went to Cristina's assistance. She was instantly all nurse. She flipped her father on his back and checked his pulse.

"He's alive. He's alive. Call an ambulance. Hurry. His pulse is weak, but he's still alive. Thank god, he's still alive."

She placed her head on his chest and listened to his heart.

"He's covered in sweat. I think he's had a heart attack. Please, help me get him inside."

The men grabbed him at once and moved him carefully through the back door. Cristina directed them to his bedroom.

"Put him on the bed, pull off his waders, and spread a blanket across him. I'll try to find some aspirin."

"I just called dispatch. An ambulance is on the way," said the sheriff.

"Thank you."

"It looks like he burned his hand," said Cory.

"I know. I saw that," said Cristina as she raised his forearm, rotated it, and scrutinized her father's hand. "It's only the one hand. I don't know what he did."

The ambulance arrived inside of fifteen minutes. Cristina rushed outside to greet them as soon as she heard the vehicle arrive.

"Hello, my name is Cristina Walker. I'm a registered nurse and the daughter of the patient. His name is Jack McGrath. I believe he may have suffered a heart attack. He's unconscious, but appears to be stable and comfortable."

Cristina escorted the paramedics into the house. She stood back as the medics took some vitals and then prepared to move her father. The medics placed Jack McGrath onto a gurney and removed it to the ambulance as Cristina followed. She climbed into the back of the vehicle and assisted the team in securing her father for the trip.

"Where are you taking him?"

"Closest place with a full-time cardio staff is Mercy in Cadillac."

"How long?"

"About fifty minutes. I wouldn't be overly concerned at this point. As you can see, his EKG looks abnormal, but it appears— how can I put it—*abnormally* stable."

"Let's go."

Cristina remained in the back of the ambulance without invitation. No objections arose from the crew. An EMT closed the doors, and within minutes, the vehicle sped away with lights flashing. Jack McGrath began to show signs of regaining consciousness as the ambulance headed down the drive toward the road.

Cory, the sheriff, and Toby watched the flashing lights disappear down the drive, at which point they wandered down from the front yard, back to the porch and water's edge. The three stopped to study the swing set.

"What the hell is that all about?" asked the sheriff.

"I was wondering the same thing," said Cory. "Cristina had mentioned something about him dragging it out into the shallows. She was pretty upset about him asking her to help him lay that deer carcass across the swings. It was funnier than hell listening to her tell it. I was laughing good and hard, but she still doesn't appreciate the humor."

"Did she tell you why the old coot would wanna throw a dead animal across the swings to begin with?"

261

"No. But I think he's trying to bait the thing. Taking that into consideration, there's something you might want to make a note of."

"What's that?"

"Look at the condition of that carcass."

"Yeah, what about it?"

"Look to you like it's been sitting there for a couple of days or so?"

"Couple of weeks, maybe."

"Try three days."

"Impossible. I've cleaned up my fair share of dead animals. As rough as that looks, two weeks minimum."

"Three days max."

"No way."

"Sorry to disagree, but she told me all about it again this morning. They picked the carcass up off the shoulder of the road, off 127 just north of 400, and hauled it back three days ago. He couldn't handle it himself so tricked her into going with him."

"I ain't buyin' it. I can see ribs from here. Must've been mighty rough when they dragged it out there. That's probably why she was so upset. I'd say it got nailed by three or four cars before they got to it. Vultures probably had a good go at it before they got it."

"I get why you think that. Your reasoning's dead on. All I can say is that's what Cristina told me. Just keep in mind that I saw what was left of three fifteen-hundred-pound cows after a few days. Bones. Nothing but bones. Bones as white as snow."

"And what about those teens at the grasser? That was one night," said Toby.

"Okay. I get the point. Right now, I'd like to know what's in that bucket," said the sheriff. "If I had waders with me, I'd have a look."

Cory was also curious.

"I've got some in the back of my Blazer. They won't fit you, but I can slip them on and see if it's empty or not."

"Yeah, if ya don't mind. It'd kill my curiosity. Probably full of some kind of bait, but knowing would put an end to it."

"No problem."

Cory walked back to the upper yard and pulled out the waders. He slipped them on and walked back to where the sheriff stood. He stopped briefly to study the water. He began sniffing the air.

"What the hell are you doin'?" asked the sheriff.

"You smell that—that odor?"

The sheriff raised his head and began sniffing the air, as did Toby.

"Smells a little like bleach to me. Is that what you're all talkin' about?"

"Yeah, it's faint right now, but I've been around the water when it's plain overwhelming. I don't pick up on the bleach. Smells more like some kind of acid to me."

"It's always the same smell everywhere," said Toby.

"Yeah, I agree," said Cory.

The sheriff inhaled deeply, trying his best to pick up the scent, and commented, "This must be what the EMTs were talkin' about this morning."

"Well, keep your eyes open," said Cory. "A faint smell is too much smell for my liking. It's a warning."

Cory looked cautiously across the basin.

"Everything looks safe enough. I guess I'll wade in. Keep your eyes open."

Cory eased his way carefully into the shallows. He walked toward the swing set.

"The smell's getting strong out here."

Cory grabbed hold of the bucket's brim and peered into it.

"Water!"

"That's it?" asked the sheriff.

"Nothin, but—"

Cory stopped mid-sentence. He sensed the slightest shift in the shallows. He stood still. He admonished himself for being skittish, but the memory of shifting water at Gloven's place, McGrath's account of the water shifting on Dead Stream, and the old man's specific questioning of Jim Conner on shifting water

263

was all too memorable. A waft of the acrid odor passed through the air at the same time a soft shushing sound caught his attention. He looked down at the half-submerged deer. It appeared to be effervescing. That was the last straw. He turned away and hastily made for shore.

"You okay?" asked the sheriff. "Something happen out there?"

"I'm fine. I got a strong whiff of that smell, and that damned deer started bubbling. I'm not taking any chances. That's the smell of death around this place."

The sheriff's eyes remained locked on Cory as he stepped onto dry land and began heading toward the upper yard. Toby joined him. The sheriff followed both. A movement to the side caught his attention. His eyes darted to his left. He saw two, no, three good-sized water snakes moving across the grass toward them. He then glanced at the ring of salt alongside his feet.

"I don't think salt will keep out snakes. Do you?" asked the sheriff to anybody listening.

"News to me," said Cory. "But Cristina said her father was having problems with rodents and such coming out of marshes and onto high ground. He claimed the salt was effective in keeping them at bay."

The sheriff stopped briefly to kick the salt with his boot.

"There's that 'such' again. Such as what? The three of you seem to believe there's something out here, and I emphasize *thing* bein' an 'it', or a 'they'. Anybody care to venture a guess on what 'such' is?"

"Haven't got a clue," said Cory as he arrived at his SUV. Toby said nothing. He looked at the approaching sheriff and shrugged.

"No idea."

"Too bad," said the sheriff as he arrived at the Blazer. "Well, if you see a 'such' or anything else for that matter, keep me informed. I'd appreciate it."

"You can count on it," said Cory.

The men said their good-byes and parted ways once they reached the open road. Cory decided to head over to the *Chronicle* and help Harold get headlines to the readers. He had six messages on his cell, and could only venture to guess Harold's state of mind. He and Cristina had gone out to investigate Bob Crandale's death first thing in the morning. Harold was probably stuck to the ceiling.

## 36

Cory stepped forward.

"Tammy, I'd like you to meet Sheriff Cooper."

The sheriff was standing alongside the booth and offered his hand.

"Pleasure to meet you, Tammy. Lord, have I been waitin' to hear from you. Been nothin' but pins an' needles. I only wish it were under better circumstances."

"I understand, sheriff. No need to explain. And let me add that I am equally impatient to get this information out to the authorities. It's critical. We definitely have a problem."

"Why don't we all sit down?" suggested Cory. He signaled for the server as Sheriff Cooper slid into the booth and Cristina moved to sit down alongside him. Tammy entered the booth and slid over opposite the sheriff. Cory sat down last. He looked across at Cristina and smiled.

"So what do we got? Tell me about this problem."

Tammy took a long, deep breath. She waited a moment while collecting her thoughts and then spoke.

"There is no way for me to say what has to be said without being dramatic, I can't help myself. But I promise there will be no exaggeration. So, let me begin by *emphatically* stressing a single point."

Again she hesitated.

"You have no idea... how insidiously horrific is this thing that lives in the swamp. Believe me, you cannot imagine. If we don't act fast to eradicate this life form, we will be facing a disaster of unprecedented proportion. Your worst nightmare in every way. This invader has the potential to essentially devour all life within the Great Lakes watershed."

Cory wondered if everybody at the table had the same suffocating sensation, or if it was only him. Did everybody's faces just go white? Was he the only one with a knot in his gut? He wondered if the sheriff was open minded enough to accept the legitimacy of Tammy's opinions in light of her credentials and connections. He studied the sheriff's face.

"Not what I wanted to hear," said the sheriff. "But I suppose you better give us an idea. Horrific or not, ignorance is still the worst enemy. We'll wanna know what we're up against."

The waitress interrupted the conversation when she returned to lean over the table and place coffees. Nobody said a word until she stepped away.

"Please. Continue," said the sheriff. "I gotta know. We all have to know."

"Okay. Where to start?"

"Seeing as how I'm the only one at this table who's in the dark, how 'bout we start from the beginning? I need to get my footing."

"Okay. The beginning. Let me see."

Tammy lowered her eyes and arranged her thoughts. She then looked up at the sheriff.

"Okay. Let's start with this. I guess, first you have to understand how ARL came to be. So, let's begin a few years before ARL opened. At that time, there was a great deal of concern within the DNR and a number of other public and private organizations involved in Michigan's inland fisheries, involved in its conservation, about matters of invasive species and changes in the ecosystem of the Great Lakes watershed. Back then, it was the hottest topic of the day.

"In particular, these organizations were under growing pressure from commercial fisheries and sportsmen. Charter boat operators, highly vocal fishermen's clubs, and like-minded groups were calling for relief from the increasing prevalence of sea lamprey in the lakes and inland waters. These groups had immense support around Cheboygan, Mullett Lake, Burt Lake, Black Lake, pretty much any water in that area, anything along the Black or Indian Rivers, or the inland waterway.

"Whether true or not, the public outcry reached its peak when it was presumed that the sea lampreys were no longer migrating back to Lake Huron, but staying entirely within the inland lakes throughout their life cycle.

"To make matters worse, they began showing up in greater numbers farther south in the Higgins and Houghton watershed, the Dead Stream Swamp, and, more importantly, the headwaters of the Muskegon River. That was especially troublesome due to the fact that the Muskegon traversed the entire state, forming the Croton and Hardy Dam backwaters, and emptying out into Lake Michigan."

"Yeah, I'm reasonably familiar with what you're saying, bein' that most of us around here are cradle-to-grave fishermen."

"I'm sure you are; it's been a major issue for many years. But what you're less likely to know unless you were on the inside is this. A number of prominent public organizations, such as the Great Lakes Aquatics Commission, the Lakes and Fisheries Canada, the Fish and Wildlife Service, along with research departments in the Universities of Michigan, Wisconsin, and Minnesota, and at least three in Ontario, such as Toronto and Algoma, formed a partnership with a number of private firms for the purpose of attacking this issue of invading species. A sizable federal grant prompted the formation of this partnership. However, to capture funds, the participant's primary focus had to be combatting the sea lamprey.

"That is where Aquatic Research Laboratories, or ARL, came into the picture. IGI, which is International Genome Industries, one of the larger private concerns, established ARL as a subsidiary.

"ARL was to work directly with these governmental and public institutions. By agreement, those organizations designated ARL as the primary research facility, the hub. It was located in the Dead Stream Swamp where it could easily monitor its work in close proximity to the endangered ecosystems. The facility was on the west side of Dead Stream Swamp and was accessible only by a gas pipe trail. Obviously, I don't have to tell you how far back those trails go into the swamp."

"Actually, I know precisely where ARL used to be," said Sheriff Cooper. "I was on site through the worst of it, working with the crews that fought the fire. I watched ARL go down."

"Wonderful. Then you probably know that the laboratory was completely gutted by that fire—a total loss."

"Yes, I do. I remember it well."

"Needless to say, that wasn't a good day for ARL."

"No, it certainly was not."

"Up until that untimely ending, ARL directed its energy toward finding or creating an organism that would flush out and destroy sea lamprey ammocoetes. The larvae live buried in the sand for a number of years. They sift through it for food until they mature into fish. ARL and its partners sought to attack the ammocoetes while in the sand, before the larvae morphed into fish that could swim away. They believed that would be the easiest and most efficient way to eliminate the invasive species. That belief held true before ARL, and still stands today.

"With that in mind, the tanks at ARL held a wide variety of marine specimens that were chosen for possessing one or more of the traits needed to exterminate the ammocoetes. For example, *Conus geographus* spends its time buried beneath the sand waiting for something to swim by and then nails it. Problem is it only nails one thing at a time, and has to digest it before killing again, as do all things, but it's slow. Now, *Chironex fleckeri* can kill a number of fish at once, and it does swim about the sandy bottoms at times, but not beneath the sand where the ammocoetes live. You see, everything is a give and take.

"For that reason, one of ARL's ambitions was to spearhead a project that designed the organism from the ground up, a genetically engineered organism that incorporated the best features of those marine animals suited to perform the task. But we never succeeded. The fire occurred before we made any real gains. Ironically, the biggest hurdle was the saltwater to freshwater adaptation that the prey we hoped to eradicate so successfully mastered on its own. It was almost like God's way of saying, *'Don't kid yourself. You aren't me, yet'.*"

"I'm with God on this one," said the sheriff. "Doesn't it scare the wits outta ya, playin' with nature like that?"

"There's nothing to be scared about. It's rudimentary, procedural, and a lot easier for me to understand than how to fix my car. You don't question a mechanic when you take your car to him. You trust him."

"My mechanic never tweaked my car to commit mass murder or destroy the environment."

"Sheriff, you might want to rethink that."

"Yeah, that didn't come out quite right. But you understand what I'm sayin'."

"I do. And you have to understand what I'm saying. We knew exactly what we were doing. Our scope was to produce an organism that could live under the sand, was aggressive by nature, and possessed the needed toxins and delivery system. Most importantly, it had to have a pre-determined life span, and it had to be sterile so it couldn't replicate. Those were the safeguards.

"An organism of that design would allow us to cordon off an area where it could be introduced. There it would be free to roam, hunting and killing ammocoetes but nothing else. Once the area was free of ammocoetes, the organism would starve to death or, after a set time, its biological clock would terminate it.

"We would then re-open the area to the public and proceed to the next treatment zone. In the end, precise targeting would assure only ammocoetes were affected. Because the organism would be a bottom dweller, most fish would remain unthreatened. In any event, the onslaught of lamprey poses more of a threat to fish and the swamp by far than any possible encounter with the organisms as designed."

"If you say so."

The sheriff was clearly uncomfortable with a world that sounded too much like science-fiction horror.

269

"I do say so.  Should I go on?" asked Tammy with an expression indicating mild annoyance.  Cory took note of her countenance and imagined she could see the sheriff burning her at the stake.

"Absolutely.  didn't mean to be rude.  Obviously, what you do is way beyond me, but it doesn't change the fact that on some base level, I need to know what I'm dealin' with."

"Okay.  Well, at this point, I think Cristina should tell you about the conversation she had with her father.  It played an important role in what would happen next."

All eyes turned to Cristina.

"All right.  Dad and I were having a heart-to-heart because I wanted to know exactly what he did to land himself in the hospital.  What's crazy is that it was he who wanted to be sure that I knew what had happened, and more importantly, that I told everybody about it.  He told me about how his attempt to inform the authorities turned into a disaster and how they wrote him off as being nuts."

The sheriff grimaced.

"Don't worry.  Dad doesn't blame you.  He said if he were on your side of the fence, the outcome would probably have been the same.  But he did say that something strange to these parts was living in the swamp.  He was sure of that.  He had seen it as a blue glow at night, or a disturbance in the water that was visible in the daytime.  He believed it could move about the swamp of its own volition, and was not subject to the current.

"Dad thought that this thing could even *leave* the water if it rained hard enough to keep the ground wet.  He believed this was how it left the shallows to kill his dog on the porch.  I questioned him about the porch being under a roof and dry, and he said he didn't know what to say other than the thing might've had an ability to draw swamp water or rainfall into itself by some form of osmosis, and then squeeze it out where needed, like wringing out a sponge, and sliding across the puddle.

"Once he saw this thing glowing at night, he saw his first opportunity to track it.  Later he realized that there were also signs during the daytime.  In particular, the shifting or effervescing of water, or large areas of dead vegetation. These were the clues to finding out what it was, or possibly trapping it. There were places where bones littered the banks. All these things convinced dad he could prove its existence, and disprove his senility.

"That was the reason he was so tightlipped with me. He figured our relationship was fragile enough without him sounding like a man losing his mind. The fact that he had been throwing roadkill, or whatever his dog dragged home, into the shallows was something I never questioned. To me it was just fish bait, and dad was content to leave it be at that. He wasn't about to tell me that it had turned into monster bait. In fact, Cory is the one who came to that conclusion and suggested it to me.

"Dad's last idea was to bait this thing by suspending a deer carcass or something similar at the surface of the water, and keep a submerged bucket as close to the bait as possible. He intended to keep watch at night and if he saw the blue glow about the carcass, or if he saw the water bubbling during the day, he would hoist the bucket up out of the water and hopefully snag something of the thing.

"I can tell you this. My father was wary of whatever was out there, but he wasn't afraid of it. He was afraid for everything else in the swamp. He knew something was very, very wrong, as he put it, because the snakes and vermin skedaddled from the marsh to high ground every time he smelled the odor or saw the signs."

"From what I've heard, he didn't suffer a heart attack," said the sheriff. "Maybe he should've been afraid. I heard he got poisoned."

"That's what they're saying. There was no elevation of protein in his blood, and his EKG was relatively normal considering that the poison attacked his nervous system. Lucky for us, he survived to tell us about it."

"Lucky for us, he wanted to talk about it," said Cory.

"So what else did he say?" asked the sheriff.

"Dad said that he arrived home from running errands, and as soon as he walked around the cabin porch, he immediately spotted a disturbance in the water surrounding the deer. He said the

271

water was shifting. He said it swelled up as if trying to engulf the carcass. He said the water was effervescing quite noticeably.

"Dad immediately ran for the rope that was attached to the bucket and yanked it up out of the water. He then put on a pair of gloves and his waders, and went out to see what if anything was in the bucket.

"Dad said that he looked into the bucket, and there was nothing inside but water. That was it, just water. However, he sniffed it, and it had that same acrid or bleach-like smell that we've been talking about. Dad said it was faint as best, but it confirmed his suspicions about something being in that water, or having been in the water. It made him wonder if the water itself was changed. He wondered if the viscosity of the water was thicker, or if it was slimy, or if it was in some manner different aside from the smell. For that reason, he reached into the bucket to feel the water's consistency.

"My father said the reaction was instantaneous and excruciating—like a bad burn. Instinctively, before thinking about the mistake he was about to make, he yanked his hand out of the bucket, pulled off the glove, and plunged his hand into the lake to rinse it. The pain instantly went from a burning sensation in his hand, to what felt like an electric shock that shot straight up to his chest. His only thoughts were to get out of the water and call for help, but he never made it past the porch.

"Dad said he grabbed an old pair of gloves, but he didn't see anything wrong with them before he put them on. He said the rubber probably cracked when he was working to pull his waders up. The water entered the glove, and his ripping it off to rinse his hand only make things worse. A lot worse.

"When I told him that Cory waded out to the bucket, dad nearly had a cardiac for real. When I told him that Cory had looked into the bucket, but had not touched the contents, he was visibly relieved. Anyway, he left me with some very specific instructions. He said he believed there was something in the water that was invisible. He believed it was a poison or venom of some kind. And if it was venom, then there might be something living in that bucket that needed to be fed.

"Dad told me to get with Cory, buy a new pair of rubber gloves at the hardware store, and then pour some of the water from the bucket into a mason jar. He was adamant that I place a small piece of fish or meat from his freezer into the jar as well, seal it, and send it all off to somebody who could examine it. I told Cory what dad wanted me to do. We got the gloves, poured the water into a jar, tossed in a piece of fish, and gave Tammy a call."

Cristina handed the conversation back to Tammy.

"I took the water sample that Cristina gave me and delivered it to Andrew Martinelli, a professor over at Central Michigan University. I studied under him and later we became friends. The man is a genius. His specialty is molecular ecology, but more specifically molecular surveillance and detection of invasive species. He's an expert in genetic connectivity and molecular systematics. What I'm trying to say is that you won't find but a few who are more qualified to determine what we are dealing with than Professor Martinelli.

"Along with the sample, I gave him my notes with the information I obtained from Mr. McGrath, Cory, and Cristina. Andrew contacted me a couple of days later to say we would be presently facing a Level 4 biohazard if there was a clear identification of the life form and determination of the potential ecological threat. He also said, make no mistake, it would be soon in coming, and asked to meet with me at my earliest possible opening. I left work straight away and drove to his office.

"Andrew also affirmed there was a high probability that DNA from the Aquatic Research Laboratories' facility escaped into the Dead Stream Swamp ecosystem. He matched fragments of the DNA from the sample and traced some to *Chironex fleckeri*. However, that was only its predominant DNA. There was also a prevalent fragment of DNA from *Conus geographus*.

"As I have said in the past, ARL studied both of these marine animals extensively, and we had a good deal of raw DNA from each. For your benefit, sheriff, they were perfect specimens for experimentation due to their exceptionally potent venom and their preference to scour the lake and riverbeds. These traits

273

made them ideal for killing ammocoetes, and we did a lot of work with their DNA. There's no disputing that."

The sheriff leaned back in the booth and frowned.

"Soooooo… you're tellin' me that we got some sort of poisonous marine animals, whose names I can't even say, breeding in our swamp."

"No, no, no, much worse than that." Tammy looked at both Cory and Cristina.

"Oh, Christ. You're killin' me with suspense, Ms. Tagart. What *are* you tellin' me? I can barely understand half of what you're saying. At least tell me it's something I can shoot. Make me feel good."

"I wish I could, sheriff, but I can't."

"Well, what the hell are we dealing with?"

"I believe that in spite of insurmountable odds—maybe trillions to one—the DNA, the genetics of these marine animals along with genetically engineered building blocks created in the ARL labs, and random molecular structures that are part of the swamp's natural ecosystem combined to produce an unknown life form. All we can say for sure is that the roots of its DNA are closest to *Chironex fleckeri,* or what we commonly call the box jellyfish."

"What?" The sheriff sat up with a hint of indignation. "A jellyfish? A jellyfish? You're kidding me, right? It's some sort of stupid jellyfish?"

Cory was himself thinking how silly that sounded, but he knew there would be more, and he was certain the sheriff's mind would soon change.

"Oh, lord, no. I wish," said Tammy. "Rainfall would kill a stupid jellyfish. No, this is something that has jellyfish signatures, jellyfish origins and traits among other things, but it is about as much like a jellyfish as an avalanche is like the snowflake that started it.

"This organism is deadly beyond comprehension. For starters, Jack McGrath was right on the mark when he told Cristina to put some meat in the sample container because it wasn't some inorganic poison, but rather venom from something alive.

That conviction ensured the organism was still alive when we received it. In fact, we were able to promote further growth at once by simply feeding it—anything... anything digestible, anything protein based.

"Like the jellyfish, this organism is mostly water, but whereas *Chironex fleckeri* is about ninety-five percent water, this is closer to ninety-eight or ninety-nine. A step removed from pure water. In the lab you can see it. It gives water a slightly tawny color, like adding a few crystals of instant coffee to a glass of water. But it is virtually impossible to see in the outdoors. You would never see this in a flowing river or streambed, or in a lake under any circumstance unless, as Cory mentioned, it effervesces, or at night by its luminescence if it's signaling. That's the only way to track it."

"Signaling?"

"Yes, this is another distinctive trait of *Chironex fleckeri* that the creature has inherited. We think that it uses pulses and patterns of light to attract fish in the nighttime. The kill ratio for fish is one hundred percent. Nothing survives an encounter. Fish have excellent eyesight under water but never see it. They swim into the bloom and suck it through their gills before they realize it. The fish are envenomed, instantly paralyzed, and quickly die. The organisms digest their catch from both the inside and outside, leaving very little if anything behind."

"Tell me somethin', Tammy," asked the sheriff. "The witnesses in the search party said them boys dropped like flies. By the sound of it, they were dead, or at the very, least unconscious within seconds, less than a minute according to their testimony. That seems to be another trait of this thing. You got any idea how it kills so fast?"

"Yes. We definitely have ideas. This life form uses venom that attacks the nervous system with a large spectrum of neurotoxins and cardiotoxins. The neurotoxins appear linked to *Conus geographus*. Now, *Conus geographus* as we know it only has one replaceable barb. It kills one by one. Its venom consists of a litany of neurotoxins and it is appropriately nicknamed the

275

cigarette snail as an indication of the amount of time you have left to live.

"As for the cardiotoxins, they've been matched up to *Chironex fleckeri*, as is the delivery mechanism, which makes use of microscopic nematocysts. In jellyfish, these nematocysts are cells that contain a small, coiled, thread-like barb. When the cell is sensitized, it explodes and drives the barb into its prey with a twisting, screwing motion. The barb is highly toxic, and in the case of the box jellyfish, can drop a man in a matter of minutes.

"The singular organism doesn't appear to have, or at least have as pronounced a barb, but it does have the cells that explode. It may not be as dependent on the barbs because its nematocysts are so small that they easily enter the pores and cracks of skin or other ports of entry to envenom prey.

"Because the number of these organisms sporting nematocysts are in the millions, or more likely, billions—literally a soup of toxicity—their collective attack is far more deadly than their genetic forefathers' individual or more limited strikes.

"One would experience confusion, agitation, unconsciousness, collapse, and almost immediate respiratory failure and or cardiac arrest. Death could occur within seconds of a massive envenomation. The life form doesn't have the ability to chase its prey, so it renders it helpless or dead on contact."

Tammy said nothing further and everybody sat in silence. It was almost too much to take in, to fathom. Heads were spinning as Tammy's audience tried to contemplate the danger that loomed, not just over the flooding and swamp, but all the creeks, and possibly Houghton Lake.

Cory preferred not to be pessimistic, but he was not the least bit encouraged by what he heard. His mind was churning out headlines for Harold because he could not help himself. However, it was thinking about those outrageous headlines that drove him to ask a question that had been bugging him since he first saw the cows.

"Can you explain the bleached bones? I've been trying to figure that out since day one."

"I think I can. The life form produces copious amounts of hydrogen peroxide. We saw it in the lab. Now, that isn't an uncommon occurrence in animals. Even humans produce hydrogen peroxide as a defense mechanism.

"For example, there exists an event that we call a respiratory burst, or an oxidative burst. It occurs when the lungs are under attack by bacteria, or viruses, or even cigarette smoke. The lungs go on the defensive and produce hydrogen peroxide, which is extremely destructive to living cells. It's the body's way of instantly killing off the intruder.

"Unfortunately, it's equally damaging to the body itself—you know, free radicals and that sort of thing. For all we know, based on the amount of hydrogen peroxide this thing produces, it could be its defense shield as well as a means of decontaminating food before digesting it. Who knows?"

Cory responded to her explanation.

"That brings up another question. How do you figure this thing manages to dissolve its prey in a matter of hours... well, realistically days, but having said that, after a couple of days there's nothing left but bones.

"It must use some hellacious acid or something, but I don't get how it can. With so much water, how can an acid or alkali remain potent? It should just dilute. Yet, when I was at the McGrath place, I stood alongside that deer on the swings and it was bubbling, fizzing like crazy. You know, like millions of bubbles. Cristina's dad said his hand burned."

"Yes.... Well, I suspect you may be confusing two different things that are taking place. As I said, the hydrogen peroxide explains the white bones. I suspect it also accounts for the fizzing. As I just mentioned, hydrogen peroxide is as deadly to a friendly cell as an intruder cell.

"For that reason, most all living things that have exposure to oxygen possess an enzyme called catalase. It's prevalent in blood, but also found to a lesser extent in tissue. Its purpose is to protect friendly cells from hydrogen peroxide by breaking it down into harmless water and oxygen. I'm guessing that it's the oxygen produced by the hydrogen peroxide's encounter with catalase that you're seeing bubble up to the surface.

"As for the speed and severity of decomposition…. Well, I would have to remind you that, contrary to common belief, stomach acid does not digest food. It kills dangerous bacteria and viruses in food just like the hydrogen peroxide may do for this life form. We're talking about hydrochloric acid here, and its real purpose is to provide the proper pH levels for activating enzymes, unraveling proteins, and producing pepsins that break down those proteins found in food into amino acids that can be absorbed by the body and reconstructed.

"I would bet my paycheck that this organism flushes its prey with hydrochloric acid for a number of reasons, but primarily to activate some very potent digestive enzymes. Jack McGrath said his dog was virtually stripped overnight. Cristina said he was experimenting with roadkill and that would also disappear overnight. The Palmer children were remarkably decomposed considering their short exposure. There was nothing left of the grasser teens after about twenty-four hours. The pattern is the same.

"What you have to consider is that this life form doesn't possess a stomach or gut whereby it can conveniently carry its food around for whatever time it takes to digest it. It also doesn't move about much faster than a floater in your coffee. For that reason, it must kill or paralyze its prey instantly. That keeps it from running off. Now, the prey is easily digestible without interruption.

"It explains why we're finding bones in perfect position on the ground. It would explain the acrid smell that is noted in the vicinity of the victims. I'm inclined to see this life form flooding over and around its victim, bathing it in hydrochloric acid, hydrogen peroxide, and enzymes that digest its prey in entirety at once. That would be my guess. I'll give you this. That type of digestion would make quick business of a meal. It is a very aggressive digestive process, unlike anything we know."

"So can this thing reproduce? Does it reproduce?" asked Toby.

"Professor Martinelli is still looking into that. Right now, his best guess is that it duplicates itself, much like the polyp stage of its jellyfish ancestor. In that life cycle, it is asexual and produces buds that shed and grow into new polyps. It's replicating itself without mating."

"Oh, that's just great. Terrific. So if this is a thing, if it does exist, how do we kill it?" asked the sheriff.

Tammy shook her head. "I don't know. We can't just arbitrarily dump piscicides or poisons into the flooding and swamp. Right now, we wouldn't even know what to use, or how much to use. We can't net it. We have no idea of the organism's collective size. Its closest genetic counterpart, the jellyfish, has no brain, at least not in the way we think of a brain. You might say, its entire body functions as a brain. You can't just shoot this thing in the head and kill it. Not to mention that you couldn't see it to shoot it in the first place."

"Well, are we dealin' with one or a million of these things?" asked the sheriff.

"Both. An interesting example may be the Portuguese man-of-war, which is not a common jellyfish. Instead of being a single entity, this animal is a collection of minute individuals called zooids that attach to one another and integrate socially to the extent that they are unable to survive independently.

"Or we may have a bloom or possibly a colony. A bloom to jellyfish, is a flock to birds, or a herd to animals. Each organism can function independently as one unit but also collectively like a school of fish or a murmuration of starlings. It can split without negative effects. It can combine without rejection.

"In August of 2006, a bloom of sixty million jellyfish approached Spanish beaches and stung more than seventy thousand swimmers, closing beaches for the entire region. In 2000, scientists discovered a bloom of Australia's spotted jellyfish that covered fifty-seven square miles.

"In 2007, a bloom of baby jellyfish estimated to be ten square miles long and more than forty feet thick approached the coast of Northern Ireland and repeatedly attacked a salmon farm. Boats working in the area complained of being bogged down as they struggled to make headway through the invasion.

279

"Within the space of a few hours during the night, the bloom wiped out the country's only salmon fishery. It totally destroyed the company's stock of one hundred and twenty thousand salmon by stinging or suffocating them to death. The company, helpless to ward off the attack was itself financially wiped out.

"That particular jellyfish was called a mauve stinger. As a matter of interest, it is famous for its purplish glow at night in the warmer waters of the Mediterranean, which it normally inhabits thousands of miles to the south.

"These creatures have survived for more than five hundred million years because of their unprecedented ability to adapt. There are more than two hundred species, some the size of a dime, others eight feet in diameter with tentacles a hundred feet long. They are the most efficient swimmers of all animals."

"It is believed some jellyfish are able to smell chemicals in water and possess a sense of taste. This may be a factor in what we are dealing with. That is to say, if food on shore is close enough to the water, it may be able to sense it. The life form may identify prey with protein sensors that it uses as we use our nose. It may explain why so many bones are littering the banks of the backwater.

"Jellyfish are also one of the most dramatic examples of invasive species. The American comb jellyfish invaded the world's seas by way of ship ballast tanks and hull-fouling to wreak unprecedented ecological damage on a global scale.

"The one thing that all jellyfish have in common is their voracious appetite. The American comb can sift through a gallon of seawater a day to filter out food. Multiply that by millions of jellyfish occupying up to 25 jellyfish per cubic foot of water. They starve out all other life. The box jellyfish, which is closest to what we seem to be dealing with here, is an apex predator. Like humans, it's at the top of the food chain.

"When it comes to adaptations, Professor Martinelli noted that when this organism feeds, due to its microscopic size, it possesses one very interesting property, and that is the ability to coalesce. In other words, it can dramatically increase density at will in order to thicken its collective mass at one side of a container. It does this to engulf prey. This has never been observed before and may have serious implications. Even more interesting, if a piece of food is dropped into its tank, it will coalesce toward it.

"Remember, Mr. McGrath insisted that something scaled his porch and killed his dog. His description of the dog's remains is consistent with what was seen in the lab on a smaller scale. If what Mr. McGrath said proves true, it means this organism has a well-developed ability to coalesce, to increase its density to the point of traversing land. If it has the ability to escape the confines of water, you have to ask yourselves how much more hellacious is this life form."

Tammy gave the others a chance to consider her question.

"This is so science fiction. I mean, this is just too weird," said the sheriff. "It's so easy to get sucked into believing rumors an' stories from grandma about ghosts an' monsters. You know what I'm saying? The town will jump on this in a heartbeat, but I can't afford to do that. Tell me this, Tammy. Do you honestly believe something is actually out there? I mean, for Christ's sake, we're adults sitting here talking about monsters."

"Sheriff, it really isn't about what I do or do not believe. It's about the facts as I know them. It's no different than how you approach a mystery in your line of work. Right now, based on what I've seen, the signs all point to it. Everything I've said is based on my years of education and research, or what was easily observable in the lab within a day or two. And I must point out that when Cory and Cristina came to me with their suspicions, I laughed at them. It was just too preposterous to consider. Not anymore."

"And it's that dangerous?"

"Science fiction would be hard pressed to concoct a monster of this caliber. This thing goes way beyond any horror flick you've ever seen. It makes the Alien or Predator look like a toddler's toy. Considering its invisibility, its exceedingly toxic venom, its fluidity, its movements not only in waterways but also potentially on land, our suspicions that it can smell protein, and we end up with a creature that could literally devour every protein-rich creature within the Great Lakes watershed. And what's to stop it there?"

"You're saying it would eat everything in sight?" asked Cory.

"Everything in sight and more. In general, when we look at the interaction of life in nature, a big part of that action is feed or be food, eat or be eaten. Yet, *eaters* are generally specific in what they eat. Most animals don't find everything in sight to be tasty. But this thing does.

"It doesn't differentiate between its sources of protein. It can be herbivorous as well as carnivorous. It's an opportunist. It consumes everything, digesting whatever its enzymes can break down. Unfortunately, in the food chain, this is the new apex predator possibly replacing humans. There is nothing we presently know of that will feed on it. Ironically, it shares that distinction with the sea lamprey.

"This thing doesn't have a stomach. It doesn't get full. What's to stop it? What might contain it? It's not constrained by size. It could grow as large as a lake if there was enough nutrition. Try to imagine a lake so toxic that by simply sticking your hand into it, you die. Imagine if by some bizarre circumstance it got sucked up into the supply lines for our drinking water in the Great Lakes. What if its venom passes through a treatment plant? Do you take one gulp and hit the floor? At this point we don't know."

The notion was mind-numbing. It left everyone speechless and in deeply worrisome thought until distracted by the siren of a volunteer's truck that raced past the restaurant.

"Now you understand why Professor Martinelli had to report these findings to his superiors. He forwarded his findings to the state police forensics lab, being that they are performing the autopsies. I'm sure the business community would like to keep this under wraps, but—"

"So what do you think will happen?" asked Cristina.

"I think there's going to be hell to pay until some bacteria or a virus is filled with glee upon stumbling into this for dessert. But until then—"

A second siren filled the air. This time the sheriff looked down at his side and dropped his hand. There was a faint click followed by a blast of static. An unending stream of chatter erupted from a mouthpiece clipped to the shoulder strap of his uniform. The sheriff looked blindly at Cory as they listened to the stream of calls clicking in and out.

A third siren and then another and another filled the air. The vehicles were racing past the restaurant headed toward the highway, headed west in the direction of the swamp. It was just as Sheriff Cooper decided to rise from the table that his radio sounded the first indication of a tragedy in the making.

*"... at least twenty bodies... maybe... thirty or more dead at Reedsburg Dam..."*

"So much for under wraps," said Cory.

## 37

Sheldon Young wedged his camper back in between the trees. He had rented a lot for the week at Reedsburg Dam State Forest Campground. It was a small rustic campground with fewer than forty sites. There were no power hook-ups, and water had to be ferried from hand pumps.

Sheldon had not taken the camper out for two years. In fact, he had invested much of winter and all of spring thinking about unblocking the camper wheels, picking out mice nests, and towing it down the road to shake out the dust. In so many ways, the anticipation lifted his spirits. In so many ways, the camper made him cry. Repeatedly he asked aloud in his empty house whether camping by himself would bring days of peace or nights of torture. He was so unsure of the outcome that he could only hitch up the trailer and find out.

Backing the trailer into position was more difficult than in the past because his wife of forty years, Pamela, was no longer there to guide him. Together they had gone through this process so many times over the previous decades that he trusted her calls and hand gestures without question.

A couple of bare-chested men who walked over in his direction and offered their unspoken support lessened Sheldon's loss. Like most campers, they were eager to help without being asked. They did not impose, they did not offer assistance; they merely stood guard to offer a sense of security and understanding. Once he put the truck into park and shut it down, the men nodded and moved on.

Sheldon stepped out of his truck and sucked in a deep lungful of pine-scented air. There was no substitute, no deception or trickery, the scent of pine meant one was free. He looked out across the backwaters of the Reedsburg Dam. It was as rustic as any Upper Peninsula state forest bivouac. Here the only signs of civilization were campers and smoky fires.

"Oh, Pamela.... It's a beautiful day."

Sheldon's face began to fold in on itself as the day's first pang of loss stabbed his heart. He was quick to address it.

"Baby, I welcome your presence, but don't crush me with your absence," he whispered, wiping away a hint of tears.

Sheldon made a point of going to a campground that he had never visited. It would allow him to escape sights that evoked memories. It was not an easy feat. Thirty years of camping with Pamela meant seeing most every park and campground in Michigan and states nearby. It was the rustic lesser-known places like Reedsburg that now attracted him. Sheldon took in the unfamiliar views, took note of his surroundings, and then focused on the trailer stands.

Once Sheldon leveled and stabilized the trailer, he cranked out the canopy. He positioned a couple of chairs and a table. He brought out a few other items, including some party lights that he strung up for later. He loved to sit under their glow in the darkness of a make-believe wilderness. He then went inside to put his home in order.

The rest of the day went without incident. He prepared supper inside, making the best of his tiny two-burner stove. Dinner and book in hand, he went outside and sat back into his lounge chair. He cracked open a fresh novel and drifted away, returning now and then to glance over the top of his book and cash in on whatever activity erupted beyond his crossed feet.

Sheldon found himself particularly attentive to the women that passed by. He grinned as he thought about how he only found older women attractive. It was not about the sex anymore. It was about women of interest. It was about women who had lived through good times and bad. It was about older women who could relate to his world, a world fast buried by music and entertainers and celebrities and technologies that he did not know and did not care to know. Unfortunately, there were no older women in the campground.

Nightfall came at long last. Sheldon flipped on his party lights and sat back down. It was too dark to read so he was content to study the smattering of lights and the glow of campfires that flickered through the pines and shrubs. He felt the onset of sadness. He felt the weight come down on his heart. He allowed only so much.

"Oh, sweetheart. God, I miss you."

Sheldon spoke to no one. It wasn't that he didn't care to, but he understood he was now the *"old man over there."* He recognized himself from the decades of camping with Pamela and the kids. He had seen himself many times and joked about it. He had wondered if he was widowed, divorced, or a drunk without friends.

Sheldon had not felt the desire to build a campfire, so when he arose from his chair, he had only to grab his book, turn off the party lights, and go inside. He placed the book on the kitchen table, closed the drapes, washed his face and hands, climbed into his pajamas, and called it a night. He turned off the nightstand light. There were no streetlights. There was nothing but the darkness into which he stared. He was looking over to where his wife might have been sleeping unseen in the blackness.

"Good night, Pamela."

## 38

Sheldon awoke the following morning, and lay still in bed, listening to the rise and fall of unintelligible chatter from campers preparing breakfast. The sounds of silverware and the smell of bacon were sufficient to push him out of bed. He washed up, clothed himself, but passed on the cooking. Instead, he went for a bowl of cereal and his book. He picked up from where he left off the night before, reading the same book, sitting in the same chair, watching the same campers, and hoping to see an attractive older woman. He did this until noon, at which time he arose to make a sandwich.

With a baloney sandwich now packed into his belly, Sheldon went back to his bedroom and took a nap. It was about one in the afternoon when he awoke, this time to the sound of children in the distance. They were laughing and screaming. He knew they were probably playing around the dam.

Maybe it was the sound of life in the distance, or the stillness of late afternoon with its melancholy sun that fed feelings of depression. Whatever the reason, it made the camper feel suffocating. The feelings drove him outside for fresh air or for a walk—anything to leave his shell and enjoy a brighter side of life.

Sheldon walked along the drive until he glimpsed a path that ferried campers to the dam. He turned to follow the path and soon stepped up onto the structure. As he stepped slowly along the wooden planked walkway, to his right, on the high water side, he looked down and smiled at the children playing and laughing, the same children he had heard while in the camper. Their voices mixed in with a handful of older children and teenagers who were either diving off the abutments, or lying on floats and sunning about the spillway.

To Sheldon's left, the water poured over the stoplogs. There were eight bays, eight separate waterfalls, and a fish ladder with water cascading down its flight of steps. Here he watched the older campers standing beneath the free-falling water. Many held tots in their arms or youngsters in their grip, who thrilled in a good dunking.

Sheldon smiled as he passed through all the activity. He crossed the dam and continued walking along a footpath that followed the crest of the earthen embankment built to keep water from flowing around the dam itself. The embankment reached out a ways from the dam. It contained the waters of the flooding, separating them from countless quiet pools of dark, stagnant, water that dotted the thickets beyond. The path continued onward from the embankment, leaving the backwaters behind as it headed deep into the woods.

Sheldon followed it a ways, stepping over a number of purposely placed logs positioned to keep people from venturing farther. At the third barrier, he stopped and slowly turned around. He observed every detail of the ground near and far. It felt like earth that barely tolerated the intrusions of man. He was afforded the hard pack of the path, but nothing more. If he had been a young boy, he would have been entirely spooked and high tailing it back to his friends swimming at the dam. Now he merely enjoyed the peace, turned about, and started walking back to the camper.

Sheldon took his time strolling in return along the path atop the embankment. He looked to his left, far out across the flooding. There was nothing beyond the distant edge of water but regions of marsh and swamp. As his eyes followed the shore of the flooding as it snaked its way to the vicinity of the dam, he noted the trailers and tents, and the colorful tables and toys that stood out here and there at water's edge and farther inland.

Sheldon's focus ended up back at the activity surrounding the dam. He could not yet see those standing at the low side of the dam. They were standing or frolicking in the overpour of water at the bays below his line of site. Only those children floating atop the quiet surface of the backwater, the high water, were in plain view.

The scene brought back memories of his own children when they were young and camped with him and Pamela. He watched three boys jump in unison from the dam. They hollered loudly for that one second of flight, and then disappeared into the blackish blue. He watched those on the rafts splashing about and screaming, and carrying on like wild things. It did his heart good. This was an afternoon of smiles.

As Sheldon strolled, he contemplated the expanse of wilderness that surrounded the dam. He understood he lived in Michigan, and that it was a populous state, but one would never know it by looking around. It not only looked wild, but it felt wild. Michigan was not the same as places out west where one saw nothing across endless miles of expanse. Michigan was about how forests closed in on you to instill a primal concern about all that you could not see. It prompted you to rush secretly back to the campfire at night, no matter what your age.

Sheldon's thoughts gave way to a man and woman running up the incline on the opposite side of the dam. As soon as they reached the abutment, they jumped into the high water. Something about their actions struck him as odd. Usually people screamed like Tarzan before taking a dive. His eyes shifted to the movement of three people running across the campground and diving into the water. They were swimming toward the dam.

Sheldon could no longer see the swimmers because they disappeared behind the concrete walls of the abutments that funneled water into the spillway. Annoyed by a sensation that something was going on that he was unable to see, he quickened his pace. He reached the top of the dam just as four more adults leapt into the water from the opposite embankment.

Finally, Sheldon could look down from the dam. He saw the pond now littered with stilled bodies. Bodies floating face down. Bodies suspended within the depths. He recognized two bodies belonging to the couple that had just jumped off the abutment. The bodies were all drifting toward the dam, all being pressed up against the stoplogs that formed the crest of the spillway.

Sheldon took stock of the horror before him. Something was terribly wrong. He scrambled mentally for an answer or a way to help. He looked ahead and saw dozens of people running toward the pond. They were coming in one massive wave across the campground. They were running up the trail to the embankment. They were about to enter the high water.

"No! No!" he screamed while waving his hands in the air. "No! Don't go in the water! Stay out of the water!"

Sheldon raced across the dam to stop those coming up from the other side. His effort was pointless as the crowd pushed him out of the way. He was an old man readily dismissed. He stepped aside and watched adults now screaming for loved ones as they plunged into the pond.

Sheldon went numb as he absorbed the mayhem that ensued. He looked to his right, below at the bottom of the spillways. Down there adults and children were splashing, laughing, and playing in the roar of the cascading water. They remained oblivious until a body washed over the stoplogs and landed on the concrete slab at their feet.

It took a minute before anybody understood what had just taken place. The adults were still laughing as they looked at the body lying there. The kids were yet running past it, too caught up in games to be concerned. Then came a second body and a third. Another two or three minutes would pass before those unknowing folks would realize that only six feet above their heads was a floating graveyard.

## 39

Cory, Cristina, and Tammy sat in the back of Detective Quinn's patrol car. They were among the very few outsiders allowed to flow into the campground with the influx of emergency vehicles. Cruisers from the Michigan State Police, the Roscommon, Missaukee, and Clare County Sheriff's Departments, and the Denton and Gerrish Police Departments clogged the campground roads. Emergency vehicles, fire trucks, Hazmat vehicles, ambulances, and more were arriving from all the neighboring counties.

The collective din of emergency radios, many being broadcast over external speakers, furthered the mayhem of blinding red, blue, and orange lights, themselves disrupted by fit-inducing flashes of brilliant white strobes.

Detective Quinn left the three to their own devices. Cory led the way, his camera firing off a stream of clicks. Although voice service did not extend to the campground, he was able to email the pics to Harold. He packed images of men in full Hazmat gear removing bodies from the backwater into his messages.

"Is this the beginning of the end?" asked Cristina.


## 40


Cory saw Detective Quinn's car pull into the Little Boots parking lot. He waited for him to enter the front door.

"Toby!"

"Hey, Cory."

"I was wondering if we'd catch you here."

"You got company?"

"Cristina's on her way, but c'mon, join us. Slide in."

"How's Jack doing?"

"From what Cristina says, he's doing great."

"Is he gonna make it to the meeting tonight?"

"From what I understand, he is."

"Good. I'm glad to hear it."

"Sit down, Toby. Join us."

Toby slid across the booth to enjoy the view from the window. He shook his head and commented.

"Damn. Look at the traffic."

"Yeah. I know. I was thinking that when they were pulling the bodies from the dam, Cristina asked if this was the 'beginning of the end'. You'd never believe it by looking around. When the hell was the last time we had a traffic jam in Houghton Lake?"

"Can you believe it? I've never seen so many reporters and curiosity seekers in my life."

"The dam made national news. Harold told me we're rated the number one national news story and holding. It isn't going to be a flash in the pan. All the hotels for forty miles around are booked, and it looks like they will be for some time to come."

"I'll bet Harold is on cloud nine."

"Oh, my god. You can't imagine. Harold and me both. I'm embarrassed to admit how profitable this has been. I don't think the *County Chronicle* will be going out of business anytime soon. Thanks to you, I got about as close to exclusive shots as humanly possible. Harold had them in the media faster'n I could blink. On a side note, we discussed our good fortune. And there is a lot of steak or whatever in your future."

"Thanks. I appreciate that."

"I gotta tell you, just before you walked in, I was sitting here thinking. Do you know what really bothers me about all of this? The one thing."

"No. What?"

"There is so much going on, so much money passing hands, so much profit being made here in Houghton Lake, that I just know people are forgetting we got a monster on our hands. The town is looking at this as if we have our own Lock Ness. The whole world is smiling while something out there's devouring Houghton Lake by the day."

"I hear ya. Now that the feds are in control, I think the rest of us have stepped back a little too far to take a breath."

"That, my friend, would be a false sense of security."

"Yeah, I know. I don't even want to think about it."

"That's the problem. Neither does anybody else."

291

## 41

Those not blinded by all the money passing hands, packed the school gymnasium wall to wall. They were not smiling or laughing about Lock Ness. They represented a nervous, if not frightened, gathering.

Sheriff Cooper stepped up behind the podium to address the crowd. The chatter was incessant. Numerous small groups of folks stood around drinking coffee while engaged in excited conversation.

"Folks, if you would please take a seat, I would like to get this meeting back underway. Folks. Break is over. Folks. May I have your attention? If you would please take your seats... thank you.

"I'd like to begin the second half of tonight's town hall meeting by saying once again that there are a number of these meetings taking place around the area. Just like here, a number of federal and state experts in ecology and invasive species are making the rounds. Let's not forget that these folks volunteer to attend these meetings in order to enlighten us and keep us up-to-date on progress in the fight against this threat. We appreciate the time and effort they've given.

"Having said that, our next guest had to be more or less dragged to this meeting when asked if he would address you and give his account of what he witnessed in the flooding and swamp.

"To those of you who are newcomers to Houghton Lake, I would like to say that the person I am about to call up next is a lifelong member of the community. More importantly, he has lived within the boundaries of the Dead Stream Swamp for the better part of fifty years. I doubt the man takes second seat to anybody when it comes to understanding intimately the ways of that expanse.

"I would also like to say that it was a good while back when I first encountered Mr. McGrath personally. You see, he showed up at the station with some very important information... information that sounded utterly insane. He did everything in his power to reach us, making an emotional plea for our attention. Had we listened to Jack instead of writing him off as being three shades beyond blonde, we might have been a whole lot better off tonight.

"Well, trust me. I listen to Jack now. We've discussed this threat at great length over the past few days. Even though you have heard from a number of experts this evening, I have asked Jack to present his own opinion on the best way to eradicate this monster. At present, there are no plans underway. All proposals are open to review.

"Understand, nothing suggested by Jack is sanctioned by the federal or state authorities. It doesn't mean this is the way we'll approach the problem. The feds have the final word. But I doubt there's a person in Houghton Lake who has given more thought to this problem and ways to solve it.

"I am standing here to warn you that at least one part of this plan will sound as preposterous as Jack's first emotional plea... when those of us at the station laughed him back onto the street. Please don't make the same mistake. Give him your ear and a polite welcome. Jack."

Jack rose from his chair and walked up to the podium. Sheriff Cooper shook his hand and left him to face the crowd and speak his mind. He began by clearing his throat.

"Ahem. Good evenin', folks. Ahem.... For those of ya who didn't catch my name, I go by Jack McGrath. Most of ya are young enough to be my kids. Most of those old enough to know me personally... well, they can't remember that far back or are pushin' up daisies.

"I guess I'm tryin' to say that I been around a good long time. I seen a good many things, but I ain't never seen anything the likes of this. Never. And like the sheriff said, I been livin' in that swamp for the better part of fifty years. I spent most of my days fishin' those backwaters an' eatin' boatloads of the best damn fish God could put on a plate.

"Well, I don't have t' tell ya how all of that sounds more like a fairy tale than reality, cuz tryin' to pull a fish outta the backwater is 'bout damn near impossible nowadays."

A chorus of agreement rose up from the crowd.

"I was mighty confused about what was happenin' for a long time. Havin' spent so much of my life fishin' the creeks an' backwaters, it was obvious to me that somethin' was amiss. There's never been a lack of fish in the backwater. There's always been good days an' bad days, but never an absence of fish. It took a while for it to sink in, you know, for me to realize this was different than anything I'd ever seen.

"Truth be known, ya can thank my back for the realization. I was leaned over nearly upside down fishin' around the bottom of my freezer for a filet to fry up, an' I remember thinkin', *'Mercy me, where the hell is all my fish?'* My stash of frozen fish was down to 'bout nothin' an' anybody livin' in these parts knows that ain't right."

A murmur of understanding moved through the room.

"I suspect by now, many of ya have heard about the bones that been croppin' up all over the place. An' not just reg'lar bones, but bones lookin' clean as fresh cream. Well, you folks inland can't appreciate the truth of it. Stories are still gonna be just stories. But for me, and those of us fishing the backwaters, we been livin' it. I was spendin' my days floatin' out there and seein' bones scattered thick as hair on a kid. They were lining the banks like dead seaweed. Everywhere I went. Everywhere I looked. Far as I could see. Believe me, there ain't a fisherman in these parts that don't know what I'm sayin'. They may not know the extent of it like I do, but they know what I'm sayin'. Ya just gotta hang around Stagg's bait shop to know the truth of it.

"I know when I got hospitalized, they ran an article on me in the *Chronicle*, so most of ya either read or heard the story of my dog, an' how I woke to find him lying next to me on the porch. Fourteen years that pup slept alongside me and one day I wake up an' he's in his place as always, but it ain't him. It ain't nothin' but a pile of bones with my pup's tag on a collar.

"When I got over the shock, when I got past blamin' kids for pranks, when I accepted that my Scrub went from bein' full of life to nothin' but bones, I knew there was a demon lurkin' out there somewhere. Trouble was, I didn't know who to tell. When I failed t' get the authorities' attention, I set out on my own t' find out what was goin' on. Sunup to sunset, figurin' this out become my only business.

"Been lots o' stories 'bout hookin' fish that put up a good fight, only to net 'em an' discover they're dead when you pull 'em out. Or maybe they're covered in slime or half-digested. Been a lot of that goin' on. Another story every bit as unsettlin' is the one about getting your hands burned when ya try to unhook fish. Well, folks, it's all true. All of it. I've experienced it all an' kept blamin' it on the oil and gas rigs.

"That all changed one night when I fell asleep in my rocker out on the back porch. I awoke in the middle of the night t' see this thing they call bioluminescence. I call it blue glow, or the abomination. It's about as dark as dark can get in the swamp come nighttime an' you can see light a mile off, like seein' a star in the night sky. This blue light was plain as a porch light. Ya couldn't miss it. You could see it glowin' through the thickets, an' seein' it brought home a real scare.

"This abomination wasn't just some floatin' carpet of plant life that bumped up against an oil well, got contaminated, an' drifted downstream. I know this because the swamp has a flow. Anyone who fishes the backwaters knows the flow. Houghton Lake, the Dead Stream, Haymarsh, Cole, an' Deer Farm Creeks, that water moves north to south, finally reachin' an' passin' over the Reedsburg Dam. If this were some kind of floatin' algae or chemical spill it would've flowed with the current and piled up against the dam.

"But it didn't. I watched it come down with the flow an' I watched it go against it. I watched it move purposely in the shallows as if scouring the marshes for food. An' that's exactly what it was doin'. It was cleanin' out whatever fish might yet be found in the beds. It was movin' around the shallows in front of my cabin lookin' for the fish I'd always kept well fed.

"To test my theory, I began to collect roadkill, a pastime that I been told has carned me the nickname *Roadkill Ralph.*"

The crowd exploded into laughter. The sound was a break from the silence that surrounded the audience now hanging on Jack's every word. It was as if he was standing tall in the quivering light of a great campfire, a haunting face fully aglow before rows of children whose upturned faces framed eyes opened wide and full of inner visions.

"Now for you young un's, who think I'm nuts, I want ya to know that years back, farmers that had fish ponds weren't opposed to hangin' a cow's head over the pond to rot. It would attract flies. And flies produced maggots that would feed, grow fat, and fall into the pond. The fish were all waitin' in line for treats. Cow livers were hard to sell, so they were chopped up an' tossed into the pond to make fish healthier. Roadkill went into the pond like everything else. I learned it from the ol'-timers. They wasted nothin'.

"So, now ya know I was cleanin' up the roads for good reason. By my way of thinkin', if it was hard for me to catch fish, it couldn't be any easier for this devil. I figured if I kept tossin' meat into the shallows, the fish would gather, an' it might show up t' feed.

"Well, just as I figured, after a time, it began showin' up in the shallows around my place and devourin' everything I tossed its way. In a manner of speakin', it got to be a regular. I suspect it has a simple thought process: repeat whatever works. Go to my place, eat; go back, eat more.

"My next plan was to try and figure out exactly what this demon was. Ya see, I'd only seen signs of it. That blue glow at night. I'd never actually seen it proper. Not once. I had seen some strange things on a number of occasions, but it's hard to explain. I'd see the water shift. For the longest time I thought my eyes were playin' tricks on me. But after a while, I come to make associations.

"For instance, those times I reeled in dead fish or got my hands burned were the same times my eyes were givin' me fits. Eventually, when I reeled in a dead fish, I'd look for this movement, and in time I could almost predict it, dependin' on where I was or what I was doin'. For example, tossing a fish into certain small bayous, that kind of thing would seem to trigger it. But nighttime was the best time to find this thing. And I spent a lot of nights headin' out in my boat lookin' for it.

"Now, I'll be honest. Between all the stories goin' around an' my dog endin' up dead on my porch, I had no intention of motorin' my boat into that glow. No, sir. I didn't know what it was an' I saw no reason to get stupid.

"An' that's why I enlisted the services of my lovely daughter, Cristina, to help me hang a deer carcass 'cross swings on a swing set that I had dragged into the shallows. It wasn't really that ripe, but I don' mind tellin' ya she had a mouthful of words for me to be sure. Ya wanna talk about blue."

Again the crowd laughed. Their expressions revealed an immediate affection for Jack. He possessed a roughness that seemed to protect a good and truthful heart. Cory was certain that he would be given their full respect when he made his proposal.

"Don't get me wrong. Cristina had every right to chew me out. That carcass wasn't a pretty thing, but it did its job. It attracted the abomination into the shallows to feed. I know this because I came home one afternoon an', lo an' behold, the water had shifted. It was swelled, standing somewhat higher as if trying to flow uphill over the carcass.

"At the same time Cristina and I placed the carcass on the swings, I also sank a bucket alongside it, so that when next I'd see the blue light or the water swell around the carcass, I could yank the bucket up out of the water, an' maybe catch somethin'. And I did.

"I'm told it's no secret that I ended up in the hospital. Nearly got myself killed. It's true. Ya see, the deal was, when I looked into the bucket there was nothin' in it. I mean, all I saw was water. So that left me wonderin' if the water was different, you know, thicker or slimy, or somethin' that would tell me more. I stuck my hand in the bucket, an' ya might've heard, it was no cookie jar. My glove had a hole in it, and so I was promptly poisoned with neurotoxins that kicked my ever-lovin' ass. But... The devil didn't want me, so I'm standing in front of you tonight."

Some of the crowd broke into sporadic applause and cheers.

"Yeah, ha, ha. I'm not sure everybody shares your enthusiasm." This time the room filled with laughter. Jack continued. "I also learned that this thing we're dealin' with is no joke. It can kill ya in the blink of an eye. I got a taste of what killed all those unlucky souls over the past couple of weeks. I know firsthand why an' how it's killed off just about everything in or near Dead Stream.

"But I also know for fact that we can draw this thing to wherever we want. It's always hungry an' hard pressed to find nourishment. Ya have to understand, this thing is huge. Maybe an acre or so in size. I believe the only thing that keeps this thing from getting even larger is it already ate up most of the fish. It's been held at bay by a lack of fish, but it's also gettin' desperate, an' that probably led to its learnin' how to edge up onto shore an' pick off animals drinkin' water and such. Probably the reason there's so many bones about the shoreline.

"Ya might be askin', why not let this thing just starve itself to death? Personally, I don't think that'll ever happen. It may start dyin' off. It may get down to the size of a dinner plate, eatin' nothin' but bugs, but once the fish rebound, so will it. If it ever gets out of the swamp, there'll probably be no stoppin' it. We need to kill it, pure an' simple. We need to kill it once an' for all. We need to kill it, folks. So... how do we do that?

"Well, years ago, I used t' deliver top soil to a developer who built homes around Houghton Lake, around Roscommon, Missaukee, Kalkaska, and Crawford Counties. I scraped off one hell of a lot of good rich topsoil and wound up with one gigantic hole, which has since filled up full of water. Water flows into the basin from one of the trenches that I dug along the length of my drive. When I was young, my buddies and me would fish this trench while sitting in lawn chairs an' drinkin' beer on the driveway. My buddies got to callin' it Jack's Creek, or Jack Creek, and Jack Creek Basin. An' it's been known as that ever since.

"From what I've seen, I believe this thing is yet small enough to fit in the basin. I'm thinkin' we can lure it in from the shallows down along Jack Creek and an' into the basin where we can seal it off from the swamp. We backfill the creek so it's got no way out, and then spray the basin with something like rotenone or whatever the DNR thinks best. Ya won't have t'worry 'bout killin' anything else because once that thing enters the basin, there won't be anything in there left alive.

"I believe that could work, but if it doesn't, our last alternative will sound every bit as insane as Sheriff Cooper warned. If it doesn't work, our only option is to drain the swamp, all ten or twenty thousand acres."

"Do what?"

"Drain the swamp?"

"How the hell...."

"Are you kidding?"

In spite of the forewarning, the crowd was hardly ready for something that sounded so outrageous, as to be impossible. The din had to be subdued. The sheriff stood up.

"Okay, folks, we understand your shock. But we have to entertain all opinions. Please give Mr. McGrath your respectful attention."

"As to your question, the answer is no, I'm definitely not kidding. The experts have already said privately that if this monster gets out of Dead Stream an' into Houghton or Higgins Lake, or into the Muskegon River, it could spell disaster across the whole state. And after that? What? The Great Lakes?

"I say we must be prepared to drain the swamp an' stop it in its tracks—now. Can't swim if it ain't got water. Can't float, can't feed. Let the sun bake it to death. Remember the flooding is big, but it's manmade. You open Reedsburg Dam and it goes dry."

The room was silent. Old man McGrath wasn't a fool. But the swamp was so large, any idea of draining it seemed too preposterous to be taken seriously.

"An' exactly how would we do that?"

"We would have to cut off Houghton's overflow into the swamp at the head of the Muskegon. We would have to reroute the lake overflow into Knappen Creek on its south bank and pump it southward into the east branch of Wolf Creek, and from there back to the Muskegon River some fifteen miles below the dam. That would effectively detour the overflow around the swamp and flooding.

"We absolutely cannot risk this thing getting into Houghton Lake. If that happens, we'll be forced to drain Houghton Lake. Just to refresh your memory, that would be more than thirty

299

square miles of water. We also would have to block 'The Cut' that connects Houghton Lake to Higgins Lake."

The concept sounded plausible, but left the room of attendees stunned. Jack recognized the look on their faces as the same expression he witnessed when pleading with the deputies at the station. A drained Houghton Lake and or Higgins Lake would spell certain death to all of the surrounding counties. What little money that existed in the region came by way of Houghton and Higgins Lake tourism. But Jack was one of the few who fully appreciated the apocalypse that was ready to break loose.

As outrageous as Jack's plan seemed, nobody was making fun of it. In fact, the room was uncomfortably quiet as the town folk considered the difficultly of such an undertaking. At the back of the room, a man stood up.

"Who's gonna pay for this? It ain't gonna be cheap."

"Compared to what?" said Jack. "Lettin' this monster get loose to wipe out the lakes?"

The room remained silent. Sheriff Cooper rose from his chair.

"Folks, let me remind you that Mr. McGrath's proposal is just that. A proposal. It hasn't been sanctioned by any authority. We're not here to take votes. If anybody else has an idea or suggestion, please feel free to speak up now or after the meeting. We will entertain and forward any and all suggestions."

A few more questions aired, but for all intent, the meeting was over.

Jack returned to his seat. The crowd grew louder as people commenced to discuss openly the information presented during the meeting, Jack's proposal, and their own opinions and concerns.

Cory, Cristina, Tammy, Harold, Toby Quinn, and Jack McGrath met afterward in the parking lot. They were also sharing their observations when two men dressed in suits approached. One called out.

"It's Tammy Tagart. Correct?"

Tammy turned around.

"Derrinnnnn—"

"Henderson."

"Yes. I thought that was you. I saw you seated at the back of the room."

"I thought you recognized me. It's good to see you. Tammy, this is Johnny Davida. Among other things, we work together in the Invasive Species Group."

"Pleasure."

"Mine as well."

"Actually, I just wanted to stop by and say that a copy of Dr. Martinelli's report crossed my desk. I was duly impressed. Nice work."

"Thanks."

"It gave us a leg up on the situation. We're currently drawing up plans for containment. Also, you might want to know that based on your conclusions and description of the consequences, should this thing get loose, we've already started formulating the framework for RFQs, and funds requisition and allocation. I also forwarded your suggestions from tonight's meeting.

"And, Mr. McGrath, both of your plans were outstanding. I hope you won't mind if we send a crew out to your place and look over Jack Creek and the basin."

"Not at all. If there's anything else I can do, lemme know."

"Thank you. We'll also be taking a hard look at those southern outlets for Houghton Lake and their potential for diverting the overflow. I didn't think the idea was at all outrageous. In fact, it's one of the best ideas put forward to date. Whereas everything I've heard so far sounds like a bandaid fix, you've taken the bull by the horns and faced it head on. I admire that. I may have to disagree with you on using your idea as a last resort. I prefer anything to a Hail Mary pass."

"I appreciate ya sayin' so. Thank you."

"Well, that's all I've got. Just wanted to say hello. We're on our way back to Ann Arbor. It was great seeing you again, Tammy, and I hope to see you in the near future—maybe grab lunch or something."

"Same here. Thanks for the support."

"No problem. Keep us posted. Take care."

Tammy turned around to see everybody looking at her with large grins.

"What?"

"Nice work," said Cristina.

"What are you, famous or something?" kidded Toby.

"He hopes to see you in the future, grab lunch or *something*," said Cory jokingly.

"Oh, please, just shut up. All of you. Just shut up."


# 42


Cristina ran out onto the porch.

"Dad! Dad!"

Jack looked up from the dock.

"Yeah, baby."

"They're going with your plan. I just got a call from Cory. He said that after the consortium had reviewed their options, your plan came up as the most cost effective and doable."

Jack studied Cristina and nodded his head as she walked across the dock to meet him.

"Come here. I want to give you a hug."

She looked into his eyes.

"Aren't you going to say anything?"

"Not much to say, Cri. I'm thinkin' 'bout what I gotta do to make sure the creek an' basin are free of obstructions. We' gotta get backfill in somewhere along the drive—"

"Geez, dad. You worry too much. Stop worrying. In fact, Cory said that the only thing that has to be done will be done by the consortium. They've got all the engineers and all the experts to handle it. They want to cover the bottom of the basin with a liner or something.

"Cory said they'll be out this afternoon or tomorrow at latest with drag rakes to clear the bottom. They can't have any stumps or fallen trees and branches lying under the water. He said they'll rake out anything they find to make sure the bottom is smooth. He and Sheriff Cooper are on their way over."

"Okay."

Cristina laughed, "I don't know, dad; you just have a way. You exude exuberance. Why don't you come inside? I made you some lunch."

Cristina and her father were just about to scale the porch steps when they heard the sound of a vehicle approaching. Cristina stepped away from her father to walk around the side of the house. A smile broke across her face just before she disappeared from her father's view. He heard her call out from the other side of the cabin.

"Hi."

"Hi. Did you tell Jack?" asked Cory.

"I did."

"And?"

"And he just took it in stride. I had to laugh. C'mon, we were just about to sit down for lunch."

"Oh, I'm good, Cristina, but thank you anyway. Sheriff Cooper's right behind me."

"Well, at least have some coffee. I'm sure the sheriff will want some."

"Now, that I can do."

Cristina looked past Cory to see the sheriff's patrol car heading up the drive.

She waited alongside Cory until the sheriff walked up. The three then walked together to the backside of the cabin.

"Hello, Jack."

"Hello, sheriff, Cory. How are things?"

"Good, thank you. I understand that Cristina told ya the consortium's goin' with your idea."

"She did. I was thinkin' about how long it's been since I fired up the ol' D4."

"D4?"

"Yeah, my dozer. It's back alongside the shed."

"Oh, yeah, I remember seein' that on the way in. I imagine it's fun to play with, but from what I'm told, the consortium's bringin' in all the equipment and manpower. All you gotta do, Jack, is sit in your rocker, smoke your pipe, an' cash one big fat check for lettin' 'em tear up your yard."

"That is the way I like to work. Yes, sir. So tell me, when's all this gonna take place?"

"Fast," said the sheriff. "My understanding's that the equipment is on its way over. Should be here today or tomorrow at the latest. And the crews will be here tomorrow. They're lookin' to set up a portable site office here, I imagine on your side yard, so they can monitor the shallows, and another back by the road to overlook work on the basin."

"C'mon, coffee's inside," Cristina insisted.

The four went inside to relax and discuss plans for eradicating Jack's abomination. They were laughing and conversing when they heard the sound of another vehicle coming up the drive. Cristina arose from her chair and walked to the kitchen window.

"We got company," said Cristina "He's walking toward the cabin."

Everyone stood up from the table and walked out onto the porch. A young man rounded the corner. He appeared slightly taken aback by the sight of everybody standing on the porch looking at him.

"How do. Lookin' for a Mr. Jack McGrath."

"You got 'im."

"I'm supposed to ask if I can set up the site-office here on your side lot."

"You go right ahead, son. Do whatever ya gotta do. No need to ask."

"Thank you, sir."

The man started to turn away.

"Say, are they doing anything at the basin?" asked Cory.

He turned back to face them.

"Ahhh, they brought down the other site-office and a boat to rake the bottom. That's all I know."

"Thanks."

The four finished coffee on the porch while watching the worker construct and level a base of timbers. Soon thereafter, he dropped the portable office on the base. He fiddled with the building and then tested a small generator. The man stepped inside and flipped on the lights. He then turned them off, exited the building, waved good-bye, and drove off.

"Well, folks, I should be on my way as well. I'll be back tomorrow to see how things are progressing. So until then, enjoy your afternoon."

"Same to you, sheriff," said Cristina.

Cory immediately felt the pressure of wearing out his welcome.

"I guess I better be on my way as well."

"Why?"

"Pardon?"

"I think you should stay for a while. I like your company. Unless of course, you have urgent matters to attend."

Cory chuckled. "Yeah, that's me, all right. I have a list of urgent matters. What is it you have in mind?"

"Cards. What else. You, me, and dad."

Jack was keenly aware of his daughter's attraction to Cory. He was also determined to assist her.

"Tell ya what, Cory. Cristina says you write bullshit for the tabloids—alien stuff an' things like that."

"Dad! I never said that."

"Well, maybe not in those exact words, but ya didn't say he was writing political commentary."

305

"It's okay, Cristina." Cory looked at Jack. "She could've used those exact words and pretty much nailed it."

"Well, tell you what. If you give me a hand movin' some stuff from the back of my truck, an' stick around here 'til dark, I'll give ya somethin' to write about."

"Something what to write about?"

"Ya wanna see the abomination?"

"Dad! Isn't that dangerous?"

"Not if ya stay in the boat."

"Dad."

"I'm in. I've been trying to get a picture of that thing forever. All I get is black. What do we need to move?"

Cristina piped up. "Just remember what happened when he asked me to give him a hand."

"Don't mind her. She's prone to exaggeration. C'mon."

With Cristina's warning still in the air, Jack led Cory around the cabin and up to his truck. He pointed into the back.

"I knew I wouldn't be able to find enough roadkill to keep this thing around the creek, so I drove over to a chicken processor an' talked 'em into givin' me a barrel load of chicken guts an' scraps. I was gonna ask Cristina t' give me a hand gettin' it into the boat, but to be honest... After that bit with the deer.... I'm not so inclined."

"I get your point. But I have to tell you, there's no way I'm going to be able to lift it. I haven't got the back."

"No, we ain't carryin' nothin'. I got a tractor. I'm gonna lift it with the bucket. I just need your help wrappin' a strap around the barrel an' holdin' it in place while I lift it. Just make sure it doesn't slip off the barrel."

"No problem."

"Wait here."

Jack went across the yard, and fired up an old orange Kubota. He drove it around to the truck. He situated the bucket over the barrel. Cory looped the strap around the barrel and fastened the free end to the bucket.

"Take her away."

Jack eased the barrel up off the bed of the truck.

"That should do it. Why don't ya go down to the dock? I'll be right behind ya."

"Got ya."

Jack followed Cory down the yard and parked the Kubota at the water's edge, leaving the barrel to swing from the bucket.

"Let's untie the boat an' pull it ashore. I'll drop the barrel into it, an' then we can tie it back up to the dock."

Cory followed Jack's lead. He held the boat in place as Jack climbed back onto the Kubota. Jack eased the Kubota into the water and positioned the barrel above the boat, at which point he lowered it carefully onto the bottom planks.

"That should do it."

"You think the boat'll be stable enough?"

"Mercy me, I hope so. I hate swimming."

"Even with the two of us on board?"

"Actually, it should be more stable with us on board. We'll be lowerin' its center of gravity. I'd be more worried about it goin' through the bottom planks. It's heavy."

"Whatever you say."

As Jack got off the tractor, Cory slipped the strap off the bucket. Together they maneuvered the boat back to the dock. After securing it, Jack stepped aboard. He released the barrel lid clamp and lifted it off.

"Oh, my god," exclaimed Cory as he turned away for fresh air.

"Like that smell, huh?"

"That's enough to make me toss cookies right here, right now."

"Get used to it. It won't be any better tonight."

"Oh, Jesus. Are you telling me we're going to be ladling this stuff?"

"It's only gonna be 'we', if you still think it's worth what ya might see."

"Mmm. Like I said, I'm in."

Jack replaced the barrel lid and slapped it with his hand.

"C'mon, Cory. Cristina's waitin'. Let's go play cards."

## 43

"You absolutely have to go out there?" asked a worried Cristina.

"Sweetheart. I been goin' out there at night for years. It's okay."

"Dad.... That thing hasn't been out there for years."

"Well, actually I'm thinkin' it has. It's been out there since ARL burned down. It's just that it took this long for it to grow big enough to be noticed an' wreak havoc."

"Okay, so it didn't used to be big, but now it is. And now I worry."

"Sweetheart, it isn't like this thing jumps out at ya or grabs your boat an' pulls it under. For the most part, it just floats around an' feeds."

"I thought you said it goes where it wants?"

"I did. And it does. But it's more like you floatin' on your back an' paddlin'. It putts around in an' out of the marshes an' shallows."

"And up porch steps...."

"We'll be fine, Cristina," said Cory.

"Do what you want. I just don't see the need. All I'm going to do is worry. So don't be dawdling. Don't be out all night."

"Give us two hours. Just enough to spread the chum."

"All right. Go. Please, be careful."

Cristina walked down to the dock with her father and Cory. She watched with concern as they settled into the boat.

"Are you sure that boat is going to hold you? It's awfully low in the water."

"Yeah, we're loaded down pretty good, but we should be fine. There's no waves in the backwater."

"Be careful. Watch you don't tip that boat over. You watch out for him, Cory. You never know what the ol' coot's gonna do."

Cory laughed, "You have my word. We won't be out long."

With that, Cristina quieted and watched as Cory and her father pushed off from the dock. In the blackness, the whirr of an electric trolling motor was the only sound, the sweeping beams of flashlights the only sight, until they disappeared beyond the trees.

"D'you have a particular place in mind?" asked Cory.

"No. My concern is that the damned thing is upstream. That will make it harder to lure down to the creek. If we're lucky an' it's downstream, we can float chum down to it an' let it feed its way toward us. I know it'll follow the trail back to its source. It'll follow us back."

"Are you looking for the glow?"

"That's all we got."

"What if it isn't glowin'?"

"Then we make it."

"How?"

"I think it glows to attract fish. But I believe it takes a fish or something that feeds it to trigger the glow. It's sort o' like findin' a dollar on the floor and yellin' to your friends, 'Hey, look what I found'."

"So if we toss in some chum, it should start glowing."

"Yeah. That's what I'm hopin'. I've seen it happen a number of times when I threw fish back. But let's not get ahead of ourselves. Most likely, it's already glowin'. We just gotta find it."

"When do we start spreading chum?"

"Now."

"Oh."

"Do me a favor, Cory. Open the lid, dig out a can full and toss it. Sittin' here at the back of the boat, I'm the only one downwind from that stink so don't leave the lid off any longer than ya have to, okay? I'll be holdin' my breath."

"Got it."

Jack powered the boat all the way down the flooding until they reached the dam. Cory had tossed canfuls of chum to no avail. Chicken slime dripped off of his hands.

"Jesus, I can't take this anymore."

Cory plunged his hands into the lake and rinsed them off. Jack raised his eyebrows.

"I wouldn't be makin' a habit of washing your hands in the lake."

"I hear you. If I'd have seen any glow, I'd have dealt with the stink."

"Long as ya understand."

Cory shook the lake water off his hands, and dried them on his jeans. The trip back up the flooding yielded equally dismal results. They found nothing.

"Well, I guess we're headed up into Dead Stream," said Jack.

"Is that a bad thing?"

"It's not a great thing. I know this swamp. Once we leave the open water, there's only streams. Then we're dealin' with currents. They ain't strong, but we'll be comin' up on that thing from downstream."

"Is that a problem?"

"I don't think so. Shouldn't be. But we'll have to get a lot closer, maybe even right on top of it, before we find it."

"I don't especially like the sound of that."

"Just remember this. No matter what happens—not that I expect anything should—just remember to keep out of the water. Don't go stickin' your hand in to wash off chicken shit or anything else unless ya wanna die or somethin'."

"Okayeeeeeeee."

Jack and Cory continued in silence that was only broken by the occasional splash of tossed chum or a large fish in the shadows. They traveled up the headwater of the Muskegon River until reaching Dead Stream Creek. They steered left at the fork and continued upstream until reaching Deer Farm Creek, where Jack turned off the motor and let the boat begin to drift. They sat in silence until Cory spoke up.

"Something wrong?"

"I got a bad feelin'. A really bad feelin'."

"About what?"

"If this thing went the other way, you know, followed the fish trail up the Muskegon to Houghton Lake, we're in serious trouble. If it enters the lake, we may never get it back down to the basin."

"What are you thinking we should do?"

"I say we go back to the fork, an' then boat up the Muskegon toward the lake. We'll just keep our fingers crossed an' hope we don't see anything glowin' up that-a-way."

The two men said nothing more as the boat drifted quietly back down Dead Stream Creek. It was not long before it reached the confluence. Jack switched on the electric motor and headed up the Muskegon toward Houghton Lake. Fifteen minutes later, the lights of the community and traffic on 27 came into view, along with something much more sinister.

The water about the boat took on a faint glow. Cory saw it. He turned to look back at Jack, who glanced down at the motor control and moved to shut it off. Jack then looked at Cory.

"Damn."

"You saw it."

"This is about as bad as it can get."

"What are you thinking?"

"Well, I'm thinkin' that the lake's less than a thousand feet ahead. The fish comin' down the overflow are drawin' this thing toward the lake. If it's not already there, it hasn't got far to go. We gotta draw it back into the swamp. An' that ain't gonna be easy."

"What d'you have in mind?"

"Empty the barrel. Empty the barrel out here an' work our way back to the swamp. If that thing gets into the lake, it's over. I don't even wanna think about it."

"Should we start shoveling this shit in here?"

"Yeah. Don't stick your hand in the water or let it splash up on ya."

Jack stood up slowly, and carefully pulled the lid off the barrel. He reached for a can.

"You got your camera ready? You might be surprised at what happens when I toss in this chum."

"Ahhh. Hang on.... Okay."

311

Jack scooped out a can full of chum and tossed it into the water. The water lit up at once. He tossed in another scoop, and another, and then a couple more off the opposite side of the boat.

"Unbelievable," uttered Cory as he raised the cell phone to snap off one picture after another. I hope it shows up this time. The last time I tried to get pictures, all I got was black."

The boat now surrounded in the soft eerie blue glow of light turned the figures of both men into silhouettes. Cory was reviewing images on the screen of his cell when the boat rocked without warning.

"Whoa!" said Cory. "Don't be tipping us over."

"That wasn't me."

"Well, it wasn't me. I'm just standing here."

"I know. That's the shift in the water I was tellin' ya about."

"What?" Cory looked around with alarm. "The coalescing?"

"If that's what it is. Yup."

"That's a little unnerving."

"You get your pictures?"

"Yeah, I think so."

"Good. It's time to head back toward the backwater. You need to start spreadin' chum. We gotta lure this thing farther back from the lake even if it takes all night."

"Okay. I'm in."

Cory pocketed his phone and began shoveling out the chum in earnest.

"Wow. Look at the size of the glow. It's growing. Hey, look, Jack. It's pulsing. I gotta get a video of this if I can. Just give me a moment."

Cory was on his feet adjusting his cell phone when Jack gave him a warning.

"Be careful, Cory. You're rockin' the boat. Believe me, you don't wanna lose your balance."

"Sorry. Can you toss in another can from where you're sittin'? I'd like to get some video of this thing pulsing. See if you can get it going."

Jack did as Cory asked.

"Wow. You really got that thing wound up. Look at those patterns."

Cory was busy shooting video when, without warning, the boat pitched hard to starboard. Cory crouched at once to stabilize it. He looked at Jack, who was clutching both sides of the boat.

"Christ almighty! We hit something or what?"

"No. The prop would have hung up. Felt more like a wave coming from your end."

"A wave or a whale?"

Both men had the same thought and reached for their flashlights. They turned them on and trained the beams into the water. They studied the perimeter of the boat.

"I don't see anything," said Cory.

"I'm not surprised. Keep shovelin' that stuff an' I'll keep us headin' away from the lake. Don't get too close to the water."

Cory tossed in another four or five canfuls of chicken parts before the boat was struck by another wave, and then a third, which was far more pronounced.

"Jesus! I didn't like that," said Cory, who fully collapsed upon his knees in order to stabilize the boat.

"Yeah, that was a bit much. We can't risk gettin' tipped. We can't have water comin' aboard. We don't want that water in the boat. This barrel is making us too top heavy," said Jack.

"Shit!" said Cory while frantically looking about. "Shit!" he repeated.

Cory looked into the beam of light that came from Jack's flashlight, which pointed into a thicket of cattails and reeds alongside the boat. He watched as the cattails began to bend away from the boat, which was rising up along their stems.

"That thing is pushing us over! The boat's going to flip!" Cory hollered.

313

"Quick, give me a hand! Dump the barrel. Throw it over! Throw it over!" yelled Jack.

Both men dropped to their knees and struggled to lift the barrel over the side. It was still too heavy. Trying not to panic, they studied the situation in what seconds remained.

"Drag it back, Cory. Lay it on its side an' dump the contents."

Cory didn't question Jack's intent. He helped slide the barrel to port, the high side, and with Jack, grabbed the upper rim. They laid it down across the gunnel and up-ended it. The chicken parts began pouring out. Once it lightened enough, Jack yelled out.

"Flip the barrel over! Flip it over!"

Cory did as told, and together they flipped the bottom of the barrel up over the side of the severely canted boat. Their quick actions resulted in two simultaneous developments. First, the boat shot upward like a bobber freed by a fish. Second, the boat shot upward as the result of a massive surge of blue water from below. It lifted the boat above the marsh grasses that had trapped it in place.

"Grab an oar!" shouted Jack. "Push us off the reeds an' back toward the water."

Cory acted out each of Jack's instructions without question. He grabbed an oar and plunged it through the watery slurry until it reached resistance, at which point he struggled to help Jack stabilize the boat. Together, they forced the boat against the slime. Jack leaned hard into the other oar until the boat slid down the surge and away from the reeds back into open water.

The short-lived but intense event left both men speechless and fixed on the barrel that was moving about by some unknown force. Cory realized that he was shaking from the rush of adrenaline.

"That was just too damn close. Did you know that could happen?"

Jack was busy fiddling with the control for the trolling motor and answered in a distracted manner.

"Yes an' no. I've seen it happen a few times, but never to that extreme."

"What the hell was with that? It was like that thing just rose up out of the water—just rose up. Christ almighty, I thought we were done for."

"Yeah, that was a tad unsettling."

"*Tad unsettling?* That's one way of putting it."

Cory shook his head in disbelief. He was riding an adrenaline high. He continued to talk, subconsciously releasing stress, while Jack concentrated on piloting the boat back down the backwater and toward the cabin.

"Did you see the way we got lifted up and pushed over on top of those reeds? The fact we didn't flip over was nothing more than just pure luck. Pure luck. I can't believe it. I mean, we'd've been dead right there. That sonovabitch would've dissolved us and that would've been that." Cory looked back at Jack. "You never saw it do that before?"

"Not like that. The only thing I ever saw was a sort of shiftin' of the water. For the longest time I thought it was my eyes givin' me fits. After a while I began to suspect that it had some sort of mass, but I never realized it could do anything the likes of that."

"Jeeeeeesus." Cory let out a long breath.

"You still got your cell?"

Cory checked his pocket. "Yeah."

"You should have service here. We're still close to the highway. Call the sheriff. Tell him that sonovabitch is at the mouth of the Muskegon an' may or may not already be in Houghton Lake. Tell him we might've bought him a few hours, but he's gotta get hold of a chopper an' have it seed the backwater with chum to keep that thing feedin' within the flooding.

"Tell him to fly that chopper over to Missaukee Poultry an' load it up. Then fly back here an' dump it in the river startin' at Higgins Lake Road Bridge, right there at that landin' an' spread it downstream toward swamp. Tell him he's gotta do it now. Not to wait 'til mornin'. That'll be too late."

Cory placed the call. The sheriff was half-asleep, but finally grasped the gravity of the situation, and assured Cory he would get on it. Cory put away his phone.

315

"It's in Cooper's hands now."

"That it is."

"So what d'you think?"

"I'm thinkin' we had a good twenty or thirty gallons of chicken guts left in that barrel. It would take a fair number of fish to equal that meal. I'm hopin' it's enough food to hold that thing back from the lake. If that chopper gets its ass in gear an' seeds the backwater, and if we can get that devil farther south, then we should be able to draw it into Jack Creek."

It was too dark for Jack to see Cory nod in understanding.

"Is there anything else we can do?"

"I don't know what. No. Just go home an' get some sleep. The consortium has to finish this out tomorrow. Liner or no liner, they gotta get that thing into the basin an' kill it. I hope we're not too late."

"What do you mean?"

"Well, for starters, if it gets into the lake, it's free. There's nothin' we can do. If we're lucky enough, an' manage to draw it away from the lake, and down to the basin, I'm wonderin' if it's too big to be contained. This thing got really big, really fast."

The men sat in silence, and as Cory contemplated what Jack said, a notion came to mind.

"You know, Jack. I was just thinking... you remember Cristina and me telling you about Gloven and his operation?"

"Yeah."

"I'll bet you this abomination, as you call it, exploded into monster proportions because Gloven started hauling in diseased cattle and dumping them into the shallows. I wouldn't be surprised if he intentionally fed this thing so that it was big enough to quickly strip clean all the crap he was dropping into his nets. That would have increased its size faster than anything it would have found on its own to eat in the swamp.

"Boneman had quite the Internet business going. I mean, you wouldn't have believed your eyes had you seen the thousands of bones in his trailers and littered around his place. I mean, honest to god, he paved his drive out to the swamp in bones. I'll bet ya anything you wanna bet that's what kicked this whole thing into overdrive."

"Mercy me, that's the most sensible thing I've heard so far. I couldn't figure out how the hell that thing got so big. I mean there's nothing left in the swamp to eat. At least not around my place. You start lobbing in cattle—that would answer it. Sure as shit."

Cory and Jack settled back into silence a second time. Only the whirr of the trolling motor sounded across the water.

"Jack?"

"Yeah."

"How long will that motor last?"

"This? Oh mercy, this is a multi-battery motor. I can run it five or ten hours, dependin' on how hard I push it."

"So, no problem getting back."

"No problem at all. Ya needn't worry."

"Good."

Jack and Cory eventually made it back to the dock. They hadn't said much about the incident mostly due to being tired. But Jack did have his concerns.

"Cory, will ya do me a favor and not say anything to Cristina about what happened. You gotta know, she'll never let me out in a boat again. I ain't bothered by it, an' you look to be doin' fine. So, why put all the worry on her. Ya know what I'm sayin'?"

"Absolutely."

Cristina had been sleeping in her father's rocker. She awoke at the sound of them talking on the dock.

"I didn't think you were ever going to get back. Would you like me to put on some coffee?"

Cory saw Jack wince.

"Don't worry, I doubt she heard anything. She's still half asleep."

Jack nodded at Cory and then responded to Cristina, "Sounds good, Cri."

317

The three had a quick cup of coffee after which Cristina walked Cory to his truck and said goodbye. When she returned to the porch, Jack was rocking gently in his chair and smoking his pipe.

"Good night, dad."

"Good night, sweetheart. Sleep tight."

In the silence of night, Jack pored back over the near-fatal mishap. No matter how he remembered the event, it always ended up with him seeing the abomination rise up out of the water and lift the boat onto the marsh grasses. There was no escaping it. He wondered if this would become a problem, but the answer never came. His arm lowered gently to the side, his pipe still gripped firmly within his hand, as he fell into the dreams of sleep.

## 44

The following morning Jack awoke early, but nowhere near his usual hour. He reached down and picked his pipe up off the wooden planks. He leaned forward and tapped his pipe on the banister until satisfied the ash ejected. He rose to his feet, aligned his back, and entered the cabin to take his morning piss. He stopped short to make a pot of coffee for Cri, and then wandered off to use the toilet and wash up.

Jack's movements about the bathroom awoke Cristina, and she was soon on her feet. She entered the kitchen and reached for a couple of mugs, which she placed on the counter. She looked first at the clock, which read 6:10, and next out the window, where she studied the portable office that sat in plain view. Somebody was already inside.

"Good morning, Cri."

Cristina turned away from the window.

"Good morning, dad. Did you spend the night in the rocker?"

"Yeah. Mercy me, I swear, it's never my intention, but it always ends up that way. It's a hurtful thing."

318

"I can't figure out how you do it. Here, have some coffee."

"Thanks. How 'bout you? You sleep well?"

"Slept hard. I think it was a little cooler last night."

"I think you're right."

Cristina sat down at the table. Jack followed suit. She took a sip of her coffee, and then looked over to her dad.

"So, what do you think this day's gonna bring?"

"Hard to say. But I'll bet ya it won't be boring."

The two conversed lightly until interrupted by the sound of a vehicle coming up the drive.

"Company."

Cristina stood up from the table and walked over to the window.

"Somebody else just went into the office."

"Yeah, I think I'll go say good mornin'."

"That's fine. I'll make up some breakfast, and give you a call when it's ready."

"Sounds good."

Jack stepped outside and made his way toward the porta-office. He noted that three men had arrived instead of just the one Cristina had seen from the window.

"Good mornin'," he called out.

"Morning. You must be Mr. McGrath."

"Call me Jack."

"Jack, my name is Ron Spelling. I'm one of the site managers. After I finish assisting down at the basin, I'll be stationed here in the yard to keep an eye out for this thing's approach. I'll do my best to stay outta your hair."

"Aw, you don't have to worry none about that. In fact, I just came up to see if there's anything I can do for you folks. If ya need coffee or anything, jus' let me know."

"Thank you for offering. Fact is, these porta-offices are well stocked, so we should be good. I understand you had quite a night last night."

"Shussh."

Jack turned to look back at the cabin, and then at Ron.

"My daughter doesn't know a thing about that. It got a little dicey, so I'd prefer we kept it to ourselves."

Ron smiled. "No problem."

"But you're right. We had a time of it. I don't think my second mate's gonna forget the night anytime soon. I was really concerned about that devil gettin' into the lake. I'm still worried about it."

Ron nodded in understanding.

"And for good reason," he responded. "But my understanding is that the crew on the chopper could see the glow quite clearly from above. They spotted it right where you said it would be. They baited it, and according to them it moved southward following the chum line just as you had hoped."

"Outstanding. So what happens today? I don't think we can afford to waste any more time."

"Well, we're raking the basin right now. The project team is adamant about gettin' a liner in place if at all possible. We got about fifty yards of fill on its way here to block off the creek. We're gonna have to dump that on your drive, which may make getting in and out of here a bit tight. There won't be a lot of room on the drive."

"Well, tell the idiots not to dump it on the drive. Bring it up here by the house. They can still access the creek, an' there's plenty of room for trucks to get in an' out around their dumps. I don't really see any of us goin' out today. We're fine. Besides, I'm thinkin' all the action's gonna be around here anyway, an' I don't plan on missin' any of it."

"I'll mention it. Well, I got a few instruments to set up here and then I'll be headed over to the basin. You're welcome to come by and watch the work."

"I probably will. Not much else goin' on. Maybe I'll walk down with my daughter."

"Okay, well, you're welcome to stick around, but bear with me, I have to get this stuff hooked up."

"Go right ahead. Don't let me get in the way. If ya don't mind, I'd love to watch while I'm waitin' around for my breakfast."

"Nope. I don't mind."

Jack watched the team set up some monitoring equipment that would communicate with sensors placed in the shallows. Ron was generous with his information and explanations. Jack gave him his undivided attention until he saw Cory's truck pull up in the yard. At that point, he excused himself and walked up to meet Cory.

"Cory."

"Hello, Jack. Did you manage to get some sleep?"

"Some. You?"

"Some. That little episode last night kept me from getting any real sleep. I spent most of my night writing."

"What did you call your article?"

*"Dead Stream Swamp Monster Rears Its Liquid Head."*

Jack laughed, "I like it. I can see myself gettin' sucked in at the check-out line."

"That's good. If the rest of the world feels the same way, I might make a few more bucks."

Jack continued to laugh. He liked Cory.

"How's Cristina this morning?"

"Good. Go on down an' say hello. She's makin' up breakfast. Join us if ya want."

"I think I will. See you in a bit."

Jack watched Cory head toward the cabin. He decided to walk across the upper yard and look over the D4. It hadn't been started in quite a while.

"Cristina?"

"Cory?"

"Yeah, good morning."

"Good morning. C'mon in."

Cristina walked over to meet him at the screen door.

"Hi. What brings you this way?"

321

"How are you?" he asked.

"Good. Slept hard. Would you like some coffee?"

"Sounds good."

Cristina retrieved another cup and filled it. She handed it to him.

"Thank you. So are you ready for the day? It should be a crazy one."

"I guess."

"Are you nervous?"

"Oh. I'm fine," said Cristina. "A little anxious about what's going on."

"Are you afraid?"

"No. Should I be?"

"No. I don't think so. Looks to me like everything is under control."

"What's the plan?"

"Nothing's changed as far as I know," said Cory. "They're still spreading chum, keeping it close by. This evening, when it starts getting a little darker, and they can see the thing, they'll attempt to draw it into the shallows, into Jack Creek, and then into the basin to trap it."

"How do they plan on killing it?"

"I'm not sure. The Environmental Protection Agency is here. I saw their trucks down on the road when I pulled into the driveway. Cooper told me there was talk about pumping out the water with some kind of super-duper filter and dehydrating it.

"But there's also been talk about spraying it with a piscicide like rotenone. That has to be done by a specialist. Normally, it takes months to undertake anything of the sort. I suppose they have half the government here to assure every *t* gets crossed. There's a whole lot of important-looking people standing in the road, and somewhere within all that brain power there must be a plan."

"Let's hope they get it right. Because, if they don't, then what?"

"Then what? Then we don't even want to go there."

"Would you care for some breakfast?"

"I would love some breakfast. I'm starved."

"Would you mind chasing down dad? Tell him it's time to eat."

"Will do."


## 45


Jack finished his breakfast, and left Cristina to Cory. He strolled down the drive past the D4, and on toward the basin. He stood his ground as a train of dump trucks started up the drive in his direction. The back brakes on the first truck squealed fiercely as it eased to a stop. Jack walked around to speak to the driver.

"How ya doin'?"

"Good, man. What's up?"

"I heard ya got some fifty yards to dump an', if ya wanna make clean work of it, drive up to the yard an' ya can dump on the left side where the drive opens up. The creek's right there an' you'll get in an' out a helluva lot easier. Same with the dozer."

"Great. Appreciate it."

Jack snapped off a salute of sorts and resumed his walk toward the basin. He was studying the creek to his right, looking for potential problems, when his eyes caught something that hollowed out his heart. His awareness had dismissed it a million times over the years, but today it held fast.

It was the one other weathered post with a plank nailed to it. It looked much like the 'McGrath' sign at the end of the drive, only it suffered to stand tall in the waters of the trench. Pale flaking bits of color were still sufficiently visible to spell out 'Jack's Creek'.

The vision instantly brought back a flash of Jack's two oldest friends sitting in lawn chairs with cold beers and fishing rods. They represented the best of memories, the best of times. One died in his forties—a car crash. The other made it just past sixty before cancer took him.

Jack preferred not to dwell on the past. It could do little more than remind him of what he once had, how rich his life once was, how little was left, and how depressing it could now be if he chose to allow it. Instead, he smiled and let the rush of bittersweet feelings pass through him. He half-saluted the ghosts of his friends and continued walking. He did not care to look back.

Once he arrived at the basin, Jack was quite surprised at the number of people milling about. A quick count totaled near thirty. He noticed cruisers belonging to the sheriff's department and the state police, cars belonging to the Department of Natural Resources, the Environmental Protection Agency, the University of Michigan, and Central Michigan University, according to large decals on the sides of the doors.

Jack watched with interest as a boat crisscrossed the basin repeatedly while dragging a rake that quite effectively hauled out dead branches but little else. The basin was relatively clean. When he saw large rolls of plastic lined up alongside the basin, he realized that the consortium was pushing for the liner. He wondered how or if they would seal the plastic strips together.

"Hello, Jack."

Jack spun around to see Tammy Tagart smiling at him.

"Well, hello, Tammy. How are ya?"

"I'm good. And you?"

"Good. Just watchin' all the activity. These boys got their work cut out for 'em. D'you think they'll make it by nightfall?"

"They should. Their biggest concern was the basin being full of fallen trees, but I guess there's only one. They're bringing in some equipment to haul it out, and all should be good. They're going to start laying the liner even before the tree is out."

"Well, hearin' it makes me feel better."

Jack and Tammy stood side-by-side in silence watching the work for a moment before Tammy spoke up.

"I suppose I should get back. I just wanted to say hello. You look like you're doing fine. I'm happy to see that."

"Thank you, Tammy. Say, there's somethin' that's troublin' me. Can I get your ear for a moment before you leave?"

"Of course, what is it?"

"I remember when you were tellin' Sheriff Cooper about this thing. Ya said it had the ability to...—I believe you said *coalesce*."

"Yes, that's the right term—'coalesce'."

"Yeah. Well, I think this ability to coalesce might be far stronger than anticipated."

"What are you saying, Jack?"

"Well... did ya hear about me an' Cory tryin' to locate this thing last night?"

"I got the gist of it, yes."

"Well, soon enough there's this tabloid article goin' to print that's titled, *Dead Stream Swamp Monster Rears Its Liquid Head*. Trouble is, unlike a lot of bullshit that gets printed up in those rag sheets, this one's dead on. I don't know what we ran into last night, but it lifted our boat up out of the water an' set us down on a thicket of reeds an' grass.

"God was lookin' down on us, Tammy. The boat didn't capsize. If it had, I wouldn't be standin' here talkin' to ya. Anyhow, the point is this. I'm thinkin' it did the coalescin' thing an' that may become somethin' we better take into account. Ya know what I mean?"

Jack awaited Tammy's comment, but she was staring at him with a distant look in her eyes. Her mind was racing. Finally, he could see himself come back into focus.

"That's interesting. Can you tell me anything more about it?"

"No. It was pitch black out there, so there was nothin' to see 'cept what passed by the beam of my flashlight. I'll tell ya, speakin' frankly, it scared the shit out of both of us. We were about as close to getting dead as you can get. Took a bit for us to get our wits back."

"I bet. Okay. I'll pass that info along. I'm glad you shared it with me. Ahhh, I don't mean to be rude, but I gotta go, Jack. You take care of yourself now."

"Thanks, I will. Go. Go."

Tammy patted him on the shoulder a couple of times and then turned to seek out her party. A short distance away she turned to address Jack.

"Jack! How high did it lift the boat?"

"Realistically, maybe a foot, or a foot an' half. But it felt like five or ten."

"I'll bet it did. Thanks."

Tammy went on her way, and Jack had seen enough. His curiosity was satisfied. Now, more than anything else, he felt the need for a second cup of coffee. He started back for the cabin. He noticed that the trucks dumped their loads precisely where he had instructed. That was smart. He spent had enough years dumping soil and dozing it to know.

Inside the cabin, Cristina handed Jack a fresh cup of coffee and persuaded him to join her and Cory at cards. He played until the short night's sleep took its toll. Overcome with drowsiness, he excused himself from the table and retired to his bedroom.

## 46

Jack was shocked to have awakened during the last throes of daylight. He was somewhat annoyed in knowing he had missed a good deal of the day's activity. He got up from his bed and headed for the kitchen.

"Well, look who's returned from the dead."

"Dead doesn't seem to be the word for it."

"That'll teach you not to play outside all night. Coffee?"

"Please. Where's Cory?"

"Well, after dozing off at the table, he decided to go down to the basin and look around. The *Chronicle*'s paying him for stories, and, according to Cory, this one's the mother lode."

"So, did I miss anything of interest?"

"No, not that I know of. They brought down a couple of boats that have been out into the swamp and back three or four times. The helicopter's been flying overhead every fifteen or twenty minutes. How you slept through all that I don't know."

"Old-man ears."

"There's been plenty of traffic next door at the office. They've been walking the creek. That's about all I can see from here."

"You wanna get out, take a walk over to the office with me?"

"Sure."

Jack set his coffee down on the table and held the screen door open for Cristina. They stepped off the porch and crossed the yard.

"Hello, Jack."

"Ron. Have you met my daughter, Cristina?"

"I have not. My pleasure."

"Hello, Ron."

"So, did ya get your monitors in place?"

"We did. In fact, we're already picking up signals."

"Really? What're ya pickin' up?"

"Changes in pH levels. It's moving this way. We're picking up the rise in acidity as it approaches."

"It's feeding?"

"I'm sure of it. They've been dropping food from the chopper all day. We're taking our time, hoping that we've drawn all of it away from the lake. We're trying to put down enough bait to keep it from breaking up and going off in different directions. We haven't baited the shallows as of yet. We're gonna wait 'til dark."

"Good idea. You'll be able to see it."

"Actually, we see it really good right now. The monitors are very sensitive. Not only does the bloom keep close to the bottom when it feeds, but the hydrochloric acid it uses for digestion is half again as heavy as water. The acid settles to the bottom and our monitors immediately pick it up. We know right where it's at.

"It's more about us being the *only* ones who can see it. So, we'll wait 'til after dark before baiting the shallows to make sure that the rest of the world can see your pet. That's the safest approach. Everybody will know when it has entered the shallows, then the creek, and finally when all of it is contained in the basin."

"I don't think you'll have any trouble with that."

"I hope not."

"Any idea how long after dark before you'll bring it into the shallows? About what time you're plannin'?"

Ron looked at his watch.

"About three hours. Somewhere around ten-thirty or eleven. Should be sufficiently dark by then."

"Eleven o'clock."

"Right around there. At least that's the plan."

"Well, I guess there's plenty of time for me to get myself somethin' to eat."

Jack looked at Cristina. She took his arm and led him back to the cabin.

"You spoil me rotten."

"I do. And the worst part is, I really have no idea why."

Cristina warmed up some leftovers. She and Jack sat down at the table to eat and chat as the activity outside began to pick up. An unexpected pounding of footsteps on the porch startled them both. They turned in unison to see Cory and the sheriff looking in through the screen door.

"Hi. We didn't hear your car."

"Hello, Cristina. Yeah, we walked up. Getting hard to move a car around. May we come in?" asked Cory.

"Of course. Hello, sheriff."

"Hello, Cristina. Jack. How you two doin?"

"Good. C'mon in. Have a seat. Got plenty o' coffee."

"Help yourself to some leftovers if you wish," said Cristina.

"Oh, that looks good," said the sheriff. Cory was already reaching for a chicken leg.

"Let me get you some plates."

"Sleep well, Jack?" asked Cory.

"Ya think? I heard you were doin' some dozin' yourself."

"Yeah, you heard right. I couldn't keep my eyes open for anything. I finally had to go out and get some fresh air."

Cristina set two cups on the table and poured coffee.

"Oh, thank you for that, Cristina. Cory did say that if I followed him, I'd find a good cup of coffee."

"He should know. He was drinking plenty of it earlier. Those two were out screwing around in the swamp all night."

"So I've been told."

"Well, what's happenin' out there?" asked Jack.

"Oh, I'd say we're pretty much ready. They got the liner in place. They were just baiting the basin and creek as we came up. Lots of people. Lots of commotion," said Cory.

"Lot of traffic," said Sheriff Cooper. "We've got roadblocks set up all over the place. Half the county's tryin' to get back here. If I were to take a guess, I'd say there must be a hundred reporters milling about. Gonna be a lot of litter."

"Long as you guys clean it up."

After some conversation, Toby Quinn's name came up, and it caught Cristina's attention.

"How is Toby? We haven't seen much of him as of late."

"He's doin' good. Hold on." The sheriff reached for his radio. "One twelve, channel four."

The radio crackled. "One twelve, go ahead."

"Detective Sergeant, can you stop by the McGrath cabin? Over."

"Affirmative. Things are quiet for now. Gimme five minutes. Over."

"Copy that. Will be waitin'. Over and out." The sheriff smiled. "I guess we'll be needin' another cup."

"I guess we'll be needin' another pot," said Cristina.

A hearty welcome awaited Detective Sergeant Quinn when he made his way up the porch steps. He joined the party for coffee and finger food. The conversation was lively as he brought everybody up to speed on both what he'd been up to during the past few days, and what was currently taking place over at the basin.

"And so, here I am having coffee and waiting around like the rest of the world. Once they finish baiting the pond, it's just a matter of waiting for dark."

"It's gettin' close," said the sheriff.

Detective Sergeant Quinn looked at his watch, which triggered a chain reaction. Sheriff Cooper looked at his watch. Cory looked at his cell phone time. Jack looked at the clock on the kitchen wall.

"Finish up, Toby. We should've been back half an hour ago."

The men stood up.

"So what's on *your* agenda?" Cory asked Jack.

"I'm stickin' around here. I wanna see that devil enter the shallows an' then I'm gonna personally walk the sonovabitch down the creek an' send it to its grave. I wanna make sure I see that abomination die with my own two eyes. Then it's back to a peaceful life of fishin'."

Everybody laughed.

"Sounds like a plan to me," said Cory. "Okay. Well, I'll see you a little later. I'm going to head back to the basin with these gents and take notes and pics. Gotta keep Harold in the pink."

"No problem. I'm sure I'll see ya in a bit."

"Cristina, would you like to join me?"

"Oh, Cory, I would, but I'm staying with dad."

"No, no, no. You go, Cristina. I'm fine."

"Cory, I'm staying with dad."

The look in Cristina's eyes left Cory with no room for attempting persuasion.

"I'll talk to you later."

Cristina smiled. "I'll walk you up to the drive."

The four departed, leaving Jack seated at the table. As soon as they stepped off the porch they looked upward.

"It's sprinkling," said Cristina with surprise. "Was it supposed to rain tonight? It's so hard to see the sky from beneath all these trees."

"Isolated showers, nothin' heavy," said the sheriff.

As if to make him a liar, the sprinkles turned more to a light rain. The sheriff's and detective sergeant's two-way radios crackled through the night air. All five stood silent as an announcement was aired. Command dispatch repeated that the operation was underway. The order went out to extinguish all lights.

"I guess they're starting a little earlier than I thought," said the sheriff.

"I think it's because of the cloud cover. It got darker sooner than expected," said Toby. I'll bet they don't want that chopper up there in the rain any longer than necessary."

"I'm sure of it," said the sheriff. "Quinn, can I get a lift back to the basin?"

"Jump in."

"See you two later," said the sheriff as he opened the door to Quinn's car.

Cory and Cristina both raised their hands and waved.

"Later."

Cory turned to Cristina.

"You better go back, Cristina, before you get soaked."

Without thinking, Cory took Cristina's hand and lifted it up. He kissed it. The gesture was so quick that it caught both of them by surprise.

"Oh, I'm sorry," he said as he shook his head. "I don't even know why I did that."

Cristina laughed. "It was sweet." She rose on her feet and kissed him on the cheek. "Byeeeeee," she wailed as she turned to run back through the rain toward the cabin.

Cory stood momentarily in place, watching her silhouette shrink before the cabin lights. He felt off balance. He felt as if unseen doors had just opened. He shook his head a second time and

331

attempted to focus on the events at hand. He headed for his truck to get an umbrella.

## 47

"Dad?" Cristina called out.

"Yeah, sweetheart."

"Turn out the lights. They've started."

Cristina walked past Jack, still seated at the table, and began turning off the lights. She entered her bedroom and returned with a blanket over her arm.

"C'mon, we'll sit on the porch. You can smoke your pipe."

"Good idea."

Jack rose to his feet, and they stepped out of the kitchen. The screen door slammed shut behind them. Cristina positioned a chair close to her father's rocker. She looked about the porch to make sure all was in order. She looked at her father to assure herself that he was seated and comfortable, and then she reached inside the screen door and slid her hand down the wall. A switch clicked, and the porch light went out. She took her seat and spread the blanket across her legs.

"You cold?" asked Jack.

"No, not really. I'm wet."

"Oh."

"To be honest, I think it's more about security. Remember when you were a kid, and a blanket had the power to fend off anything?"

"No. But it's nice to know you still can."

Amid the suffocating darkness, low voices, and sensations of shadows moving about, Cristina was content to sit alongside her father. Another shower broke loose, prompting her to pull the blanket up to her neck. She closed her eyes and enjoyed the patter of rain on the roof along with the aroma of cherry-blend tobacco.

Nervous conversations and hushed voices carried through the night air. Unseen faces barked out orders or erupted into laughter, sometimes singularly, sometimes in groups. The sound of human voices was strange and invasive by its own nature as it replaced the eons-old drone of swamp life. It continued this way for the better part of an hour until a cold electronic voice broke the relative peace by hailing across the yard from the porta-office speaker.

*"May I have your attention?! May I have your attention please? The subject is approaching the shallows. I repeat... the subject is entering the shallows. Take all prescribed precautions. All unauthorized personnel are to stay clear of the water. I repeat... all unauthorized personnel are to stay clear of the water."*

The darkness went dead silent. The stars disappeared behind the clouds. Cristina tightened her blanket about her. She shared the anticipation of the strangers that stood about the yard awaiting something to emerge from the featureless black void.

"Cri?"

"Yeah."

"Have you seen the blue glow?"

"Yes. Once with Cory when we were out at Gloven's place. I was so scared I thought I was going to pee my pants."

"Well, keep an eye open in that direction over there. Just a little off to your right. You should see the blue glow slowly appear through the thicket. That's where the open water is. It'll come from that direction."

"Okay."

"D'you want to hear somethin' funny?"

"What's that?"

"There's gonna be a lot of mighty upset folks around here in a little while."

"Why? What do you mean?"

"The surest way to know if that abomination's in the neighborhood is by the number of snakes an' rodents that come scurryin' across the yard. I don't know who's out there, but I do know they're in for a hell of a surprise."

"Well... we're okay up here, right?"

"We're fine."

"Thank god."

The glow of Jack's pipe was the most notable feature in the absence of light. Cristina watched patiently off to her right. As her eyes gradually adjusted to the dark, she defined and sorted out the features of the shallows and beyond.

"Dad! I see it!" Cristina whispered loudly. "At first, I thought it was one of those weird trails that remain in your eyes after you see something bright. But it wasn't. I saw it. The light flickered across the water. Over there, just where you said. Did you see it?"

"No, sweetheart, I didn't catch it. Ya gotta remember, your eyes are a lot younger than mine. But keep watchin'. Pretty soon the whole area will glow."

"You're right," whispered Cristina. "It's getting brighter, just like you said."

Jack strained to see the gentle glow in the distance, but he was beat out by another. By the time he saw the blue glow at least four other strangers had beat him to the punch.

"Oh, yeah."

"Do you see it?"

"Oh, yeah. I do now. It's pulsin'. It's feedin'."

"So what happens now?"

"If it holds true to form, it'll enter the shallows an' come right up to the bank, right here in front of us lookin' for roadkill."

"Is that safe?"

"I hope so."

"Seriously? Did you just say that?"

"What I'm sayin' is don't get too relaxed under that blanket. That thing did come up on the porch an' kill Scrub. That was a while back, when it was just a kid."

Cristina flung off the blanket and jumped up out of the chair.

"Where're you goin'?"

334

"I don't know, but I'm not getting cornered in a chair on this porch. That's for sure."

Jack started laughing. He stood himself up.

"Actually, you might be smarter'n ya think. Who knows what that thing can do now? But it doesn't like salt. All those idiots out there think that's funny, but I'm tellin' ya, it doesn't like salt. I don't think it'll cross the ring."

"I don't care what you think. I'm not staying this close. You can if you want, but I'm going farther up into the yard."

"Really?"

"Yup. You do what you want."

It wasn't but a second later and Jack's prediction rang true. A woman somewhere behind the cabin let loose a blood-curdling scream. A riotous clamor of shrieks, cries, and general commotion immediately followed.

"Told ya."

Cristina started laughing as flashlight beams began slicing through the dark. The blinding light only served to make matters worse. Now what was formerly unseen appeared in plain view—a yard full of swamp life. The yelling and commotion grew worse, and all of it followed the sweeping patterns of laser-like rays that retreated toward the porta-office.

"Hey, turn out those flashlights! You're ruinin' my night vision."

Jack had no qualms about projecting his feelings, and lights quickly extinguished or dimmed at worst. The screaming continued to come and go.

"Do me a favor, Cri. Call out when all the snakes have passed through."

There was a brief period of profound silence.

"Very funny, dad. Whatever happened to being stuck between a *rock* and a *hard spot*? How do I end up stuck between a *monster* and a yard full of *snakes*? Unbeeelievable."

Cristina could hear her father trying to hold back.

"I don't have old-man ears, dad. I can hear you snickering plain as day."

"Look. Ya wanna give it a little more time until that thing gets right up front here. By that time, whatever crawled out of the swamp on this side will have gone back into the swamp on the other side. Besides, if they bait that thing right, it's goin' to be far more interested in following the food trail down the creek."

"Okay. If you say so. I hope you're right."

"I'm right. Trust me. Here."

Jack took the blanket dangling from Cristina's hand and draped it over her shoulders.

"There. You're invincible... and you can still run."

"Mmmm." Cristina let out a whimper of resignation as she shrugged her shoulders. "I wish I could run from that smell."

"The swamp critters do."

The two of them stood side-by-side at the banister and watched the creature slowly drift into the shallows. It was pulsing with intensity due to active baiting by people along the shore.

"Okay, Cristina. We can go up into the yard if ya like."

"Well, do you think we're safe here?"

"I don't think it'll cross the salt line. But it doesn't matter. I plan on walkin' it down the creek."

"Oh. All right. Do you want me to pour a couple of cups of coffee to take with us? There's still some left."

"Good idea. Hurry up. It's comin' in close."

The two walked over to the center of the porch where Cristina entered the cabin for coffee, and Jack waited at the top of the steps. Cristina emerged with two mugs.

"Here you go."

"Thanks."

"Wow. So that's it."

"That's it."

They stood at the steps and stared into the blue pulsating light that was now filling the shallows before them.

"I can't believe how soothing that is to watch."

"If you only knew how many times I kicked myself in the ass for fallin' asleep while tryin' to watch that blue devil. It used to really piss me off."

"It's so peaceful."

"Yeah, but looks are deceiving. In this case, really deceiving."

"Yeah."

Jack and Cristina stepped off the porch and walked along the bank on their way to the side yard. Jack turned to yell toward the shallows.

"Make sure you guys stay back from the water. Stay inside that ring of salt!"

With that said, Jack led Cristina around the cabin, staying inside of the salt perimeter. At the back of the house, they crossed over the line and walked in the direction of the creek. A sizable number of others were gathering in anticipation of watching the life form coaxed toward the basin. There was a lot of bait in the creek.

"Here it comes," someone yelled out.

Jack and Cristina watched as the bioluminescence surged and retreated, back and forth along the banks of Jack Creek.

"Wow."

"What?" asked Cristina.

"That thing's gotten really big. That's the biggest I've ever seen it. Makes you wonder how much food they used to bait it."

"Will it fit in the basin?"

"Mercy me, I hope so."

Cristina took her father's arm and walked with him along the creek. The silhouette of the old cedar post came into view as the blue glow swirled around it. Letters spelled out on the plank now were visible only in Jack's head.

"Well, I guess it's officially in Jack Creek."

"That's a good thing, dad."

"Maybe. That thing's movin' faster than we're walkin'."

"That's not a good thing?"

"I don't know. I do know there's not much of a current in the creek. So, it's not just floatin'. It must be coalescing."

The signpost fell back into the shadows as they made their way toward the basin. They watched the life form slowly overtake them and continue ahead as it devoured a creek full of floating chicken parts. The creek was fizzing. The effervescence could be seen everywhere. The smell was agonizing.

"Dad, that thing is thoroughly mesmerizing. It's like staring at sparklers on a summer night. It's like—"

"Whoa."

Jack forcefully pulled Cristina back from the bank of the creek.

"What! What happened?" asked Cristina clearly unnerved.

"Did ya see that?" he whispered

"See what?"

"The water. Did ya see it shift?"

"What do you mean shift? I didn't see anything."

Jack didn't answer. He was transfixed.

"Dad."

Jack stood motionless. He studied the creek with total concentration.

"Dad. What's the matter?"

"The water's shifting. It's shifting, but they don't see it. They're too close. Those fools are too close. What the hell's a matter with those idiots? Everybody was told to stay back from the water. Damn it."

Jack began walking along the creek. His pace was quickening. Cristina was trying to keep up.

"Well, they're not staying back. Looks to me like they're taking water samples."

"Idiots. Oh, shit!"

"What!"

"Look at the water. Look at the water! It's shiftin'." Jack started running. "Hey! Get back! Get back from the water! Get back from the goddamned water!"

Jack's outburst, his screams, shattered the relative calm of the night. A few people looked his way. Some were puzzled, some disinterested, but all seemingly oblivious to the danger. They appeared unconcerned.

They were the first to die.

Jack stopped running as his mind worked exclusively to register details. Cristina's hand reached out for her father's arm and locked onto it with a fearful grip. In the space of a second, the water rose to slide up the bank and inundate the lower legs of those standing too close. They toppled over at once, rolling down the incline of earth to disappear into the blue glow of chicken soup.

The swell engulfed those down on their haunches and those bent over the creek pulling water samples. They disappeared in like fashion. The brave but ignorant who jumped into the creek to help the unfortunate were immediately paralyzed, torture frozen on their faces, and unable to jump back out. They went under with the rest.

Beams of light stirring across the creek's surface revealed countless bodies submerged within the bloom. The water was fizzing from bank to bank. The scene stole Jack's breath. Cristina's voice snapped him out of it.

"Oh, my god. Oh, my god. Oh, my god. Dad. Dad. Do something!"

Jack took stock of the situation, but understood he was helpless to do anything more than yell. He again took off running in the direction of the chaos. Cristina followed in pursuit.

"Stay back! Stay back! Get back from the water!"

Jack understood the crowd could no longer hear his pleas. The night, now filled with hysteria, worked like a social magnet as the mayhem fed furiously on itself. The unaware came running out of the darkness, twenty, thirty, forty, and more. They came to help. They came to see. They came to die.

"Mercy me, look at them! Look at them! They still don't get it! They don't understand. They're gonna die."

Jack stopped running in order to catch his breath. He bent over.

"Are you okay, dad?"

"Yeah, I'm fine. Just need to catch my breath. Listen, Cri, we can't do anything for this crowd. There's too much confusion. People are acting on instinct. C'mon."

He led Cristina toward the basin at as quick a pace as he could muster. Cristina now yelled at the crowd. Her voice was lost in the din, drowned out in an atmosphere of tortured screams.

"Get back! Get away from the wat—"

Cristina watched in stunned silence as the bloom again surged up the bank and flooded past another group of onlookers. They went down at once. There was an escalation of despair, a freshened chorus of screams from the bystanders, but little more than yelps from those lives snuffed out too fast to fathom.

Now, every light available was seized to focus on the disaster. To the horror of all, the lights illuminated and highlighted the grizzly spectacle of corpses both in and out of the water. The blue glow of the bloom was lost to the intense beams of emergency lighting, but the bubbling of decomposing bodies was both visible and audible.

The sound of hydrogen peroxide fizzing pervaded the night air along with the accompanying acrid odor of hydrochloric acid. The burning scent was overpowering the crowd and forcing them back from the creek. In a fashion of pure irony, the organism itself proved most effective in saving lives by the repulsive nature of its digestion.

"We gotta get to the basin. This thing's way too big. They must've been feedin' it tons o' shit to bait it all the way down here from the lake. It's huge. Ron said they used a lot of chum to keep it from fragmenting. I'm thinking too much."

Jack grabbed Cristina's arm and pulled her as he fought both old age and the crowds. He stumbled ahead, detouring around the back of the crowd now packed in tight and focused on the activities along the length of the creek. Once past the crowd, once past the trees, Jack got his first look at the basin. He halted.

"Oh, mercy. Oh, mercy me, we're done for."

"What's the matter, dad? What is it?"

Jack turned to look at Cristina. Fear was in his eyes. He looked back across the basin.

"What is it, dad?"

"That pile of bait. Look at that pile of bait. They must have emptied three or four truckloads into the basin. What were they thinkin'? We're screwed. We're screwed, Cri."

"But I thought you had to bait the basin. I thought you said we had to draw that thing into the basin. You said we had to make sure and get it all."

Again, Jack turned to look at his daughter. In the glare of all the emergency lights, it was easy for Cristina to see the dread etched into her father's expression.

"Cristina.... I said we had to bait the sonovabitch, not force-feed it. Not dump truck-loads of industrial waste on top of it. How did this happen? How could this get past Tammy? Don't you remember what she said? This thing has no stomach. It doesn't get full. It only grows. Look."

Jack pointed. Whereas the majority of people were flocking toward the creek to take count of the dead and dying, the few that remained were taking note of the massive swell of pulsating water as it eased its way up to envelop the towering pile of chicken waste.

"Look at it, Cristina. It's huge.... It's enormous. Look at the water. The whole basin is sloppin' back an' forth."

Jack and Cristina, along with a few stragglers stood watching with numb fascination as the food pile shifted and settled beneath the thick coating of syrupy water.

"What now, dad?"

"What now, indeed?" said the sheriff.

Jack and Cristina turned to see Sheriff Cooper standing behind them.

"We got us some real trouble here, sheriff."

"Yeah. I been watching that thing slither up over that pile of food and thinkin' about that story you told us about your dog. Ya think that thing would have any trouble scalin' a porch?"

"Not much. I also don't think it's gonna have any trouble sliming its way out of the basin."

"Are you serious? Seriously?" asked a sober wide-eyed sheriff.

"Dead serious. Look at the size of that thing. Look at the water level. It's goin' down. That thing is suckin' up water. Hell, the water ain't even flat. What'd Tammy call it? Coalescing."

"Holeeee christ. What do we do now? Should we get ahold of Tammy or somebody?"

Jack turned and looked straight in the sheriff's eyes.

"I doubt there's time for that. Listen to me, Cooper. Get a hold of MDOT. Their winter supply of road salt should be in stock. Their yards should be piled high with that shit. Tell 'em to load up as much of that salt as they can, an' get it over here now. You tell 'em life as we know it around here is gonna depend on how much an' how fast they get that road salt over here."

The sheriff reached for his radio. His voice trailed off as he stepped back and away from Jack and Cristina. Jack returned his attention to the creature.

"What are you thinking, dad?"

"I'm thinkin' about every nasty thing Tammy had t' say about this abomination. We can't let this devil get outta the basin, Cri. There's nothin' out there to take it down."

"Don't say that, dad. There has to be something."

"Oh, eventually somethin'll come along. It always does. We don't have the Spanish Flu anymore, but it cost us forty million people before it disappeared. We can't let this sonovabitch get out."

Jack stopped talking as soon as he heard a dozer start up on the drive near the cabin. He looked in that direction and could see the lights.

"They're sealin' off the creek. Thank god. However big it is, I guess it all fit. Thank god for that. At least somethin' went right."

"Is the basin going to hold it, dad?" asked Cristina.

"God, I hope so. I'll tell ya this. If it doesn't, we're doomed. Life as we know it around here is finished."

"Jack."

Jack turned around to look into the glare of additional lights. Sheriff Cooper's silhouette emerged.

"MDOT is loading their trucks now, and sending 'em out one by one as soon as they're filled. What are ya plannin' on doin' with all that salt?"

"Sheriff, ya got a lot of educated sorts standin' around—maybe a few less now than before. And I understand that Tammy an' that Doctor Martinelli friend of hers may know what we're up against. But they watch this thing in a beaker or a test tube. I been watchin' it in the swamp, an' I'm tellin' ya, it don't like salt.

"Its best chance of escape is across that low swampy stretch between the basin an' backwater. It's been raining, and that ground's gonna be plenty wet enough to give it an escape route.

"We gotta get salt spread across that ground. It's gonna kill everything. It's gonna lay waste to that land for years to come, but we gotta do it. We can't let this thing get back into the backwaters. Not now. I mean, look at the size of that thing."

"Where d'ya want it dumped?"

"I heard the dozer backfillin' the creek up by the cabin, sealing it off. We can cross over the creek by using the backfill as a bridge. Tell 'em to dump the salt alongside the piles of backfill. Right where that dozer's workin'. We can push salt back into the swamp from there and form a barrier that will border the entire west side of the basin. That'll cut it off from the backwater. It wouldn't cross salt at the cabin. I'm bettin' it won't cross it here."

"I'll let 'em know."

"Sheriff?"

"Yeah?"

"You tell everyone that if they see a massive drop in the water level, run like hell—time's up. It'll suck up as much water as it can an' use it to propel itself across the lowland."

"Got it."

The bloom was mowing down through the pile of bait and even though bright lights seemed to be coming from every direction, the bioluminescence grew visible. The acrid, biting odor of

343

hydrochloric acid hung heavy in the air along with the scent of bleach. It was irritating to the sinuses, almost choking, and people everywhere could be seen holding handkerchiefs to their faces and spitting.

"Dad, what happens if it gets out?"

"I suspect they'll spray rotenone, or something similar all over it. First, you sacrifice everything in the basin, then you poison the flooding, and finally the swamp. Next comes killing off everything in the Muskegon River downstream of Houghton Lake, which I cannot even fathom. After that... well, after that sacrifices are irrelevant."

"Geez, dad."

"You know, Cristina, the worst part, the real problem is this. How would you ever know if ya killed it off or not? What's t'say it wouldn't break up into a million smaller organisms as a means of survival? D'ya see why I'm sayin', it can't leave this basin."

"Dad, look at the water."

Jack's eyes immediately shifted to the shore. The water level was dropping.

"Damn it."

"What now?"

"I have no idea."

Five minutes later the first of the MDOT trucks turned onto the driveway and headed toward the cabin. Jack flagged down the driver and showed him where to dump the salt alongside the earthen dam that now sealed off Jack Creek. Soon after, a second, a third, and a fourth truck roared past to dump loads in a like manner.

Jack watched as an operator climbed aboard the dozer and began carving into the salt pile. The dam turned white in the pollution of emergency lights as the operator pushed material across it. Slowly, a raised white road of salt began taking shape. Jack led his daughter back along the drive toward the cabin.

"I don't think that dozer's gonna make it."

"Why?"

"It's gettin' bogged down. I can hear it. The rain's made the ground too soggy. Shit. I know it. I know it. He ain't gonna make it."

"What does that mean?"

"You wait here, Cri. I'm goin' to fire up—"

"What's he doing, dad?"

"Huh?"

"He's running back to the drive."

"I knew it. Damn it, I knew that was gonna happen."

Jack looked into the woods to see the operator running back along the salt line. He started running to meet him. He yelled out to the stranger.

"Is she bogged down?"

"Yeah. The more I tried to get out, the deeper I sank. I need to get it towed out."

"Lemme see if I can get my D4 fired up."

"Are you kiddin' me? You got a D4 sittin' around here?"

"Always have had. She's old but she's faithful."

"A friend of mine's got one of the older D4s. They can be a real bitch to crank over. D'ya need a hand?"

"If you've done it, sure. That pony motor breaks my balls."

Jack turned to Cristina.

"You wait here, sweetheart. That D4'll bust your eardrums. It's probably the reason I can't hear."

"Okay. But be careful. Dad!"

"What?"

"I said be careful."

"I will, honey."

Jack and the operator disappeared into the shadows.

"Name's Mason."

"Jack McGrath."

"Pleasure to meet you, Jack."

They headed for the shed. Once inside, Jack grabbed a flashlight, a can of starting fluid, and a rope. He led the operator out of the shed and over to the D4.

"You got youth, so you get the honors. Here's the pull rope."

"No problem. You set 'er up an' I'll pull. We ain't got much time or you'll need more'n this D4 to pull me out."

"Let's do it."

Jack checked to make sure the cat was in neutral and the clutch was engaged. He turned the ignition switch to ON, set the choke, pulled the throttle out to half-speed, engaged the compression release, and turned on the gas to the pony motor. He sprayed a couple good shots of ether into the carb intake.

"Pull!"

Mason pulled on the pony motor twice. The second time it fired up and the noise was deafening. There would be no talking at this point. Jack engaged the brake for the pinion shaft, and pulled up the lever to engage the pinion. He checked his fuel pressure; he checked his oil pressure. He released the compression release and let the main engine crank. It would need to warm up if it was ever to come to life.

"C'mon, c'mon, c'mon, c'mon, baby, fire. C'mon, we ain't got all day. C'mon, you piece of shit. Fire!"

Jack engaged and released the compression release a number of times. The main was firing on one cylinder and finally a second. Smoke was billowing out of the stack. He released the compression release and the third cylinder kicked in. Jack let it spin. Thankfully, the fourth and final cylinder kicked in and the engine smoothed out. Jack opened the throttle, released the clutch, and shut down the pony motor, which eliminated most of the noise.

Mason turned to Jack and hollered, "I'll meet ya at the salt pile."

Jack nodded and climbed aboard. He put the D4 into gear and engaged the clutch. It started down the drive toward the salt pile. A cloud of dense diesel exhaust permeated the area as it hung low in the air. Jack spun the dozer to the right and started across the earthen bridge. He followed the salt trail until coming up on the back end of the other dozer.

Jack tossed down a chain, and Mason quickly hooked the two dozers together. Jack waited for Mason to climb back onto his seat and give the ready sign. At that point, Jack eased the levers back. The D4 began pulling. He popped the other dozer out of the mud with little effort. Once safely backed out of the swamp and on the hard-packed driveway, Mason signaled Jack to step down. He did and they spoke.

"Listen, Jack, I can't go back in. The ground is too soft and I haven't got the wider tracks like you. The only way to do this is for you to go in. What d'ya think?"

"Ahh, that ground ain't nothin' for this baby. Done that an' much worse over the years."

"Great. Have at it. You know your equipment and the terrain better'n anyone. You keep pushin' salt, an' I'll prep the piles for pushin'. I'll stand by with the chain in case ya need a pull."

Jack nodded and went back to his D4. He climbed aboard, set the throttle and blade, and took his first swipe at a salt pile. He started pushing the load along the salt road. As he reached the hole that trapped the other dozer, he filled it in with salt and went back for more.

The MDOT trucks continued to roll in and dump their loads. Jack continued to swipe the piles and push salt back into the marsh. It was on his eighth or ninth trip back into the swamp that Jack caught an especially strong whiff of acrid air and sighted something to his left.

He looked between the trees and picked up the reflection of emergency lights flashing across a wet surface. He knew at that moment the abomination had surged out of the basin and was spreading out in his direction. He put the D4 into reverse and went for another load of salt.

By the time Jack plowed another dozen loads to the end of the salt line, the creature was clearly visible about forty feet from the barrier. The air was biting; it irritated his sinuses. In spite of the distant emergency lights flickering through the trees, in spite of the working lights on his dozer, he could see patches of blue. It prompted him to turn off his lights.

In the ensuing darkness, as Jack's eyes grew more sensitive to light, he could see blotches of blue mottling across the entire expanse of swamp between him and the basin. It reminded him of the patches of snow yet unmelted in a spring thaw, snow that looked blue in the light of a bright moon.

A pang of hopelessness stabbed Jack to his core. The life form was soaking up the many stagnant pools of standing rainwater. It was drawing up water from the ground. It was devouring all the invisible creatures that serenaded him to sleep night after night as he rocked on his porch. The thing was exterminating all life. It had no conscience as it headed toward him.

Jack flipped a switch and the dozer lights shattered the blackness. He squinted his eyes for a second to adjust, but in that short period, he was able to see hundreds of creatures crossing the salt line, fleeing for their lives. The light startled them, and for a moment, they froze in place or ran in circles, but only for a moment before their exodus resumed.

Jack went back for another load. After three more loads, the creature had made it to the salt line. It resisted crossing the salt as Jack had expected, but the forward edge was under pressure from the flow behind and apparently caused it to thicken and rise at the barrier.

It was now flowing rapidly sideways, outward in both directions along the trail. Flowing to the left would send the life form back to Jack Creek, but there was nothing to stop it when flowing to the right. Jack steered the dozer alongside the bloom, pushing the salt, extending the barrier another twenty feet with every load. But it wasn't enough. He was losing the race.

Back at the salt piles, Mason did exactly what he had promised. He prepped the piles to save Jack time. Jack watched him pull his dozer back so not to get in his way. Jack pulled the D4 alongside Mason's dozer, stopped, and jumped off his equipment. He ran over to Mason who climbed out of his seat and stood on the dozer tracks to meet him. Jack hollered out over the roar of the engines.

"It ain't happenin'!"

"What?"

Jack cupped his hands, as the operator held a hand to his ear.

"I said, it ain't happenin'! I can't keep up. It's outflanking me. It's runnin' along the barrier faster'n I can spread. This ain't gonna work. It's on its way to the backwater."

"What d'ya want me to do?"

"Get ahold of your supervisor an' tell'm to spray. Tell'm to get that chopper over here and nail that sonovabitch. We're outta time."

"Got it."

Jack ran back to his D4 and carved out another blade full of salt from the pile. He headed back into the swamp. In the brilliance of his lights, he could see the creature standing proud, pressing up against the barrier like snow plowed to the side of a road. He wondered how long it would remain penned in.

The leading edge of the bloom appeared to be breaking down, washing away, as if the salt was killing it. In turn, the watery effluent was eroding the road itself. The run-off was flowing into the salt bed, loosening the pack, and carving its way across the road.

When Jack reached the end of the line, the monster was there to greet him. It had beat him. It was flowing past the end of the barrier toward the backwater. Jack had no option but to swerve to his right. It was an impulsive act in order to intercept it. He pushed the salt as far as it would go. Once depleted, he stopped, turned off his lights, and studied the movements of the blue glow. It looked like a dam had let loose. The earth disappeared beneath its luminescence.

The thought of a breeched dam gave Jack an idea. He knew he wouldn't have time to go back for more salt. That was out of the question, but he might be able to stall the monster's advance until the chopper arrived by building an embankment. He thought of the large embankment holding back the waters at Reedsburg Dam.

Jack did not have the option of second-guessing himself. He dropped his blade and angled it. He pushed the levers forward and the D4 stormed ahead. He peeled the earth's crust and folded it back over onto itself in a long neat row. He repeated the process until his luck ran out.

Jack knew it had always been about luck. Shooting from the hip was sloppy. The shooter felt good, the rest suffered to clean up the mess. He had given it his best shot. Now, he had to deal with the mess. In this case, it was about a stand of trees that sucked him deep into its midst, until he was funneled in so tight there was barely enough room to maneuver. It appeared that his only option was to back out and go.... Where?

Jack flipped off the lights. He had gained nothing on the blue glow in his race to outflank it, but his hedge of earthen debris had held up remarkably well. In fact, there was a gentle slope to the land in this area, which penned the creature in between the embankment and the slight rise behind. The bloom, now trapped temporarily and pooling, would soon pass by what little embankment was in place.

Jack turned on his lights and studied the trees. The D4 was powerful enough to push over trees, but tree felling was dangerous business and required thought before undertaking. It was cautious business during the light of day, let alone the dark of night.

Unfortunately, Jack found himself again with no options. The trees had to come down in order for him to extend the embankment and stall the abomination from advancing farther. He assessed the situation and could see that the blue liquid appeared to be nearly two feet deep on the backside of the embankment and rising.

Jack looked up at the sky. He longed to see the chopper approaching. It was not there. Jack looked forward. In the dozer lights, he studied the blade. He reached for the controls and twisted the blade, angling its lower corner to dig and sever roots.

Jack worked the D4 with all the dexterity of a young man. He severed roots, he raised the blade and nudged trunks to fall away, pushed trees back, and he made the best of fresh earth. He n for the long haul. He thought of Scrub. The fight was al. Jack never took his eyes off the goal until something 's attention.

as loud and nobody would hear anything near the dozer itself. So, in spite of the thunderous noise licopter as it chopped up the night air, Jack heard nothing. It was only because he was in the process of nudging over another tree and looking up through its tops, through its upper branches, that he glimpsed the spotlight of the chopper heading his way.

For Jack, it brought a feeling of immense relief. It brought him a sense of hope that he needed in the worst way. All he had to do now was get the hell out the area and let the chopper rain chemical hell down on the devil itself.

The only obstacle that arose to stand in the way of Jack's retreat was the distraction made by the helicopter. The split second his focus moved *from* the branches to *through* the branches, he failed to appreciate the way the tree that he was nudging turned about overhead. As he glanced at the approaching lights in the sky, the spin of the tree changed the direction of its fall. The chopper arrived just in time to spotlight the new trajectory.

Jack watched with some apprehension as the tree angled over toward its new direction. He took a breath of relief as it started crashing its way down through the woods to his left. He watched without concern as it came down and collided with the massive rotted-out husk of an old branchless oak that was all of five feet in diameter and fifty feet tall.

Jack tensed up as the old barkless landmark unexpectedly fell back toward him. In a split second, Jack calculated he was still in the clear. His anxiety settled as his eyes followed the tree downward. Luckily, he was safe. As the earth came into view, Jack instantly understood the depravity of the deception, but this time he had run out of options.

The old barkless hulk landed square and hard, shaking the ground as it crashed just behind the embankment. The placid horizontal surface of pooling luminescent blue liquid instantly transformed into a vertical wall of venom that towered high over Jack. No slower than his rush of fear did the wall collapse upon him.

The spotlight overhead was blinding. Centered in its beam, Jack looked up into the brilliance and thought first of Scrub, and lastly of Cristina. The vision of his daughter stayed the course during those final seconds of excruciating pain that ended his life.

351

# 48

"Well, what's it going to be?" asked the waitress.

Harold looked at Cory.

"I gotta do that New Yorker one more time. There's no way around it. Medium rare."

"Make mine the same."

"Excellent choice." The waitress picked up the menus and walked away.

"So, how'd it go?" asked Harold.

"Short, sweet. Not too many people. No body."

"What about his daughter? How's she doing?"

"Cristina? I sat with her. She'll get through it. She's strong. She's intelligent. I think for Cri, it was more like the passing of an uncle. You know, someone who she knew, but didn't. Someone who could tell her something about her childhood, about her family, her home, but someone who lived an entirely different life. She'll miss Jack, but not like a parent.

"Actually, I was thinking about this, and I think it'll be toughest on her mother. Cristina told me that her mother hadn't seen Jack in fifty years. She loved him, hated him, and in the end, never stopped talking about him. The old lady was always worrying about his welfare. She's the one who takes the hit. It was the two of *them* that had history.

"Anyway, Cri's on her way back to Grand Rapids. I told her I'd give her a call. Maybe have dinner or something. Who knows?"

"You like her?"

"ᵉah. Actually, I do. I met her before. A couple of times at ᵗs in GR. We have some mutual friends. But aside from ʳht chitchat, I never had an opportunity to know her. Now, ᵈ she's quite a gal. I enjoyed her. She's got a great sense

I was told my wife had one of those, but I never ᵈ it for her affairs. I guess it makes sense.

352

When I saw some of the guys she was running around with, I laughed too.

"So, what about you, Cory? What are you going to do? Things aren't going to be the same around the office without you. I know Mary's going to miss you. She's tired of looking at me. Sure you don't want a job? I'd hire you in a sec."

"Yeah, and you'd fire me in a sec. Face it, Harold. This town isn't big enough for the two of us. One of us has to ride into the sunset, and I don't own the *Chronicle*."

"Yeah, it does tie me down."

"Besides, the way I see it, you got a ton of new material headed your way—stories up the wazoo. Much as I hate to say it, I don't think anybody's ever going to kill this thing off. I think it's going to starve itself down to something so small you can walk around with it in a shot glass. But the first time you stick your finger in that glass, it starts growing. It's a monster. Pure and simple. *Jack Creek horror*, Harold. *Jack Creek horror*."

"Did you hear about the Reedsburg Dam?"

"No."

"The DNR closed the campground until further notice. I just got the info to print up. Between the investigation, the stigma of the tragedy, and the fear of that thing lurking in the swamp, the state figured there was no point in reopening it."

"Can't say I'm surprised."

"There ya go. I'll tell you what's worse. The state's predicting a total collapse of this entire area. Right now business is way up because of all the publicity and curiosity seekers. But they're saying expect near zero room and cottage rentals for next season, or at least until this mess is put to rest. They predict zero fishing in the flooding or swamp. They don't figure anybody will enter the backwaters, Houghton Lake, or Higgins Lake for swimming or recreational boating. The campgrounds are already laying off employees.

"To give you an idea of what we're going to be up against, the real-estate market has been depressed since the recession, but my listings have tripled in the last week. Those in the know, th savvy ones who understand what's coming, are bailing as fast as they can before home values plunge for good. And the way it looks, pretty soon you won't even be able to give away lake property. I'm telling you, Cory, they have to kill that thing."

"Did they say anything about the next plan of attack? Did they say anything about rerouting Houghton Lake's overflow or anything like that?"

"From what I understand, they're back to baiting the flooding. They're hoping to attract Jack Creek into one place and draw it back into the basin like before. Only this time there's going to be one mammoth ring of salt around it."

"*Jack Creek?*"

"Yeah, everybody's suffering to call this thing something, and after all the deaths at the basin, the name Jack Creek started to circulate. People need to make it personal. *It* doesn't cut it. Neither does bloom. Jack Creek seems to satisfy."

"*Jack Creek and the ring of salt.* Sounds like a frickin' fairytale. McGrath has to be laughing in his grave."

"There ya go."

"What bothers me most about all of this are those bodies that spilled over the dam. They had to be contaminated. How could they not be? How much of the bloom washed over the spillway and floated downstream? Who knows? It's impossible for me to accept nothing made it past the dam. I just don't believe it."

"Only time will tell."

"I'm betting a year from now, maybe two, or maybe three, there's going to be a wave of panic that will make the Jack Creek horror ıok like a two-wagon carny act. You watch."

ʿarold looked at Cory with an air of resignation. He didn't ʿd.

ʿy, I gotta get going. You did me good, Harold. You hauled here to sleepy ol' Houghton Lake, and I made me more ʿey in a month than I've made in the past two years. ʿ. In fact, I owe you, buddy."

ʿ owe me nothing. I made out better'n I expected."

"Nah, I owe you, I do. Which reminds me... before I leave. I wrote my final installment last night. Here you go."

"Thanks. I think I'll hold this one for Friday's run—best circulation."

"Whatever works. Listen, you're going to have a shitload more stuff to print before this goes away, if that ever happens. You got nothing to worry about. And you got Quinn to keep you in the loop. You can't get better'n him. He's got all the whens, wheres, hows, and you name it. He's got it. Not to mention he likes a little cash on the side."

"Yeah, Quinn's a good head. I like him. He's been a lot of help over the years. I probably would already be out of business if not for Quinn."

"Buy the man a steak, Harold."

The two men were talked out. They looked at each other and smiled as they savored the final moments. Their friendship went way back, and was apparent. Cory reached for his bill and stood up from the table. He extended his hand.

"I'm out of here, Harold. Take care, buddy."

"Drive safe, Cory."

# Local Hero Dies Fighting
# The 'Jack Creek Horror'

### By Cory Ballard

Roscommon, Co., Mi. Long-time Roscommon County resident Jack McGrath died last Tuesday at his home on the backwater of Dead Stream Swamp.

Mr. McGrath sacrificed his life while engaged in emergency operations at Jack Creek basin. He was attempting to contain the unintended genetic creation terrorizing the Reedsburg Dam backwaters, and believed responsible for numerous deaths in the area.

In the face of much ridicule and accusations of mental instability, Mr. McGrath was first to

355

sound the alarm on one of the most insidious predators so far discovered by man.

McGrath collected roadkill to draw the creature into the shallows surrounding the cabin where he lived, for closer study, earning himself the name "Roadkill Ralph".

Mr. McGrath was not a member of the team responsible for the containment and extermination of the invasive species. When the operation failed to go according to plan, and the organism breached the containment basin, Mr. McGrath mounted a dozer, and in a singular act of heroism, fought back the entity until overtaken.

Mr. McGrath gave up his life for good reason. From personal observations, he knew better than most that a failure to contain the life form would prove disastrous for the environments of Roscommon County and neighboring watersheds. A threat now expanded by federal authorities to include the entire Great Lakes watershed.

Numerous federal and state agencies are currently involved and fully committed to eliminating the threat at whatever cost. Efforts are underway to track the organism day and night by all means available, including a variety of high-tech sensors such as those that monitor pH levels of the backwater.

Sources speaking off the record state targeting the life form with aerial spray applications of highly concentrated rotenone piscicides is the current plan of attack. Considerable collateral damage is expected.

A contingent of scientists in opposition to mass application of piscicides are investigating the possibility of changing the pH level of the backwaters in order to disrupt the organism's digestive mechanism. They emphasize lessened environmental impact under their proposal.

As disastrous as the situation appears for ¬scommon and Missaukee Counties, a group ¬nvironmental scientists headed up by Dr.

Chakor Chopra stated that "The three bodies known to have washed over Reedsburg Dam were likely contaminated." He also stated, "...odds were high that the organism was introduced into the Muskegon River below Reedsburg Dam as it starts across the state toward Lake Michigan."

Dr. Chopra, added, "by comparison, the potential cataclysm will make the Exxon and Deepwater Horizon oil spills look like little more than cake smeared across a baby's face."

According to information supplied by another anonymous source working closely on the case, the potential threat could affect the entire Great Lakes water basin ecosystem, which makes up 18% of the world's fresh surface water and 84% of North America's supply. Collectively, it is the largest supply of fresh water in the world. The Great Lakes ecosystem also feeds the St. Lawrence ecosystem.

"The enormity of the problem can barely be described." The Great Lakes encompass more than 94,000 square miles of water, contain 5,500 cubic miles of water, and encompass a watershed covering 295,000 square miles of rivers and streams that empty into it.

The lakes form 35,000 islands that include high proportions of endemic and endangered species, fish spawning areas, nesting water-birds, and migratory waterfowl. "The task of tracking this invasive species amid these safe havens would be entirely impossible," said the source.

The source also noted that this invasive species has the potential to shut down the lakes' supply of drinking water to 40 million people, and restrict the 56 billion gallons of water provided daily for municipal, agricultural, and industrial use.

Currently, no contingency plans or procedures have been proposed or deemed effective in combatting the now infamous and lurking 'JACK CREEK HORROR'.

A special thanks and note of appreciation to Gary Gilman and Paul Lehman for their technical direction. Also, Nancy Smith and Martha Hart for their selfless support and editorial assistance.

Additional thanks to Cynthia Guy, Terri Johnson-Nausieda, Gerrie Vennesland, Pamela Kellogg, Roberta Crawley, Kristy Cygan-Jenks, and Matt & Sandi Nelson for their generous assistance.

Most importantly, I thank my wife, Nancy, for allowing me to act on my dreams instead of my responsibilities. God bless her..

OTHER BOOKS IN PRINT BY

# C. JOHN COOMBES

CLAUS: A CHRISTMAS INCARNATION; THE CHILD VOLUME 1
ISBN 978-0 9822213-2-7
CLAUS: A CHRISTMAS INCARNATION; THE WOMAN V2B1
ISBN 978-0-9822213-6-5
CLAUS: A CHRISTMAS INCARNATION; THE WOMAN V2B2
SBN 978-0-9822213-7-2
CLAUS: A CHRISTMAS INCARNATION; THE DISCIPLE V3B1
SBN 978-0-9822213-8-9
CLAUS: A CHRISTMAS INCARNATION; THE DISCIPLE V3B2
SBN 978-0-9822213-9-6
FULL MOON STO
SBN 978-1-941623-90-9